# Artist

## Devlyn & Shelly

A FRIENDS TO LOVERS, SLOW BURN ROMANCE DUET



# PERSEPHONE AUTUMN

BETWEEN WORDS PUBLISHING LLC

# Books by Persephone Autumn

## <u>Lake Lavender Series</u>

Depths Awakened

One Night Forsaken

Every Thought Taken

## <u>Devotion Series</u>

Distorted Devotion

Undying Devotion

Beloved Devotion

Darkest Devotion

Sweetest Devotion

## <u>Bay Area Duet Series</u>

### <u>Click Duet</u>

Through the Lens

Time Exposure

### <u>Inked Duet</u>

Fine Line

Love Buzz

### <u>Insomniac Duet</u>

Restless Night

A Love So Bright

<u>Artist Duet</u>

Blank Canvas

Abstract Passion


<u>Novellas</u>

Reese

Penny


**<u>Stone Bay Series</u>**

Broken Sky—Prequel

Shattered Sun

Fractured Night


**<u>Standalone Romance Novels</u>**

Sweet Tooth

Transcendental


**<u>Poetry Collections</u>**

Ink Veins

Broken Metronome

Slipping From Existence

Poisonous Heart

Beneath Wildflowers


# PUBLISHED UNDER P. AUTUMN

**<u>Standalone Non-Romance Novels</u>**

By Dawn

# *contents*

BLANK CANVAS

# ABSTRACT PASSION

# Blank Canvas

BOOK ONE

*For those who have been broken by people and circumstances
beyond your control. For those who decided to take a leap
and be selfish for the first time.*

*Four Years Ago*

"We should break up."

I rear my head back as if Kelsey slapped me. Did I hear her correctly?

The crowd continues to cheer and dance as high-volume music plays around us. A tassel smacks my cheek as another graduate from our senior class squeezes through the throng of bodies.

Leaning in, I speak next to Kelsey's ear. "Sorry, didn't hear you over the noise." At least I don't think I heard her. "What'd you say?"

Kelsey takes my hand and guides us through hundreds of our classmates and their families. Her hand in mine feels different, colder, less comforting. Nothing like the girl I've known the past three years. The abrupt change has me queasy and unsettled.

Once we reach the outskirts, she stops and spins to face me. The downturn of her lips is an instant red flag. A warning sign telling me I didn't mishear what she said a moment ago. But I refuse to believe it. Not until I hear the words clearly from her lips and the reason why.

"Devlyn, I'm sorry." Her bottom lip juts out as her eyes droop at the corners.

*She's sorry?* You have got to be kidding me. Her *sorry* appears a little too forced, a little too practiced.

Kelsey and I have been practically inseparable since Andrew Bishop's "We survived freshman year" party three years ago. It wasn't an instant love connection, but she carried herself unlike other high school girls. More mature and less catty. She had this air about her; a strength I gravitated toward. Plus, she made me laugh. A lot.

We had hung out all summer. By the time sophomore year started, Kelsey Martin was officially my girlfriend. Not a single day passed where I doubted our relationship or its backbone. We were solid. Practically attached at the hip. In love.

Or so I thought.

"You're sorry?" The words leave my lips harsher than intended, but I don't regret the severity of my tone. Not when the girl who has owned my heart for three years says she wants to break up. I glance off to the side, too stunned to see anything. When I return my gaze, every soft line of her face—the ones I drew from memory with pencil and charcoal—blur into a blob of unpleasant colors. "Doesn't seem like you're sorry," I choke out.

A hand grazes my forearm and I yank it from her grip. Her head falls forward as she sniffles. "Please don't hate me." Sadness laces her voice and makes me question reality. Makes me question the reason behind this sudden change.

"How did you expect me to feel?" I shiver, cross my arms

over my chest and hug myself. "Did you expect me to be okay with this?" I close my eyes, take a deep breath, and open them on the exhale. "You gave no indications. We see each other every day and you've never said or shown you're unhappy."

"I'm not," she says quickly.

Our eyes meet and I shake my head. "Then why?" I want to touch her. Want to reach out, wrap my arms around her, and mold her to my frame.

But I won't. Never again. Doing so only muddles the water more.

She stares off toward the crowd, laughs without humor then meets my doubtful eyes. "Graduation day," she murmurs. "Today should be one of the happiest days of our non-adult lives." I nod but keep my lips sealed. Right now, I don't trust my voice or the words I might spew. "Last night, as I got everything ready for today, it blindsided me."

My brows pinch at the middle. "What did?"

Kelsey waves a hand toward the massive gathering, as if I should automatically know the storm of thoughts brewing in her head. "This!" She points to random people, then waves a hand at the room. "Graduation. The end. And not just the end of high school, but the start of what follows."

This isn't hot off the press news. Most of our senior year was spent in assemblies discussing what would happen this year and what it all meant. Most of junior and senior year was packed with college discussions and plans for after high school. Kelsey and I had discussed all this at length with each other. Us taking different paths after high school wasn't anything new. And we talked, on more than one occasion, about our relationship post high school.

Our conversations never revolved around breaking up. Of

course our relationship would be different, but we planned to stick it out.

Yes, hundreds of miles would separate us—Kelsey starts Florida State in the fall while I start at Ringling. Less than a day's drive away, our plan was to spend as many weekends and breaks together as possible. We had it all mapped out.

Or so I thought. Obviously, unbeknownst to me, those plans flew out the window.

"And?" I drag out the single-word question. "We talked about this."

She shakes her head, not wanting to hear what I have to say. "No, Dev. We talked about our fantasy life, post high school." Her eyes close a beat, then meet mine. Another shiver racks my body at the coldness in her eyes, the stiffness in her posture. "Reality check, we aren't kids anymore. Even if we met in the middle, seeing each other on off days would be exhausting. Both of us will get behind in our studies. It's just too hard."

She averts her eyes to the senior class twenty feet from us. Her spine straightens as she wipes all emotion from her face. Bile rises in my throat as I take in this new side of her. A side I have never seen. A side that makes me sick to my stomach.

How long has this part of her existed? How long has splitting up been on her mind? I refuse to ask because I fear learning the truth. That she has considered the idea of breaking up for much longer than a day or two.

"Breaking up is for the best," she says without looking my way. "We should get to experience college and this new phase of our lives. Make new friends. See the world… without fear of hurting each other."

All I hear is… *I want to have fun and be open to new*

*experiences without being tied down. Better to break up now than cheat on my boyfriend and feel guilty.*

I won't throw the words in her face, but I am no fool. Well, maybe I *am* a fool. A heartbroken idiot who believed the girl he loved would want to be with him for years to come. A naive guy who thought his girl cared for him as much as he did her.

What the fuck is wrong with me?

What boy believes he found his soul mate at fifteen? Trusting boys with moldable hearts, that is who.

Kelsey continues on her tirade of why our breakup is for the best, but I don't hear a word she says. Her voice is white noise in my ears. The words scrambled and vacant and pointless. When I don't respond to something she said, she pats my shoulder, mouths something else, then walks off.

Week-long seconds pass as I stand in the same place and stare at the fuzzy basketball championship banners over the collapsed bleachers. A warm hand settles on my shoulder, a perfume I have known since childhood fills my nose. My mom says something beside me, her voice saccharine and insincere yet firm. A woman not to be crossed. I have no clue what she said, but I nod.

I exit the gymnasium with my parents, thankful when Dad's arm hooks around my shoulders, and walk to the car. Our drive to the restaurant is a blur. Graduation dinner goes by in a haze of disbelief. With each passing minute, a black vignette clouds my periphery. Blankets my vision. The thumping organ in my rib cage beats with less enthusiasm. And it doesn't take long before the pericardium around my heart shrinks. Withers. Splinters into thousands of jagged pieces and stabs the vital organ it holds.

With each new wave of darkness, I make a new vow.

I will never let anyone in again. Never let someone close enough to ruin me with such severity. And never will I give another my heart. The agony in the fallout isn't worth the risk. No one is worth this endless heartache.

Then, I give in. Let pain and darkness swallow me into the abyss. Let my world go numb.

## SHELLY

I love pink. Much of my wardrobe consists of various shades of the hue. But seeing this much—balloons, streamers, cake, clothes, drinks—has me nauseous.

Another round of oohs and awes fills the room as Cora opens another gift and holds up an infant-sized black dress with tiny pink hearts. Then she pulls out a pair of black Mary Jane's, small enough to fit in her palm, and her eyes glaze over.

The smile on my face is genuine. The joy in my heart is real.

I am happy for my best friend and her husband, Gavin. They deserve nothing *but* happiness and love after the journey their relationship has endured. I never pictured them as parents, but since finding out Cora was pregnant, they smile more than ever before.

Truly, I am happy for them.

The last two and a half years have been a whirlwind. For everyone in our circle. Everyone except me.

My best friend since forever—the woman we are here to

celebrate joining motherhood soon—reunited with the love of her life. Gavin. Their reunion tipped the first domino.

Watching Cora and Gavin come back together and fall in love all over again, was magical. Like something from one of the romance novels on my bookshelf. I sat front and center with popcorn in hand. Consoled my friend when she needed someone to listen and give advice. Offered my shoulder when she needed to cry. But deep down, anyone who knew them before knew their relationship would stand the test of time. After more than a decade apart, their love was timeless. Genuine. The real deal.

"Oomph." Cora sets down the gift bag, shifts on the couch, and rubs her growing belly.

Elizabeth, more affectionately called Mom by more than just Cora, rises from her seat in the living room and wanders down the hall. Not a minute later, she strolls back in with an office chair lumbar pillow and offers it to Cora.

"Might make you more comfortable."

"Thanks, Mom." She tucks the cushion behind her, leans back, and sighs. "She has been so active the last week. I swear she's rearranging my organs in there." Cora laughs and we all join in.

My eyes drift around the room. Take in the small group of women gathered to celebrate the impending arrival of Cora and Gavin's bundle of joy. So much love resides in our close-knit circle, and I am blessed to have these women in my life. Women who will drop whatever they are doing to help one another. Friendship and family like ours cannot be bought. It brews over time and strengthens with each passing day.

Cora continues to rub her belly, then sucks in a breath. "She kicked." A pained smile lights up her face as her gaze shifts from one person to the next, until she reaches me, her best friend. Cora is the one person I know better than anyone else walking the earth, and vice versa. "Come here, Auntie Shell. Check out Miss Clara's latest dance moves. Something tells me she'll be our karaoke choreographer one day."

I laugh and shake my head as I cross the room and plop down beside Cora. "I have a feeling this little girl will change us all." Looking over at Autumn, whose belly has just started to round as well, I smile. "Just as Clementine did."

I lay my hand on Cora's belly and she guides me to where baby Clara kicks. The second her little foot punts my hand, tears pool in my eyes. Feeling this sweet girl stretch her limbs warms my heart. She will be loved and spoiled, not by just her parents, but by us all. Especially me.

Cora sucks in a breath and looks to me for confirmation. "Did you feel that?" I nod but don't answer, too scared my voice will be sandpaper. "Girl is one tough cookie. She'll exit the womb kicking her legs."

Elizabeth and Autumn laugh. Of the small group of women in attendance, only two have experienced pregnancy and childbirth. Elizabeth, of course, and Autumn. Gavin's mom didn't fly out for the shower but will be in town a while once Clara joins the world. Erin, Penny, Peyton, and I sit in silent awe. Motherhood has never been big on my radar, but I don't discount the idea. If the right person came into my life and our relationship became serious enough to travel down that path, the possibility of motherhood would be given merit.

But motherhood, let alone love, is such a distant reality in my life. Not intentionally. I love the idea of finding the one and falling in love. I love knowing, one day, I will have someone special at my side.

*If anyone listens to my inner ramblings, go ahead and send him my way. Please.*

"Can't wait to meet her," I say, then look to Autumn. "And your new addition too."

Little Clara settles and Cora resumes opening gifts. We play strange baby shower games for hours. Tasting jars of baby food while blindfolded and trying to guess the flavor—which is disgusting, in case you were unaware. Guessing the number of candies in a baby bottle. Speed changing diapers on dolls while someone covers our eyes. Each game is equally fun and weird, and the laughter never lets up.

Once the games are done, we scope out the massive buffet of food.

Peyton—my soon-to-be sister-in-law—told her mom about the baby shower and Tracy insisted on catering the day. No complaints here. I file into line near the end, pick up a pink paper plate with "It's a girl!" swirled in the center, and pile food onto my plate.

Being that it is Cora's day, Tracy got a list of her favorite foods and things she steered away from while pregnant. Needless to say, much of the buffet has Asian flavors. A variety of vegetable sushi, rice noodle dishes, and spring rolls. But there are also macaroni and cheese balls, lettuce wraps, muffin-sized fruit tarts, and large trays with fresh vegetables, fruit, cheese, crackers, and dips.

Tracy is awesome in the kitchen and made enough to feed three times the people present. She also made two dozen chocolate cupcakes with white-and-pink frosting. No doubt we will all leave with tons of leftovers. Again, no complaints.

With Micah and Peyton's wedding only three weeks away, I am eager to see what Tracy makes for her only daughter's reception.

Another nail in my love life coffin… my brother is getting married. To the woman who crushed on him in high school. Who also happens to be the woman he bullied in high school. The entirety of their relationship leaves me baffled.

When Micah and Peyton started hanging out as acquaintances-slash-friends, I never expected it to go anywhere. Their history was a hot mess. Not only had my big brother been her high school bully, Micah had been burned by his one and only serious relationship. And Peyton was far from interested in finding love after past losses. As a romantic couple, they were wobbly and jagged. Destined to fall apart.

But they found a way to grow beyond the horrible parts of their past. Developed an irrefutable friendship. Then slowly, they fell in love. Their love story was rocky, but neither of them gave up. What they felt for each other superseded every obstacle thrown their way.

Is there anyone in my life I *don't* envy? *Someone send help. Please.*

All I want is to find *the one.* Have a boundless love that captivates me from the start. A love that makes you forget anything and anyone else exists. A love that consumes every molecule of air you breathe. That owns every beat of your heart. A love you would crumble without.

That's not asking for too much, right? Wanting someone to look at me like I am the reason they breathe isn't asking too much. Wanting someone to take hold of my hand and never let go isn't asking too much. Not from where I stand. My friends have that type of love. It's only fair I have it too.

Sure, my notion of love and romance and happily ever afters are skewed by the countless romance novels I read. So what? There is nothing wrong with a woman knowing what she wants. There is nothing wrong with setting emotional expectations. There is nothing wrong with wanting immeasurable love.

Could I have dated half the county by now? Sure. Plenty of men have flirted and let me know they were interested. And who knows, maybe I would have found *the one* had I put myself out there more. Of the men I flirted with and casually dated, my *the-one* alarm never rang. Not once was there a whirl in my belly. No instinctual voice to tell me *give this one a chance*.

Does this make me pathetic? Not in my eyes. Does this make me a sad excuse? Depends who you ask. But I would rather be single than exist in an unhappy relationship. I'd rather be single and sad than tied to a person and dismal. Period.

Most of the men I dated were nice. Gentleman. Never pushy or angry I didn't give it up—which shocked me more than expected. The men in my everyday life—family and friends—are mixed bags in this department. That is, until they got hit by Cupid's arrow and settled down. My brother was the worst of them all, but only because of how things went down with his ex. Can't say I blame him.

Out of the inner circle, the original group—Cora, Micah, Jonas, Erin, and me—I never expected to be one of the last standing solo. The woman who preaches love and fate is one of the last to find it herself.

Erin has been dating on and off, but stays too focused on work for a relationship to stick. Leading a solo life doesn't bother her. At least she gets out there and makes an effort, which is more than I can say for myself.

"You okay?" Cora parks in the chair next to me and wraps an arm around my shoulders. "You're quiet all of a sudden. Which is not you."

I twist in my seat and smile at my best friend. Neither of our lives has been perfect. The years she and Gavin were apart were harsh and painful—for her and those of us who cared for either or both of them. All the nights I spent hugging my best friend and shushing her cries were tough. At the time, I didn't understand her heartache. How losing Gavin caused her to cry for days and weeks and months. Couldn't comprehend how her soul ripped in two at the loss of him.

And I still can't.

Not because I have a cold heart or am numb to emotion. Simply put, I have yet to experience an all-encompassing love. A love that owns every piece of you. I also don't know what it feels like to lose something so profound. To have your heart torn in two.

Instead of moping at her baby shower—one of the most joyous moments in her life—I should be giddy. The excited aunt showering my most loyal and lovable friend with pink frilly outfits and pacifiers and boxes of diapers. I should be hyping the party, not bringing it down.

Unfortunately, the small cynical part of me refuses to relinquish my selfishness. Refuses to spread false joy.

I take her hand in mine and meet her sincere, bright gaze. "I'll be okay. Just in a funk."

"Say no more." A very pregnant Cora hobbles out of her chair and tugs me upright. Before I admonish her, she hugs me tight to her body—a challenge in and of itself. My arms wind around her frame as I bite the inside of my cheek to halt the threatening tears. "I love you, Shell," she whispers in my ear. "No matter what, you can always come to me with whatever. You know that, right?"

Biting my cheek harder, I nod. "Yeah," I choke out. "I know."

She leans back enough to look me in the eye. Swipes my hair from my cheek. Studies my glassy irises. Tips up the corners of her lips slightly. "Whenever you want to talk, I'm here. Always. Doesn't matter what time or what it's about, I'm here."

I nod again. "Okay." I swipe beneath my eyes and sniffle. "But not today. Today is about you and"—I rub her belly—"Miss Clara."

Cora narrows her eyes for a split second, then drops her gaze to her swollen belly and rubs large circles. "Can't wait for us all to meet her, Shell. Pregnancy has been the most astonishing and uncomfortable experience." We laugh. "But I wouldn't trade a second of it." Cora lifts her gaze and locks me in place. "One day, you'll know too."

"Yeah, okay," I scoff. "Procreation requires a deposit, if you catch my drift. And no one's stopped by the bank."

Cora snort-laughs and braces herself on my shoulder as a hand holds her belly. "Oh my god, Shell. Finances have never sounded so dirty." She laughs harder, then stops abruptly. "Shit. I gotta pee."

I giggle to myself as my best friend waddles down the hallway as fast as her feet and belly will allow. What an interesting sight.

The rest of the shower goes by with more food, baby talk, and laughter. I smile and laugh at all the right times. I am happy for my friend. Happy that the stars in her life have finally aligned. Happy she and Gavin reconnected and rediscovered their love.

In many ways, their love story gives me hope. Tells me all things are possible.

Now, I need to *believe* it.

If romance novels have taught me anything, it is that love

happens when you least expect it. Not all love is explosive. Not all love hits hard and fast. But… love happens for us all. In one way or another. I just need to practice patience while I wait for mine to show.

No matter how long it takes.

## DEVLYN

Bars are not my scene. The noise and unruly behavior make my skin crawl. Hundreds of desperate people vying for attention. Countless others drowning their sorrows and problems with a temporary numbing agent. The occasional few just here for food and a laugh with friends.

Like me.

I wouldn't be sitting at this high top if not for the guy across the table. Chet Yarborough. The man who got me through some rough days at Ringling. Days I avoid thinking of at all costs. Chet graduated with his Bachelor of Fine Arts spring of last year and moved to New York a month later to pursue his career. Since arriving in the Big Apple, his name has splashed the artist headlines a few times. In our world, having your name in the headlines is a big deal—no matter how big or small the media outlet.

When Chet called last week and said he would be in town, I jumped on the chance to hang with him. Even if that means sitting in a bar and shirking away from swaying bodies. It isn't often I leave the house or my studio. Not without a reason. Some might call me a hermit. I don't really care.

There is no point in wasting gas or time or money if my leaving serves no purpose.

Chet dunks an onion ring in an odd but tasty barbecue-ranch sauce. Before it reaches his lips, he asks, "How've things been? Tell me what's new."

Before I get the chance to avoid and spin the question back to him, he shoves the onion ring in his mouth. If I say nothing, the empty time while he chews will be awkward. Not that I care about uncomfortable situations—life is full of discomfiture. I just go with the flow.

But Chet is the opposite. A rarity among our kind. The extraverted artist. The guy who paints and sculpts and draws for others more than himself. A people pleaser artist with a chatty disposition.

"Not much, man. Graduation was a few months back. Still doing my own thing—side projects, special requests, and whatnot—like before. Staying busy. What about you? How's New York?"

He finishes chewing and washes it down with a swig of beer. "New York is its own world. Bustling and alive and nothing like Florida. Like all places, it has its ups and downs, but I love the energy. It inspires me in ways I never expected."

New York is arguably one of the best places for the arts, in all forms. I never picture myself in places like New York or San Francisco, Los Angeles, or Miami. They are fantastic cities, hands down. Artist friendly and more welcoming than most. But the constant crowds, people in my space and nonstop business make me queasy. Bad enough I already live in one of the most populous areas of Florida. No need to up the ante and suffocate myself.

"That's great, man. I hope to move away too. But somewhere less crowded. Somewhere I can sit outside with an easel, a blank canvas and my brushes, and get lost without interruption."

Chet nods and then stares off into the crowd. Zoning out and getting lost in the idea. "Sounds nice," he mutters.

More than nice, actually.

Before either of us gets in another word, a man's voice booms from the far wall. "Good evening, ladies and gents. Welcome to another night of glory and excellent renditions. Also known as karaoke night."

The night went from a three out of ten to a five with this announcement. I don't necessarily love karaoke, but at least it may simmer down the crowd nearby. Have fewer people in my personal bubble for the rest of our time here.

A server arrives at our table, offers refills, and asks if we need anything else. With Chet more than happy to talk all night, I order something more substantial than an appetizer. She scribbles down my turkey burger and fries, our drink refills, and Chet's buffalo wings on a small notepad, then wanders back to the bar.

An older man steps up onto the karaoke stage and the crowd roars to life with wolf whistles and rapturous applause. Obviously, he is karaoke famous in this place. A local favorite.

I study the man as he takes the stage. Old enough to easily be my grandfather, the man sports attire of someone half his age or younger. His vibrance captivates and holds your attention. For a beat, I picture him in a swirl of blues and reds and whites on canvas. The wrinkled lines of his face a testimony of a life well lived.

Across the dining area, a voice screams above all the rest and steals the spotlight momentarily. "We love you, Karaoke Grandpa."

The old man blows kisses to the masses. "I love you too, sugar."

I scan the sea of excited bargoers in search of the woman who called out to him. Not sure why, but I need to put a face to the voice. I crane my neck and survey hundreds of men and women, looking for the one face excited to see this man grace the stage and microphone.

And then I land on her.

Familiar and not in the same breath. Sun-kissed golden skin. Dark, twinkling irises fanned by long lashes and accentuated with bold brows. Thrill on her naturally pouty lips and at the corners of her eyes. A slim yet prominent nose. Thick, dark-blonde waves swing from her ponytail; the occasional stubborn lock grazes her cheek, but she doesn't swipe it away.

Where do I know her from?

I dig through my mental archive and search for her face. Run the contours of her cheekbones and lips and nose against my mental database. Scour all the places I frequent and the jobs I have done. And it doesn't take long before I get a hit. Before her familiarity becomes crystal clear.

Last year. The mural I painted outside Petal and Vine Florist before fall semester. The woman more vibrant and spectacular than all the blooming buds in the shop. The woman I spent hours sneaking glances at, only to get small snippets of her profile or the way her hair glowed in the sunlight. The woman whose name I never learned because our paths barely crossed.

No matter how many peeps I got of her partial profile, I wanted more.

I had never spent so much time on such a simple project. Never purposely dragged out my art to spend more time in someone's presence. I may not know her name, but the fading memory of her had been a muse for much of my art this past year.

How odd I didn't recognize her right away. Must be the lighting or this place; both so very different from the flower shop.

Fingers snap in front of my face and I jerk back. My eyes snap to Chet and his shit-eating grin. I don't crumble under his scrutiny. Nor do I feel shame or guilt. Instead, I stare back with a look that asks why he got all snappy.

"Who is she?"

I shrug. "Don't know." Not a lie. We never shared a conversation. Far as I know, she has no clue who I am either. "Looks like someone I've met but can't place." Half-truth. But that is all I plan to give Chet. Last thing I need is a long list of intrusive questions I have no answers to.

He glances over his shoulder at her profile; too long for my liking. I bite my tongue, stow the possessiveness simmering in my veins, and wait for him to break his stare. Thank goodness, for his sake, I don't wait long.

"You should talk to her." I raise my brows at his suggestion. He shakes his head and laughs. "I have no intention of hooking up with anyone while I'm home. Not my style. You, on the other hand, will be around. And she has obviously caught your eye."

*You have no idea.*

I pick up my water and sip it to avoid responding for a moment. Before I set the cup down, the server comes to the rescue. She deposits red plastic baskets lined with red-and-white-checkered paper beneath our food. Soon as she steps away, I pluck my burger from the basket and take a monstrous bite.

The entire time we eat, neither of us says a word. I pretend to listen and focus on the crowd favorites. Chet appears to enjoy the entertainment.

While he does, I sneak the occasional glance at my anonymous muse. Take in her smile. The brightness with a hint of shadow. A touch of shade not all eyes would detect.

But I see them all. The light, the dark, the spectrum in between.

There is something beautiful about capturing all the facets of another person. Without words, without touch. Just what the naked eye sees. Translated through the mind of another. An unspoken truth sketched in graphite, scrawled in charcoal or stroked in oils.

Nothing speaks louder than the voice of art. A transcription of one's mind interpreted differently by another.

Five karaoke performances later, I eat the last of my fries. The server deposits our bills on the table and we pay. Chet has long since moved on from provoking me to talk to the woman. Hallelujah.

"How long are you in town?" I ask as we step into the balmy, late-September air.

"Few more days. If my folks don't shackle me to the house, maybe we can hang again before I go."

Neither of us is an idiot. Chet will spend half his time with his parents and the other half catching up with other friends, but I nod anyway.

"Sounds great, man. Let me know."

One backslapping bro hug later, we go our separate ways. I hop into my car, exit the lot, and speed down the road. My fingers twitch with the need to be in my studio. To bring the golden-haired beauty to life on paper or canvas.

Her image had faded in my mind's eye. Not much, but enough. Tonight, though… I did all I could to memorize every angle of her supple skin and flushed cheeks. The way her locks escaped from the elastic and framed her face. How her cheeks rippled near the corners of her lips as she pushed them upward. The subtle arch of each brow as it highlighted her already ethereal appearance.

I park in the driveway, jump out, and stop myself from running inside. Not that I care what the neighbors think. Surely, they already find me peculiar. They wouldn't be wrong, but I own my awkward nature. All artists are quirky in their own way.

I kick my shoes off at the door, weave through the house, and take the stairs two at a time. The closer I get to my studio, the stronger my pulse pounds. Scents of the earth filter through my nose—the fibrous sixty-pound sketch paper, the metallic tinge of graphite, the pungent, piney odor of turpentine. I inhale deeply as I step through the studio. Breathe in the smells so familiar and comforting.

Snatching a sketchbook from the long table along the wall, I go to the drafting table, sit down on the stool, and pick up my pencils on the side table. With ease, I sift through the sketchpad to the first blank page and run my palm down the endless possibilities.

Closing my eyes, I see her again. Beauty. Charm. Abundance. Sharp and soft angles. And a hint of melancholy.

That small dash of despair calls out to me. Begs me to bring it to life and set it free. Spill the hurt onto paper and release it from her soul.

I press the tip of the pencil to the paper and begin. In a matter of minutes, I already have the rough contours of her heart-shaped face and jaw definition. Hunching over the table, I shift the pad this way and that, over and over. I zone out. Let the art pull me in. Possess me and flow through my fingertips.

With each line drawn, each stroke of a softer or harder lead, each brush of the pad of my finger to shade, I breathe easier.

It isn't purely about bringing her to life with my fingers and a set of tools. It is about connection. A connection so foreign, yet so intimate. A connection I crave, yet don't know how to manifest.

This woman wakes up the lost pieces of my soul. Stirs the biochemistry in my brain and paints it with color. Draws me into her orbit and locks me in with her gravity.

The scary part?

I want to stay there. In her bubble. In the one place I don't have to imagine the twinkle in her dark, mysterious eyes. Or the subtle pout of her bottom lip. Or the sadness that emphasizes her stellar smile.

I want to stay in her bubble and never leave. Exist in her space and breathe her air. Stand at her side and lace my fingers with hers.

But I won't. I can't.

Being in anyone's bubble isn't in the stars.

Not for me. Not ever.

# Three

## SHELLY

No place I'd rather be than right here.

Petal and Vine wasn't always my dream job, but I consider myself lucky to have this place. In a world full of craziness and uncertainty, standing in the middle of this florist shop gives me purpose and eases the stress in my life. Working here started off as an accident, but I don't regret a day I walk through these doors.

Early junior year of high school, my aspirations lie in interior design. For homes and businesses alike. As far back as I recall, I had an eye for design and flow and symmetry. Oftentimes, I rearranged my bedroom when the air felt stagnant. Rearranged my clothes in the dresser and closet. Hung posters and photos in new places. In change, I discovered new life. Energy invisible to the naked eye, yet it made the hairs on my arm vibrate with intention.

On a Friday girls' night, years ago at Cora's house, her mom interrupted our hundredth *Lord of the Rings* marathon. I didn't mind, though. That girl and that movie—cue eye roll. Anyway… Elizabeth asked if we would help her at the shop the next day. She had a huge wedding order to fulfill and her employee called out sick. Like the good daughter and daughter's friend, we obliged.

That was the day I learned to love all things floral related. It wasn't only the natural perfume that woke me up, but also the way I could create something beautiful. How something so small and simple could bring a smile to someone's face. Improve someone's day with a gift. A single bloom or three dozen.

Working at Petal and Vine has been a long journey. I have worked here half my life. Literally. This career, this life, has gifted me so much over the years. Stress. Tears. Days when I wanted to throw in the towel. But also joy. Courage. Strength.

Most of all, opportunity.

In little more than a year, my name will appear as the owner of Petal and Vine. In a year, I will own a business. Elizabeth and I have gone over all the fine print little by little, so neither of us is overwhelmed by the transition. But this step is huge—for us both—and thrilling.

"Got another online order," Elizabeth says as she steps up to the arrangement table.

I wiggle a dahlia between a fern stem and baby's breath, then look at Elizabeth across the table. Without question, Cora is a younger, spitting image of her mother. Working with Elizabeth has been like working side by side with my best friend. With my family. Within the walls of Petal and Vine, it feels like home. Warm and comfortable and welcoming. Over the years, Elizabeth has transitioned from mother figure to boss to coworker to friend. But she instantly snaps back into mom mode when any of us needs that side of her. I count my lucky stars to have such a wonderful woman in my life.

No offense to my own mother. Nicole Reed is a lovely woman. Strong and brilliant and thoughtful. I wouldn't be who I am today without her. She and Dad raised my brother and me in a loving environment. Taught us to go after our dreams and never give up.

But as of recent, Mom has been a bit overbearing. Intrusive and suffocating. The incessant probing started before Micah and Peyton became official. Questions about relationships and love. And babies. God, has it been agonizing. No one would ever accuse me of being anti-baby, but the pressure Mom puts on us for grandchildren has me double-locking the chastity belt.

Which is why it is a blessing to have two mother figures in my life. Elizabeth balances out the crazy Mom puts on my shoulders. Gives me another person to express what has me bogged down when I feel Mom may go off the rails.

"Great!" I survey the full vases in the cooler behind her. All orders waiting to be delivered or picked up today and tomorrow. "Business has been picking up steam. Not sure if it's the ads or word of mouth. Whatever it is, I'm here for it." Majority of our orders are online, but we have regular foot traffic as well.

I get back to work on the current arrangement and Elizabeth starts the online order. Setting it in the cooler when I finish, I stare at the abundance of lavender, yellow, and white rose bouquets, boutonnieres, table arrangements, and more. All for one momentous occasion.

Tomorrow, my brother is getting married. Never thought I would see the day. With his track record, I sure as hell thought I'd marry before him. But life had other plans and I am so happy for him. Thrilled he found love.

Micah and Peyton have come a long way since high school. A year and a half ago, when I'd learned Micah had started hanging out with Peyton, Cora and I jogged his memory of who she was and what he'd done to her. I had never seen my brother so petrified in his life. Horrified by the ghosts of his past. Ghosts he created. He did anything and everything to right his wrongs, stepped up and became a better man, and Peyton forgave all his past transgressions.

Every time I see the two of them together, their dopey, lovesick eyes, I know love can overcome every obstacle. And if *they* can defeat history with love, all things are possible.

Which means I, too, will find love one day. I only hope it happens before a full head of gray hair and a dozen cats.

"Is everything set for the wedding tomorrow?" I ask, although I know the answer. We finished the last of the arrangements before close yesterday. But the stress of my brother's impending nuptials makes me ask anyway. Last thing I want is to forget an arrangement and throw the whole day off.

Elizabeth steps up to my side, places a hand on my shoulder, and strokes her thumb back and forth. "Yes. Never thought I'd see this day."

I turn to face her. "What do you mean?"

She shakes her head and laughs. "I remember all the stories Cora shared. *Shelly's brother is gross. He's always staring at girls and licking his lips*," she says in a mocking tone.

I tip my head back and laugh.

Cora and I have been friends since elementary school. It wasn't odd for our families to hang out together on weekends to appease us. Which also meant my annoying brother was around. Two years wasn't a major age difference, but it was enough to steer me away from him before entering middle school. Rumors of my brother kissing most of the girls in middle school before my first year there spread faster than

STDs. It was nothing compared to the year before he and Peyton became an item. I have no intention of walking down that dirty alley again.

"He was gross." I laugh harder and Elizabeth joins in. "But I'm glad he and Peyton found each other. It was questionable for a bit, but they came out stronger on the other side. She makes him a better man."

Elizabeth pats my shoulder. "Agreed." She goes back to the table and continues the online order.

Rounding the table, I clean up my mess and put the pruning tools back in place. I start for the small office in the back corner of the store when Elizabeth speaks up.

"Oh, I almost forgot." I turn around and give her my full attention. "Patty from my book club asked about floral arrangement classes. What do you think?"

Petal and Vine has had more business in the last two years than the previous five years combined. We aren't hurting for business or income. But as a small business owner, it is always wise to have other sources of revenue. Anything could happen to taper off orders. Supply shortages, economic changes, clients unhappy with the ownership transition. The last one seems less than likely considering we hide nothing from our clients, especially those that have been loyal from the beginning.

"Classes are a wonderful idea. Floral arrangement, buying for the seasons, how to maintain planted and trimmed flowers. The possibilities are endless."

"Excellent. The ladies will be thrilled." A smile brightens Elizabeth's face.

"I'll do some research, come up with a list of classes to offer and when, price them reasonably yet still be competitive with the market."

A list forms in my mind of all the options we could offer. Different skill levels. Showing attendees how to artfully decorate their space with one bundle of flowers. Ways to use flowers for special occasions such as birthdays, anniversaries, holidays, and gatherings.

I smile and spin to face the office. I don't make it three steps before Elizabeth stops me again.

"Also…" I pivot on my back foot and meet her gaze. "Remember when we had the mural done last year?"

What an odd question, but I roll with it. "Yes, of course." I don't add anything else, unsure what to say.

"I spoke with the artist last week. He'll be by in a couple weeks to do some touch-ups on the mural and add a thicker layer of sealant. To help prevent fading from the elements."

Oh. My. God. Ohmygod.

A thin layer of perspiration blankets my skin. At the rate it seeps from my pores, I will undoubtedly look like I walked in the rain without an umbrella in no time. My heart does this bizarre somersault in my rib cage before bounding into fifth gear. Then my stomach flip-flops beneath my diaphragm.

*Is it hot in here?*

Will Elizabeth be weirded out if I stand in the walk-in cooler for the next half hour? Probably not. We go in there so frequently, she won't bat an eye. But if she sees me without a jacket, she will ask questions.

"And since he'll be here," she continues as if I am not having an existential crisis, "I asked him to paint a mural on the west wall inside the shop." Her gaze shifts to the wall she references. "When the morning sun hits it, it'll feel like we're in a meadow."

Elizabeth's eyes light up as she envisions said meadow-like mural. Meanwhile, I seem to have forgotten how my lungs operate. *Inhale through the nose, hold it, exhale through the mouth.* Is it too much to ask my heart to settle? *Jesus.*

*The Artist*—that is what I call him since he never introduced himself and I was too chickenshit to ask his name—consumed too much of my free time last year. Not to mention my dreams for months after. Elizabeth hired him to paint the mural on the outer east wall. The entire time he was here—twenty days to be exact—I made up every possible reason to step near the small east window panes, just to sneak a peek at him. When I ordered lunch, I asked if he wanted anything… just to hear his voice.

We didn't exchange many words in those twenty days, we barely looked at one another, but there was just something about him. Not a physical feature, per se—although, he was easy on the eyes. But he had this zeal. A vibrancy that radiated off him. Anytime my eyes landed on him, anytime I stood within ten feet of him, my brain shut down. My motor skills went on vacation. Every outgoing function I possessed hid in the shadows.

I don't know what it is about *the artist*, but he feels familiar. Not in the sense that I had seen him at the grocery store every Wednesday after work. No, his familiarity resonates deeper. Rooted in layers of past lives. Memories of a time lived lifetimes before this one.

And now, he will be here again. Adding more to the flowery garden scene on the outside of our building. Creating an indoor meadow for all to admire, for me to admire, every day.

"Sounds lovely." I clear my now dry throat. "Can't wait to see the outcome. It'll be beautiful, I'm sure."

Before Elizabeth reads too much into my suddenly scratchy voice, I turn on my heel and pick up the pace as I head for the office. Once inside, I close the door behind me, lean against the grain, close my eyes, and take deep breaths.

*Get it together, Reed. He's just a guy.* I repeat the words until they turn into Scrabble squares in my head. *He's just a guy.*

Out of nowhere, a new voice whispers in my mental ear. *Keep telling yourself that. He isn't just some guy, and you know it. Why else would you be freaking out?*

"Ugh!"

I stomp over to the desk, wake the computer up, and sort through emails to distract myself. It works… for a little while. But it isn't long before my mind drifts back to the man with floppy brown-and-golden hair. To the way his body moved with the art. How *he* was as much the art as the brushes and paint and strokes.

A year has passed since he was here. A year since I have seen him in person. Yet, the image of him is quite predominant when I close my eyes. Tall and lean, his jeans and T-shirts loose on his frame. His quiet demeanor as he focused on the art. The soft timbre of his voice faded long ago, but just the thought of hearing it again forms a bubble of anticipation beneath my breastbone.

I drop my head in my hands and sigh. "God, I'm hopeless," I mumble into the empty office.

Hopeless or not, *the artist* will be here in two weeks. Time to prepare myself to not look the fool. On the outside, at least. The mess brewing inside me will undoubtedly magnify between now and his arrival.

Where are you, inner zen master? Because I definitely need to locate my inner calm. Stat.

# four

## DEVLYN

*Get out of the car. It's just a job.*

The same nine words cycle my mind for the sixth time. Yet I remain glued to the driver's seat. My grip tightens on the steering wheel as I stare at the flower shop through a trellis of jasmine, beyond the three-foot wooden fence. One breath. Then another. My fingers loosen and I unbuckle the seat belt.

*Get out of the car. It's just a job.*

I open the car door and get hit with more than a dozen floral fragrances. The exterior of Petal and Vine is unlike any other florist shop in the area. Similar to a small business outdoor nursery, except the plants outside are for visual appeal, not purchase. The shop has an old-world feel. An impression of simpler times and forgotten contentment.

Walking under the jasmine-woven lattice, my sneakers crunch the gravel as I come to a halt. Clusters of flowers greet me with their version of good morning. Butterscotch yellow and boysenberry purple. Blush and fuchsia pinks. Apricot and tiger orange. Sage and rosemary green and several shades between. Bushes and vines decorate the earth and the store with foreign strategy. The gravel path weaves between the plants for visitors to see and smell and touch. Bright and subtle. Sweet and pungent. Smooth and prickly. The occasional bench or chair along the way, parked beneath tall crepe myrtle and oak trees, so one can enjoy more time with the blossoms.

Past the blooms and slithering greenery is the shop. The exposed cinder block on the east wall is slathered in layers of paint. An image of another garden beyond this one. Cobblestone frames the cinder block and gives the feeling you are stepping through realms, into the place where only flowers and plants exist. The color hasn't faded much, but the paint isn't as bold as it was last year. To the right of the cobblestone, two tall windows with wide black borders frame glass-paneled French doors. Black lacquered wood rests above the windows and doors with *Petal and Vine* written in white script.

*It's just a job.*

Taking a deep breath, I start for the doors. Brush my fingers over soft rose petals and wispy grass shrubs along the way. Turn the knob and step inside, a blast of cool air hitting my skin. The shop is the equivalent of a three-bedroom, single-story home, minus several walls. Dried lavender hangs in twined bundles from the ceiling. Before I take in more of the shop, a voice calls out.

"Devlyn." Elizabeth steps around a rack of flower bins, wipes her hands on an apron at her waist and offers one to shake. "Good to see you again."

"You as well, Ms. Davies."

A smile lights up her face as a hand rests over her heart. "Please, call me Elizabeth." She drops her hand, but her smile remains. "We have gotten several compliments on the mural.

Thank you for coming out to touch it up and give the inside a little face-lift."

I tuck my hands in my pockets and rock back on my heels. "My pleasure. I'll add a better sealant to the exterior this time. Should preserve the color for years to come."

"Elizabeth," a voice calls from farther back. My blood fizzles in my veins. A whirl forms beneath my sternum. *It's her. My otherworldly muse.* "Is the delivery truck here?" Her words fade as she enters the main floor and spots me with Elizabeth.

Her feet jerk to a stop as she goes rigid next to Elizabeth. Her twinkling eyes capture mine and I get the first *real* glimpse. Twilight-blue irises hold me prisoner for three breaths. During each inhale, I notice something new.

*One*... her eyes literally twinkle.

*Two*... the gold flecks resemble constellations.

*Three*... she is *my* constellation. *My Andromeda.*

She shakes her head and addresses me with a smile she no doubt grants everyone. But this is not the smile I want. Or the smile I need.

"Didn't mean to interrupt."

She goes to step away, but only takes two steps before Elizabeth speaks up. "Shelly, this is Devlyn, the artist who painted the mural."

The glimmer in her eyes arrests me. As if she wished on a star to learn my name. And today, her wish came true. Guess you could say mine did as well.

*Shelly.*

I scan through the random wealth of knowledge I stowed over the years and remember, in some beliefs, Shelly means "meadow." How fitting. In a blink, the meadow I plan to paint inside the shop has new meaning. A new purpose. A life all its own. I won't paint the meadow solely for the shop, but more so for her. A place of beauty, but not more beautiful than her. Scenery to let her imagination wander. To let her escape.

Blush tints her cheeks and she swallows.

Another random fact about the name Shelly… it means one of purity in Hebrew. Although Shelly has youthful features, the way she carries herself indicates maturity. Most women with her level of maturity don't blush. The fact she does is intriguing.

"My apologies." She offers her hand. "It's nice to meet you formally, Devlyn."

I slip my hand from my pocket and place it in hers. Soft skin with the occasional nick from a thorn and callous from the floral shears. But otherwise, smooth and warm and perfect against my own.

"Nice to meet you as well."

I don't want to free her hand, but know holding it captive makes for an unpleasant first encounter. So, like a gentleman, I slip my hand from hers and stuff it back in my pocket. I do my best to ignore the tingle still on my palm. The lingering warmth where our fingers touched and hands clasped.

*It's just a job. Just stop. Getting romantically involved is a bad idea. Always.*

"At the end of next year," Elizabeth starts, snapping my attention back to her, "Shelly will take over Petal and Vine." A smile lifts the corners of Elizabeth's lips and eyes. Thin lines accent her cheeks and temples; years of wisdom and joy evident in those creases. Pride and delight and maternal love echo from her aura as she beams at Shelly. Within minutes, I learn Shelly is more than just an employee or coworker. She isn't just someone buying out a business. Shelly is family, even if not by blood.

"Congratulations," I say. And I mean the sentiment. Owning a business is no simple feat. "Elizabeth picked a wonderful woman to carry on her legacy."

*Whack.*

I need more than a mental slap.

*What the hell am I saying?*

First, I don't know Shelly. Not really. Sure, I caught a glimpse or two of her last year while painting the outside mural. Caught her from the corner of my eye, checking me out through the shop windows. Seeing her two weeks ago at the bar doesn't count.

Second, I barely know Elizabeth. I stumbled upon the job last year after my mother stopped by the shop to have an arrangement delivered to a grieving friend. She'd instantly fallen in love with the *cute flower shop*. Bragged about it for weeks, months. She also bragged to Elizabeth about her son who made everything more beautiful with a paintbrush. Not long after, I received a call and was asked to spruce up the outside of Petal and Vine.

I love my mother. Assume her intentions are honest and come from a place of deep affection for her only son. That is what I have told myself over the years. I have yet to convince myself it's true. Much as I appreciate her effort, she needs to stop meddling. Give me the opportunity to spread my wings. Find my way on my own. Let me be my own person. Without her.

As a child, her words and actions seemed harmless. I always thought of her as a role model, a strong woman with sheer determination. She didn't get to where she is today by standing quietly on the sidelines.

But as an adult, my lens of perception has changed. With age comes wisdom. With wisdom comes enlightenment. And with my developed awareness comes perspective and uncertainty.

I love my mother, but as more time passes, I learn with each word she speaks and act she commits, it is only to benefit her. To put her in the limelight. To make people fawn over her. To elevate her onto the shiny, stage-lit pedestal. She brags about her son because, in return, she gets praise for raising such a wonderful and talented young man. She glows under that praise and slowly transitions those conversations to focus solely on her.

In this one instance—tossing my name out to a prospective client—I make an exception.

*Because, Shelly.*

But god, I pray her meddling stops, and soon.

Another dose of crimson paints Shelly's cheeks and heats my blood. I memorize the color. Stash it away for the next time I have a brush in my hand and canvas beneath the bristles.

"Thank you. That's very kind of you." Her eyes pull me into her orbit and hold me steady. Her chest rises and falls in my periphery, over and over. Then she blinks and breaks the spell she cast. "I'll be in the back." She shifts her gaze to Elizabeth. "Let me know when the truck arrives."

"Will do."

Before another word is said, Shelly spins around and vanishes behind a wall of flowers. The second she disappears, I miss her presence, her energy, her aura. All things eidetic memory cannot replicate. At least the image of her is carved into my memory.

I blink a few times, shake myself back into reality, and look over at a smiling Elizabeth. Her smile speaks volumes, whereas her voice remains silent. The eye of an artist picks up on these small idiosyncrasies and uses them to convey deeper meaning in their work. As for now, I ignore the hidden message in her smile.

"Show me where you were thinking of placing the indoor mural," I say to steer the moment back to business.

In a blink, Elizabeth transitions into proud businesswoman and owner. She guides me to a wall opposite the entrance. Several tin pails, large and small, occupy the floor space. Eucalyptus stems, wheat sprigs, grassy bundles, lush greenery, cattails, and more fill the taller baskets on the floor. On a short shelf behind them, shorter pails are filled with lavender, sprigged red berries, oblong fiery flowers, blue thistle, baby's breath, fern stems, and wispy twigs with pink flowers that remind me of weeping willows and cherry blossoms. Off to the left, white and blush roses grow on a wooden ladder.

Visions of the meadow pop into my head. Various greens, hints of gold and brown, small splashes of violet and honey and berry, and subtle touches of white and indigo. With a slight shift of the pails, the illusion of a natural slate path in the mural will give patrons a feel of stepping into the meadow while shopping.

"It isn't much to work with…"

I hold up a hand and shake my head. "No, it's perfect." Beside me, Elizabeth beams. "Do you mind if I shift things around? Obviously while I paint, but also for when the mural is finished."

"Not at all. I trust your vision."

Hearing those words never gets old. When a client trusts you to bring the art to life, it is the ultimate gift.

"Thank you." I give her a sincere smile. "Also, a suggestion." Her brows lift as she holds my gaze. "When I finish the touchups outside, you may want to invest in a small awning.

Nothing extravagant. But something that will shade the mural from the midday sun. It'll add years to the painting after I add the extra seal."

"I will look into them immediately. Thank you for the tip."

Elizabeth guides me back to the shop's office. I don't miss the opportunity to smile at Shelly as I pass. Her cheeks pinken again, then plump as she returns the smile. I don't know what it is specifically about this woman, but she steals my attention when we exist in the same space. Her aura controls the room and says *look at me*, and I cannot help but oblige.

But I shouldn't be caught looking at her like some creeper. So I shift my gaze and focus on the task at hand.

Elizabeth and I look over our schedules and coordinate— not as if my schedule is packed, but no one needs to be privy to such information. Minutes later, we both mark our calendars for the project to start in a few days. I give her a guesstimate of how long the entire project will take, mentally stretching the time frame longer than necessary.

*Because, Shelly.*

We walk out of the office and Elizabeth pats my shoulder. "Thank you again for doing this. Your art will add an elegant touch to the shop and make everyone's visit more pleasant."

I stop us near the table where Shelly studiously works on an arrangement, desperately trying not to make eye contact. But I need one last walk under the stars before I leave.

"If you don't mind, I'd like to bring you ladies drinks on the mornings I work. A token of my gratitude for the additional work."

Elizabeth waves off the idea. "Not necessary." Shelly peeks through the sunset-colored petals with a small smile on her face. I let her hypnotize me for three wobbly heartbeats.

"True, but I'd like to anyway. So, what is your beverage of choice?"

"Relentless," Elizabeth mumbles, and I laugh. "If you insist, coffee. No cream or sugar." She pats my shoulder again. "You're too sweet, Devlyn."

Shelly steps aside and out of the arrangement's protection. And for two breaths, we don't speak. I don't know what it is, but this woman crosses my wires. Makes me forget how to function on a day-to-day level. For whatever reason, it doesn't bother me in the way it would with anyone else.

"What about you?" I ask, desperate for more than just her eyes.

She swallows, then wipes her hands on her apron. "I'm more of a tea drinker." She clears her throat. "Not sure where you'll be going, but I'll take any type of tea drink. With oat milk, if it comes with milk. If it doesn't, no milk is okay too." She purses her lips and attempts to hide a huff. Obviously upset with her slight rambling after being silent so long.

But I like her rambling. I like everything about Shelly. Even how different she is near me than she was when I saw her with friends not long ago. I like her shy side, but hope I get to know her outgoing side as well.

"Tea it is." I tip up one corner of my mouth, lightly tap the table between us, and take a step back. "I will see you ladies on Thursday."

Elizabeth gives an enthusiastic goodbye. But it is the quiet farewell from Shelly I hear the loudest.

I have zero intention of involving myself in any type of romantic relationship. With Shelly or anyone else. But non-romantic relationships aren't off the table. And I would very much like some type of relationship with Shelly. The fair-haired beauty with stars in her eyes.

# *five*
## SHELLY

Lavender London Fog. That is the name of the tea Devlyn brought me today. The last four days at the shop, he has brought me something different. Hot teas. Cold teas. Tea lattes. Some florally, others earthy.

And I love each one of them.

Elizabeth smiles like a schoolgirl when Devlyn hands over her coffee and deposits a brown bag with fresh baked goods each morning. The bakery items are unique and different each day. Today, he brought two lemon-frosted lavender scones with a side of honey butter. Yesterday, it was brown butter pear galettes.

With his arrival each morning, my cheeks sting and neck heats. No doubt he sees the flustery embarrassment on my skin. But he doesn't say a word. Just smiles and says good morning.

I have never been so enamored with someone. Enough to blush like an adolescent.

And it is so freaking odd.

Shy is not my typical style. Sure, I quiet down on the first two or three dates with a guy, but I am not *quiet*. Not like this.

Not as if I fear fumbling over my words or saying the wrong thing.

And let's get one thing straight, I am most definitely not dating Devlyn. Not that I wouldn't want to.

Devlyn is attractive with his sun-streaked, floppy brown hair, sharp, square jawline, and reserved nature that has me wanting to know more. To ask countless frivolous and meaningful questions. Without effort, Devlyn easily garners my attention. Lures me in. Holds me captive with unrestrained interest.

If Devlyn asked me out, my brain would conjure a hundred ways to word vomit yes in a heartbeat.

*Someone stop my internal rambling. Jesus.*

Devlyn is a nice guy. Quiet in ways different from my sudden shyness. His muted words and subtle smiles seem more his true nature. His way of processing the world around him without breaking it apart with meaningless words. In less than a week, I feel a sense of comfort from his taciturn nature. Like a warm hug you never want to end. This bewilders me in inexplicable ways. Drives my curiosity further. Makes me want to share more hushed moments in his presence.

When Devlyn exists in the same space as me, I see and think and process the world differently. Give myself a moment to *really* take in my surroundings. The bow of flower petals. The jagged edges of leaves. The soft brush of dried bunny tails. The potent scent of clove and cinnamon for the upcoming holidays. Each strikes me with new perspective. They aren't just plants in a shop to sell, but also a part of something more. Something bigger.

I sip the tea and sigh. "This is wonderful. Thank you."

Devlyn gives me his boyish smile, one that makes me, without hesitation, smile in return.

"My pleasure. Glad you're enjoying it."

Then he walks through the front room and out the door.

My brow furrows as confusion runs rampant. Not from what he said, but how I feel. The way I miss his presence the second he disappears. Such an off sensation. Is it weird that I enjoy the jittery calm only he delivers? Probably.

I sigh and sip my tea.

The touch-ups Devlyn has done to the outside mural have been minimal thus far. During my occasional work near the window, I have seen him add touches of fresh paint where the colors have dulled the past year. Blues and reds, but nothing extensive.

For the last four days, I fabricated reasons to be near the windows. Like I am right now. Stealing every opportunity to sneak a glance at the wall he paints. To daydream as I watch his arms flex and his head tilt as he works the brush over the concrete.

Watching Devlyn work is art in and of itself. The way his hair flops over his temple with each tilt of his head. The way he studies the wall with the end of a paintbrush pressed to his chin. How he zones out and becomes one with the art. How he only adds paint where he deems necessary.

Devlyn fascinates me in ways I never thought possible. Not solely how he views art, but also his physical presence.

I gawk at him way longer than appropriate. But no one stops me because no one is around to witness my lewd behavior. Hell, Elizabeth would probably encourage me. Tell me to spark a conversation with him. Push me to do more than spy on him through the window.

But she is in the office with a stack of bills and invoices.

So, I sip my tea, swirl the lightly sweet, floral flavors on my tongue, admire the man outside, and pretend to tend to the flowers at the front of the store. Flowers that need no organization whatsoever.

When lunchtime approaches, Devlyn steps inside. Perspiration glistens his brow, his temples, the line of his jaw, his philtrum, and I forget how to use words in the correct order. At least I stop myself from speaking early enough. No need to embarrass myself further. My hot cheeks have already done more than enough.

"I'm ordering lunch," he says before dabbing his mouth on the sleeve of his shirt. "Would you like anything?"

The leftover spaghetti I stowed in the fridge calls out. Tells me I should save my money and not waste food. Whispers that I should gracefully decline his offer. Especially since I need to save every penny with the shop purchase next year.

"I… uh…" I fumble for the answer. *No, thank you* sits on the tip of my tongue, yet the muscle won't curl properly to say the words. *Dammit.*

"It's my treat," he adds, a half smile pushing up the corner of his perfect lips and tempting me further.

My cheeks heat and I tuck my lips between my teeth. The action does nothing except make my embarrassment more evident.

*Way to go, Shelly. He probably thinks you're batshit.*

*Get it together. Jesus. Take a deep breath, thank him and carry on.*

"You don't have to buy lunch. I brought leftovers." I point toward the back, where our office-slash-break room resides.

Many moons ago, the shop was a house. But when the streets widened and the neighborhood became more commercial than residential, some of the houses turned into small businesses. At first, it was odd seeing houses turn into real estate agencies and restaurants and veterinary offices, but it didn't take long to become normal.

When Elizabeth purchased the building, it still had many of the interior walls. The previous owner ran a beauty salon. Hair, nails, facials. They may have had a massage room too. Completely understandable why the previous owner wanted the separate rooms.

Elizabeth had a vision when this place became hers. To have it as open and airy as a field. To make the atmosphere inviting. For the business to not look like an old home, but a unique storefront. Slowly but surely, she brought her vision to life. Watching the changes, small as they were, happen over the years has been wonderful. And I am so fortunate to have such an amazing business to step into when it changes hands.

The only original walls Elizabeth left intact were ones for a bedroom, bathroom, and the short hall leading to the garage. Now, the bedroom is the office-slash-break room—the bathroom en suite—and the garage is set up for storage and cooler space. All other walls were removed. Beams were erected to stabilize the ceiling wherever necessary. But now, over two thousand square feet are an open, usable storefront.

"Will they last another day?" I scrunch my brow, confused. *What were we talking about?* "Your leftovers," he clarifies, deepening that small half smile.

Right. *Dumbass.* "Oh, yeah. Probably. It's just spaghetti."

"Then eat it tomorrow. Let me get you lunch today."

Three. Freaking. Letters. Say yes. You know you want to eat lunch with him. Not just to sneak closer looks, but maybe to strike up a conversation. One where you use your words. In order. And not too quickly.

*Say it!*

"Uh, yeah. Yes. Lunch would be nice. Thank you."

He retrieves his phone from his back pocket, unlocks it, and scrolls. All the while, I simply stare at him. Watch as he hunches over the phone, the thumb of one hand scrolling while a finger of the other hand presses his lips. *Oh, to be that finger.* His head pops up and heat hits my cheeks at being caught.

He simply smiles.

"Sandwiches or sushi?" I laugh a little too hard and he leans closer. His scent hits my nose and I stop laughing. Remind myself to breathe, slow and steady breaths. *God, he smells good.* "Maybe over lunch, you can tell me why that's so funny."

Suddenly, lunch feels like a date. But I don't know Devlyn. Not really. Not that I knew the guys I dated either. So I brush off the notion and think of it as two friends eating a meal together. Like I would with Gavin or Jonas or one of the guys from the tattoo shop.

"Sandwiches. And yes, I'll let you in on the joke."

Devlyn picks a delicatessen two miles up the street and we both choose sandwiches. He asks what Elizabeth likes and I give him her typical order.

*See, Shelly. Just friends. He's buying Elizabeth food too.*

He places the order for delivery, then says the food will arrive in a half hour.

The next thirty minutes take hours to pass.

Devlyn goes outside to clear some of his supplies from foot traffic. Me… I wander the store and pretend to straighten the already clean and organized shelves and flower buckets… while watching Devlyn… through the windows.

Am I a lost cause or what?

I force myself away from the windows and head for the office. While we wait for lunch to arrive, I clean the small card table we eat at in the break room. Spray it down with all-purpose cleaner and wipe with a little too much gusto. After I straighten the napkins in the holder and resituate the salt and pepper shakers, I exit the room.

Elizabeth busies herself with bouquets and table settings for an upcoming Halloween wedding. Seeing the bride's vision come to life has been impressive. Dark red and vibrant orange roses mixed with black calla lilies and black wispy spirals. As usual, Elizabeth places each stem in the perfect place. Her arrangements are always immaculate. Perfection.

My goal is to one day create bouquets and arrangements as coveted as hers.

I step up to the tall banquet-length table we use to arrange. Classical music plays in the background, loud enough to hear, but not so loud it hinders conversation. Elizabeth is in the zone as she shifts and adds stems. I don't want to mess with her chi, but I don't want her to miss lunch either. We generally don't eat at the same time, but I always give her the option to go first.

"Hey," I say softly. She peers up from the flowers, gives a small smile, then returns to the piece in front of her. "Devlyn insisted on buying us lunch. Got you cheddar and turkey on rye. Should be here any minute."

"He's so sweet. You eat first." She snips the end of a rose and feeds it into the vase. "I still have a bit to go until this one is finished and I don't want to leave it half done."

"Are you sure?"

She leans back from the flowers, twists the vase left then right, scrutinizes the arrangement from every angle, then returns to her original position. Although I have learned a wealth of knowledge from Elizabeth over the years, seeing flowers the way she does isn't a skill you learn. It simply exists. Elizabeth has an uncanny eye for arranging. A true gift.

"Yes." She lifts her gaze. "By the time you finish up, I should be done with this one."

I nod and watch her work.

In the beginning, I followed her every move for hours. Observed the way she selected flowers. The precision in which she clipped the stem. How she started an arrangement or bouquet, then brought it to life as she added one flowering stem after another.

In some regards, watching Elizabeth with flowers was similar to watching Devlyn with paint and a brush. Both mesmerized me with how they viewed the piece and how their fingers seemed to move without instruction. It isn't a job to them. Put simply, it is an extension of them. Their creativity brought to life.

Devlyn steps up to the table with a large brown sack in his hand. "Lunch arrived."

"You two enjoy. Just set mine in the fridge and I'll get it soon." She slides a black calla lily into place then looks at Devlyn. "Thank you for lunch. Was kind of you."

"You're welcome."

Without a word, I lead the way to the break room. Take a seat near the wall and am surprised when Devlyn slides the chair out to my left instead of across the table.

*Is it normal for friends to sit so close?*

*Don't put the cart before the horse. Is Devlyn my friend?*

He digs through the bag, oblivious to my internal inquisition, and pulls out three sandwiches, individual bags of potato chips, small paper cups of fresh fruit, and bottled waters. He picks up Elizabeth's sandwich and sets it in the fridge, along with her fruit and water.

Brown butcher paper crinkles in the otherwise silent room as we unwrap our lunch. I use the paper as a placemat and dump out my chips. Then pop the lid off the fruit cup and water, ready to dive in.

The first few minutes of lunch pass in silence as we satiate our stomachs. Covertly, I side-eye Devlyn as he eats. Watch the muscles of his jaw work as he chews. Lick my lips when he swallows.

Do you believe what you eat says something about your personality? If so, what does the Cuban without mustard or pickles say about Devlyn? While on the topic, what does the roasted veggie with brie and orange marmalade say about me?

Most of my guy friends eat anything you put in front of them. Does that mean they are more open? Can't be sure. I mean, I am kind of picky with food—eating familiar dishes to avoid change. Is that a personality trait that extends into the rest of my life? Is that why I am picky with men? Not that men are the same as sandwiches, or food of any kind.

"How long have you worked here?" Devlyn asks, startling me back to reality.

I swallow my bite then sip my water, praying I don't have a piece of spinach stuck between my teeth. "Sixteen years next month. It's the only job I've had, but I love it. Wouldn't change it for anything."

"Wow." He pauses and stares at the pressed meat and cheese in his hand. "You don't look old enough to have worked here so long." He bites his bottom lip and I don't hide my blatant stare. His bottom lip looks tastier than my sandwich. "If you don't want to answer, I'll understand..." He swallows and my eyes refuse to look up from his throat. "How old are you?"

Some women lose all sense of reason when someone asks

their age. Me? I don't care. Age is just a number. Age happens to us all. No sense in dwelling on something that happens regardless of how you feel about it. I say, never be ashamed of all you endured in your lifetime. Scars from years past can be painful, but they also remind us how far we have come. What we endured to get here. Own yourself—age and body, scars and wrinkles.

My gaze drifts up his throat and finally lands on his eyes. "Thirty-two. You?"

He tilts his head to the side and studies the contours of my face. On cue, my cheeks heat. His stare doesn't unnerve me. It is more like he *sees* me. Sees the parts no one else does. It intrigues me more than unsettles.

"Twenty-two."

A myriad of emotions swirl through my chest at hearing his age. Devlyn is *young*. Much younger than I suspected. A voice in the far corner of my mind says he is *too* young. Ten years is a big difference. Maybe not when the younger person is in their thirties, or older, but that isn't the case.

Should I be uneasy with my attraction to Devlyn? Hell, when I graduated high school, when I stepped into the adult world, he was finishing third grade. It feels… strange, wrong, to find him physically appealing. To watch him through the window as he works because of some newfound mental addiction. To think desirous thoughts about him and what his lips would feel like pressed to mine.

It feels wrong. Yet, it doesn't.

We are both adults. Yes, I have a decade on him. Yes, people might stare longer than usual or say off-putting statements. But societal standards are absurd. Invisible lines drawn to make others feel guilt or shame for loving someone or something that others deem controversial. In general, I am not the type to buck the system. But when it comes to pivotal topics, I am front and center.

Is age difference one of those topics? Potentially.

No one I know has been in this particular situation. The opinions of others have never bothered me in the past, but this feels different.

"Does that bother you?" he asks, jolting me from introspection.

I meet his gaze. Stare at his translucent green irises, so similar to stained glass. For the first time, I study their depths close up. See beyond the man. Deeper. Through the window, getting a glimpse of his soul. Without a doubt, his soul has lived more than one lifetime.

"No," I answer just above a whisper. I sip my water then speak with more confidence. "No, it doesn't bother me. You?"

He shakes his head. "Nah. Age is a number, tossed out every year by someone who wanted to mark time. I don't let it rule how I live."

Such a profound statement from someone barely in adulthood. Quite philosophical.

The room quiets and we go back to our lunch. I do my best to not blatantly stare at Devlyn. Every few breaths, though, I glance to my left. The more I get to know Devlyn, the more fascinated I become.

"So," I start, wanting more conversation in our limited lunchtime. "When are you starting the interior piece?" I stab a tangerine segment and study the piece of fruit longer than necessary.

"Tomorrow."

I perk up at the news. Granted, he was only touching up the exterior, but I assumed the exterior would take another week.

"Oh," I squeak out. Heat blooms over my cheeks at my juvenile response. "Thought you'd be outside longer."

Eyes on his water bottle, a hint of a smile glints his face then disappears just as quickly. "No. After lunch, I'm applying the sealant. Then it's finished." He pops a potato chip in his mouth then meets my wide eyes. A confident yet laid-back vibe rolls off him.

I like the feeling more than I should.

Then a sudden burst of panic infiltrates my bloodstream. With Devlyn inside the shop eight-plus hours a day, for the next week or longer, will I be the creepy voyeur lady? Yep, that sounds like me. The woman who stays in his periphery at all times, gawking. The woman trying to put the Devlyn puzzle together. The woman asking endless questions to learn everything about him.

Ugh! Please don't let him find me as disturbing as I do.

"That's great. Guess I expected the touch-ups to take longer."

I finish my fruit cup and stare down at the brown butcher paper, wondering if my embarrassment will swallow me into the pits of hell.

Devlyn strikes me as the intuitive type. Aren't most artists? That said, there is no possible way he doesn't pick up on my attraction toward him. Or my occasional self-consciousness, which is most peculiar. Ask any of my friends if I am shy, laughter would fill the room. Every one of them would say I don't have a timid bone in my body.

Until Devlyn, that statement held truth.

"Some colors fade easier in the elements. I touched them up. The sealant will help, and Elizabeth is adding an awning."

Why does it sadden me there won't be a reason for Devlyn

to return in a year or two? Unless I figure out some other project for him.

"That's great." Is that the only response I am capable of speaking? My words lack enthusiasm, which makes him smile. I really like his smile. It isn't artificial or something he hands out to everyone.

He crumples up his sandwich paper and deposits it in the bin with his other lunch trash. All too soon, conversation time ends. Rather than feel down, I inwardly smile at seeing him inside for the next week. Fingers and toes crossed it will be longer.

Devlyn keeps to himself for the most part, and I don't mind. The trait adds to his allure. Gives me ambition to learn more about him through conversation. Devlyn may be quiet on the outside, but something tells me the inside is the polar opposite. Eclectic and mysterious and affectionate. Perhaps a little loud and overzealous.

Maybe, just maybe, I will find out.

## DEVLYN

The past ten days at Petal and Vine, constantly inhabiting the same space as Shelly, reminds me of *The Mulberry Tree* painting by Van Gogh. Subtle hints of color illuminating vitality and brilliance. A hidden fire, out in the open, waiting for the right kindling to set it ablaze.

Oh, how I want to be her kindling.

But after years of solitude and single-minded focus, I feel so out of my element in personal conversation. Sharing pieces of myself with someone, especially an attractive woman.

It isn't the actual conversation I find challenging; I speak with strangers often.

Conversations related to business flow with ease. Someone purchases or praises my art online or in the community, my introversion takes a back seat. The typical interaction at exhibitions, some might say I don't shut up. Shoptalk doesn't make me uneasy.

But talking about something other than art—my pieces or someone else's—isn't something I do often.

While Chet was in town, even our conversations were clipped. Not that we didn't have anything noteworthy to share, we just understand each other. Understand the inner workings of the creative brain. That we don't necessarily voice everything we think or feel or perceive. Instead, we digest it in our head and translate it via art. Some on a sketchpad, others on canvas, and many with another medium.

Oddly enough, I enjoy conversations with Shelly. Conversations about something other than work or art. With each passing day, she opens up more. As do I. Like the petals of a morning glory. Slow and steady, then all at once.

Since walking through the doors of Petal and Vine, I have learned a lot about Shelly.

Her preference for pink is unrivaled. Pink isn't the only color she wears, but it is somewhere on her person each day. Whether it be accents in the attire or the elastic securing her ponytail.

She prefers tea lattes over tea with a splash of milk, but won't disclose this. There was no disguising the twinkle in her twilight eyes when I handed over the extra spicy chai tea latte. Never had I seen someone so excited for a drink.

Which is why I bought her the same drink today.

"Enjoy the rest of your day," Shelly says to an older man leaving with a bundle of flowers in paper and twine. The bell over the door jingles, the man waving goodbye as he exits. My eyes are glued to the door when I feel Shelly sidle up to my right. "Looks dreamy." Her voice soft and fantastical.

I twist and take in her profile, her gaze lost in the meadow on the wall. *Her meadow.* The one I painted with her in mind.

Whimsical weeping willow branches in the foreground. Tall grasses a pale green and golden brown. Wild purple flowers and sunset-colored echinacea buds. Common daisies and bold-blue cornflowers. And a small cobblestone path that starts at the floor and trails a few feet into the meadow before disappearing.

"Good. Was the impression I wanted to give."

She stares at the meadow. Studies the intricate lines and detailed strokes. Meanwhile, I revel in the contours of her profile. The minor slope of her forehead and prominent arch of her brow. The subtle angle of her nose, slight flare of her nostrils, and dip of her philtrum. The plumpness of her lips, the bottom fuller than the top. And the strong yet soft line of her jaw and chin.

Shelly is real-life art. An artist's model. A muse. A goddess.

I shake my head. Shake away the fantasy of something more.

*It's just a job. Nothing more. Never anything more.*

Shelly snaps her gaze away from the meadow and meets my stare. The usual sparkle in her twilight eyes is muted, duller, less dazzling. I want to ask her the cause of her sudden mood shift. What brought on her melancholy?

But I don't, fearing I already know the answer.

After I leave Petal and Vine tonight, I won't return. Not for work, anyway. And this fact displeases her.

A twinge expands in my solar plexus. Reminds me not seeing Shelly every day will be difficult for me as well. Something I am not used to… missing another person.

What alternative is there?

I don't want this to be it. The end. The last day I see her. But I don't want to give her the wrong impression. Don't want to lead her on and spread false hope. It wouldn't do either of us any good. Still… this can't be it.

"Would you want to hang out sometime?" The words leave my lips in a rush. Then I mentally smack myself as they replay. *What the hell are you doing?* But it is too late. The offer has already been extended. Perhaps I should amend it. "As friends," I clarify.

Her eyes dart between mine, searching for unspoken clues.

*Good question. If you find answers, let me know.*

"Uh…" Her teeth nibble at her bottom lip. In the periphery, her fingers tug at her waist apron. "Sure, I guess. Sounds nice."

God, how does she make apprehension look adorable? Her hesitation makes my heart beat faster and breath come in bursts. Spreads warmth in my veins and stirs me to life. Gives me an inkling of hope for something more. Something I swore off years ago.

But it shouldn't give me hope. It can't.

Shelly is a friend. Only a friend. Plenty of men and women have strictly platonic friendships, and so can we.

*Keep telling yourself that. Maybe if you repeat it enough, you'll believe it.*

"Before I leave, we should exchange numbers," I say, then add with too much enthusiasm, "To coordinate." *Take a fucking pill already. Jeez.* "What do you think about lunch and a museum?"

Seriously, this feels like more than friendship. Asking her to lunch and the museum sounds more like a *date*. But what do I know? I haven't had many female friends since high school. That is what happens when you keep to yourself. So what do adult, opposite-sex friends do?

The museum sounds like a safe atmosphere to visit with a friend. Lots of people. Plenty of distractions.

At least it isn't my house, on my couch, with the bedroom in close proximity. Or worse, my studio. Although my desire to be intimate with a woman is minuscule, I fear the tempta-tion of having Shelly in my space. Near my bed. Near my creations. Her scent in the air and on fabrics. The image of her permanently etched in each room she enters. God, it would make my home my own personal torture chamber.

"I haven't been to a museum since I was a kid. I'd love that."

Her smile is worth every questionable thought. Worth the agony of where we go—as friends—from here. If a day at the museum excites her, I wonder what other places will?

"Great." I almost slip and add *it's a date*.

For a moment, we stand there, unsure what to do next. The corner of her mouth twitches, and I drop my gaze. Before temptation gets the better of me, I face forward and start cleaning up my mess. This snaps Shelly into action and she goes back to her workspace and cleans up the table. As I gather the last of my brushes, she fills the low-stocked flower pails with more blooms and tidies up the shop.

When she locks the front door and flips the welcome sign to closed, I wilt like a thirsty flower. She does a few last-minute tasks and then we exit through the back door.

After I stow my supplies in the back of my SUV, we stand unmoving, unspeaking, between our cars. I barely know Shelly, but today feels like goodbye. Like letting go of someone important. And I don't like the pang beneath my diaphragm. The ever-increasing twinge between my ribs.

"Talk to you later," I say as I reach for the door handle. "Drive safe."

"You too. Talk to you later."

We get in our cars and I wait for her to leave first. When her car is out of sight, I drop my head on the steering wheel and close my eyes. Take a deep breath. Then another as I wrap my fists around the wheel.

"What *are* you doing?"

Of course, I don't answer myself. What the hell would I say? I have no legitimate answer. Wish I had an idea of what happens next. Wish someone would give me advice on where I go from here. I don't need step-by-step instructions, but a look in the crystal ball wouldn't hurt.

If I keep the boundaries clear, keep us both on the same page, everything should be fine.

Shelly and I are friends.

*Only friends.*

I stare at my phone screen, waiting for a response like a needy teenager. Like a boy desperate for attention or affection or both. No matter how hard I stare, no matter how long I keep the screen awake, a response doesn't come.

And I hate how much this bothers me. I hate how I can't look away or put the phone down.

Three hours have passed since we left Petal and Vine. Three hours is both too long and not long enough.

I wanted to wait longer to text her to set up our "friend date." I hate the word *date*. But what else do I call it? Casual meetup? Get together? An engagement or rendezvous? None sound right. Especially the word *date*.

I hate myself.

Hate the inner workings of my mind and how I overanalyze every little detail. Hate that she hasn't answered me, and it has only been ten minutes since I sent the message. Hate how I have worked myself up over something I deem friendship.

Have I ever been so frantic to hear from a *friend*? No. No, I have not.

Rising from the couch, I lock my phone, stow it in my pocket, and head up the stairs to my studio. If anything distracts me, it is a pencil or charcoal or brush in my hand.

As I reach the landing, I laugh at myself. A little too hard. Why? Because I plan to use my art as a means to escape the thought of Shelly. But as soon as I fill in the blank canvas or heavy stock paper, it will be her I see. Best if I own and accept facts… there is no escape. Not when it comes to Shelly.

I am sick. Sick in the head and a glutton for punishment. My own worst adversary.

Sitting on the stool at my drafting table, I flip to a new piece of stock. Grab my charcoals and blending tools. Turn on the repeat playlist I listen to in the studio. Then, I hunch over the paper and let my fingers and mind roam freely.

I smudge a lock of hair near the corner of her eye and angle of her jaw when my phone chimes. Jolting at the sound, I sit up and set down the blending stump. Staring down at the table, I know the profile of the woman on paper is the person who just texted.

It is no secret I keep to myself. Not that I don't have friends or socialize with people. I simply prefer solitude. Family and friends know this about me, and only reach out when something noteworthy happens. Texts and calls are never just a *hey man, how's it going?*

So, when I pick up the phone, I know exactly who texted. The woman I messaged over an hour ago with a date, time and place for us to meet for our non-date.

Sunday works. I haven't been to the Black
Cat Tavern yet.

Perfect. Meet you there at 12:30.

Meeting Shelly at the restaurant versus picking her up and riding together sends a clear message. *This is not a date. We are just friends.* Opposite-sex friends who enjoy each other's company. That is all. Period.

In college, I had female friends. We shared meals and philosophical conversations all the time. So I know friendship with Shelly is possible. I can do this.

If I tell myself this enough times, perhaps I will believe it into existence.

I'll be the cute one in pink. See you then.

Her comment is meant to be funny or endearing. But of course, my mind veers down every other path. Searches for every hidden meaning in her words. Focuses on the way she refers to herself as cute. Pictures of different pink tops or attire she has worn in the short time I have known her.

And I hate that my mind does this. Sends me down a road I should not travel.

Why? Why do I torture myself? Overthink and scrutinize every word someone says. Look for a double meaning that, more than likely, isn't there. Look for reasons to reschedule or cancel. Or worst of all, look for clues that say this is a *good* thing. That a friendship with Shelly is exactly what I need. To feel alive again and get past the shadow masking my heart.

Since the day Kelsey put my heart through the shredder, I refuse to believe romantic happiness is an option. The heartache she inflicted still haunts me. It sets the tone for every interaction I have with a woman. Causes me to doubt the intention of every woman. Causes me to question my own feelings. Destructive as it is, what Kelsey did changed the way I perceive romantic relationships. The harsh way she ended our relationship, the way she threw our love in the trash, it made me turn my back on love and trust.

It irritates me she still has this power. Over me and the way I live life. Over my happiness and future. Over my heart and the love I could give another.

My mother and her frigid, heartless temperament toward me didn't help matters.

Maybe Shelly is the key. The one person to unlock this darkness that has consumed me for far too long. The sunshine after the storm. The light at the end of a very long, dark tunnel. Hope. *My hope.*

My relationship with Shelly doesn't have to be romantic to be fulfilling. Romantic ideals cloud what matters most. Connection. Trust. Loyalty. All components of a solid friendship.

*Repeat the word friendship enough times and you might spur it into existence.* Eat, sleep, rinse, repeat.

"Play it by ear," I mumble as I stare down at her charcoal profile. "Maybe Shelly is exactly what you need."

More than I realize.

# *seven*

## SHELLY

I scream and all but evacuate my skin as Gavin laughs inches from my trembling frame. "Jerk!" I slap his cloaked form and he laughs harder.

"Your expression was priceless."

"What? My *I almost pissed myself* face? How sweet of you."

He lifts the terrifying mask from his face and juts out his lower lip. Not fair. Just because he is my brother's best friend and my best friend's husband, it doesn't mean he gets a free pass. He needs to learn his lesson. And grovel a bit.

"I'm sorry, Shell." His pout becomes more prominent, but I really want him to work for it. So I purse my lips and narrow my eyes, then firmly plant my hands on my hips. "Really, I'm sorry." The corners of his eyes downturn, a telltale sign his apology is genuine.

Relaxing my stance, I nod. "Apology accepted." I jab a finger in his chest. "But don't do it again."

Cora waddles toward us, one hand on her rotund belly and the other carrying a bottle of water. She surveys the situation, then gives Gavin a stern yet affectionate look. "What did you do?"

He holds his hands up in surrender. "Nothing. Just some Halloween fun. I swear."

"Mm-hmm," she mumbles. "And your version of fun versus mine and Shelly's is totally different. Please, don't give my friend a heart attack. Or I might have to hurt you." Gavin gives Cora a look that says *oh, really*. She arches a brow. "Don't press your luck, mister. I may be ready to pop any day, but I'll still go to bat."

For a second time, and for Cora's benefit, Gavin apologizes. "Sorry, Shell. Just trying to liven up this party. If Micah didn't have to work, I'd have someone else to joke with."

My dear, sweet, sometimes pain-in-the-ass brother. Over the last year and a half, he has become a new man. A better man. Mature and caring and respectful. But put him in the same room with Gavin—best buds more than half their lives—and all levelheadedness disappears. I love my brother. Love Gavin like a second brother. And like any sibling does, they both get under my skin from time to time. I always forgive them, but it's fun to watch them squirm first.

"Yeah, yeah." I narrow my eyes and give him my best death glare. "Next time, I may not be so forgiving." Lies.

Panic fills Gavin's eyes. Beside him and a step back, Cora clamps her lips impossibly tight to not laugh. Cora knows me better than anyone. Which is how she knows I am messing with him. Knows I am giving him shit, just like he did to me moments ago. She loves it as much as I do, if not more. My cheeks sting as I fight the urge to laugh. My faux seriousness on the verge of crumbling any second.

Thankfully, it doesn't have to.

"Promise, Shell." Surprising me, he hauls me in for a hug.

Forces the air from my lungs. "Won't do it again." He releases me and holds me at arm's length. I pat his shoulder in acceptance. "Let's eat."

"I vote yes to food," Cora answers and I agree.

Gavin wraps his arm around Cora and kisses her temple as we wander toward the spooky-themed buffet.

Tonight is similar to our Sunday night get-togethers. Tons of food. Music in the background. Good conversation between friends. Not everyone is here, but most of the group has gathered. Tonight's festivities will end with cobweb cleanup and candy inventory instead of leftover burgers and talks of seeing each other in a week. With Sunday around the corner, we will gather again in no time.

Halloween is different this year. Still fun, but more adult than previous years.

With Cora pregnant—very pregnant—her costume of choice is more about comfort than fun this year. Black maternity leggings and a top that says *The goblin stole my candy* with a cute, animated goblin baby on her belly.

Autumn is also pregnant. Although her belly is less round, her outfit is practical as well. She and Jonas will welcome their new bundle of joy a little more than two months after Cora and Gavin. They decided not to learn the gender ahead of time and, every once in a while, I hear their whispered exchanges of baby names. Some male, some female, and a handful of gender neutral. Watching both couples share openly affectionate moments and fawn over their upcoming additions warms and jump-starts my heart. Has me wistful as I think back to missed opportunities. Has me questioning when my life steered down this path. The lonely path.

I sound envious. To say I am not, would be a half-truth.

So much has changed in such a short period of time. For everyone. Everyone but me.

My friends and family seem to have their lives figured out. On track. Moving forward. Marriage, cohabitating, starting a family, buying a home. They have it all figured out.

Me… I feel stuck. Stuck in singledom. Stuck in place. The next phase of my life in my sights, but just out of reach. And I hate how immovable life feels. In a continuous loop with no forward motion.

As with our Sunday get-togethers, tonight's shindig is at Jonas and Autumn's place. Their new house. Their gorgeous, *we are definitely adulting*, new house.

The house isn't grandiose, but it is a big step up from the small two-bedroom they lived in previously. Now, they have two stories and double the bedrooms, which they will need once their new addition arrives. Clementine, Autumn's first-born, has been the sweetest helper since learning she will be a big sister. Doing extra chores, talking to Autumn's belly, getting drinks or snacks or blankets for her mom.

Her sass makes an occasional appearance, but she makes up for it with pampering later.

Tonight, Clementine plays hostess. Tidying up the buffet table, greeting everyone, offering drinks. Jonas and Autumn rave over Clementine helping with the decorations too. Hanging fake cobwebs with plastic spiders. Carving ghoulish faces into pumpkins and toasting the seeds. Stabbing fake tombstones in the front yard and stringing tattered sheets to large oak tree limbs. And instead of the usual rock music we listen to, haunted house music plays from the front porch.

"Aren't you trick-or-treating?" I ask Clementine as we fill our plates with finger foods. Some actually look like fingers.

"Yes." She munches on a deviled egg that looks oddly like

an eyeball. "Mr. Jonas is taking me out soon. I'm super excited, Miss Shelly." She bounces on her toes. "One of the kids from my new school said our neighborhood gives out *whole* candy bars. Like the big ones you get at the store." Her eyes widen and jaw drops.

Oh, to be young again. To have simple things—like regular-sized candy bars given on Halloween—bring you joy.

"That's amazing!"

"I know, right?"

"When I was your age, we would trick-or-treat around our neighborhood, then go to my friends' neighborhood. If it was a weekend, we went to as many houses as possible. Some years, we had candy for months."

"Wow." Clementine peers up, awe in her expression. "Maybe Mr. Jonas will do that for me next year, after my baby brother or sister is born."

"Maybe. Just make sure you ask days before. You have to make a plan."

Clementine salutes me. "Yes, ma'am." Spartan appears out of nowhere and sniffs along the edge of the table. "No, Sparty. Mama said you can't eat the people's food. It upsets your tummy. Come on." She steps away from the table and Spartan follows without another word. "Later, Miss Shelly."

"Later, cutie Clementine."

I load more food onto my plate and head for the living room. Plopping down on the couch between Cora and Autumn, I scoop up spinach artichoke dip that came from a carved pumpkin mouth. Listen to my friends discuss pregnancy and pending motherhood. Sit in silence and wonder if I will experience more than solitude one day. If I will experience the pangs and joys of pregnancy and motherhood.

Part of me still envies their lives. The natural progression. Attaining happiness and love.

My inner romantic reminds me I will walk the path too, when the time is right. To just be patient. Quit looking at every guy I meet as a potential love interest. Let nature run its course. Things will pan out on their own. Bloom when the time is right. That I just need to stay confident and calm.

*My time will come.* I want to believe this. Need to believe this. But some days, convincing myself is more of a challenge than not.

Jonas hooks Spartan on his leash before he and Clementine kiss Autumn goodbye.

"Don't pick up anything heavy while we're gone, Mama," Clementine says with a stern expression. I swear that girl will make others bow to her one day. Once Autumn agrees, Clementine skips out the door, telling Spartan they are going to get the best candy stash ever.

"Is it wrong to be happy I don't have to do the trick-or-treating this year?" Autumn laughs and Cora and I join her.

"I'm just waiting for all the Halloween candy to go on sale tomorrow, so I can buy my own stash," I admit. "That's the only trick-or-treating I'll do." We laugh again.

"Get me some," Micah says, entering the room with Peyton at his side and surprising us.

"Thought you were working, big brother."

He kisses me on the forehead. "I was. We got out early. The owners decided to give management an early night." He waves a hand around the room. "So, here I am. Ready to indulge in mountains of sugary, ghoulish treats and torture people I love." I narrow my eyes at him and he sticks out his tongue.

"Help yourself. There's food and drinks in the kitchen and

dining room," Autumn says.

Peyton gives us hugs, then she and Micah wander toward the buffet hand in hand.

I stare after my brother and his wife of less than a month, and smile. More than anyone else in our circle, they give me the most hope. If they were able to forgive and let go of the horrid history they share, overcome crazy obstacles thrown at them, find love and a happily ever after together, how can I not believe in a happy ending for myself?

Autumn rises from her seat next to me and dashes for the hall, grumbling about the constant need to pee as she walks off. Not a second later, Micah plops down and knocks my arm with his.

"What's up?" I ask.

"You look better."

I cock a brow at him. "Thanks, big brother. You really know the way to a woman's heart."

He rolls his eyes. "Ugh, you know what I mean. You're smiling more since I last saw you." He sets his plate on the coffee table then wraps his arm around my shoulders. "No offense, but you look happy. What changed?"

Everything. Nothing.

My life is pretty much the same. Work eight to ten hours a day, five to six days a week—depends on time of year, orders, events, and staff. Each day, I go home to my empty apartment, eat something simple or order delivery, and watch an episode or two of my current television drama. On occasion, I sneak in a romance movie on Hallmark or Passionflix.

Oh yeah... I also have a new friend. A new male friend.

Is that what Devlyn is? My *friend*? That is not a question even *I* can answer. Devlyn feels like more than a friend, yet not a romantic interest. At least, that is what I tell myself.

Over the past two weeks, I have gotten to know a fraction of what makes the man. But Devlyn is still a mystery, and I feel a bit like Nancy Drew trying to figure him out.

"Work's been good. Tonight's been fun with everyone." I bite the end of a dough-wrapped mummy dog. "Just so happy for Cora and Autumn."

Micah narrows his gaze; his twin eyes study mine in search of falsehoods. But nothing I said was a lie, so…

He lays a hand on my shoulder, his thumb stroking back and forth as his eyes resume their normal shape. "You know you can talk to me about anything, right?" I nod but don't say a word. "Just need to know everything is okay. That *you're* okay. I need you, Shell."

I don't miss the undertone in his words. Fear. Worry. Love. The backs of my eyes sting. An expanding ball of emotion forms in my throat. A tsunami of love builds in my chest. Micah isn't emotionally detached, but he also doesn't freely share how he feels. For him to openly express such things, it hits harder than expected.

I never lie to my brother. Not about the important stuff, anyway.

As of now, there isn't much to share with him about Devlyn. When something notable happens, he will be one of the first to know. After Cora.

Now, though, Devlyn and I are friends. Nothing more.

"I need you too, big brother." Twisting in my seat, I snake my arms around his torso and hug him hard. "Love you."

"Love you, too." He feigns a cough and I shake my head. "Sorry. Trouble breathing." He smacks his chest over his lungs.

In the affection department, Micah and I have been opposites for years. Since he and Payton became serious, he leans more toward the mushy category and I don't think he knows how to handle it. So I give him a free pass. Let him fake his cough rather than own his emotion. But I love how Peyton has made him a better person. Caring and soft and more sensitive.

The night carries on like our Sunday get-togethers, with added special treats and a mountain of candy. With each new conversation, bout of laughter, and hug given, I am thankful to have this tremendous group of people in my life. People I love and who love me in return.

Perhaps one day, I will have someone special at my side. Someone new to our inner circle.

One day.

Fifteen minutes early. Better than being late, I suppose.

I park in the lot for the Black Cat Tavern, but don't shut off the car. It may be the beginning of November, but the cool weather won't hit this part of Florida for at least another four to six weeks. So, I scroll through social media and clear notifications while the air conditioner blows my hair and dries out my skin. I click the heart reaction on a few Halloween photos friends posted. Comment on those same posts with praise for costumes or treats or candy hauls.

Then I look out the windshield and spot Devlyn's black SUV. A BMW as mysterious as the artist himself. *How does he afford such an expensive car?* Maybe artist incomes are better than I realized. Murals on flower shop walls don't pay for cars like his. With his talent, he probably commissions work often, sells pieces online, and isn't hurting for paychecks. Or women.

I shake my head at the errant thought.

Devlyn is a good-looking guy, no sense in denying it. Beautiful in an unconventional way. Some may disagree due to his lack of thick muscles, but I see beyond the outer layer. Sure, I can lie to myself until blue in the face, but doing so is pointless.

I enjoy looking at him. Being in the same space as him. Talking with him.

Our conversations, even the most mundane, are my favorite. Less than twenty words might be shared between us and the conversation feels profound. Those brief, meaningful conversations are one of his most attractive features. One of many.

I cut the engine, stow my phone in my purse, and step out. Before I close the car door, he spots me across the lot. He stops walking and locks on to me with his sunglasses-covered eyes. As if my mere presence is a beacon. And that notion does strange things to my head and heart. Makes me dizzy. Has my stomach in knots and my pulse jumping hurdles. Makes my knees weak.

My reaction to him gives me pause. Has me unsure how to proceed after such an emotional response. On unsteady feet, for sure.

Devlyn has given me no indication he likes me more than a friend. All the kind gestures—drinks, lunch, conversations—weren't only bestowed upon me. Elizabeth was included in those treats, although she may argue that he included her to disguise his true intentions. That said, he also hasn't given any signs to state the opposite either. When he suggested we hang out, spend time together, just the two of us, he emphasized the word friend. A little too much. Like he needed to stress the word before I agreed. Still not sure if the emphasis is for my benefit or his.

I try not to give it much landscape in my head.

His stride resumes, picks ups steam, and he reaches me five breaths later. "Hey," he says. "Sorry you had to wait."

I shake my head, then swallow past the dryness in my throat. "No need to apologize. I haven't been here long. Didn't want to be late. So I occupied myself with the black hole that is social media." Cue rambling Shelly. God, he must think me an idiot. I sure as hell would. The babbling woman who blushes more than any person her age.

I bite the inside of my cheek to stop myself from blurting more nonsense, and I swear he notices. A half smile flashes on his lips and has me biting a little harder.

"Hungry?" I nod, not trusting myself to speak without blathering, and he gestures toward the restaurant. "Let's eat."

We step into the restaurant and I silently thank whoever manages the air conditioning in here. You would think it was the peak of summer at the rate I am sweating. The host seats us, hands over menus and indicates the server will be with us in a moment, then walks off.

Devlyn and I lift the menus like shields and I almost laugh at our identical behavior.

*Is he as nervous as I am?*

Devlyn is always cool and collected. A perfect example of chill. Him on edge is unimaginable. Impossible. Preposterous.

We place our order, and now the only thing we have to shield or distract us is two glasses of water. And I should try to pace my drinking. Take small sips and not too many. Repeated trips to the bathroom will do nothing but kick my anxiety into overdrive and embarrass me to no end.

"How was your Halloween?" he asks as I study the ice cubes in my water.

I peer up and spot genuine interest on his face. His gentle

smile and pale-green eyes calm me a fraction. "Good. Hung out with friends, had spooky-looking food, handed out candy. You?"

He plays with his straw, but his eyes don't deviate from mine. His stare isn't intense or uncomfortable. If anything, eye contact with Devlyn feels automatic. Natural. Effortless. As does his company. And this poses question after unanswered question. Because I get the sense he doesn't want anything more than this. Lunches and trips to museums and whatever else it is non-romantic, platonic friends do. Together... but not.

I think back to all the times I'd hung out with Jonas before he and Autumn were together. Our friendship came naturally. Our connection more like siblings or cousins. Things have always been straightforward and comfortable with Jonas. The definition of our relationship always clear and never tricky or confounding.

Not like with Devlyn.

Don't think I will ever regard Devlyn with that same brotherly mindset. The idea is ludicrous.

"Quiet. Not a lot of kids live in my neighborhood. So I get a small bag of candy and make sure it's something I'll eat eventually." He laughs and I follow suit.

"I hand out candy if I'm home, but it's minimal too. But don't be fooled, the day after, I'm the lady raiding the shelves. For myself and the shop."

"Hmm. Too bad I didn't start the mural later. Bet you have good taste." My eyes widen a fraction. "In candy choice," he adds.

I love how he feels the need to clarify. As if I didn't know he meant the candy.

Lunch arrives and silence settles over the table. I dig into spring greens piled high with turkey-craisin salad, feta, veggies, and sweet dressing.

Every now and then, I peek up from my food to find Devlyn staring. Not the creepy type of staring that makes my skin crawl. But the type that makes my chest and neck and cheeks hot. The type that makes my throat dry and causes me to swallow over and over.

The server returns as we finish our lunch. Her eyes dart in my direction, a big smile on her face. "One check?" she asks.

My brows pinch together as to why she asks *me* this. Not that I am the type to assume the guy always pays or that Devlyn will pay for my lunch. But something in the way she looks at me while she asks has me thinking there is an underlying assumption. One I am not privy to.

"I'll take the bill," Devlyn speaks up.

The server shifts her focus to Devlyn as her cheeks pinken and eyes widen. "Oh. God." She closes her eyes a beat and shakes her head. "I am so sorry. I just assumed he was…" Her eyes come back to me, her blush darkening. *What am I missing here?* "Your son or little brother."

What. The. Fuck?

I stop breathing. Stop every motor function I control.

*She thought he was my son? She thought Devlyn was my son?*

Jesus. How old do I look?

Yes, Devlyn looks young. Maybe a year or two younger than his actual age. But there is no possible way we look that far apart in age. That I look sixteen-plus years older than him. Do I?

How many people over the years have told me I look young for my age? How many have asked what skin regimen I use because of my youthful appearance? Far too many to count. So, how is it this woman thinks I am Devlyn's *mother*?

Soon as Devlyn hands her a card with the check, she bolts from the table. No doubt she is as mortified as I am. Just for different reasons. Bet this curbs any future assumptions she'd voice aloud.

"Hey," Devlyn says from his seat across the table.

I want to look up. Want to stop staring at the same drop of condensation on the water glass. Want to unhear that my lunch partner, the guy I have an undeniable crush on, looks young enough to be my *son*. Or that I look old enough to be his *mother*.

My stomach flips and I close my eyes. Take a few deep breaths and beg the contents to stay down.

Calmer, I open my eyes and look up. Meet his gaze and try to read the unspoken thoughts in his expression. But the server returns, hands Devlyn the check presenter, apologizes again, and wishes us a good day before she dashes away.

Exiting the restaurant is a blur. I barely hear or register Devlyn telling us we can walk to the museum. I just follow alongside him, trusting he won't let me stray or bump into anyone.

Most opinions don't hit me like this. Don't render me speechless. Don't muddle my thoughts so thoroughly.

But her assumption is a slap in the face. A punch to the gut. It makes me question myself. Makes me question if hanging out with Devlyn, as friends or something more, is a good idea.

I want this—us—to be a good idea. I want it to be more.

Ten years may divide us, but I have never felt closer to another person. Does that make this—us—wrong? If only I had the answer.

# eight

DEVLYN

I hate this. Hate that something so trivial bothers her this deeply.

Yes, there is a ten-year age difference between us. Yes, I look younger than my actual age. But damn, I sure as hell don't look young enough to be Shelly's child. And Shelly sure as shit doesn't look old enough to parent a grown-ass adult.

What bothers me most is how deeply the woman's preconceived idea sticks. How Shelly has let it sink its claws in, make roots, and sour her mood. And the mood for the day.

More than anything, I hate how much I care. How my mind won't let the matter go. And how much I want to storm back into the restaurant and complain. Question the server's ability to see clearly or think before opening her mouth. My heart isn't cold. Cruelty isn't how I approach situations. And dammit, I shouldn't care this much.

I *can't* care this much.

Things between me and Shelly should stay casual. For her sake and mine. Shelly is my friend. *Just a friend.*

Friend or not, I damn sure won't let anyone drag her down or make her feel less than. Intentional or accidental.

Distress turns her aura stormy gray, and I don't like the shift in her energy. I much prefer the raspberry red I often see around her. The passion and strength and love. Qualities that magnetize me to her.

I bump her arm with mine as we walk past storefronts. "Hey." She doesn't lift her gaze. Doesn't answer. Just keeps her eyes ahead and semi-downcast, still in a daze. So, I bump her again. "Hey," I repeat, a touch louder.

She snaps out of her momentary fog and grants me her full attention. A nameless emotion burns white hot inside me as I stare back at the dulled color in her irises. Eyes that would no doubt shimmer in the sun. Radiate and add a new layer of appeal. An appeal I work hard to shut down.

*Just a friend.*

"Sorry," she says just above a whisper. "That was just…" Shelly leaves the rest unsaid. Leaves me mentally bereft.

Nope. Not having it.

I reach for her elbow, steer her away from other people on the sidewalk, and stop us under a store awning. "Was just what?"

I shouldn't care this much. Shouldn't worry about a statement from someone neither of us will see again. But it isn't so much what the woman said that bothers me. It is the fact Shelly is so thrown off by the misunderstanding.

"Does it not upset or frustrate you? What she said." She points down the street toward the restaurant.

Please don't let her think I am dismissing her feelings. "Actually, no." Her forehead scrunches in confusion, disbelief, hurt. I hurry to explain my reasoning. "Shelly, if I let other people's opinions rule my life, I would be disappointed or depressed or irritated more often than not. I'd rather spend my energy on what makes me happy." I glance down the sidewalk, let my eyes lose focus. "The last time I let someone's words consume me, it almost cost me my life." Blinking, I turn back to her. "And I won't do that again."

Her dazzling twilight irises glass over. Breathtaking and tragic at the same time. The idea of Shelly in pain—whether physical, mental, or emotional—bothers me on an unhealthy level. But seeing her exposed and vulnerable, seeing her look at me with hundreds of questions in her eyes, has my soul begging for more. More of her heart. And me giving her more of mine.

I should not want either.

*I cannot want either.*

She lifts a hand and sets it on my forearm, giving a light squeeze. "I'll do my best to let it go."

A strand of her hair catches the wind and grazes her cheek. And god, do I want to tuck it back into place. Brush my knuckles over the apple of her cheek and reassure her. Tell her everything will be alright.

But I leave my hand at my side. Refrain from speaking such reassurances. Don't move an inch. Because friends don't touch each other that way. Not the way I want to touch her.

"Good," I choke out, then clear my throat. "Shall we?" I offer her my elbow and smooth out my expression. Act as if we didn't just share emotional intimacy.

She loops her arm with mine and straightens her spine. "We shall."

We walk two more blocks, our steps leisurely as we take in the city. Most of Downtown St. Petersburg is plastered in art. Paintings by local artists on the sides of buildings. Sculptures in front of local businesses. Even some of the older structures are art without effort.

Soon, I steer us toward the Morean Arts Center, where the

local Chihuly Collection is on display. Although sculpture and glasswork are not my specialty, I appreciate the love and labor and artists who construct such astounding masterpieces.

"Oh, wow." An air of awe occupies Shelly's expression. "I haven't been here, but I've heard wonderful reviews about the exhibit."

"Well, then I'm glad we came."

Gone is her morose mood from the restaurant. Now delight and anticipation set her aura on fire. Excitement and a hint of passion. The shift soothes something deep inside. Something I won't question or spend time trying to figure out. Not now.

After we go through check-in, a curator in the museum explains the rules while inside. As with most museums, there is no touching. Unlike most museums, you have permission to take photos.

Without hurry, we go through each room. Read the placards and learn about Dale Chihuly and his glasswork. Stare at the blown glass that defies logic or gravity. His pieces are pure imagination brought into existence. His gift to the human eye. Globes in various sizes. Bowls resembling ocean waves. Spirals and pillars and tentacles.

With each room we enter, each new piece we see, I study not only the displays but also Shelly. Really study her. How she reads about each display thoroughly. How she steps back and looks at the display from afar. Then steps closer and takes in the intricate details. The fine lines and layers of color woven into each piece. The unprecedented design and craftsmanship.

She sees each piece as more than just *pretty* or *neat*. She finds inspiration in the work. Looks at it from one angle then another. I would swear she *feels* the art. Immerses herself in the mind of the man who created each piece and display.

When we walk beneath the *Persian Ceiling,* I swallow past the dryness in my throat. Breathe deep and work to calm the ever-expanding organ beneath my sternum. The one that should *not* be beating so profusely. Yet, I can't stop what happens naturally.

Not when it comes to Shelly.

Under the lights and strategically placed glass pieces in the *Persian Ceiling* is a rainbow of color. The space is a sea of stained glass and wonder. The sight of Shelly beneath the art, reds and blues and yellows splashing her cheekbones and neck and jaw, stuns me. Renders me speechless. Bonds me to the floor where I stand. Robs me of breath and reason and practicality.

And I do nothing to stop or fast forward the moment. I can't. Not when I see her like this. Not when it makes me eager to dip a brush in pigment and paint her in this new light. A spectrum in a world of gray. A myth brought into existence.

"I found one," she whisper-shouts.

I snap out of my Shelly-induced stupor and step closer to her. "Found what?" With my fantasizing, I have no idea what it is we are looking for.

"A cherub."

Ah, yes. Chihuly and his affinity for the childlike angel. "That you did."

While Shelly scans the ceiling to locate more, I remain a step back and watch her. Watch her fascination, her excitement, her eagerness to find the next special piece in the art. I don't need to search for cherubs. My eyes on her is all I need in this magical place.

Once we leave the *Persian Ceiling,* the rest of the museum

tour speeds by. Wraps up far quicker than I would like. In the gift shop, we each buy a small token to remember the museum and our visit. Not that I need a token to remind me of today, or any day with Shelly.

We step out into the warm November air and pause. After getting swept up in the whimsical world of Chihuly, we both need a minute to reset ourselves. Find our footing back in the real world.

A voice in my head tells me to ask Shelly to dinner later. Well, only a couple hours from now. The words are on the tip of my tongue. Ready to spill out and be heard by someone other than myself.

As I open my mouth to ask, another voice speaks up. Reminds me of the last time I gave too much of myself to another. Reminds me of the heartache and pain and dark, dark days that followed when she ripped me apart. When she left me to waste away. When she abandoned me without care.

And the fear from that singular moment is why I bite my tongue. Why I seal my lips and close off my heart. Because if I ever let anyone that close again, if I allow myself to be truly vulnerable, it sets me up for loss. For anguish. For the darkness.

I can't go back to the darkness. Not again. Never again. Who would pull me out?

"Ready to head back?" I mutter. This time, I don't offer my arm. Don't add pep to my voice. Don't glance in her direction.

And she picks up on the sudden mood shift.

Shelly wraps her arms around her middle and looks in the direction of where our cars are parked. "Sure."

No doubt, she probably wishes we didn't have to walk back together. Not after my abrupt coldness.

But shutting her out like this is the only way. The best way. All I know. She may not be grateful now, but she will eventually thank me. When she moves on and finds someone worthy of her smile and warmth and heart. Someone who won't love only the idea of her.

All too soon, we arrive back in the lot. The lukewarm goodbye we exchange is pathetic. Friends give better farewells than this. Usually a *see you soon* gets said at some point. But not with us. Not today. And I hate that I did this. Put a damper on our *friendship*. Ruined a perfect day.

But it has to be this way.

Not a complete asshole, I wait until her car starts before walking to my own. Behind the protection of tinted windows, I stare, stare, stare at Shelly's red Beetle. Watch for any sign of dismay; a look of disgust toward my car. But nothing comes. So I wait impatiently for her to drive away. And maybe flip me off. But she sits idle a moment, and I wonder if something is wrong with her car.

I narrow my eyes and look through her windshield. With the blinding sun, it is difficult to see her. See what she is doing. If she needs help.

Maybe she is waiting for me to leave. Wants me gone before she drives away. Just as I give the thought merit, her car rolls forward and exits the lot. No slow down to smile or wave. She just… leaves.

My knuckles pale as I grip the steering wheel tighter. I close my eyes, bang my forehead on the leather, and berate myself. Mentally slap myself upside the head.

"Did you really need to do that? Did you really need to fuck up something good?" I ask myself aloud.

Yes, I did. Because although I keep telling myself Shelly is just a friend, my thoughts continue to step over the invisible boundary. The boundary dividing friends and lovers. A boundary I dare not cross. A path I refuse to travel down. Not again.

If Shelly and I don't cross the boundary, if we remain strictly friends, neither of us will get hurt. Defining the line today was for the best. For me and her and our friendship.

Did I need to be so cold when defining said line? No. But I don't know how else to set the tone for our relationship. Our friendship. And the definition of us definitely needs to be precise. Black and white. No gray. No color.

Lifting my head from the wheel, I take a deep breath and attempt to clear my cluttered thoughts. I put the car in gear, exit the lot, and drive home in a fog. I speed down the road faster than responsible. Faster than safe. And in no time, with no memory of the trip, I park in the driveway. Amble out of the car. Unlock the front door. Kick off my shoes. Wander through the house and take the stairs two at a time. Step into my studio.

And breathe.

I close my eyes and inhale. Find comfort in my safe space. In my solitude. In my art.

Then I pick up a blank canvas, park it on the easel, sit on my stool, and paint. A woman in full spectrum with wonder and delight and amazement in her twilight eyes. A woman, no matter how hard I try, I can't erase from my mind. A woman I will apologize to sooner rather than later.

Because there is not a chance in hell I won't be seeing her again.

Even if it hurts.

Even if it breaks me.

Even if I should walk away.

# *nine*

## SHELLY

"Ouch!" I bring my thumb to my lips and suck on it.

When was the last time a thorn stabbed me? Years ago. Probably not since the first or second year I worked at Petal and Vine.

Yet, here I am. Getting stabbed by flowers with a vendetta. Really, they have no discord with me. But picturing a flower with revenge in its veins gives me a reason to laugh. Imagining every thorn prick brings the flower joy is the only humorous way to deal with the sting.

Why do some of the smallest wounds hurt the most? Thorn pricks, paper cuts, the slip of a needle tip while you sew.

I step back from the arrangement table and study the full vase of blooms. Contemplate adding more filler or flowers. Maybe a little of both. Anything to keep my hands and mind busy. To distract me from what I have been waiting to hear. What we all are waiting to hear.

Baby Clara is on her way.

Any second, Cora will go into labor. Baby Clara will

make her debut. Everyone in our circle is on edge, eager and ready.

Elizabeth and I decided not to take on any major orders in the two-week window of her due date. Which happens to be tomorrow.

Our part-time employee, Francine, is on standby. She typically works two days a week, less than sixteen hours, to help out when either Elizabeth or I am alone, or we have major events to work on. She will work more hours if either of us is under the weather, but prefers the lesser hours. Plus, she told Elizabeth early on, her minimal time here each week gives her a sense of purpose.

Our delivery drivers, Joe and Melanie, won't be affected much. They come and go with orders, but keep an eye open for delivery and store updates.

With the impending arrival of her first grandchild, Elizabeth has busied herself more than usual. And driven me a bit crazy, to be honest. For the last twenty minutes, she has swept the same section of the shop repeatedly; not a speck of dirt to be seen.

But I don't blame her.

If I were in her shoes, I would be jittery too. On edge. And I am, but my anxiety is nothing compared to that of a parent waiting to become a grandparent.

Any minute now, my niece will enter the world. We may not be genetically related, but Cora is one hundred percent my sister. Always.

The arrival of baby Clara will change all our lives. In a good way. I never thought it possible, but her birth will bring us all closer together. Bond us in a way we never imagined. Start a new phase of our lives and expand our friendships.

"You okay?" Elizabeth points to my hand.

"Yeah. Just zoned out and the thorn attacked." I narrow my eyes at the thorny flower in question.

Elizabeth laughs. "They get you when you least expect it."

I go back to the arrangement, one of several premade bouquets we have available. Elizabeth and I wanted an abundance of grab-and-go flowers in the case so Francine won't be overwhelmed in our absence.

Elizabeth switches from sweeping to dusting, mumbling to the flowers as she moves through the shop.

I insert the next stem into the vase, then twist the arrangement left and right to see where I need to put the final flowers. My gaze drifts toward the front of the store. Toward the beautiful meadow painted on the wall. The wispy grass and abundant wildflowers. And I zone out again. Imagine myself in a magical place like the one Devlyn created.

A little more than a week ago, Devlyn and I shared the best and worst day. Between the age mentioned by the server and his aloof behavior after the museum, I considered throwing in the towel on our friendship. Everything about us is new. So breaking ties with Devlyn wouldn't be the same as losing a friend I'd had most of my life.

At least, this is what I've told myself every day I'd considered texting him.

Then Devlyn took me by surprise. The next day, he reached out.

When the notification popped up on my phone, I expected to see a text with *it's been fun* somewhere in the bubble. Those words were nowhere to be found. What I saw instead was an apology. A real apology. More than the basic *I'm sorry.* His message read… *I didn't mean to be such an ass. It's a long story. But I'd love another chance at friends. Please.*

I have never been the type to hold on to anger toward

another person. Not unless they did something major. Something unforgivable. Ninety-nine percent of the time, I forgive easily and let the past roll off my shoulders.

With Devlyn, though… the man needs to figure out what he wants.

He dishes out the word *friends* more than an all-you-can-eat buffet. Not sure if the constant reminder is for me or him. Either way, it leads me to believe two things without hard evidence.

One—he fears anything beyond friendship with a woman. The thought hurts my heart on so many levels and stirs up a list of questions as to why. Two—part of him wants more than that with me. More than friendship.

More than once, I've wanted to ask who broke his heart. Who made him so anti-love. To love someone is human nature. His vehemence to avoid love has to stem from past hurt, past pain. Putting him on the spot, coming out and asking him who did this to him, won't yield answers. And with our friendship so new, so on the edge of tipping one way or the other, asking would only push him away.

In his own time, and however he processes things, Devlyn needs to work through his emotions. I simply ask him not to rake me over the coals in the process.

Since his apology, we text or talk daily. No philosophical or life-altering chats. Just normal day-to-day stuff. Conversations similar to those I have with any other friend. Chats about work, strange clients, weird conversations we overheard at the grocery store, great jokes someone shared. And like all new friendships, we learn each other's quirks and boundaries.

Another change since the apology… we hang out a lot. Like every other day. For my own sanity, I compare time with Devlyn to hanging with Jonas or Gavin. We meet up at restaurants, eat pizza or Chinese or sandwiches. Talk, laugh, and ask questions. Nothing too deep, though.

My cheeks have stung more over the past few days than any previous time. Devlyn makes me smile. Often. More often than a friend.

Our late-night phone calls—Devlyn is anti-text whenever possible—aren't like the calls Cora and I shared as kids. The kind where you stay on the phone all night, trying to find something, anything, to talk about. Conversations between Devlyn and I hold more definition, more purpose.

Last night, we talked about college. How my experience compared to his. The way he spoke about art school and the people—professors and student body—enthralled me. His experience sounded otherworldly. In a sense, I suppose living and breathing art is a different way of life.

I shared my time at college, which was boring in comparison. How I originally studied interior design, then switched gears to get my bachelor's in finance and business. Working at Petal and Vine fulfilled my creative heart. Learning how to successfully own a business was more important for my future.

Time and conversations with Devlyn are a nice change of pace. A change I didn't see coming, but enjoy more than expected.

I take the finished vase of flowers to the open-air cooler, then return to the table and clean up. As I brush stem bits off the table into the bin, Elizabeth appears out of nowhere.

"It's time!"

My eyes widen. "*Time*, time?" She nods and I drop the can to the floor. "Okay. Shit." I fumble with my apron strands. "Grab our purses. I'll flip the sign and lock the door."

A minute later, we dash across the lot. I tell Elizabeth I

will call Francine on the way. We hop into our cars and speed toward the hospital. Most of the drive is a blur of bumper-to-bumper cars, red lights, and finger taps on the steering wheel.

Cora consumes my every thought until we reach the hospital.

Is she in pain? When did her labor start? Is she all deep, practiced breaths and cool as a cucumber? Or is she detaching Gavin's hand from his limb and screaming at the hospital staff? Will she be in labor ten more hours or two?

I park a few spaces down from Elizabeth, jump out and press the lock button on the fob, then jog to catch up. She presses the button for the elevator car more times than an impatient child. I don't say anything to stave off her anxiety. Instead, I lay a hand on her upper back and draw small circles. Soothe her as best I can while she worries over missing this monumental moment.

The doors whoosh open and we dart inside the elevator. Elizabeth smashes the button once, twice, then takes a step back as the doors close. Seconds later, the elevator doors open to the labor and delivery floor. Elizabeth runs to the nurses' station while I go to the waiting area, where I spot Jonas, Autumn, and Erin.

"Any news?" I ask when I reach everyone.

"Gavin came out to update us a few minutes ago. She's eight centimeters dilated. Shouldn't be much longer," Jonas shares.

Admittedly, I know nothing about pregnancy or having babies or motherhood, except for the basics and what I have heard recently. This whole centimeters-dilated thing is jibber-jabber. A foreign language only parents and parents-to-be know. I want to ask how many centimeters she has to be dilated before she has the baby. Babies are big, so it has to be a lot. Right?

Autumn chuckles at my deer-in-headlights look. "Shelly, ask me anything."

Autumn must have a sixth sense. Probably hears my inner monologue and confusion. In another couple of months, our friends will gather here again. For Autumn and Jonas and their new arrival. Probably best to ask now.

"The centimeters thing…" I pause and Autumn nods for me to continue. "What's the magic number? Like twenty?" Sounds legit.

Autumn laughs, then grabs her belly and stops. "Don't make me laugh. I'll pee." My eyes widen. Do I ever want to be pregnant? The big belly, the whole squeezing a watermelon from your body thing, the fear of peeing your pants. The more I think about it, the more I don't think I want to be. "Ten. Ten is the magic number. She's almost there. Which means it won't be long. Within the hour, most likely."

Oh. Well, that is good news. But how the hell does such a big baby come out… No. I don't want or need to know. I zoned out during that part in health class for a reason. The entire concept is just too painful.

"I'll get us drinks," I offer. "Any takers?"

With everyone's drink order, I head downstairs in search of the hospital cafeteria. It isn't long before I pop two coffees, two hot cocoas, and a pile of creamers, sweeteners, and stir sticks in a cup carrier. When I step off the elevator in labor and delivery, Jonas is pacing with a larger-than-life smile on his face.

I rush over to him and Autumn, noticing Elizabeth's absence, and set down the drinks. "Is she here? Did I miss the excitement?"

Jonas shakes his head. "No, but she's pushing now. Elizabeth went in the room while you were gone."

For the next thirty-seven minutes, Autumn, Erin, and I sit in uncomfortable chairs while Jonas continues to pace. Autumn and I sip hot cocoa while Erin drinks coffee and Jonas takes the occasional sip. I continue to watch my friend. Watch as he wears a new pattern into the shiny, bleach-scented linoleum. Watch as he picks at the edges of his nail bed with other nails. Listen to the scuff of his boots and occasional huff from his lungs.

No doubt, he is envisioning the day he and Autumn return to this floor. What it will be like when his girlfriend gives birth. How his family will be as they wait in this very room. What their smiles will look like when they meet their new grandbaby or niece/nephew.

I rise from my chair and step into his space. He pauses his trek and meets my eyes with his antsy ones. "You okay?"

He nods. "Yeah. Just trying to absorb it all. It'll be different when Autumn's on the hospital bed and I'm in the delivery room." He takes a deep breath. "I'm just trying to not freak out."

Hooking my arm with his, I steer him toward the chairs. "Sit." He obeys. "There is nothing to worry about. We've gotten happy and healthy news about their baby and yours." Autumn laces her fingers with his. No doubt, she has dealt with his anxiety more than either will admit. "And I can't wait to meet my next niece or nephew." The three of us laugh.

"Who would've guessed?" Jonas's question is rhetorical, but I answer anyway.

"What?"

"That we'd all be here. Less than three years ago, we hung out at the bar every week. Listened to horrible, but hilarious karaoke. None of us were where we are today. In relationships. Having children."

Erin glimpses my way and I spy the subtle, quick wince. I want to say, *"I feel you, girl."* But I keep my lips shut. Jonas rambles because his nerves are shot and his thoughts are scattered. Although Erin and I are definitely not the same women we were three years ago, neither of us is in a romantic relationship or expecting a child. His comment isn't meant to offend, so I don't take it as such.

"We're adulting," I tease. "You guys"—I point down the hall, then between Autumn and Jonas—"are just adulting hard core."

Erin laughs and we follow suit. Then Autumn stands up with an *oh-shit* look on her face.

"Where's the bathroom?"

Jonas is at her side immediately. "I'll walk you." I love how sweet my friend is. How attentive he is with Autumn. Jonas has always been such a good man. And it makes my heart happy he and Autumn found each other.

For years, I worried about him. Long before Gavin returned to Florida, I watched Jonas pine for Cora. And Cora almost gave in to the idea of a romantic relationship with him. Almost. But Jonas was the bigger person. He put aside his feelings for her and encouraged her to follow her heart.

Karma, in return, brought Jonas and Autumn together. And I honestly believe everything went according to plan.

Sometimes you have to deal with pain and heartache before you get your happily ever after. Which is what I keep telling myself. One day, I will get my happy ending too.

Elizabeth dashes into the waiting room with the biggest smile on her face. Peter—a.k.a. Mr. Davies—appears out of thin air. *Has he been here the entire time and I ignored him?*

His smile is as big as Elizabeth's and I have my answer. Obviously, he arrived before us and was in the room.

"She's here!" Elizabeth says louder than ever before. "Seven pounds, eight ounces. And she is perfect." She steeples her fingers in front of her lips. Her smile locked in place. A smile that will never fade.

"When can we see them?" Erin asks.

"In about fifteen minutes. They're getting cleaned up and settled," Peter states.

By the time Jonas and Autumn return, we are allowed to see Cora, Gavin, and Clara. We wander down the hall and, one by one, enter the room.

The hospital room is unlike any I have seen. So spacious and welcoming. Cora lies in a hospital bed that looks more comfortable than most regular beds. A rocking chair and stool take up the corner by the draped window. A small sofa and table sit opposite the bed. And tucked in the corner near the door is a collapsible bed. The room has everything for the new family.

A small, clear bassinet sits parked next to Cora's bed, empty. I step farther into the room and locate my best friend. And she is positively glowing. Baby Clara rests peacefully in her arms, snug to her chest, fast asleep. Cora stares down at her in what can only be described as pure amazement. Gavin watches them both with similar awe in his eye.

And I want to cry. Shed a million tears for my friends and this newfound joy in their lives.

Cora peers up and sees me near the foot of the bed. "Hey," she whispers.

"Hi."

"Does Auntie Shelly want to hold her niece?"

I nod because I can't seem to find my words.

Elizabeth appears at my side then guides me to the rocking chair. Gavin scoops up Clara so gently, I mentally gasp at how different he is as a father. Such a beautiful sight. He sets Clara in my arms and reminds me to support the back of her head. And we just rock.

Clara doesn't wake. Her eyelids flutter now and again. Her lips twitch just as often. She makes the sweetest little sounds. And she smells amazing. All I do is stare at her and whisper how lucky she is to have such a wonderful mommy and daddy. That she is loved by so many. And when she gets older, I will do all the fun stuff with her.

"Do you want a picture?"

I peer up to see Jonas waving his phone in the air. "Please."

He snaps several pictures and then Clara goes to the next set of arms as I evacuate the chair. Jonas sends me the pictures and I ooh and awe over them. Then, I send a photo to Devlyn.

> My best friend just had her baby. Isn't she precious?

The small bubble pops up and dances a beat.

> Two beauties in one masterpiece.

I stare down at the screen. Read his response. Then read it again. And again. Question if I misunderstand the message. But no matter how many times I read it, I decipher it the exact same way. Each time I read it, I hear Devlyn's voice telling me I am beautiful. That I am a masterpiece.

And it confuses me. *Devlyn confuses me.*

One minute, he says the sweetest things. Compliments me like a lover and not a friend. Leans in closer, hooks my arm with his, watches me from a distance. He inserts himself in my life in ways unlike any other friend.

Perhaps he doesn't know I notice his eyes on me more often than not. That I don't feel the weight of his stare on my profile. The slight shift in his posture or held breath. But I notice every glance. Feel the way his eyes scorch my skin. I see it all. Feel it all.

Then, abruptly, he gives me the cold shoulder. Skirts around a past he hasn't gotten over. A past that keeps him from moving forward. When it comes to love and trust and his heart on the line, anyway.

So… I remain his friend. Act as I do with Jonas or Gavin or any of the guys in the tattoo family, and maybe sometimes with my brother. Try not to say anything flirty or dreamy or lovey. Do my damnedest to remain neutral.

But when he says stuff like this, when he tells me I am beautiful, I don't know what to think or feel or say. Do opposite-sex friends compliment each other's appearances? Sure. But Devlyn isn't like any guy friend I've had. When Devlyn tells me I am beautiful, the sentiment is layered with complexity and hidden meaning. So hidden, I don't think he even knows what is underneath.

Gah! Devlyn is a frustrating man.

Since I sent the picture of me with baby Clara, since I provoked the conversation, talking baby-related stuff wouldn't be awkward. Would it?

Thanks. I've never given thought to having kids. You?

Not so much. Even if I did, I'd want to be in a long-term relationship first. Don't see that happening anytime soon.

This man is like a damn seesaw. A mood swing waiting to happen. I press a loose fist to my stomach as nausea begs for relief. His text is another reminder. A reminder I don't need, but receive almost daily. A reminder that feels like a constant slap to the face.

Friends. Devlyn and I are only friends.

His random sweet words, charming smile, and desire to spend time together throw me off balance. Make me question my sanity and perspective. Make me ask myself if I am interpreting his words through a romanticized lens. Because I have no clue.

God, he makes me dizzy.

> Well, they're asking us to go. Talk to you later.

Later.

No one asked us to leave yet, but probably will soon. Cora and Gavin must be exhausted. No doubt baby Clara is as well.

The conversation with Devlyn needed to end, though. We haven't known each other long, but part of me *knows* him. And every once in a while, I want to smack some sense into him. Tell him to wake up and see what is right in front of him. Ask him what I can do to help heal his heart.

But I don't. I won't.

As always, I keep my eyes forward, mouth shut, and just go with the flow. And I pray one day it will all work in my favor. That I will find the love I have been looking for. Without mixed signals and crossed wires.

If that person happens to be Devlyn, I would be surprised.

If that person happens to be Devlyn, I would show him what being loved is really like.

# *Ten*

## DEVLYN

Did I fuck up?

For days, Shelly has been in a funk. Absent is the timid yet passionate woman I met more than a month ago. In her place is a more lackluster woman. She gives no indication I am to blame, but the pang in my gut says otherwise.

I want to ask what happened. What has her more hesitant and quiet? What has her avoiding eye contact?

But I don't say a word. I won't.

Asking questions leads us down a path of uncertainty. A path where I ask the questions, but won't answer hers. A path that muddles the lines of friendship, once again. And as much as I'd love to wipe the friendship line from existence, my heart trembles at the idea.

I am not a cold person. Not empty or devoid of emotion. Not intentionally. I do *feel* things, emotions. Love and happiness. Hurt and sadness. Joy and pain. The good and the bad. I feel it all.

Years back, prescribed by my dear mother, I visited a therapist regularly. My mother had it in her head that I was empty inside. Soulless. The irony isn't lost on me, but maybe she assumed this because I didn't express myself in a way that made *her* happy.

With each therapy session, my mother sat in the room—something abnormal on all accounts, but she insisted upon it. With each session, I opened up more. Expressed what I dealt with in school and how it made me feel. Mother wasn't keen on my responses. Perhaps they didn't suit *her* needs. She told the therapist she'd done her own research and was convinced she knew what was *wrong* with me.

Thanks to my mother, in one session, the therapist teetered on the idea of me having anhedonia—the inability to feel pleasure.

What a crock of shit—the doctor and the prognosis.

For years, all I felt was the good, the wonderment, and the delight in the world. There had never been a dark cloud in my sky. Sometimes, I experienced the pleasure a little too much.

And perhaps, that is the problem.

I feel *too* much.

But isn't feeling too much part of being a creative? A fault in the genetic makeup of an artist, any artist. We feel *everything*. Which is why we create. Why we draw or paint, journal or write, sculpt or build, play instruments or sing. So we have a way to release the pent-up emotion, a way to express what consumes our mind and soul. So we don't lose our minds. Mostly.

Shelly and I walk along the park trail. I stay just a hair back so I have my favorite view of her profile. The one I stare after too much, yet not enough. Sunlight filters through the trees and dances over her prominent cheekbones, her toffee-blonde ponytail, the column of her throat. The play of light heats my skin more than hers. I lick my lips, swallow, then avert my eyes forward.

*Don't go there, Templar.*

"Hey." I bump her arm with mine. Her gaze shifts from the path, but only for a second. "Everything okay?" A shiver shakes her frame, but she tries to disguise the action by tucking a nonexistent stray hair from her cheek. A cold front swept through yesterday. The air a touch crisper today, but not cold. The sun warms us as we walk through the park. A hoodie on me, as well as her. "We can head back if you're cold."

She stops walking and I follow suit. In the front pocket of her hoodie, her hands squirm. Too fidgety to be from the temperature.

*Is she nervous? Why would she be nervous?*

Before I open my mouth to suggest we turn back, she speaks up.

"I'm not cold. And…"

She lifts her eyes to the trees. Her twilight irises twinkle in the sunlight as she thinks of what to say next. Moments such as this, I wish for telepathy. The ability to hear her thoughts. Hear them unfiltered straight from the source. To know what confounds her so deeply.

Then, I nix the idea. Because with the thoughts I want to hear comes the sentiments she keeps to herself. The ones I want to hear, want to reciprocate, but refuse to accept or return.

"Sorry," she says after a long pause.

"Why are you apologizing?"

She lowers her gaze and I come eye to eye with Andromeda. Immerse myself in her starry eyes. Swallow past the expanding lump in my throat. Berate myself for leaving my sunglasses in the car because, right now, I feel completely vulnerable. Exposed. Nude in a crowded room. I love and despise the feeling. I crave and evade the eddy beneath my diaphragm. Beg for more while wanting to bury myself deep in the earth.

"Sometimes, it's hard being your friend."

My brows tighten. What does she mean?

Yes, I have been wishy-washy. Been open and interested one minute, then cold and reserved the next. I know this. But the stony mask is my shield. How I protect myself. How I protect her.

"Not sure what you mean." I truly haven't the slightest idea. And guessing will only dig a deeper hole.

Her steps resume and lead along the path again. Without hesitation, I follow her. "You confuse me."

"How?"

"I've had guy friends all my life. When you have an older brother, it just happens." I nod and hum, although siblings are foreign territory. "And none of them have been like you."

Is this a compliment or an issue? Her tone gives nothing away.

"Thanks," I say on a wince.

She laughs and knocks my arm with hers. I take it as a good sign. "Don't be a weirdo."

Laughter bubbles in my throat. "It's who I am." I shrug as if my awkwardness is common knowledge.

"What I mean is, none of my guy friends really connect with me." I stop breathing for one, two, three strides. "We have stuff in common," she continues as if her declaration is no big deal. "But they never seemed to get me. Not like you do."

I do get her. With Shelly, everything clicks into place.

At one point, everything clicked with Kelsey too. Or so I thought. Then, she pummeled me with her proclamation and I lost sight of all perspective. Doubted every gut instinct I felt. Because how did I not see that coming? How did I not know my girlfriend of three years, who seemed happy and in love with me, wanted to break up?

Is this where things are headed with Shelly? Down the path of promises and hearts on display. Souls exposed and futures on the line. Not sure I can walk down that path again. Not after where it led me last time.

Shelly is not Kelsey. Shelly has years of wisdom and heart guiding her. But if I let her all the way in and lose her, the end would be pure devastation. For us both.

"Not sure what to say."

Part of me wants to nix our friendship. Call it quits before it becomes something more, deeper, unbreakable. Before either of us navigates this irreversible path.

I should walk away now, say goodbye as we go our separate ways. But abandoning Shelly is impossible. Just the idea of walking away steals my breath. Forms a fault line in my heart. Has me mentally bending at the waist and retching.

I hate the piece of me that needs her. Needs her aura and light. Craves her smile and warmth. Begs for her timid conversation and unrelenting attention.

I also love how much I need her.

She spins around, walks backward, and grants me the smile I see every time I close my eyes. "You don't need to say anything. I just wanted to tell you." She spins back and walks beside me again.

The next quarter mile of our walk around the lake is blanketed in silence. Our pace leisure. Her arms swing at her sides as she glances up at the trees. I shove my hands in my hoodie pockets to avoid reaching for hers. Wouldn't be surprised if my body did it involuntarily. Not with the level of gravity Shelly harbors.

Her behavior the last few days wiggles its way to the surface. The uncomfortable, tense silence. Her stiff posture and dejected body language. I work to force the memory away but fail miserably.

"Can I ask something?"

"Yes."

Deep breaths. It's just a question and I am probably over-reacting. Still, my stomach twists and flips. "Did something happen?"

"Not sure I understand?" Her gaze falls from the trees and heats my cheek, my jaw, my neck.

"The other day, you texted about your friend having her baby. You seemed really happy. Since then, not so much. Did something happen?"

A chill blankets my skin the second she looks away. Shelly stays quiet for several paces, and I wonder if the question was too personal or somehow upset her.

We happen upon an empty bench by the lake. She ambles off the path and goes straight for the bench without a word. I stay a few feet back until we both sit. Out of the corner of my eye, I watch how intently she focuses on the lake. Watch as she searches for a way to tell me what occupied her mind. What had a gray cloud floating over her.

"This is going to sound stupid." Her eyes scan the bank of the lake as she works her jaw back and forth.

When she doesn't continue, I bump her shoulder with my arm. "Nothing you say is stupid."

She laughs without humor. "Just wait." I grant her the time she needs. Don't interrupt while she compiles the words in her mind. And then she spills her secrets. "I read too much into your response after I texted you that day."

"When your friend had her baby?"

"Mm-hmm."

*What did I say? Think, think, think.*

I go back a few days in my memory bank. Remember the picture she sent of her with the baby. Recall the way I stroked her cheek in the image before I replied. Then, I hang my head. Mentally slap myself for the responses I sent her. I'd let my mind wander and didn't think before typing either text. *Shit.* No wonder she has been distant. If our roles were reversed, I would be too.

I complimented her. Told her she was beautiful. Which is true, but could be taken out of context. Considering I define the friendship line every time we see each other, my words undoubtedly confused the hell out of her. Then I drove the nail deeper and told her I wouldn't have children without full commitment. Followed by my disinterest in serious relationships. With two texts, I went from one extreme to the other. Said something wonderful, then followed it up with distance and heartless words.

God, I am a fucking idiot. And a goddamn mess.

"It wasn't my intention to upset you."

"I know."

"Seems I can't help myself when it comes to you."

She twists on the bench, props a leg up on the seat, her knee grazing my thigh as she faces me head-on. "Like that." She jabs my arm with a finger. "You sound as if you can't stay away from me. But one false move on my part and you go cold. Feels like I can't win."

Unfortunately, she is right. No sense in denying it. No matter how many times I remind myself Shelly and I are only friends, the voice in my head, the one I stomp down often, laughs and calls me a fool for believing such hypocrisy. The number of hours I think of Shelly… I am a moron if I believe we will remain strictly friends.

But I keep that to myself.

"Sorry," I say, hypnotized by her sparkly blues. "I'm too selfish for my own good. And yours."

She opens her mouth, ready to respond, but my phone rings and cuts her off. Her lips form a tight line before she smiles and twists to face the lake.

Immediately, I hate the lack of eye contact. Hate that she shifted away.

I pull my phone from my back pocket—the number not in my contacts—and answer. "Hello?"

"Good afternoon. May I speak with Devlyn Templar, please?"

"This is he."

The woman on the other end goes into a well-rehearsed spiel. For a moment, I zone out. Don't listen to a word she says. Until I hear her say, "We'd like to feature some of your work in the exhibition. I realize it's last minute. My apologies. Another artist gave us your information and, after seeing your pieces online, we'd love to showcase your work with other local artists."

"You've piqued my interest. When is the exhibition again?"

"Saturday. In a few days. If the notice is too short, I understand."

"Count me in."

"Wonderful," she says with jubilance. "Can I send details to the email listed on your website?"

"Yes, that'd be perfect."

"Thank you, Mr. Templar. We'll see you on Saturday."

I disconnect the call and stow the phone in my pocket. Last-minute calls for exhibitions are few and far between, but they happen. When the email hits, I will read up on the exhibition. Whether or not there is a set theme. Either way, I know which pieces I will show.

And I would like if Shelly saw them.

"Do you have plans Saturday?"

She studies the lake without a word. Takes a deep breath. Tightens her grip on the edge of the bench seat. Then meets my gaze. Left then right, left then right. Her eyes dart between mine. Seeking, hunting, searching for clues or answers to a question she has yet to speak aloud. Feels as if I know the question, but I refuse to give it a voice. I won't jeopardize time with her. I need every second she grants me.

Clamping down on her lips, she shrugs. "I work a few hours in the morning. Other than that, no. Why?"

Inviting Shelly to the exhibition with me sounds like a date. A legit date. Unlike the *friend non-dates* we share more often than not, there is no avoiding implications with this. No matter which way I spin it, asking her will suggest we are more than friends. Call me cruel or self-centered or destructive, I don't care. I want Shelly there. At my side. On my arm. To see my art on display. To decipher what she sees and feels. To watch her gravitate toward each piece. To decipher how she sees what I see.

Our friendship is still in the infantile stage, yet she consumes much of my day.

I ache for and detest how she rattles my heart. How she makes my breaths uneven. How she spins a tornado in my head. Each day, I wake up with Shelly as my first thought. It gives me life and scares me to death.

"Was just invited to display some of my work at an exhibition." I pause for two breaths. "And I'd love it if you came."

*Shit.* Should not have used the word *love*. Maybe she will bypass it or think of it in the general sense and nothing more. Hopefully.

"I'd like that, thank you." Her toothy smile is infectious. As is the way it lights up her eyes. Like a visual hug.

God, I want to conquer my demons, my insecurities. For me. For her. For us.

Shelly is the first woman to truly monopolize my every thought. The amount of time I spent thinking of Kelsey years back is child's play compared to the hours and days I think of Shelly. Often, I chastise my obsession with Shelly. Tell myself it isn't healthy to spend every waking—and non-waking— minute with one person invading my thoughts.

Art is how I cope with this obsession. How I release the emotions growing, building, expanding exponentially inside. The emotions I don't expose to anyone—at least not verbally.

Will Shelly pick up on the underlying emotion I don't— can't—voice when she sees my art?

Part of me hopes she sees it all. Part of me begs her to solve the big mystery. To put an end to my constant indecision. The other part of me pukes at the possibility.

"The curator is sending me the details. I'll share more when I get the email. Most exhibitions are casual. The food is hit or miss. Might be a good idea to eat before or after, depending on the showtime."

Yep, definitely making this sound more and more like an official date. While I didn't outright suggest dinner together, it won't shock me if she interprets it as an invitation. I won't deny her if she does. I will never deny Shelly.

*Keep telling yourself it's* her *you're not denying. You know* it's you.

"Okay." She looks back out at the lake, her smile still firmly in place. "We should head back. I smell rain."

We look up simultaneously. Looming overhead is a cluster of gray clouds, slowly drifting in from the coast and stealing the blue sky.

Rising from the bench, I wait for Shelly to lead. Her eyes scan the lake one last time as she takes a deep breath. On the way back, the rustle of leaves and clap of our shoes on the path chase away the silence. Our pace faster with the impending storm.

Peeking at her profile, I will her to speak. Will her to tell me what is on her mind.

Does she think Saturday is a date? Or just two friends hanging out, one supporting the other, while possibly sharing a meal together? Not like we haven't shared several meals or spent time together. Regardless, the list of questions grows longer with each step forward.

But I don't ask a single one. I won't ask.

Because more than anything, I fear her answer. Fear she believes Saturday is a legit date. Fear I will have to cut ties with her because being emotionally vulnerable scares the hell out of me. Fear that I feel more for her than I am willing to admit to anyone, including myself.

I care for Shelly. More than a *friend* cares for another *friend*. And no matter how hard I try to define our relationship, the lines are blurring. From where I stand, they blur more each day.

The biggest question of all... do I let those lines disappear completely? Or do I draw them sharper in the sand?

God... how I want that line to disappear.

# eleven

## SHELLY

We reach the parking lot as the first drops of rainfall.

I dig the fob out of my pocket and unlock the car. Feet away, I slow my pace. Ready to turn on my heel and tell Devlyn I will talk to him later. Before I get the chance, his fingers lightly brush my lower bicep. Curl into a firm yet gentle grip above my elbow. Stop me in my tracks.

Heat radiates from the spot where his hand touches me through the hoodie. Briefly, I close my eyes and take a deep breath. On the exhale, I open my eyes and slowly spin to face him.

"Shelly…" His voice is soft, scratchy, hesitant. His pale-green irises a touch darker and loaded with unspoken emotion.

I lick my lips and his eyes drop to follow the action. "Yeah?"

His eyes flick north as he swallows. Drizzly rain kisses our skin, yet neither of us attempts to escape it. And it is in this moment that I see it. The emotion he works so hard to keep hidden. The feelings simmering in his veins that he refuses to give control.

Since Devlyn and I fell into friendship, I questioned how he really felt. Not that I need more than he gives, but it oftentimes feels as if he holds back. Restrains himself from temptation. Resists what he truly wants. What we both want.

I have no idea what it is Devlyn wants—for himself, from me—but I wish he wouldn't fight his heart.

He scratches the back of his neck. His brows pinch together for a split second before he smooths his expression. "Come back to my place?" Of all the things to come from Devlyn's mouth, that was *not* what I expected to hear. "The weather and that call"—he tosses a thumb over his shoulder—"cut our time here."

This right here, this exact moment, is why my brain is a scrambled mess. We have hung out several times, but not a single occasion has been at my place or his. Probably his method of keeping our *friendship* in check. If we don't step into each other's personal space, the wall between friends and lovers stays upright. Solid. Permanent.

Not to be presumptuous, but him asking me to come over... did a few bricks from his highly erected wall just tumble?

"Uh..." I drop my stare to the hoodie strings near the hollow of his throat, swallow, then lift my gaze to his. "Yeah. Sure."

For someone so adamant about keeping us indefinitely in the friend zone, it seems as if Devlyn handed me an exclusive, *I never give these to anyone* invitation to the next step. I don't want to feed my inner romantic—the one currently singing and doing backflips—and think more into what all this means. But ignoring this gesture is asinine and ignorant.

"I'll text you my address. Give me an hour to clean up the

house?" His fingers finally unravel from my arm and I miss the warmth of him immediately.

I nod. "Sounds good." If this was any of my other guy friends, we'd plan food or movies or games. "Need me to bring anything?" A small crease forms between his brows. "Takeout or a movie?"

He steps back, inching closer to his car and farther from me. "Nah. We'll figure it out."

*Who is this guy?*

Everything with Devlyn has always been on the straight and narrow. No room for deviation. Sure, the occasional misunderstanding occurs, but he is quick to put us back on the path he finds most comfortable.

In the span of an hour, the space around us feels bigger. Expansive. Ever growing. Like a new side of him has emerged. One he kept locked away. Hidden. Safe. And I am not sure how to feel about the change. Should I welcome it with open arms? Or should I remain rooted and hesitant, arms hugging my chest? I'd rather it be the former, but mentally prepare myself for the latter.

"Okay." I open the driver's side door. "See you soon."

Devlyn throws me a half smile. "See you." Then he is in his car and driving out of the lot.

Minutes go by in a haze. I start the car but sit idle in the lot. The oak tree near my front bumper blurs into a blob of brown and green. The music on the radio fades into a low hum. Rain smacks the windshield in fatter drops, mottling my vision more as I get lost in thought.

*What does this all mean?*

Spending more time with Devlyn—in his home, no less—has my mind in a spiral. I don't want to overthink the invitation—to his house or the exhibition. Overthinking is the enemy of happiness. But I need some form of clarity before taking another step.

What if this is just an extension of what Devlyn deems friendship? What if it's not?

Devlyn is a great guy. Different than anyone I have met. More reserved, but it suits him. Occasionally cold, but I think him acting distant is a front to protect his heart from whatever —whoever—hurt him. Most of all, he has this complex, sensational energy. A magnetic field that pulls you in and holds you captive.

I don't want to set myself up for heartache, but I don't want to ignore the shift between us.

My phone dings with an incoming text, snapping me from my introspection. Unlocking it, I read the message with Devlyn's address. I connect my phone to the car and map his address. *Twenty minutes.* Should be enough time to get my brain in the right headspace.

"God, I hope so."

With a huff, I put the car in reverse and back out. I make a quick stop at home. Change out of my damp clothes. Eat a few pieces of chocolate. Give myself a pep talk in the bathroom mirror as I fix my ponytail. Then, I jump back in the car and drive east, toward the unknown.

*"The destination is on the right."*

I park in the driveway behind Devlyn's SUV and stare at the moody blue house. In the dark, with how far back it sits from the road, I'd easily miss it. The house a single story along the front with an additional story over the rear of what I assume was once a garage. Tall crepe myrtle trees fill the spacious front lawn—minimal foliage on the branches and bare of flowers.

Exiting the car, I shoulder my purse and walk toward the front door. Along the front of a small screened-in porch is a kaleidoscope of flowering plants. Dark-pink coneflowers and sunny bright coreopsis. Vibrant orange gerbera and purple shooting stars. Behind them, fountain grasses butt against the porch and fill in the space.

Before reaching the door, I already have a new perspective of Devlyn. One I never expected. Comprised of a large house and an even larger yard. Of plants to tend to and patio furniture on the porch. It all feels… odd. But in a good way.

I lift my hand and tap my knuckles on the door. Clattering echoes on the other side of the door, followed by a *dammit*. A soft chuckle spills from my lips as I shake my head.

Then the door whips open and I remind myself to breathe.

Devlyn finger-combs his hair a beat before gesturing to the space at his back. "Come in."

I duck my chin as a rush of heat blooms across my cheeks and I step over the threshold. Entering Devlyn's space is taking a step into the inner workings of his mind. Sure, he didn't construct the house, place the walls or windows, but his touch is everywhere.

The entry is a formal sitting room. Rustic wood floors as far as the eye can see. A simple yet sleek pale-gray sofa against the right wall, several throw pillows in various colors consume most of the sitting space, a khaki throw blanket draped over an arm. A white rug with eccentric black lines parked beneath an ashy oak coffee table. On the table is a thick book of artwork, a black three-wick candle and a small vase of common daisies. Two white lattice-woven chairs with frames matching the table sit on the opposite side of the table, facing the sofa.

Moody paintings on canvas hang on the gray wall above the sofa. The images purposely staggered, but all part of the same portrait. A woman walking in the distance, trees and flowers and tall grass in her surroundings. The image reminds me of the meadow Devlyn painted in the shop, only the observer stands farther back.

"You have a beautiful home."

Devlyn shuts the door, sidles up to me, and shoves his hands in his pockets. "Thanks. My mother insisted I get more square footage than a single person needs." He shrugs. "She isn't a woman easily ignored."

I chuckle under my breath. "Yeah, I get that. I love my mom, but sometimes she can be a little too persistent."

"Can I get you a drink?"

"Water, please." I set my purse on one of the chairs and follow him to the kitchen just past the sitting room.

A framed pass-through-slash-bar connects the kitchen and sitting room. Rather than use the bar for eating, Devlyn has another vase of flowers. This one shallow and wide and filled with magnolia buds. The fragrance a gradual scent in the air.

The kitchen is U-shaped with white cabinets, black marble countertop, dark-gray marble backsplash, and stainless steel appliances. A small window over the sink at the end looks out on what I assume is the backyard. A small basket of fruit sits on the counter in one corner, a coffee-and-tea station in the other.

Devlyn pours water from a pitcher in the fridge then hands me a glass before filling his own.

Being in Devlyn's space, without the possibility of inter-ruption, without outside means of distraction, feels claustrophobic and bizarre. Time alone with Devlyn isn't what has me worried. More often than not, our time together is spent alone.

But this is different.

There is no one to interfere. No servers or patrons or park-goers. No visual deviations such as menus or trees or walk-ways. And that realization adds a layer of sweat to my skin. Makes my breaths come in short bursts. Makes my pulse whoosh louder in my ears.

Devlyn sips his water, oblivious to my inner freak-out, and steps past me. "Come on." He glances over his shoulder. "I'll give you a tour."

To say I am overwhelmed by the time we finish the tour would be an understatement. This house is *huge*.

Five bedrooms—although he showed three, the other two I assume are his bedroom and the studio upstairs—three bath-rooms, living and dining room, laundry area, and the back-yard. The backyard is as spacious as the front, but inhabited by a large jasmine-covered pergola over canyon stone pavers with short, fine grass between each. A slate-tiled table is parked under the canopy with eight chairs. An oak tree with a trunk too wide to hug halfway shades the yard on the left, a bench swing hanging from a thick limb. Several crepe myrtles appear strategically placed in the yard to add color, shade, and beauty.

We step back inside and I down the last of my water.

The sheer size of Devlyn's home, how he has attained a level of adulthood I have yet to, sends my head into a tailspin of questions. Has me asking where I went wrong. He has acquired so much at twenty-two and I am barely able to add to my savings each month at thirty-two.

He bumps my shoulder with his bicep. "You okay?"

Am I? Yes. No. I have no freaking clue. "Yeah." I lift my

glass, then remember I have no water to quench the drought in my throat.

Devlyn takes a step and twists to face me head-on. He lifts a hand and presses the tip of his index finger between my brows. "If this spot gets any tighter, it'll never relax," he says, dropping his hand. I sigh and close my eyes. "Relax, Shelly." His voice barely above a whisper. "It's just me. Us."

I open my eyes and meet his. There, I see something familiar yet foreign. The man in front of me is Devlyn. Complex and quiet and mysterious. Only now, a darker shade of green rims his pale irises as he holds me captive. Steals my breath and has my brain foggy.

*Did a switch flip in his brain?*

My voice refuses to work. Even if it did, I wouldn't know what to say. This is yet another moment where Devlyn confounds me. Says things I easily misconstrue.

So, I simply nod in response. He rewards my bewilderment with a subtle half smile.

"Let's order food. Was thinking Asian." His smile grows. "Maybe you'll also share the story I never heard over lunch at the shop?" My eyes narrow as I think back. "Why you laughed when I asked sandwiches or sushi."

"Ah." I nod with a smile. The day comes back in a flash of colors. I was so nervous to eat lunch with Devlyn that I completely forgot. "Yeah, I'll share over dinner."

Devlyn pulls up the website for a Japanese restaurant nearby. He hands me his phone, a pad of paper, and a pen. "Write down what you want."

I arch a brow. "Before I do, you should know… I order a lot. More than a lot."

With a shake of his head, he laughs. "Doesn't matter. Leftovers always taste better."

"True." I point a finger at him.

A mile-long list later, Devlyn calls in the order. He guides us to the living room—a room he probably spends more time in, if I read the vibe accurately.

The walls throughout the house are painted the same midgray tone. Except this room. The living room is a darker gray. Cavernous with floor-to-ceiling black curtains blocking out any light from outside. Oak beams have been added to the ceiling and down the length of one wall. An oak-and-black-steel-framed bookshelf consumes the wall behind the L-shaped couch. The shelving unit decorated with small, green plants in black pots, stacked books, an eclectic wire-framed lamp with an Edison bulb, and several other statuesque knickknacks.

The L-shaped gray couch has pillowy cushions, an array of monochrome throw pillows, and a gray-and-black blanket draped over the back near the chaise. Two wooden block tables sit in the center of the room, wheels on the base, candles in the center, a drawer on one side, bolts and antique hinges and leather straps at the joints. A light tweed rug blankets the floor. Across from the couch is a black-painted brick fireplace, unburned logs on the grate, the mantel matching the oak beams. Above the fireplace, mounted to the wall, is the largest television I have seen in a home.

Devlyn doesn't strike me as someone to sit in front of the television for hours on end. But who the hell knows. We still have so much to learn about each other. Maybe Devlyn is a closet binge-watcher. Up all hours of the night, glued to endless episodes on Netflix.

Devlyn digs through the table drawer, turns on the television, then hands me the remote. "How about you find us something to watch and I'll go get us fresh drinks." I take the remote, his fingers grazing mine in the process. Heat sizzles my fingers, my forearm, my blood. No doubt my cheeks are crimson. He swallows and slowly retracts his hand. "Any requests? Water, hot tea, beer, cola."

"A beer would be great. Thanks."

The moment Devlyn exits the room, I drag in a deep breath.

*Jesus, Reed. Get a hold of yourself.*

Alcohol isn't something I partake in often, but maybe a beer will help settle my anxiety. While Devlyn fetches drinks, I surf Netflix. Would help if I knew what Devlyn likes and dislikes watching. I have no die-hard preferences and will give any show or movie a shot. With how creative Devlyn is, I assume the same of him.

After scrolling past far too many romantic movies, I scan the Netflix original series list and stumble upon *Dark*. Reznor, from the tattoo shop, raved about the show during one of our Sunday night gatherings.

Watching a mystery with Devlyn sounds a hell of a lot safer than anything else. *Dark* it is.

"You find something?" Devlyn asks as he walks back in and hands me a brown bottle.

Glancing down at the label, I laugh. "Interesting." His brows lift. "You just happen to have Japanese beer in the fridge. Like you planned this."

Devlyn sips his own beer as his eyes dart up in an unspoken answer. I laugh internally as I lift the bottle to my lips. The smooth, rich malt rolls over my tongue and cools my throat on the way down.

*He probably planned this on his way home and stopped at the store. Don't overthink it.*

"So… what are we watching?"

Oh. Right. "Since I wasn't sure of your taste, I picked something a friend recommended. *Dark.* Have you watched it?"

He shakes his head and twists to see the show synopsis on the screen. Sipping his beer, he nods. "Sounds interesting."

Next up on the list of awkward events… where do we sit on the couch?

The plush corner couch easily seats six with wiggle room. If this were my couch, I'd sit centered with the television. Which is probably where Devlyn sits when in here. I don't want to take his seat.

Should I sit in the corner spot? It's probably the most comfortable. But would I come off as distant if I sat there and Devlyn sat two seats away? Maybe I sit one off from the center. Then I appear close, but not to the point of crowding him.

Why the hell is it so damn hard to figure where to sit? Why am I overthinking couch space and seating arrangements?

*Because you're in Devlyn's home. In a dark room with minimal lighting. About to have the most intimate moment between the two of you.*

Ugh!

It may only be dinner and a show, but this is the *most* intimate span of time we have shared. Out in public, the looks and conversations we exchange don't feel as cozy or profound. In public, disruption is inevitable. It's easier to take a step back, to shy away from his stares when I can pretend something has caught my attention.

Here, in his home, all that disappears. The security blanket of distractions vanishes.

Devlyn takes a seat exactly where I knew he would, sets

his beer on a coaster on the table, then pats the seat next to him.

*Seriously, who is this guy?*

"I won't bite." A smirk tips up the corner of his mouth as he fails to hide a light chuckle. "Promise."

*What if I want him to bite?*

*Shut. Up. Shelly.*

Tossing throw pillows to the side, I sit in the space beside him. Our arms inches apart, his heat hits my skin. His scent—a blend of graphite and pine and earth—hits my nose. Head forward, I close my eyes, take a deep breath, and remind myself to breathe. To not fidget. To act *normal*.

When my eyes open, I spot Devlyn in the periphery. His gaze heating my cheek more than any flush ever would.

*Is it wrong to love his intensity? How deeply he studies every curve and line, dip and shadow of my profile?*

I rotate my head until he comes into view. I sip my beer then pick at the label. Lick my lips. Swallow when his stare falls to watch the action. Break the spell when I lean forward and set my bottle on the table, next to his.

"Should we start the show?" I point to the screen. "Or wait for the food to arrive?"

Devlyn extracts his phone from his pocket and checks the time. "Fifteen-ish minutes until food. Let's start."

As I press play on the remote, Devlyn turns off the lamp. The room goes dark. Darker than dark. The inches between my arm and his vanishes. His heat may as well smother every inch of me on this couch, in this room.

An Albert Einstein quote fills the screen in German, subtitles listed below. A second later, ominous music follows and a man's voice floods the room. And it is all I need as a distraction. The deep timbre demands my attention. The words beckon me to listen, to pay attention.

I thank whatever instinct told me to choose this show. Because I need the diversion. Need something to grab my attention more than Devlyn.

An eerie sound fills the air from a cave on the screen just as the doorbell rings. I all but jump out of my skin. Devlyn… laughs.

"Not scared, are you?" I shake my head and he laughs again. Rising from the couch, he exits the room. "Be right back."

As my heart settles back to its normal rhythm, Devlyn strolls back into the room with two brown bags, sets them down, and rolls the two tables together. As I empty the bags, Devlyn tosses pillows on the floor between the couch and table. When I eye him, he simply says, "Makes it easier to share."

Devlyn stares at the containers in front of me as if waiting for a sign to pop up with descriptions for each. I point to each dish and tell him what they are.

"Seaweed salad, veggie tempura, bulgogi."

"Bul-what?"

"Bulgogi. Uh… essentially, it's Korean BBQ. And so good." I point to my last dish. "Yaki udon. Noodle soup with veggies and shrimp."

He glances at all the food I ordered, then looks to his salmon teriyaki, rice, miso soup, side salad, steamed veggies, and noodles. His eyes dart back and forth a few times before he looks up.

"Will you eat all that?" His voice is absent of judgment but loaded with curiosity.

I shake my head. "Definitely not. I just love all the flavors and have a hard time deciding."

A smile kicks up the corners of his lips. "Will you tell me the story behind why you laughed at sandwiches or sushi at the shop that first day I ordered lunch?"

"Only if you promise to try everything."

He tips his head side to side in contemplation. "Deal."

We dig into food. The screensaver replaces the pause point of the show, and I dive into the story.

"My best friend, Cora, loves every type of Asian food. We've known each other since elementary school and she wasn't always this way. I remember when I stayed the night at her house. She begged her mom, Elizabeth—"

"Elizabeth from the shop?"

I nod. "Yep. That's a story for another day." There I go being presumptuous. "But she always begged her mom to cook us Kid Cuisine TV dinners. She always wanted the one with chicken nuggets, macaroni and cheese, corn, and chocolate pudding. That's how it was until early high school. She loved those damn things." I laugh. "Then, one day, out of nowhere, she didn't. She wanted lo mein and egg foo young. Teriyaki and phở. Sushi and katsudon. When I asked her what sparked her sudden interest, she said her dad received a stack of gift certificates for restaurants near the beach. A few of them were to Asian restaurants. Went downhill from there."

Devlyn's lips plump as he mulls it over. Longer than a friend would, I stare at his lips. Unfortunately for me, I don't look up until he clears his throat.

Cue my virginal blush.

*Someone save me from a lifetime of humiliation. I beg you.*

"So, me asking sandwiches or sushi was funny because you've probably had sushi with your friend thousands of times." I nod. "Makes sense." He takes a sip of beer. "What's *your* favorite food?"

"Way to put a lady on the spot." I chuckle while dipping a piece of fried squash in the tentsuyu. "I don't know. I like variety. Picking one thing seems impossible." Tipping my head back, I stare at the ceiling. "If I had to pick *one* food, it'd probably be bread. Any kind except white sandwich bread. And fresh out of the oven." I hum, and out of the corner of my eye, Devlyn shifts his position.

*What was that?*

"Bread, huh?" I nod. "I'll have to remember that."

*"I'll have to remember that." Why? And what does that mean?*

Devlyn picks up the remote and presses play, ending the story. Our conversation may be over, but we both wear ridiculous smiles on our faces.

When our bellies are full, Devlyn puts the leftovers in the fridge. We relocate to the couch, seemingly closer than before, and watch more episodes of *Dark*. I do everything within my power to focus on the show and not how close we sit.

Inevitably, I lose the battle and it isn't long before I lay my head on Devlyn's shoulder and press my weight into him. Never more comfortable than in this moment.

# twelve

## DEVLYN

A pinch in my neck stirs me from sleep, but I don't dare move. Not when my senses spark to life and a scent I know all too well drifts through my nose. Jasmine, orange blossoms, and patchouli. Such a unique combination. Each note detectable on its own, but addictive when combined.

*Shelly.*

I crack an eye open, take in her blonde locks, then inhale deeply.

Face buried at the base of my throat; Shelly's body curls into mine. Our legs a tangled mess. Her arms sandwiched between us, palms pressed to my chest. One of my arms supports her head while the other drapes her waist.

I close my eyes and absorb the moment, the connection, the gravity we can't escape.

Oddly, in this blip of time, fear doesn't grab me by the ankles and pull me under. In fact, fear is nowhere to be found. No fear, but anxiety bubbles just below the surface. That will never not exist when close to Shelly—physically and otherwise.

Thinking back to last night, Shelly sank into me more with

each passing minute. Our bellies full after we gorged on the living room buffet. The second she laid her head on my shoulder, I closed my eyes and fought the voice of doubt in my head. The voice I heard often when it came to Shelly.

I don't want to fight what I feel for her. I also don't want to hurt again.

Question is, how do I balance what I feel for her and the self-doubt eating at my heart?

Shaking away my thoughts, I focus on the here and now. Focus on the sleeping woman in my arms. Opening my eyes to see her in a new way, a new light, close up and unrestrained. Expression soft, hair disheveled, lips slightly parted.

God, it feels good to hold her. *Really* hold her. How many times have I pictured this moment? Well, not this *exact* moment, but a similar one. One where I wrap my arms around her frame and haul her snug to mine. One where her touch provides me comfort and not unease. One where I sweep my knuckles softly over the line of her jaw, her cheekbone, her chin just before I lean in and brush my lips with hers.

Too many times. Not enough times.

A mumble leaves her lips. Something unintelligible. By her tone, I assume it was endearing or sweet, but can't be certain. She mumbles again, a soft *please* against my skin. The heat of her breath, mixed with the weight of her plea, sends goose bumps across my skin.

Then she moves… and I freeze.

Her legs weave more with mine like vines climbing a trellis. One arm wraps around my torso and hugs me while the other fists my shirt. Her nose burrows into the bend where my shoulder and neck meet. And then she sighs. Melts into me more. Holds me physically captive. Arrests my heart. Consumes my soul.

I love and hate it equally.

I love how easy it is to love Shelly. To fall into her in ways I never did with Kelsey. To look forward to her smile and voice and presence. To feel the radiance bounding off her aura and spilling into mine. I love how her dark, starry eyes suck me in and send me soaring. Shelly makes me dream of possibilities, of the future, of a life with her.

In the same breath, I hate how easily I give in to my emotions with her. How easily I am willing to tear away the barrier guarding my heart, the one that has kept me sane and safe and whole for the last four years. The armor that shielded me from making irrational decisions based on what my heart wanted versus what my brain knew.

But Shelly isn't Kelsey.

Shelly is vibrant and charismatic, brilliant and vivacious. When she walks in a room, she brings light and laughter and love with her. More than any of that, she is wise. Wise beyond her years. Mature. She would never just drop someone because she wanted to explore life freely.

We haven't discussed our pasts—not in-depth—but her rosy cheeks every time I toss out a compliment give her away. Tell me her experience with men isn't as vast as other women her age. She is selective with who sees her heart. If that's true, it only adds to her allure.

"Stupid thorn," she mumbles against my skin.

I bite my cheek to not laugh. For a little longer, I want this side of her. To see her in the faint, dim light creeping in from the edge of the curtain. To watch her while she sleeps. While I can look at her features without restraint, without fear of being caught. Her toffee locks with hints of sunshine. Matching lashes fanned beneath her lower lid to the apple of her cheek. The three small freckles lateral to her right eye.

The soft line of her jaw and curve of her chin. And lips so soft and full and kissable.

Licking my lips, I picture what it would be like to kiss Shelly. To give in to the urge, the desire, the need to feel her lips pressed to mine.

I close my eyes and let the fantasy take over. Allow myself to daydream about how warm and supple and perfect her kiss would feel. How demanding she'd be. How demanding I'd be in return. What her moan would sound like when I drag her bottom lip between mine. What she'd taste like when she finally bloomed like a flower and let me in.

Her fingers on my lower back curl slightly, tug at my cotton shirt, and I stop breathing. My eyes fly open and I think of anything except kissing Shelly. Because fuck my life, I'm hard.

Sure, if she wakes now, I can pretend to do the same and play it off as morning wood. This is most definitely *not* morning wood.

What is the one thing that automatically sends my mood south? Is an instant buzzkill?

*My mother. Mom, Mom, Mom.*

And thank god it works. Just as my erection softens, Shelly opens her eyes. She groans and leans back. A smile slowly plumps her cheeks.

Without a doubt, this is my favorite view of Shelly. Soft and unkempt and not a worry marring her beautiful face. Perfect.

Then the corners of her mouth sag. Her brows wrinkle at the middle. Pupils go wide as realization dawns. That she is wrapped around me tighter than a koala. That she is on my couch, in my house, and we fell asleep.

Before I open my mouth to say everything is okay, she bolts upright.

"Oh my god!" She looks around the room so quick it makes me dizzy. "Oh my god," she whispers and slaps a hand over her eyes.

I sit up beside her, rest my palm between her shoulder blades, and rub small, slow circles. "Shelly, it's okay. We fell asleep."

She drops her hand. "Shit. What time is it?"

Crawling across the room, I fetch my phone from the table and tap the screen. "Five thirty-eight."

A groan spills from her lips. "I need to go. The shop. I have to go home and shower and change and eat and—"

"Shelly"—I add more pressure to my touch—"it's okay. You have time. Breathe."

And she does. She inhales through her nose and out through her mouth. Then does it again.

"Better?"

She nods.

"Before you go, let me at least make you breakfast."

"I don't—"

"Please. Promise I'll be quick." Her brows twitch. "I'll even pack it to go if you want."

"Sure. Okay. But only if it's quick."

"Pinkie promise."

She gives me her beautiful smile. Warmth floods the center of my chest, my heart thumping in a new pattern. And after I rise off the couch, before my brain can stop me, I bend at the waist and press my lips to her crown.

Neither of us moves. My pulse shifts again. Beats more erratically. Fear jolts my nerves as a dose of cortisol enters my bloodstream.

*I took it too far. Shit. Shit, shit, shit.*

Then she reaches for my hand, lifts her eyes, and shows me her rosy cheeks. "Thank you," she whispers. "I'm just going to use the bathroom."

"Right. Yeah." I step back, give her room to pass. "I'll be in the kitchen."

By the time she walks into the kitchen, I have cheesy scrambled eggs and buttered toast ready. Immediately, I want to make her a better breakfast. One that isn't rushed and we can enjoy together. But I am getting way ahead of myself.

She tugs on her shoes and shoulders her purse. I hand her the container and a fork as we awkwardly head for the door. And because I am not ready for goodbye, I follow her out to her car.

After unlocking the car, she sets her purse and the container inside then spins to face me, the door partially between us.

I won't lie… I hate it. The barrier and the fact she has to go.

"Thank you, again. For dinner and a show. It was wonderful."

"We should do it again. I do have leftovers." I lift a brow. She opens her mouth to answer, but I hold up a hand and cut her off. "Think about it."

She rolls her eyes and chuckles. "Fine," she says on a huff. "But I really do need to go."

*I want to kiss her. Right here. Right now. I want to lean forward, cradle her cheeks in my palms, and kiss her.*

But I won't. Now is not the time.

Soon, though.

"Then I won't keep you any longer." I reach out, take her

hand, and give it a quick squeeze. "Drive safe. I'll send you the exhibition details later."

She drops into the driver's seat. "See you."

"See you."

I close her car door and take a few steps back. Watch her back out of the driveway and wave as she pulls away. The moment she is out of sight, I pivot and jog back to the house. Weave to the stairwell off the dining room and take the stairs two at a time.

The moment I step into my studio, the moment graphite and Turpenoid and canvas hits my nose, I sag with a heavy exhale. Then I snap into action. Bolt into the closet and grab a fresh canvas. Set it on my easel then grab my brushes and paints.

In seconds, I get lost. Lost in the image of her face this morning while she snuggled my chest. Lost in the contours of her face. In the sunshine highlights in her hair. In the fullness of her lips.

Not for the first time, I transfer my memories of Shelly into art. Stroke the bristles over canvas and create the outline of her heart-shaped face. Well, half of it.

Barely a fraction into the piece, I see it all so clearly in my head. Half her profile—plump full lips, rosy cheekbone, twilight iris with a touch of gold, and her slightly arched brow, framed by her golden hair. Behind her, pink blossoms. Primrose and meadowsweet.

This is the moment—*the moment*—when it truly hits me. The moment I can no longer deny what I feel, even if it scares the hell out of me.

What I feel for Shelly isn't love. No, it is way too soon for such a deep emotion. But I like her. *Really like her.* A lot. More than I should.

I admit this, but only to myself. Our relationship is too new for verbal confessions. But I feel it all the same. In the turbulent beat of my heart. In the shortness of my breath. In the thick of my marrow.

Question is, where do I go from here?

It is too soon to put my heart on the line. To cut myself open and hand her my heart. Every instinct inside me says to trust Shelly, that she won't hurt me. But once upon a time, the same instinct existed in regard to Kelsey. I'd thought we were inseparable. Endgame. And then she crushed me. Broke me in half and left me without a care in the world.

I refuse to let that happen again. To be blindsided and thrown away.

*Shelly is not Kelsey. She won't hurt you. Not on purpose.*

As I paint the rich blue of her iris on the canvas, I inhale deeply. "I really hope that's true."

Surviving the breakup with Kelsey was painful and life-altering. If Shelly and I went separate ways—no matter the cause—not only would it be painful, it would be downright devastation. A crippling debilitation. Losing Shelly would be a darkness I'd never overcome. A shadowed life I'd never be able to escape. Losing Shelly... I would give up. On everything.

Shelly isn't just endgame... she is so much more.

A dangerous thought slips into the foreground. One that scares the hell out of me, but I cannot deny.

From the moment I laid eyes on her, with every re-creation of her image, I say without a shadow of doubt... Shelly is the one.

And recognizing this simple fact terrifies me more than anything.

# Thirteen

## SHELLY

I have never sweated so profusely in my life. And it's sixty degrees outside.

Devlyn picked me up for the art exhibition minutes ago. When he sent me the event details, I offered to drive myself, in case he needed to be there earlier. He insisted on arriving at my door almost two hours before the event and chauffeuring me to the exhibition.

It only took one deep breath for me to cave. To give in to his persistence. Let him take control of the evening.

Devlyn in control is one of the reasons my pores are mini waterfalls.

*Please don't let me have sweat stains under my pits.* I mentally put my hands in prayer position. *Please.*

The drive to Sarasota—the gallery near the college Devlyn attended—isn't far, but it's not right around the corner. The distance and the fact I don't know my way around Sarasota is another reason I let Devlyn drive.

The event starts at four and runs until six. Then, we have dinner reservations at a restaurant near the gallery. Dinner.

Reservations. As in a premeditated meal at a nice establishment.

*God, this feels like a date. An expensive date.*

With Devlyn, it is hard to know. My new rule with him is to never assume. Assumptions get me nowhere. After movie night the other day, and falling asleep on his couch, he seems different. More open. Closer. But assuming we are anything but friends may shut him down.

So, unless he mutters the word *date*, I will keep repeating… This. Is. Not. A. Date.

On the way, Devlyn talks more about his time at college. I lean in closer and listen with rapt attention. His willingness to share has me on the edge of my seat. Although our friendship has shifted, taken on a new persona, I don't often get this side of Devlyn. The more personal side. A deeper look into his past. Small glimpses into his life, into the way he sees the world. I soak up each new story he shares and pray it won't be the last.

My college years centered around lectures and term papers and parties. Devlyn's focused on honing his current craft, finding love in new mediums, and immersing himself in everything art related. Polar opposite lives; his ten times more fascinating.

We hit the peak of the Skyway Bridge and I stare at the bright-yellow stay cables. Blink at the strobe effect they cause as we pass at highway speed. As with all bridges, this one has history. It wasn't always this mammoth bridge supported by massive cement pillars. The old metal bridge… it had a tragic ending. It was before my time, but I remember the stories my family shared anytime we drove over the new bridge and the local history lessons taught in school.

Are Devlyn and I headed that direction? Tragedy. Not like

Romeo and Juliet's tragedy. Love that deep makes me uneasy, but not fully. With tragedy, I mean more like an ending where neither of us comes out happy.

Please, don't let that be our trajectory. A one-way road of devastation.

After the other night, after waking up in his arms, I'd like to think not. But presuming anything with Devlyn is dangerous and foolhardy. A nonrefundable ticket to heartache.

I try to forget the cold shoulder moments. The instances he shut down and said the word friends for the thousandth time. Instead, I focus on the days he has shown me tenderness. Spoken sentiments friends don't exchange. Stared at my lips or neck or body with more interest than a friend.

Would it shock me if he said I read too much into any of it? No. I may be outgoing and perceptive with friends and family, but when it comes to romance, all that awareness goes out the window. It's difficult to not read between the lines with rose-colored glasses. Especially when he looks at me as if I am his world, as if I am his next breath. To say it confuses me is an understatement.

"Almost there," he says, interrupting my inner tirade.

"Are you excited?"

A smile brightens his face—the one I love more than I should—and I have my answer. "Yes and no."

When he doesn't expand on his answer, I mentally reach across the console and shake him. "Care to elaborate?"

I love Devlyn's mysterious nature. His solemnity and zen. He sees the world like no one I've known. Sees it in black and white, but also brilliant colors. Finds the beauty in all people and places and life. Depicts emotion as if it walks among us. Adds zeal to everything he touches with the flick of a brush.

And I breathe it all in.

He guides us off the interstate and my eyes zero in on the city. Most of the Bay Area cities have similar vibes and one uniquely their own. Yes, it is another coastal city with beaches and nightlife and shops, but it feels different here. More alive. Maybe because this place is new to me. Or maybe because the history of the city is different. Either way, I love the vibe.

"Seeing my work in a gallery never gets old. I don't create to have it on display, but people seeing my art opens up doors. The opportunity to sell more pieces or create custom originals."

Like most artists, Devlyn creates because the need is ingrained in him. A deep-seated urge to spill his emotions without speaking. To express himself without becoming one-hundred-percent vulnerable.

"Sounds more yes than no."

"True." He purses his lips a beat. "The downfall of these events is being in the spotlight. People asking about your personal life. Criticizing your work. Putting their two cents in. I don't necessarily mind criticism from peers or people I look up to. They give me new perspective. Help me improve who I am as an artist. It's the snooty folks who think, because they have art hanging in their house, they know what *good* art looks like."

I reach across the console and touch his bicep. "Ignore them."

Briefly, he glances down at my hand on him. I pull it back and drop it to my lap before I spot the slight uptick of his lips. "I do my best. Isn't always easy." I don't miss his brief glance at my hand again, and I wonder if he enjoyed the small physical connection.

Since the other morning, Devlyn and I haven't touched. Friends don't share intimate touch. And until I know how movie night and the morning after makes him feel, I am doing my damnedest to stay on my side of the friendship line. Keep our physical contact to arm bumps and the occasional hooked elbows. We don't hug hello or goodbye like I do with my other friends or family. No teasing slaps on the arm or ruffling of hair. And we both know why.

To form a stronger connection—to touch easily, without second thought—our friendship would morph into more. Evolve beyond pizza lunches and walks in the park. Move beyond movie night with takeout and awkward mornings the next day. Blossom into something neither Devlyn nor I am prepared for, if I am honest with myself.

We haven't talked much about our pasts, but I know someone hurt Devlyn. I see it in the way he fights his feelings. The hidden stares followed by cold shoulders. The invitation to spend time together accompanied by the reminder of that ugly line drawn in the sand.

Hurt bruises my heart that a past relationship shook him so deeply, he refuses to let it happen again. Refuses to let love in. By choice, he shelters his heart—well, he attempts to shelter it. I do and don't understand, mainly because the subject has never come up. So, I grant him all the time he needs. Let this—us—be whatever it is while it exists. Let Devlyn set the pace. Allow him to set the tone and shape our relationship.

But I see the small cracks in his exterior. Notice how his stares last longer. Hear the undercurrent of desire and longing in his voice. Feel his warmth and impulsive need for physical contact when we exist in the same space. All of which weighs more heavily since my limbs tangled with his and he didn't let go.

Is going at Devlyn's pace fair? Not when I don't know where his head is at.

But I like Devlyn, more than he'd deem comfortable. I enjoy our time together. The brief chats as well as the lengthy conversations. The fleeting lunches and hours strolling in the park. If we remain only friends, I consider myself lucky to have him. If we become more… loving Devlyn would be sublime.

When it comes to this complex man, I set no expectations.

He parks the car, exits, and jogs around to my open door. I open my mouth to ask what he is doing, but when my eyes meet his, I zip my lips and smile at the gesture. His chivalry may be unexpected, but I refuse to depreciate the moment. Not with the way my heart flip-flops in my chest.

*This is not a date.*

We walk into the gallery, elbows hooked, and are bombarded. The event doesn't open to the general public for another thirty minutes. All the people flocking to Devlyn's side are peers and professors and fellow local artists. People who have seen or heard of his work. His fan club.

Although Devlyn doesn't care for the spotlight, he smiles and laughs and boasts about other artists whose work is *better*. Watching him here, now, I get another new side of him. He isn't necessarily more outgoing, just more himself. More comfortable in his own skin around those who share the same passion.

I love this side of him.

After a few minutes, he introduces me to the group. He doesn't introduce me as his girlfriend, but he also doesn't introduce me as a friend either. Just Shelly. A low hum whirls beneath my diaphragm. A new layer of perspiration dampens my skin. I work to not let the moment go to my head. Much. Easier said than done.

"Want a drink before the doors open?" he asks.

"Please." Lord knows I need something to temper the heat in my veins.

Drinks in hand, Devlyn guides us to the start of the exhibition. Tonight, there are seven local artists on display, including Devlyn.

Offering his elbow, my favorite smile of his makes an appearance. "Shall we?"

A fresh wave of heat blankets my skin as I hook my arm with his. I swallow past the thick swell of emotion in my throat and nod. "Yeah," I say, voice hoarse and low. Clearing my throat, I try again. "Yes."

The first showcase is Tomas Suarez. His medium of choice is watercolor and, as I gaze at each canvas, I am already at a loss for words. I never knew watercolor could be so bold. So evocative. Pops of bright blue and fuchsia. Subtle greens and soft yellow. Powerful yet subdued. Tomas paints landscapes, and this one reminds me of the meadow Devlyn painted in the shop—*my meadow*—but with softer lines. As if out of focus. We study his other pieces, digest their beauty, then move on to the next artist.

Kanesha Winston. Her three-dimensional art on canvas has me utterly fascinated. Oil paintings with book pages or paper-mache or origami added, then painted to blend in. I have never seen anything like it. The art is literally in my face, screaming to be seen. Begging me to reach out and run my fingers over it. Shifting left and right, I look at each piece from a different angle, a different perspective. See it come to life in its own way.

Akira Yamamoto and Leonard Denver are the two sculptors on display. The clay artist has softer appeal. A profile bust of a man in mourning. An ancient warrior mask. A mosaic of a woman in a garden. Each beautiful and mesmerizing in their own right. The metal pieces have harsher lines and are made of scraps. A hummingbird on a flower. A bionic cat. And my favorite—the softest of the metal pieces—is the embracing couple. Two human forms from the waist up, holding each other. One of them shiny and without imperfections. The other a mix of chain mail and luster with minor cracks.

Devlyn and I stare at this piece the longest. As if it represents us. Soft and rough. Smooth and harsh. Solid and broken. When I peek at him from the corner of my eye, I want to ask what he is thinking and feeling as he stares at the piece. If he sees the uncanny resemblance of us in the art. The strength and instability.

For now, I keep the thought to myself.

The last two artists before we reach Devlyn's work are Justine Thomas and Harrison Beaufort. Their charcoal pieces are remarkable. The art world is still so new to me, but it blows my mind how people create such beauty with paper and charcoal.

One piece, dubbed *Blue Woman*, is easily life size. Drawn on a six-by-three-foot paper scroll, the *Blue Woman* hides behind messy strands and a large sweater. Without question, the term blue depicts her mood. And I don't know why, but I *feel* her pain, her despair. So much it has me on the cusp of tears.

As if he senses my mood shift, Devlyn leans into me more. Gives me more heat and weight. Soothes the sting with his natural balm. Dropping his chin, his breath heats the skin of my earlobe and just beneath. "On to the most embarrassing moment of the night," Devlyn says, and I shiver.

He rests his free hand on my forearm and gives it a slight squeeze. For a split second, I stare down as if imagining things. The lingering sensation of his breath on my skin. The warmth of his hand on my arm. It isn't weird or uncomfortable, but it is different. New.

Without second thought, I lay my hand over his. Allow his warmth to blanket my skin and seep into my veins. Let my heart pound viciously, my lungs inhale erratically, and my nerve endings light on fire.

This feels more like holding hands. Forming an entirely new bond. A connection miles past the friendship line. Because friends don't hold hands. Not unless they are drunk or exhausted or injured. And I am none of the above.

"Don't be embarrassed," I say, voice unsteady as I peer up at him. Eyes on mine, he swallows and nods.

I tighten my hold on our connection, close my eyes for two breaths and savor how perfect this feels. Then I let him lead the way.

Ten steps and several rapid heartbeats later, we stand in front of a collage of pencil drawings. Two on larger pieces of stock, five on smaller pieces and surrounding the two larger.

I step closer to the images and Devlyn steps with me, not relinquishing my arm. My eyes graze over the first smaller drawing. Fingers, the top of a hand, a wrist and forearm, the start of a bicep. The limb feminine, soft, shaded, intimate. I swallow as heat blooms in my cheeks. A sudden sense of voyeurism hits the center of my chest. As if I am invading an intimate moment.

Taking a deep breath, I shift my gaze to the next small piece. The supple curve of a shoulder and border of the throat. Extra shading to emphasize the collarbone and subtle dip of the hollow spot at the base of the throat.

*Jesus. Is it hot in here?*

How does he make simple body parts, parts we see on people every day, so striking? Something you can't not take pause to stare at, to absorb, to get lost in. Something that makes your pulse race and your breath catch.

The next is the profile of a neck and jaw. I assume the muse for all the pieces is the same due to the feminine depiction. I want to ask Devlyn who she is. If she is the person who has him scared to move forward. To open himself to another.

But I don't ask. I fear his answer. Fear whoever this woman is, he will never move past her.

The last two smaller pieces depict a shadowed profile of her face and a pair of eyes. The eyes tug at something inside me, beg me to open my mouth and ask questions. Dark irises with the occasional shimmer resembling stars.

My eyes narrow as I step closer. Study the irises more critically. The occasional shimmer in the darkness makes me think of my sister-in-law, Peyton. How she calls my brother starlight. Because of his eyes. The same eyes that match my own.

And suddenly, I can't breathe.

My heart rattles in my rib cage. Bangs in the hopes of escape. And I do my best to settle the irrational thoughts and emotions surging inside. I don't *know* this is me, and should not assume as much. For all I know, these drawings are years old. Depictions of the woman that broke his heart. Someone he once loved, but who is no longer in his life. Someone other than me.

I try to collect myself. Calm my racing heart. Normalize my breathing. Not stiffen my arm looped in his. Focus on the rest of the images—the two larger ones I have yet to see. All while not letting on the path my mind has taken.

When I shift my gaze, when I take in the last two pieces, I stop breathing all over again.

*Confused. I am so damn confused.*

One is the back of a woman. Light wavy strands down her back. The edge of her profile on display as she looks off to the side. The second... it is the same woman. In a meadow. A meadow strikingly similar to the one painted inside Petal and Vine.

I don't know what to think. What to say. How to feel. How to function.

Devlyn leans into me, his breath warm on my ear as his body presses into mine. I might have a heart attack in the middle of this gallery. "What do you think?" he whisper-asks.

*What do I think?* What a loaded question.

My eyes roam the drawings as I ponder how to answer his simple yet complex question. A question so heavy, I'm not sure if there is a right answer. Right or wrong, I think Devlyn feels much deeper for me than he realizes. Either that or he refuses to accept how he feels.

"I... uh..." I close my eyes and swallow. How do I act myself, act as if everything is still the same, after seeing these? How do I go on pretending we are just friends? Because this—these drawings—screams more than friendship. This is passion and longing and heartache. Beauty and fantasy and hunger. These aren't just depictions of an elegant woman, they are intimacy and affection and hope. A desperate cry for more. Of what, I can't be sure.

No doubt they took weeks to draw. Weeks. Our friendship was only weeks old.

What rattles me most is that Devlyn *chose* this collection to display tonight. Purposely selected these drawings for hundreds to see. Is all but silently telling everyone we are more than friends. That I don't just occupy his thoughts, but also his heart.

Friends don't draw provocative, intimate angles of another friend's body. Friends don't focus on eyes and lips and freckles. Friends don't invite friends to see how much they think and feel and desire the other. Lovers do.

And in this moment, it feels as if Devlyn has always thought of me as more than a friend. Whether he wants to admit it or not.

"They're beautiful," I say after a long pause.

His breath wafts my hair and I close my eyes. "Couldn't agree more."

When it comes to this man, this beautifully broken, soft-spoken, timid man… I am screwed. No matter where we go from here, no matter if we remain friends or take the next step, I am, without a doubt, screwed. After all I have seen tonight, my heart no longer wants to fight what it feels. The only problem with that… Devlyn might not be ready to reciprocate. His walls may be slowly crumbling, but I doubt they will ever fully fall. Not anytime soon.

Devlyn may not be ready to confess his heart, but I am willing to push his boundaries. Willing to cross the line with him. For him. No matter the outcome, at least he will know where I stand.

*Best buckle up and enjoy the journey. While it lasts.*

# *fourteen*

## DEVLYN

I must be having an out-of-body experience. It's the only logical explanation as to why I have practically erased the line between me and Shelly.

As often as I tell myself we are just friends, that we will *only* be friends, my actions and thoughts and feelings toward Shelly supersede that of a friend. I am a walking contradiction. Saying and doing things more like a lover than a friend. The subtle touches that come off as normal, but are far from it. The whispered words close to her ear as I inhale her intoxicating scent. The constant need to be closer to her, to feel her warmth and weight.

Worst of all, I don't stop myself.

I no longer *want* to stop myself.

"Am I underdressed?" Shelly asks as we pull up to the restaurant.

I stare out the windshield at the glass-front brick structure. The restaurant gives off fine dining vibes, but is quite casual. Online reviews raved over the food, atmosphere, and service. I studied the menu long enough to learn it had decent variety. So I set a reservation.

"You look great. The website didn't mention dress, so I wouldn't worry."

She laughs under her breath. "Easy for you."

And I wonder what she means. Why would it be easy for me and not her? If anything, Shelly outshines everyone. Me? I'm the scrawny, quirky guy at her side. The person everyone will look past to glimpse her.

I park the car then jog to the passenger door to help her out. Not that she needs help. Shelly is a strong woman. Capable of standing tall on her own.

But having her at my side and on my arm tonight was a new, unfamiliar high. Something I never expected. Something I want more of. Her warm hand wrapped around my bicep, her eyes on my art. Nothing has ever felt so right and perfect and exhilarating.

Am I walking a dangerous line? Yes. I have never been on a slope this slippery. Do I care? At the moment, no. I'd tread the steepest incline for her.

When was the last time I felt a connection like this? When was the last time someone *wanted* me? It had been too long. Scary as it is, I crave Shelly. More than my next breath.

Instead of fearing what may happen, I offer my arm once more. Lock onto my favorite constellation and wait for her acceptance. And she does not disappoint. I don't think it's possible for Shelly to ever disappoint. At least not me. She hooks her arm with mine, wraps her dainty fingers near my elbow, the digits giving a gentle squeeze. I live for that squeeze. For any near or intentional touch she bestows. Each has my breath more erratic. Each little reassurance says she enjoys being on my arm.

I am so fucked. *We* are so fucked. In the best way.

We step into the restaurant and I give the hostess my

name. She escorts us through the restaurant, toward a table in the back near another set of large windows that looks out onto the Gulf. Shelly takes her seat, then I take mine across from her. As much as I would love to sit closer, to be within easy reach of her hand or knee, I love this unobstructed view. To see half her face aglow from the setting sun and the other half from a candle at the heart of the table.

There are a million and one ways to take in Shelly. To catalog her features in a new light. To discover a new angle of her delicate profile. A new light to absorb the beauty of this woman. Taking the time to learn them all has my body abuzz. Shoots thrill through my limbs and to the center of my chest.

I want to view all million and one.

"Devlyn." My name is soft and worrisome on her tongue. I snap out of my Shelly-induced daydream, lower my menu and lock onto her wide eyes. She curves the menu to the side of her face to shield our conversation from other tables. The gesture is cute. "Did you look at the prices on the menu?"

I give her a half smile. "Didn't cross my mind."

Her eyes go impossibly wider. "You may want to."

To appease her, I stare down at the menu. See a thirty-dollar chicken dish and don't think twice. Not that I eat at places with price points like this on the regular, but it wouldn't be the first time. Not with all the fancy dinners and fundraiser events I attended with my parents as a child.

Mom always has to have the best. Be the best.

Cue mental eye roll.

Since living on my own, most nights I cook at home or get takeout from small, local places. Nothing pricey or lavish. I tend to not dine out often since crowds aren't my thing.

Tonight is an exception. Tonight is a special occasion. My art in a gallery—without the help or influence of my mother

—warrants celebration. And there is no other person I would rather share an overpriced, intimate meal with than Shelly.

"It's fine, Shelly. Tonight is a special occasion and I'd like to indulge. Order what you'd like and don't worry about the cost."

She shifts the menu so it hides her eyes. After a few deep breaths, she nods and scans the menu again. Thank goodness she doesn't fight me on this. On the price of a meal. Yes, the cost of dinner here is more than I typically spend. But tonight is worth every cent. *She* is worth every cent and much more.

The server comes to the table, tells us the chef specials for the evening, takes our drink order and gives us another moment to decide. Before either of us sets our menu down, the server returns with two glasses of red wine and takes our order.

Shelly stares out the window at the fire-tinged horizon. Studies the skyline, sips her wine, and sighs. I don't hide my stare. Don't hide my eyes as they trace the arch of her brow, slope of her nose, and plump lines of her lips. I drink her in more than ever. Get drunk on her and not the wine. Love how at ease she is in this moment, at a table with me, sharing a meal after an evening on my arm.

Our easy connection has me dizzy. The comfort she gives has me wobbly in my chair.

The entire night—the drive, the gallery, dinner—is more than I expected. With Shelly, I set zero expectations. But she shocks me at every turn, with what she says and the feelings she stirs up from deep, hidden places.

The more time Shelly and I spend together, the more I want to open myself to her. Give her pieces of myself I have given no one. Not even Kelsey.

Over the last two months, Shelly has wiggled her way in.

Not with her wit or charm or beauty—although, I love these traits too—but with her magnetic energy and gravitational pull.

In our minimal conversations, we communicate more with silence and body language than most do with words. Our quiet chats reflect my introversion more than her natural disposition. Shelly lights up a room with her exuberance. Being the center of attention has never been my cup of tea, but I want to test the waters. Dip my toes in, ask the questions on the tip of my tongue, and learn more about Shelly Reed.

And share more about myself.

"Do you visit the beach much? When it's warmer, obviously."

She inhales deeply then shifts her gaze from the setting sun to me. "Not as much as I did years ago. This adulting business is bullshit."

I laugh, far louder than I should, but it can't be helped. Thinking back, I can't recall many occasions when a curse slipped between Shelly's lips. Not that I pictured Shelly as a complete saint.

"Couldn't agree more. Whoever came up with the idea you had to pay to live, to exist… I'd like to have a word with them."

Now, it's her turn to laugh. Head slightly back, hand over her heart, lips and eyes tipped up at the corners. I love how effervescent the sound is. Like carbonation and sunshine. A gust of wind on a still day. Her laughter is one more thing to like about the woman sitting across the table.

"What about you?" she asks. "Do you visit the beach much?"

"I actually enjoy the beach when it's cooler. Not the water, but bundled in a blanket on the sand with my sketchpad. A unique creativity sparks when I'm out in the elements. It challenges me in a fresh way. Changes how I interpret what I see and feel on paper, or canvas later. It also depends on my mood."

She nods then sips her wine. Before either of us gets in another question, the server returns with the appetizer—ricotta-stuffed figs with a balsamic reduction. I gesture for Shelly to taste one first.

"What's your favorite color?" The question is generic. One I probably know the answer to, based on her wardrobe, but I ask anyway.

"Pink." Correct. Shelly may not be decked out in pink daily, but she incorporates the color in her life. Polish, hair accessories, jewelry, lip gloss, pins. I see each touch, each shade and variation.

"Favorite foods? Aside from bread." We both laugh under our breaths.

"That's a little more difficult." She taps her lips with a finger and my eyes magnetize to the action. "Household staples… I *love* cashew butter. Too much for my own good. Slap it on crusty bread"—her frame wilts slightly as a dreamy look fills her eyes—"and I'm in heaven." Her exaggeration of the word love makes me chuckle under my breath. "Prepared foods, especially ones I don't cook"—we both laugh—"bulgogi. There's more, but those rank highest."

Flashes of the other night, of Shelly in my house, eating dinner with me in front of the television, pop in my head. Followed by waking up with her wrapped in my arms. I want another night with Shelly. I want another morning with her snuggled against my frame.

"Still can't believe I'd never eaten it before the other night."

"Right? I'll make it your favorite too." She winks and the corner of my mouth instantly lifts.

With simple ease, we slip into a more intimate space. One I learn to love more each time it happens. One that doesn't put me in panic mode. Doesn't have me fleeing the scene like I committed homicide. I never want to be scared at the ease flowing through my veins, at the comfort I feel being with Shelly. Ever.

After years of letting heartbreak rule my heart, I decide it's finally time to push all the negativity aside and bask in this woman. Indulge in the way she makes me feel. Give over to my heart and ignore the hushed voices of warning in the back of my head.

The more we talk, the more I let loose. Shelly pumps life into my veins. Makes me laugh more and lean in closer. Makes me smile so much my cheeks sting. She is the light I have missed all these years. A light I never want extinguished.

When our meals arrive, we eat and talk and enjoy the evening. Worry evades me and I give merit to the idea of Shelly being more than a friend. For a minute. Only a minute.

Four and a half years have passed since I relished the company of a woman. Let it swallow me whole and never let go. When Kelsey ditched me for frat boys and the *college experience*, I shut down. Closed myself off from emotion and intimacy and anything that would hurt me further. I became numb. To everything.

With Shelly, I never want to let go. Never want to spend a day without seeing her or speaking with her or knowing her. Is this healthy? Probably not. No form of addiction is. But Shelly… her brand of drug is exactly what I need. What I never knew I needed.

As our plates empty, the server comes with a tray of

desserts. Shelly ogles them with wide eyes and her lips trapped between her teeth. Much as I'd like to trap her lips with my own, now is not the time. Instead, I agree on her choice of dessert, a thick slice of chocolate ganache cake with fresh whipped cream and berries, to share.

All I will say about dessert… I have a new love for chocolate cake that has nothing to do with the taste and everything to do with watching Shelly eat it.

*Oh, how I wish to be that cake. Sweet and warm on her tongue. Eliciting the most provocative sounds.*

After I settle the bill, we walk to the car, arms hooked at the elbow. The drive to Shelly's apartment is a blur of quiet music, good conversation, and our arms a breath apart. Hushed as we are together, our talks flow with more ease now. As if we have known each other for years and not months. And I want more.

More of her. More time. More of whatever she will let me have. More *us*.

I park in the guest spot near her building and walk her to the door. The cool November night grows hot and thick and edgy. There has always been this unspoken familiarity between us. An energy that brings us closer. Since day one, I fought the sensation with every molecule I control. Little by little, I've slowly let it take over.

"Would you like to come in for coffee or tea?"

At her question, that stupid voice in the back of my head speaks up. Tells me to say no. Tells me to get in the car and drive home. To leave and not take another step toward her front door.

I hate this voice. Hate that it still creeps in and tries to sway my life in one direction or another. Tries to keep me from moving forward and moving on. Eerie as it is, I hate this voice even more because it suddenly sounds like my mother. Full of acid and judgment.

Tonight has been perfect. More than perfect. If I leave now, will it end perfect? Or will I wake up in a cloud of regret? Miserable from not doing what *I* want versus listening to the *no one will ever love you* voice in my head.

I am not ready for tonight to end. The more I have Shelly in my world, the more I want to exist in her bubble. Breathe her in. Share my life. Make her mine.

A new voice storms forward and tramples the doubt. The voice of selfishness. Soft and lovable and coaxing. She whispers, *"Go inside. Spend more time with her."* And without a second thought, the selfish part wins.

"I'd like that."

A timid smile pushes up her flush cheeks. Shelly unlocks the door and steps aside to let me in. The apartment is small but quaint. Enough for one person. Cozy enough to entertain guests. The vibe and appearance simple, but very much Shelly.

Ivory walls with occasional family photos and framed print art. Soft-pink sheer curtains accent standard blinds. A beige sofa with throw pillows to add a pop of color and a knitted blanket slung over the back. An ivory-shaded lamp on a side table farthest from the door. A rectangular, cherrywood table sits between the couch and a small entertainment center with a television, DVD player, and streaming device. Fuchsia and taffy and blush flowering buds in a vase on the table.

"Make yourself at home," she says as she hangs her purse on a hook behind the door. "Coffee or tea?"

"Tea. Please."

"I'll be back in a moment."

Shelly walks to the left, past a small dining space, and into a kitchen big enough for just her. The dining has a small, round table with two chairs. Another vase, this one smaller, with the same array of flowers rests at the heart. A chandelier fixture that doesn't match Shelly's style, and probably what comes standard with the apartment, hangs above the table. The kitchen, from my position in the living room, has stainless steel appliances, oak cabinets, and dark countertops. The kitchen appears to be the darkest part of the entire space.

I sit on the sofa, run my fingertips over the fabric, the throw pillow and blanket. Soft. But not as soft as Shelly. So much of her is woven into this small place. Although it isn't vast, it casts a warm energy. An energy I recognize any time Shelly and I exist in the same space.

While I wait, I breathe it all in. Fill my lungs with her floral and patchouli scent. Fill my heart with her kindness and radiance. After tonight, everything will be different. Everything. Yes, inviting her into my home was huge. Sitting beside her in my living room was heart stopping. Falling asleep curled up beside her was unreal. Waking up with her wrapped in my arms was life altering. But tonight… it feels… more.

"Hope you like chamomile."

I open my eyes as she rounds the couch and hands me a mug. "Chamomile is perfect." Because I need something to calm the buzz swirling in my head and beneath my diaphragm. Going from zero to one hundred may be exhilarating in a car, but with my heart…

We sip our tea and sit in silence a moment. A silence vastly different than any other we have shared. Why? Because it's in her home. Her most sacred space. And for the first time in minutes, I realize just how close we are. That her knee brushes my lower thigh. Her lips a mere foot away.

She sets her mug on the table and I mirror the action. Was

I this nervous when she came to my house? No, not to this degree. Sure, I was hyperaware of Shelly the second she set foot in my home, but her presence soothed me otherwise. Maybe it's the size of the space. How, in her apartment, I feel like I am on top of her.

"Do you want to watch something? A movie," she clarifies.

Without checking the time, I know it's late. Easily after ten. A movie would keep me well past midnight. Much as I want to entertain the idea, I probably shouldn't press my luck. The temptation is real, though.

"No, I—"

She cuts me off. Frames my face with her hands and brings her mouth to mine. Then everything goes dark as my eyes roll back. Dark and warm and euphoric.

Her lips move against mine in gentle strokes. Sweet and soft and pink. On the second wave, my lips move with hers. Perform a dance they haven't in years. I tilt my head to the side, change the angle of the kiss, and she shifts too. My hands reach for her, land on the curve of her hips. Glide up either side of her rib cage, skirt the length of her collarbones until I trail up her neck and take her face in my palms.

I need to taste her. See if she is as sweet as I have imagined.

Parting my lips, I lick the seam of hers. Like the blooming petals of a flower, she opens up and invites me in. Lets me sweep my tongue over hers. Tangle it with hers. Taste her.

And I am done.

Lost with no desire to be found.

Lost in her warmth. In the electricity. Her earthy-floral scent. Her sweet and succulent taste. Lost in the high that hits my bloodstream with my lips on hers. Obliterated by the volatile rhythm she teaches my heart.

I kiss her as if I never will again. As if she is my last supper and I am a starved fool.

*You are a fool.*

A ping sounds in my brain. A system override. A tripwire. An alarm telling me to abort. To stop kissing Shelly because we can never be anything more than friends. Because emotional attachment beyond friendship only leads to heartache. To pain and suffering. To an inevitable end. Because one day, she will decide she no longer wants me. No longer needs me. Doesn't want me at her side to touch her or hold her or give her whatever she needs.

She will throw me away.

Just like Kelsey did.

I break the kiss and scoot away from her. Eyes downcast, I shake my head and hold up a hand. "No." I shake my head again. "No, I can't. We can't. I can't do this." Finally, I meet her gaze and see the tears already rimming her eyes. "I'm sorry."

*Fuck.*

I hate myself. Hate that kissing a woman I want, a woman who wants me, a woman I *trust,* ends in catastrophe. More than anything, I hate that my brain is wired this way. Ready to ruin everything good.

It's bullshit, but I already lit the fuse.

I need time to think. Time to figure out how to fix the messed-up shit in my head. Time to make myself worthy of Shelly. She deserves better than this. Better than me.

Rising from the couch, I look everywhere but at her. Mutter my apologies over and over as I slowly make my way to the door.

*I need to get out of here. Away from her. Before I lose the strength to go.*

"I shouldn't have… I'm sorry, Devlyn. You don't have to go. Please, I'm sorry." She is off the couch, taking slow, deliberate steps in my direction. Approaching me like a scared, wounded animal.

She can't touch me. If she touches me, I will cave. Lose all willpower and give in to her pleas. And I can't. Not yet. Not now. Not until I unscramble my warped brain. Otherwise, I will just make it worse. Hurt her worse.

I meet her eyes again. Take one last look at her glassy, veiny, twilight irises. "I can't," I whisper. "I wish I could, but I just…" Two more steps and I grab the knob. Twist and take another step, this one outside. "I'm so sorry."

And then, I leave. Dash to the car, start the engine, and drive home in a fog. In my pocket, my phone vibrates over and over. Without fishing it out, I know who it is. Know that Shelly is texting or calling. And I want to answer her. Want to tell her how I feel. Want to confess how much I care for her. Explain what just happened. Why I reacted the way I did.

Just as I closed her door, I saw the first bout of tears glide down her cheeks. And now, it will be all I see when I think of her. Her pain and misery and regret. And I deserve that to be my reminder. I deserve to only see her suffering. Her pain is my punishment.

I reach a red light and pull out my phone. Thirteen text messages, all from Shelly and all various forms of an apology.

"I'm sorry too. You don't know how much." I look at the screen and shake my head. "God, I wish it was that easy. I wish I could give you more. But I can't. Not yet."

And then I power off my phone, stow it in my pocket, and finish the drive home.

Tonight started out as one the best nights in a long time. Correction, tonight was *the* best night of my life—the second being Shelly in my house, in my space. Leave it up to me to ruin it. To ruin her. To ruin us.

I fucking hate myself. But dammit, I will do whatever it takes to fix myself and make things right between us. Because Shelly... I *need* her.

# fifteen

## SHELLY

Have you ever felt like your life has been one major clusterfuck of an amusement park ride? The more time passes, the more I feel this all too deeply. And it just fucking hurts. A bone-deep ache that won't go away.

Night after night, I stare at the romance books on my shelves. Scan their worn spines and tattered covers. Books I have read over and over. Others waiting for me to pick them up. And I just can't do it. I refuse to let myself get swept up in some happy fairy tale where everyone ends up with their happily ever after. Meanwhile, I'm over here plucking the occasional gray hair, developing wrinkles at the corners of my eyes, and contemplating if I should buy one cat or ten.

Not like I don't want to experience those "all the feels" moments in my own life. For my heart to rip apart the cage holding it captive. For my lungs to burn when I forget to breathe. For my skin to heat and dampen with just his eyes on me, his body near mine. To feel each and every one of those don't-ever-let-me-go moments.

God, do I want them. *Really* want them. I thought I had

them—some of them—for a blip of time. A very small blip. But I was wrong.

And now… I am exhausted. Utterly spent. Out of gusto.

So tired of faking happy twenty-four seven. Tired of contributing one hundred percent to everything and getting shit on constantly. Tired of being paired with the other single friend in our circle, Erin, because we don't have someone on our arm.

During get-togethers—like Autumn's baby shower today —they seat Erin and me together. Why? Because we have singledom in common. Because we haven't found someone to sweep us off our feet. Because we are lepers when it comes to love. At least, that is what it feels like.

Gah! I want to fist my hair, scream at the top of my lungs, and rip the strands from my scalp. I want it to hurt more than the unyielding pain beneath my breastbone. Physical pain, I can handle. Gut-wrenching emotional pain…

Autumn unwraps and opens a box wrapped in black-and-white baby farm animals. Since she and Jonas don't know the sex of the baby yet, everything has been neutral. Light and soft tones. Khaki, gray, cream. No pink or blue, yellow or green. The gifts, the cake, the decor. All of it is just… neutral. Plain. Simple.

My life is plain. Neutral. But not simple.

I wish it were simple. That I didn't spend most of my time each day trying to fix what I broke. To mend fences with Devlyn. Unfortunately, some things can't be fixed. Not when only one person does the work and two are required.

God, I miss him.

I took our friendship for granted. Got swept up in the moment. In his earthy, artsy scent. The way his smile only popped up on occasion and not for just anyone. I only ever saw him smile at me and Elizabeth. And the smile he gave me was not the same he gave her. And I miss the contrast between his dark, floppy hair and pale-green eyes.

His eyes still linger. When I close mine, I see them with such clarity. Staring back at me. Haunting me. Crushing me. Which is why sleep has been shit recently. Distracting yourself while you dream is a bit difficult.

Why did I have to mess things up? Why did I kiss him?

No, I am not the only one to blame for all of this. I felt it. The way he gravitated toward me any chance he got. The subtle, unspoken hints of something more than *friendship*. Always wanting more time together. That night and morning at his house…

"Shh, shh, shh," Cora shushes as baby Clara starts fussing. "Someone's hungry." After a few wiggly moves, Clara latches onto Cora's breast and suckles.

Everyone in the room watches in awe. Everyone but me.

I love my best friend and niece fiercely. Would do anything for either of them. But watching them share this intimate bonding moment makes the backs of my eyes sting. Forms a lump in my throat. Makes the ache in my chest more pronounced.

Rising from the couch, I wander out of the room and mumble, "Be right back."

I step into the bathroom, shut the door and lock it, then slide down the back until my butt hits the cold tile. Silently, I weep into my sweater sleeves. Cry long enough to get it out, but short enough to not let my face puff up. Then I get up, take a deep breath, use the toilet, and rinse my face with cool water.

Minutes mimic days as I stare at my reflection. As I question my life, my past, my way of thinking. Question what the hell is wrong with me. Question why two weeks and hundreds of text messages and phone calls from me to Devlyn go unanswered.

Why? What have I done to warrant this level of extreme solitude? What karmic rule did I break to receive this overflowing spoonful of loneliness?

I love people. Family, friends, strangers. I do right by others. Help out whenever possible. Give back to those less fortunate in the community. Always contribute if possible. I care for others. Am loyal without question.

But it never seems enough, and I don't know why.

*Someone, please tell me why.*

Hell, the fact that I haven't given up my *virtue* should count for something. Give me bonus points in someone's book. Not that being a thirty-two-year-old virgin was a goal, but here I am…

*Why won't he talk to me?*

My hands hurt from wiping them so long with the towel. I hang the cloth back on the bar, give myself one last glance in the mirror, take a deep breath, then turn for the door.

Back in the living room, the crowd has thinned. Guilt seeps into my veins and rattles me.

*How long was I in the bathroom? I didn't get to say goodbye.*

After a deep breath, I sit in the same spot on the couch and try to pick up on what I missed. Which proves difficult because no one says a word. When I survey the room, all eyes are on me.

*Great. Just fucking great.*

"Shell, what's wrong?" Cora asks, her tone treading lightly.

Much as I don't want to dump my lackluster life onto my

friends, I refuse to lie. Especially to Cora. She leaned on me countless times in the past. To deny her the truth would make me a hypocrite and a horrible best friend.

If only the truth didn't throb painfully in my chest.

Eyes on my lap, I tuck my hands and fingers in the sweater sleeves. Hide them from view, so no one sees me pick at my cuticles. The room goes quiet, too quiet, but the stares I feel burning my skin scream deafening tones. And I just want the silent questions and eye-piercing volume to stop.

"Remember the guy at the shop last year?" I don't need to elaborate. Cora knows who I mean. It's not often I talk shop... or guys.

"*The artist* who did the mural?" Cora questions.

"Yeah."

"Sort of. I remember Mom talking about him. Only saw him briefly during a visit. I remember him being there, but not *him*." She rises from her chair and sets Clara—who fell asleep while I was in the bathroom—in her carrier. Then she parks next to me on the couch. "Is he the reason you're down?"

This is so weird, awkward. Maybe because guys don't stick around past date number two. Maybe because I have never had a long-term romantic relationship. Not that Devlyn and I are—were—long term or romantic anything. But he is the first person I connected with on a profound level.

Then I ruined everything with a stupid kiss.

*What a great kiss it was, though.*

"Yes and no," I say with a shrug. "He was back at the shop, touching up the outside mural and painting a new one inside." I drag in a deep breath and exhale loudly. "He was there daily for weeks and we talked. A lot. When he finished, we started hanging out. About a month and a half. Nothing serious. Guy friend stuff."

I pause and close my eyes. Fill my lungs with fresh air and swallow past the lump forming in my throat. I peel my eyes back open, but keep them on my lap and trudge forward.

"A couple weeks ago, I kissed him. He was into it. Really into it." I lift my gaze to Cora and see the wince already building on her face. All it does is amplify the pain in my chest. A pain that just won't quit. I press the heel of my palm to my breastbone and get no relief. "Then, he freaked. Couldn't leave fast enough. And I haven't heard from him since."

The spear pushes straight through my heart and lets every drop of life puddle at my feet. When did I become this woman? An emotional wreckage pile. The woman who lets the idea of a guy rule her life.

Cora scoots closer as Autumn presses her weight to the opposite side. A hand swipes my cheek. Wipes away the tears I hadn't realized were leaking from my eyes. Which makes me cry harder. Then, I am swathed tighter than a newborn. Surrounded by arms and warmth. Friendship and love. Family.

And I let it all go. Cry as if my ducts hadn't been used in years. Weep as if I lost the love of a lifetime. And I don't stop until my eyes are puffy and cheeks are hot.

"What did I miss?"

Cora, Autumn, Peyton, and Penny lean back. A whoosh of cool air smacks my face as Elizabeth steps closer. When she wasn't in the room when I returned, I assumed she left. Guess she was in the kitchen or off doing something with Clementine.

"Nothing, Mom," Cora says. "Shelly's just been a little down. So, we were giving her some love."

Elizabeth regards her daughter, then me. She may see me

more times a week than Cora, but I haven't mentioned anything to her. Just kept my head low and hands busy at work. But I see the questions in her eyes now. See her motherly armor slip into place.

"Devlyn?"

All she asks is his name. She doesn't need to elaborate. The woman isn't oblivious. Although she appeared to not notice my interaction with Devlyn at the store, she didn't miss a thing. Maybe it is her motherly intuition. Or perhaps, it is the wisdom that only comes with time and life experience. Either way, she knows. And it eases the pain a little.

At least it's Elizabeth and not my own mother. Mom's mission to see me married with children is *not* what I need right now.

I nod. "Yeah."

"Oh, sweetheart." Without hesitation, she steps closer, takes my hand, hoists me up from the couch, and gives me the best mama bear hug. A fresh batch of tears spill down my cheeks. Dampens my shirt and hers. It only makes her hug me harder. Tighter. Longer. "I got you," she says as she softly strokes between my shoulder blades. "Get it all out."

And I do. For the longest time, Elizabeth embraces me with a fierceness only mothers possess. She strokes my hair and shushes my cries. Whispers reassurances and motherly love in my ear. When my ducts run dry, we pull apart and she holds me at arm's length. Gives me a gentle smile that soothes the pain. A little.

Elizabeth and I take a seat among the others. Heat crawls up my neck to my cheeks as guilt swirls in my veins for stealing the spotlight during Autumn's baby shower. For making my personal problems more of a focus than Autumn's impending delivery.

"Sorry," I mutter, then abandon my spot on the couch to refill my glass of water. When I return, I *feel* more than see everyone's stare on my face.

"What are you apologizing for?" Autumn asks.

I park on the couch, sip my water then set it on the table, but keep my eyes trained on the glass as I lean back. This isn't my day. No one is here to celebrate me or a child I am bringing into the world. And it feels ten kinds of wrong to steal the spotlight from Autumn.

"Nothing. Can we talk about something else, please?"

"Nuh-uh," Cora says with a shake of her finger. "You've been up and down a lot recently. Then, you cry your eyes out for almost an hour. Baby talk can wait a few. Am I right?" Cora looks to Autumn, who nods.

"I'd like to talk about something other than pregnancy and babies, thank you very much," Autumn states as she purses her lips. She rests a hand on my forearm, the touch soothing yet serious. "You matter, too, Shell."

I peer down at Autumn's hand before meeting her dark-amber eyes. All I see is love when I look at her. Not an ounce of anger or frustration or jealousy that her baby shower has turned into some form of a Shelly Reed soap opera. A fresh sting bites the backs of my eyes and I tip my head back, blink a few times and swallow past the lump in my throat.

How did I get this lucky? To be surrounded by such wonderful women who support me regardless of what is happening in their own lives.

"Thank you." I sniffle. "Still don't want to be the center of attention." I laugh without humor.

"Well, then, you best get it all out now. Tell us everything weighing you down."

"Might need something stronger than water."

Autumn rises from the couch and waddles toward the kitchen. "I've been saving this ginger beer for a special occasion, but…"

Laughter fills the room, even from me, as she returns with brown bottles of ginger beer. She pops the lid off one and hands it over. I take the first sip and go into a coughing fit.

"Jesus." I cough into my elbow. "Is that just liquid ginger?"

She shrugs. "Don't know, but I love it and so does the little one." She rubs her belly.

Over the next hour, I spill my heart out to my friends and family. Tell them about every day or evening Devlyn and I spent together. Our minimal conversations and how I never knew so little could mean so much. How he always looked at me more than a male friend looks at a female friend. How he went out of his way to do nice things for me. That he always wanted more time together. And was the one that pushed us in the direction we ended up in.

"He never wanted to get me those drinks in the morning," Elizabeth chimes in. "But he did so it wouldn't look like he was showing his affections toward you."

I narrow my eyes at her. "What makes you say that?"

"Just because I've been married most of my adult life, doesn't mean I am blind to flirting and gestures."

I shake my head in disbelief. "No, he was just being nice."

"Keep telling yourself that, if it helps you sleep. But that young man sees you, sweetheart. Not just the woman on the outside, but what's here, too." She presses a hand to her heart. "He just doesn't know how to express that verbally."

Elizabeth has a point. Devlyn hasn't opened up much since I have known him. Not that I expect his entire life story after knowing me a minute. Those six-plus weeks were the best. Each week, I got a fresh glimpse at Devlyn. A new side to him. Some days, he was so deep in thought while he painted, I could've screamed and he wouldn't have flinched. Other days, we were so in tune. The slightest look my direction and it heated my skin.

The night at his house… the next morning… those memories strike the hardest. Hurt the most. Everything about that memory feels like a lead-up to the kiss.

*He wanted me there. In his home. In his space. Alone with him. Inches away in the dark. Snug to his body as we slept. He made me breakfast. Didn't want me to leave. At the car, I saw it… he wanted to kiss me too.*

But maybe Elizabeth is on to something.

"Yeah, you're probably right." I sigh and stare down at the fumbling fingers in my lap. "What do I do now? He doesn't answer my calls or texts." Tipping my head back, I stare at the ceiling and huff. "I hate how bereft I feel."

Cora wraps an arm around my shoulders and tugs me into her. "Wish I had the right answer. The one to put a smile on your face. But everyone operates differently. Especially Devlyn, from what you've told us." She gives my shoulder a squeeze and I peer up at my best and longest friend. "You either need to give him patience or…" Her eyes dart between mine for two breaths. "Let him go." My shoulders drop and Cora's lips turn down at the corners. "You don't want to, I'm sure. But you need to do what's best for you."

The backs of my eyes sting for the umpteenth time today. "Why does this have to be so hard?" I garble out.

Autumn embraces me from the other side. "Because you obviously have feelings for him. Beyond friendship." A palm rubs up and down my back. "Jonas and I went back and forth so many times because I wanted to do what was best for

Clementine. Little did I know, what I was doing wasn't best. But I had to learn that in my own time." Autumn leans her head on my shoulder. "What's meant to be will play out. But don't stop living because he won't own his feelings."

I nod, absorbing Autumn and Cora's words. Letting them sink deep and fill me with the strength I need to get past this. More than ever, I am grateful for the wonderful women in my circle. All my family, none by blood. Lucky is an understatement. I take their love and support and harness it as armor. Feel their courage pass to me as I wipe the tears from my cheeks.

"Thank you," I say as I glance at each of them in turn. "Thank you for always being there."

Cora squeezes me a bit tighter. "Wouldn't have it any other way." Her arm drops from my shoulder as she gives me a smile. "Now, let's talk about something else. Since none of the guys are here, let's talk shit about them and laugh when they get here later."

Everyone laughs, including Elizabeth, and I love how the mood in the room became ten times lighter. And for the next few hours, life is normal. Happy. Loaded with jokes. When the guys show, we make plans for another get-together. Karaoke or bowling. Something in addition to our Sunday gatherings.

I leave Jonas and Autumn's house with less weight on my shoulders and a warmer heart. Now more than ever, I need to spend time with people who make me whole. Who bring me joy.

Which is why what I am about to do is more important than anything else. I have to do this if I want to move on. If I want out of this dark place.

Parking the car in my designated spot, I cut the engine and

stare at my front door. My apartment has been occupied with the energy of that night. *The night.* The night when I kissed Devlyn, and he reciprocated long enough to give me hope. Only to squash it just as quickly.

Tonight, I am detoxifying my space. Lighting sage, opening the windows and letting all the negative vibes out. Time to make it mine again. To make it a place I love.

Exiting the car, I walk to the front door with a straighter spine. I insert the key, turn the knob, and step inside. Plopping down on the couch, I fish my phone from my purse and pull up the text history between me and Devlyn. After two deep breaths, I tap out the most difficult seven letters of my life, then hit send.

A tear splatters on the screen and the word *goodbye* blurs… just like my life. But I am taking my life back. After this final cry.

# sixteen

## DEVLYN

My phone lights up on the table, the message icon on the notification. Without leaning for a closer look, I already know the text is from Shelly. Over the last two weeks, she has texted and called more times than I care to admit. Although I haven't responded to a single call, voice mail or text from Shelly, I listen to and look at each one. She is none the wiser since I disabled my read message receipts.

Yep, I have become *that* guy. The biggest asshole in the Bay Area.

And I detest the person I have become. Hate that I hurt her. Hate that I led her on then flipped.

I opened myself up to her, let her in the slightest bit, gave her a glimpse of who I want to be, that I want *her.* Then I smashed it all with a foolish mistake.

Kissing Shelly was *not* the mistake. Losing my shit and walking out the door was the mistake. Not responding to her daily texts and calls was—is—a mistake. Sitting on this couch instead of driving to her apartment and apologizing in person is a big. Fucking. Mistake.

Now I fear it's too late to repair the damage.

*Fuck.* I hope it isn't, but I feel stuck. Unsure what to do to fix myself or how to make things between us right.

Memories of the kiss drift back in—not that they ever leave. Shelly's lips pressed to mine, so soft and warm and inviting, knocked the air from my lungs. The memory of it still does, each and every time. As does the searing pain at my epicenter. The pain that never leaves. The pain I deserve, not Shelly.

If I were the only one suffering, I would willingly take a dagger to the heart. Let it twist over and over.

But Shelly is suffering too.

Her pain spills across the screen with each word she types. Is evident in the crack of her voice when I play back her messages. Hearing—*feeling*—her pain is ten times worse.

Ignoring the nature documentary in the background, I pick up the phone, take a deep breath, and open the message.

Goodbye

*Goodbye? What the hell does that mean?*

I stare at the screen until I lose focus. Until my eyes glaze over and my thoughts swirl into a vicious hurricane. One after another, I take a deep breath. Try to settle the erratic line of my thinking. Sending a text with only *goodbye* in the message could translate a hundred ways.

*Goodbye, I no longer want to speak to you.*

*Goodbye, I never want to see you again.*

*Goodbye, we were obviously never friends.*

*Goodbye, you're an asshole.*

Or the one I don't want to think, but can't ignore.

*Goodbye world.*

I shake my head at the last one. Shake off the dark direction my thoughts took. Shelly and I may not have shared everything, we may not have fully exposed our pasts, but I don't picture her harming herself. Not with her sunny disposition. Not with the brilliant smile she flashes the world. Not with the long line of people who love her. She would never hurt herself. Right?

*Fuck.*

Why can't I be a better person? Why can't I step up and own what I feel? Tell this woman, this phenomenal woman, how I feel about *her.* Tell her she invades every waking moment of my life. That the kiss we shared is all I think about. That I still feel her lips on mine when I close my eyes. Still see her starry eyes. Still picture her in my home, in my arms, nestled against my chest. That I still smell her in the couch fabric and haven't slept in my own bed since that night.

Why haven't I told her any of this? Why haven't I acted?

Because I am a fucking coward. A chickenshit. A pathetic excuse. Rather than opening up and letting her in, I cower in the corner and shut out the world.

Any chance I had at a friendship with Shelly in the future has flown out the window. Because Shelly just cut ties with one word. In a text message, no less, because I won't speak to her. I shut her out and she locked the door for good. Threw the key in the landfill.

A red, hot dagger pierces between my ribs. I smash the heel of my palm to my sternum and curl my fingers into a fist. I drop the phone to the floor, drop my head to my knees, and rock in place on the couch. Fist my hair and tug until the pain steals my vision. Gasp for the breaths that refuse to fill my lungs.

"Aaaah!" I scream until my vocal cords strain. Then I scream again. Louder. Not giving a damn what the neighbors hear or think. I bolt up from the couch, scoop my phone from the floor, and throw it at the wall. I grab the next thing in reach, then the next, and throw them across the room.

Pain and anger are poison in my veins. Seeping slow and steady into my bloodstream, the marrow of my bones, every atom and cell. Turning everything black. Dark. A shadow of its former self. And I let it. Allow it to consume me. Swallow me into a never-ending abyss. I deserve nothing less.

I dash up the stairs, taking them two at a time. Enter my studio and scan the room. Study the countless drawings and paintings along the walls, on the floors, on my desk and easel. Each and every one of them inspired by the same person. The woman I wouldn't open up to because of past insecurities I refuse to face.

"Fucking idiot," I scream into the room. "Dumb. Fucking. Idiot."

Stepping farther into the room, I stand inches from the canvas on the easel. Stare at the stormy, dark-blue backdrop, the strategic gold splatters, the fine, faint white lines forming a half face. My Andromeda.

*No, not yours. Shelly was never yours. She never will be.*

I fist my hair and scream at the canvas. Scream at the pain I inflicted on Shelly and myself. Scream until my vocal cords shrivel and my lungs exhaust themselves. Then, I take the canvas in my hands. Grip the wood frame until it bites my skin. Rotate it in my hands, lift my foot from the ground, and crack the frame over my knee. The canvas doesn't tear, which only serves to fuel the flames of my anger.

Stomping to my tools, I dump them on the floor, drop down on my knees, and dig for the spackle knife. The wooden handle grazes my fingertips and I grip it until my knuckles whiten. I lay the floppy canvas on the ground, hold the edge with one hand, raise the blade in the other, and freeze.

The room blurs. My lungs quiver. The hand harnessing the blade trembles.

I don't want to do this.

*Goodbye.*

But I have to.

*Goodbye.*

Have to erase every piece of her.

*Goodbye.*

Have to let the idea of her go.

*Goodbye.*

I brought this upon myself. Opened us both up to heartache. Heartache Shelly doesn't deserve. But I do.

*Goodbye.*

Tipping my head back, I close my eyes and let the salty tears spill down my cheeks, my temples. "Give me her pain," I croak out. "Give me her sorrow, her heartache, her anguish. I deserve it. Not her."

I drop my head to the floor, grip the tattered canvas in my hands, and crowd it around my face. Again and again, my heart spasms. I accept the pain. Absorb every strike without complaint. Beg for more if it means Shelly feels none.

With each new hit, I rise to my feet. Take my pencils, my brushes, my oils and throw them across the room. I rip the drawings from the wall. Tear them down the middle twice and toss them in the air like confetti. I swipe my arm over the shelves and spill everything to the floor. Punch my fist through one painting after another until my fist meets drywall. My foot connects with the trash bin and scatters debris in a wide radius.

I stop and stare around the studio. Stare down at my fist

and watch in fascination as a thick layer of crimson drips from my fingertips. Gaze at the chaos, the shredded sketches, the demolished canvases, the splattered paint. The sight should throw me off balance. Should have me in hysterics. Eager to put everything back in its rightful place.

Instead, I laugh. A delirious, maniacal sound spilling from my throat. I bend at the waist and grip my knees. The hysterical laughter transitions into an unsteady wheeze. I take in the disaster that is my studio and a fresh wave of panic hits. Punches me in the gut and knocks the air from my lungs.

"Damnit."

I drop to my hands and knees. Grab the tattered drawings on the floor and try to match them up. Try to salvage them and make them whole again. I put all the pieces in a pile. Then create another pile of the decimated paintings. Frantic hands sift through the first pile, trying to match the images and edges like a puzzle. When none of the pieces fit, I move to the next pile. Try to right my wrong.

But I am too late. Just like with Shelly.

*Goodbye.*

I fucked up and now I am paying the price. "Stupid, selfish idiot. Why did you do this? Why are you ruining every good thing in your life?"

Crawling across the floor, I grab a blank canvas from the stack. Rise to my feet and pad over to my easel. Gingerly set it on the stand. My eyes dart between the debris and the blank canvas, an idea developing.

Much as I should eliminate all reminders of Shelly from my life—most of which are locked in my memories—I simply can't. So, this is my punishment. To live with mental photographs and videos of her. To paint or sketch her likeness until my digits and limbs no longer work. To torture myself, day after day, because I deserve nothing less. I deserve pain and anguish—mine and hers.

I sift through the catastrophe on the floor, locate some brushes and a handful of paints, and then I start anew. Use bits of the drawings I shredded and add them to the new project. To twist the knife deeper in my chest, of course I recreate Shelly. If this is the only way I can have her, so be it.

Parked on my stool, I paint the canvas a blue so rich, it appears black. Using the scraps, I adhere them to the damp canvas. Create a mosaic of sorts. I rummage through the room and look for other bits I can add to the canvas, tools to add other forms of texture and dimension. Before returning to the stool, I turn on music. Play something other than the typical classical music I listen to in this room. Tonight, I need something to match my mood. Beats and lyrics filled with irritation or fury. Music with grit and rage. Songs to scream and thrash and smash objects to without concerning the neighbors. In the short time I have lived here, they have adapted to the weird guy in the neighborhood.

Loud, violent rock music spills from the speaker. The growly vocals against the fast tempo crowd the room. The hairs on my arms stand on end. The bass vibrates my bones. And the noise steals all potential space for thought.

This… this is what I need.

To not think. To get lost in something. Anything. To forget about what I lost and the pain I caused us both. This may not be the cure, but it will help the time pass easier. Help ease the pain, if only the slightest.

*Goodbye.*

The seven-letter word will be one I never hear or say in the same context again. I hate it had to be said in the first place. I never wanted to say goodbye to Shelly. Part of me hoped, after enough time passed, we would find our way back to each other. As friends.

Yes, I want to be more than Shelly's friend. No sense in denying the truth now. If I felt the cosmos collide when we kissed, she felt the intensity ten times stronger. I am not emotionless. I simply feel on a different scale. A scale tipped closer toward numb. Void. But not completely.

"Goodbye." The word singes my throat and burns my lips. Leaves a rancid taste on my tongue.

I swipe up a piece of a charcoal drawing. Home in on the thick black lines. Without question, this is Shelly's brow. An arch I memorized weeks ago, when the sun shone on the lateral edge. I brush the tip of my finger over the line. Swallow the pooling saliva in my mouth. Blink and look away for two breaths. Bite the inside of my cheek until a metallic tang hits my tongue.

"Wish we could've been more. Wish I was strong enough to be who you want. Who you *need*." I close my eyes and shake my head. "You're always in here, you know." I tap my temple. "That'll have to be enough, for now." A half-hearted laugh spills from my lips. "Maybe one day, I'll get my shit together. Maybe one day, I'll be strong enough, good enough, for you."

*No! No, no, no, no, no.*

*Get your shit together, Templar. Now. And make this right. Quit wallowing in self-pity and fix this.*

My eyes drift around the studio, take in the disaster once more, then land on the fresh canvas. "I fucked this up," I say to the canvas as if it is Shelly. "Now… I need to make it right. Hopefully, you'll forgive me. Hopefully, I'm not too late."

Because this pain… I won't survive it. Not for long.

# seventeen

## SHELLY

Sleep evades me as I lie in bed and stare up at the hints of moonlight slipping through the blinds. And for the hundredth time since I sent the *goodbye* text hours ago, nausea rolls in my belly.

If letting go of Devlyn was the right thing to do, why am I sick to my stomach?

The urge to rip my phone from the charger and type out a new message hits me like a freight train. I want to delete the message. Rescind it. Pretend like the thought never crossed my mind.

In its place, I want to send my longest apology. An extensive plea for him to forgive me for crossing the line. To beg him to take me back as his friend. Something. Anything.

God, I am such a fool.

How many times did Devlyn tell me he could only be my friend? So many times, I hate the word more than moist. Did I listen and respect his boundaries? No, but with good reason.

There is no possible way I read him wrong. Right? In our last week together, he threw one hint after another. Showed me his interest with small gestures and sentiments. His romantic interest. By no means can I professionally read people, but I picked up every hint and smile and longer-than-normal stare he sent my way. Honestly, I thought it was his way of telling me he wanted more without using words.

Obviously, I am an idiot. And supremely horrible at body language and gauging others.

"Ugh," I huff out, throwing the comforter and sheet from my body. I sit up and stare at the clock on my bedside table. The dull-blue numbers stare back and mock me—3:21. "Fuck you," I whisper to no one as I rise from the mattress.

Maybe a steaming mug of chamomile will settle my mind enough to allow sleep. Even if only a few hours, some sleep is better than none.

The electric kettle comes to a boil just as I hear something outside. Flipping the switch to off, I abandon the kettle and tiptoe to the window near the door. Slowly, I inch back the curtain and part a slat of the blinds to peek out. A gasp leaves my lips.

*Why is Devlyn on my porch?*

Hands shoved in his hoodie, he paces back and forth in front of the door. Every other direction change, he stops and looks at the door. In the artificial light, I watch the lines of his forehead scrunch and flatten then repeat. It's obvious he wants to knock on my door, but refrains from following through.

After watching him pace the same ten feet several times, I close my eyes, drop my hand from the blinds, and take a step back. Part of me wants to ignore Devlyn outside my door. Ignore him and hold firmly to the goodbye I sent earlier. He hurt me when he left here without explanation. He hurt me when he ignored my obsessive texts and calls.

Until I sent the one that hurt him.

Much as I want to ignore the upset man on my porch, I

also want to fling the door open and give him a chance. Allow him the opportunity to explain why he flipped. Let him grovel and beg for forgiveness. Not that it would take much for me to forgive Devlyn. My feelings for him would override any stint of torture my mind wanted to inflict.

My fingers wrap around the door handle as my lungs take one last deep breath. *Give him a chance.* After I unbolt the lock, I twist the knob and swing the door wide.

Devlyn stops his trek past my door, his back to me goes rigid. Then his head drops, shoulders cave, and his entire frame deflates. Neither of us speaks, but the tension between us is a living, breathing entity. Harsh energy radiates off him and spills over me, causing a shiver. Devlyn is angry, but it isn't directed at me. Perhaps that is why he hasn't faced me yet.

Minutes pass before he lifts his head. Measured and hesitant, he spins around and meets my waiting gaze.

Translucent-green irises hold my blues. He takes a step in my direction, eyes darting between mine, silently asking why. Then with another step, he stands inches away. It's now that I notice the red veins hugging his irises. The puffiness around his eyes. The dampness on his lashes. The permanent valley between his brows.

"No," he whispers, his eyes holding me prisoner.

My brows bend in the middle. "No?"

He shakes his head slowly. Steps impossibly closer. Slips his hand around mine and holds it like I am his lifeline. "No goodbye."

I open my mouth to rebut him. To tell him I won't be the recipient of mind games. That I won't always wait in the wings while he melts down and abandons people who care about him—including me. That I won't let him break my heart because he is too scared to feel or own what he wants.

But I say none of those things. Don't even get the chance.

Devlyn lifts his free hand and cups my cheek. Captures my eyes with his as our breaths turn ragged. Then, ever so slowly, he leans forward and presses his lips to mine. I freeze at the initial connection but melt when he lightly sucks my bottom lip between his.

Warmth spreads through me as our lips dance together. His hand abandons my cheek as his fingers weave through my hair. I fist his hoodie, walk backward and drag him inside. The door shuts behind us and I assume he kicked it. He lifts our joined hands between us, between our hearts, and trails kisses along my jaw, my ear, my neck.

"So sorry," he mutters between kisses. "Such an ass." At this, I chuckle. His lips break free of my skin, eyes meeting mine. "I want to explain. Please, let me explain."

I drop my forehead to his and sigh heavily. His thumb on my hand draws lazy circles while the fingers of his other hand massage my scalp. The hurt side of me wants to pull away and drag out the agony. Make him feel an iota of what I felt after he ran off. But the sensible side shakes her head and tells me to hear him out. Let him talk. Let him share the pieces he keeps hidden from everyone else.

Sensibility wins.

Nodding, I pull back. "Okay." I drop my hand from his hoodie. "I was making tea. Would you like some?"

He presses his lips to my forehead. "Thank you." Why does this kiss feel more intimate? "I'd love some tea."

I head for the kitchen while Devlyn takes a seat on the couch. Filling two mugs with hot water from the kettle, I deposit chamomile in both and let them steep as I watch Devlyn.

His head falls back on the sofa. Eyes closed, he looks as exhausted as I feel. The last two weeks have obviously tormented us both, yet neither of us did anything to rectify the situation. Well, not until I sent the most recent text message. That was all it took to truly rattle Devlyn to the bone. To wake him up from whatever dream—or nightmare—he'd abandoned me for.

Whoever hurt him in the past... I have never been a violent person, but I want to strangle them. Then maybe thank them. Devlyn wouldn't be who he is now without them, but I hate that he was hurt.

Setting the mugs on the table, I take a seat beside him on the couch. He rolls his head my direction and opens his eyes. And for a minute, we sit in suspended animation. I read his every movement, every unspoken word scrawled in the worry lines of his face. See his apology in the redness of his eyes, in the defeat of his posture.

I want to comfort him. Tell him I forgive him. Let him know we will be okay.

But I won't say a word. Not until he gives me more. Explains what made him panic.

He extends his arm closest to me. Lays it palm up on his thigh. An open invitation for me to take his hand. To twine our fingers. To connect us physically while he exposes himself emotionally.

Without hesitation, I take his hand. His eyes drift shut as a heavy breath stutters from his lungs. A sad smile on his lips.

"Sorry will never be enough," he says as his eyes open and capture mine. His thumb glides up and down in gentle, measured strokes over my skin. "But it's a start." He sits taller. Scoots an inch closer. "And I promise to make it up to you. Every day of forever, if necessary."

*Forever.* The word holds a heavier weight than imaginable. And I want to let it pin me down. Blanket me in comfort.

He brings the mug to his lips and takes a sip before setting it back down. His gaze fixes on our joined hands. The fingertips of his free hand lightly dance over the top of my hand. Draw invisible lines permanently etched in my soul.

"When I think back, the reason I'm so closed off seems childish. Immature. The result of a young love lost. Something millions have dealt with, but overcome with little struggle."

He shakes his head, again and again, as if he can't believe he let someone from his youth disrupt his life with such severity.

Bringing my free hand to his cheek, I brush my knuckles over the line of his jaw. "Devlyn," I say in a hushed tone. He leans into my touch, but keeps his head down. "Your feelings are valid. Justifiable." He tips his head to the side. "Just because you were young, it doesn't mean what you felt was inconsequential. It was real. It mattered. *You matter.*"

At this, he lifts his head. Glassy eyes meet mine, unbelieving. Full of questions. I cup his cheek and stroke the stubble with my thumb. He closes his eyes and leans into my touch again, parallel tears painting lines down his cheeks.

"I don't deserve you," he whispers into the darkened space. "Your heart. Your..." His eyes pinch tighter. His head gently rocks in my palm as he swallows. "Your love."

I sweep my fingers beneath his chin and lift. "Look at me," I whisper a breath from his lips. His eyes pop open, dart between mine, flash me with worry and fear. My stare doesn't deviate from his as I lick my lips. "Devlyn, you deserve so much more. And I'll spend every day of forever proving it to you." I use his words from earlier to tell him I am in this with him.

To seal my promise, I lean in and press my lips to his. The kiss chaste, but equally potent.

I may not have long-term relationship experience, I may not be the person people go to when they need relationship advice, but I will do whatever it takes to help Devlyn heal. To show him that what we have is not the same as his past. That what he felt then and what he feels now are similar and yet completely different.

Everyone has experienced young love—whether it be a crush, deep infatuation, or heartfelt love. The only difference between the love we feel in our youth versus what inhabits us in adulthood—wisdom. And wisdom only comes with time and experience.

I may not have long-term relationship experience, but I have dated my fair share of men. From sweethearts to assholes, I have dated them all. But none of them *felt right*. None of them made me feel alive. None of them made my palms sweat or my knees weak. And none of them made me want more than a simple meal a time or two.

None except for the man next to me.

Devlyn may be young, he may be inexperienced at life and love and hardship, but he has an old soul. He sees the world through a unique filter. And I should be so lucky as to sit at his side and let him see me. Let him love me.

"I'm here. Always," I say, then kiss his lips again.

# eighteen

## DEVLYN

The next couple of hours on Shelly's couch are filled with me telling her about Kelsey. From the start of our relationship to its abrupt end. And the entire time, Shelly sits beside me, her hand encased in mine, in silent support.

How am I worthy of this woman?

"Thank you for telling me," she whispers, eyes closed as she rests her head on my shoulder.

I kiss her forehead. "Thank you for listening." I tighten my hold around her waist and inhale her sweet and earthy floral scent. "Should get some sleep," I mumble as my eyes drift shut.

Shelly curls into my side, fists my hoodie above my heart and snuggles into my neck. "You too."

I startle awake, Shelly nestled in my arms. Without waking her, I dig my phone from my pocket and check the time. Quarter to seven. Must have drifted off. Thank goodness it's Sunday and Shelly doesn't work today. Neither of us is mentally capable of much right now.

Shifting on the couch, I scoop an arm beneath her knees and haul her into my lap. She groans slightly and I bite the inside of my cheek to resist laughing. Rising from the couch, I walk down the small hall and step into her bedroom. A space that suddenly feels more intimate than a place to rest.

With the curtains drawn and a small amount of light peeking through the blinds, it's difficult to make out the intricacies of her space. But the energy radiates Shelly the farther I step inside.

Sidling up to her bed, I lower her onto the side I assume she sleeps on since the covers are pulled back. The moment I set her down and remove my arms from around her, she reaches for me.

"Stay," she says in her groggy state.

The single word weighs heavy on my mind the more it sets in. I am in no condition to drive, but I don't want to invade her privacy.

Bending over, I kiss her cheek. "I'll be on the couch," I whisper in her ear.

Her head moves side to side in slow motion. "Don't be silly." She yanks at the covers on the opposite side of the bed then pats the sheet. "Lie with me." When I don't move for a beat, her eyes crack open. "Please," she adds and gives my hand a gentle squeeze.

*Sleeping. You're just sleeping.*

"Okay," I acquiesce.

Once she frees my hand, I move to the other side of the bed and sit. I toe off my shoes then ditch my hoodie and shirt. Something as simple as removing clothes has never felt this rousing. Heady. Potent. Although I hear the soft cadence of Shelly's breathing as she drifts off to sleep, every nerve ending in me is wide awake. Ready to feel and consume every physical touch shared.

Considering we slept on my couch weeks ago, I shouldn't be this antsy. Shouldn't feel this on edge.

But Shelly isn't just anyone. And as much as I wanted to keep things between us black and white, Shelly showed me how vivid and glorious and breathtaking life can be when you fill it with color.

We have spilled our pasts. Exposed our hearts. And now… we move forward.

I slip beneath the covers and turn on my side to face her. The moment I stop moving, she shifts from her side of the bed. Scoots impossibly close and curls into me, face to face, like the night on my couch. I wrap her in my arms and snuggle her closer. Breathe in her scent and tangle my legs with hers.

Not a minute later, her body relaxes completely. Her breathing slows and quiets. Her palms on my chest lax and leg between mine slack.

With one last kiss on her forehead, I let go of every worry and drift off to sleep with the most incredible woman in my arms.

The rest of Sunday is spent on Shelly's couch with takeout and more episodes of *Dark*. With Shelly curled into my side, I have never felt more comfortable in my own skin or life. By no means is my life perfect, but she makes each day better than the previous.

Shelly tells me about the upcoming classes she and Elizabeth will offer at Petal and Vine in the new year. Nothing elaborate, maybe five to ten people, and only once a month.

"Do you have plans for the holidays?" she asks around a

mouthful of fried ravioli.

I shake my head with a laugh. "Not yet, but I'm sure my mother will text the day before and demand my presence." I aim for it to sound like a joke, but with the way Shelly stares at me in the periphery, I must not have succeeded.

I love my mother. I do. But sometimes—okay, a lot of the time—she can be a bit much.

As a child, I never paid attention to her insistence. Never put much thought into her need for perfection. Honestly, at the time, I admired her desire for everything to be in its place or exactly how she wanted it. Friends would come over and describe her as a neat freak or controlling. I shrugged it off and said she just didn't like dysfunction or disorganization.

Now, as an adult, I see her differently. Especially after college and living on my own, making new friends and meeting their parents, I have a new perspective.

My mother isn't just a perfectionist. She isn't your classic control freak. There is more to it. I picked up on it the first month home after college graduation. She invited colleagues from the museum to dinner. Hours before their arrival, she walked into my bedroom, went straight to my closet, plucked clothes I only wore for dressy occasions from the hangers and handed them to me with a sour look on her face.

*"We have dinner guests this evening," she'd said. "You will wear this and be downstairs no later than five thirty. You will be well-groomed and behave like a proper young man. Do not speak unless spoken to. Do not say anything untoward or questionable. They are not coming to hear your opinions. They are coming to talk about the museum and what I'm doing."*

That night, I saw my mother in a whole new light. She'd spoken to me like a disobedient child. As if I never used manners. As if I didn't grasp common courtesy. At first, I played it off as nerves. Gave her the benefit of the doubt. These people must have been important. Probably on the fence about donating funds or art to the museum and this dinner might seal the deal.

But as I dressed that night and combed my hair, one piece of her tirade stuck out. Playing on repeat and unnerving me in a way unlike any previous occasion.

*What I'm doing.*

Since that night, I paid closer attention to our conversations. The more I listened, really listened, the more I heard it. The constant me, me, me. Anytime Mom called to "catch up," she led the conversation. Talked about everything driving her crazy, followed by the incompetence of everyone around her. Anyone not doting on her or lifting her up or making her life easier was unworthy in her eyes, and she voiced as much during our one-sided conversations.

As it stands, I ignore most of her calls. Let them go to voice mail. Listen to them when I am mentally prepared. Call her back when I have the energy but cut her off after thirty minutes. My mother isn't just an energy vampire. She is something entirely different. And after hours of research, I gathered my mother is a narcissist. Or something along those lines, since she hasn't been professionally diagnosed. Unfortunate for me and everyone who encounters my mother, we will never live up to her standards. And my father—sweet man that he is—is her enabler.

"My mom can be a bit much too," Shelly states. "Before my brother Micah started dating his now wife a little more than a year ago, Mom wanted to start having these regular family dinners." She sips her wine. "At first, we both thought it was no big deal. Just our parents missing us."

"Why do I sense a but coming on?"

Shelly laughs without humor. "They did miss us. But Mom also wanted to pester us about our love lives, or lack thereof."

"Ouch."

"Yeah." Her lips kick up in a meh half smile. "Nothing like sitting down for dinner and your mother asking if you've been dating or plan to give her grandchildren before she dies." Shelly rolls her eyes then twists in her seat. "What if I don't want kids?"

"Then that's your choice."

She spears another ravioli and eats the edges off before stuffing the rest in her mouth. "Have you ever thought about it? Having kids, I mean."

If any other person would have thrown this question at me, I'd probably fly off the handle. But with Shelly, I know this is her curiosity. Us still getting to know each other.

For a split second, I remember the texts I sent when her friend had a baby. What a damn fool I was.

"Honestly, I haven't given it much thought. Like I said that day when you texted from the hospital, I'd have to be in a serious relationship before the idea ever crossed my mind. And since I avoided relationships—until you—there was no sense in thinking such things."

Shelly nods. "I get that. The guys I dated before, none lasted past date two." The look on her face says there is more, but she doesn't add anything else. She shrugs and pokes at her dinner.

"Why does it feel like you want to say more?" Her cheeks stain pink, a color I haven't seen on her in weeks. There is more. "You don't have to tell me if you don't want to."

Her lips tip up at the corners. "I appreciate you saying

that." She takes a deep breath and exhales slowly. "But I'm going to say it anyway."

She grabs her wineglass and downs the remaining half glass. *Whoa.* "Shelly, you don't—"

"I'm a virgin," she blurts then smothers herself with a throw pillow.

*Wait, what?*

No way I heard her right.

By the way she is actively trying to cut off her oxygen, I'd say I heard her perfectly fine.

How is that even possible? I mentally roll my eyes. Okay, I *know* how it's possible. But how in the hell does someone as stunning and magnificent as Shelly reach her early thirties and not lose her virginity? Not that I have loads of experience, considering Kelsey is the only sexual partner I've had.

I reach for the pillow and pull it away from her face. She resists me at first but finally lets me take it.

"Shelly…" I encase her hands in mine. "You have nothing to be ashamed of or embarrassed about." She tucks her lips between her teeth and rocks her jaw side to side. "If anything, the trait makes you more attractive. Not because of some male need to claim you. It says more about your character. Defines you as particular, selective. That you associate the act with love and not physicality. That you don't just hand your heart or body over to anyone who shows interest."

She releases her lips and looks up. "No one ever felt right. Not before."

*"Not before."* I will not overanalyze Shelly's words. Will not read into them and conjure up my own fantasies. But I also won't leave here tonight until I ask what she means.

"Not before?"

Her cheeks turn crimson, but she doesn't try to hide it. "I

make no assumptions." I narrow my eyes in question. "About you or me or us."

I nod. "Neither do I."

"And…" Her hands fidget in mine. "With you, things lean that way." I tilt my head and beg her to elaborate. To shape her thoughts into words. "They feel… right."

I free her hands and bring mine to her cheeks. Before she gets another word in, I pull her to me and press my lips to hers. Kiss her gentle and slow. When a moan spills from her lips and down my throat, I deepen the kiss. Wrap my arm around her waist and drag her onto my lap. Fist the hair at the nape of her neck and hug her body flush to mine.

The kiss lasts forever and not long enough before I break it. Before both of us gasp for air.

It is in this moment that realization hits. This very blip in time that I finally believe. In paths and fate. That everything happens for a reason. The struggles of our past align us for the beauty of our future.

Kelsey may have been my first love. The teenage girl I pictured with me for eternity. Although she broke my heart, although she threw my life into a tornado, I wouldn't be in this very moment if none of it happened. I wouldn't have Shelly or this constant swell beneath my sternum. I wouldn't appreciate and reciprocate the emotion spilling from my heart without first experiencing the cracks and aches.

If I bump into Kelsey one day, I will thank her. If it weren't for her need for freedom, I wouldn't have stumbled upon the woman in my arms. If it weren't for her selfishness, I wouldn't have fallen in love. Real love.

Yep, I said it. In love. Although, I may just keep that to myself a little longer.

# nineteen

## SHELLY

Lights twinkle from every direction. Red and green, blue and white. Rainbows and blinking and solid strands. Some wrapped around tree trunks and limbs. Others clinging to bushes and rooflines. Animals on lawns with robotic animation. Blow up snow people—because actual snow doesn't happen here—and cartoon characters on the grass and rooftops.

Each year, the amount of holiday decorations people add to their homes is mind blowing. Every Christmas, I ooh and ahh over the displays. Drive slowly down my parents' street to glimpse each setup. Note the new additions from the previous year. Hem and haw over my inability to put up exterior lights, with the exception of my small porch. Complain how I wish I had a blow-up reindeer or Santa to put outside.

I love Christmas. Well, I love all holidays. They all have their own kind of magic. Christmas just happens to be the one I go the most bonkers over.

But this year is a bit different.

This year, the lights twinkle brighter. Candy canes have a little more zip in the peppermint. Balsam firs smell fresher and more piney than any previous year. And the slight chill in the air puts a smile on my face.

During the holidays, I add a minimal amount of decorations to my tiny apartment. A small artificial evergreen. Citrus and clove-scented candles as well as balsam fir. Strands of white fairy lights. Garland made of evergreens and cranberries. An evergreen wreath on the door with blue thistle, white berries, eucalyptus, holly berries, and lightly wrapped gray ribbon. Festive bouquets on the coffee and dining tables as well as the kitchen and bathroom counter. Festive towels hanging from the oven door.

If I had the space, my home would be a holiday mecca.

Every year, I purchase gifts weeks before the holiday. Lug the bin out from under my bed and riffle through rolls of festive paper and ribbons and bows. Play cheery Yuletide music and sip hot cocoa as I write jolly messages in cards. Decorate the tree and light candles.

For years, this has been my ritual. Not down to an exact science, but pretty damn close. This year, everything changed.

A month ago, things with Devlyn went haywire. Out of nowhere, I kissed him and he kissed me back. Then, he panicked and disappeared for two weeks... until I sent a text that scared him more. The night he paced outside my apartment, I had no expectations of what would happen when I opened the door. I definitely didn't expect our relationship to manifest into what it is now.

Devlyn has shifted himself out of the friend category and sits firmly in the boyfriend category. And over the last few weeks, we have been solidifying that new status. Spending every free moment together. Kissing... constantly. And losing track of time.

Which is why, two days ago, I was frantic. One of those

berserk people in Target searching empty shelves for the perfect gift. I scored a few small gifts but caved and bought gift cards for the rest. Gift cards are not my style. They feel so impersonal. But I'd rather give a gift card than nothing at all.

"Hallelujah," I whisper as I park next to Peyton's car in my parents' driveway.

I love my parents. Really, I do. From time to time, though, Mom gets a little pushy. Not in the way Devlyn described his mother. Mom has a big heart and means well, she just gets a bit overwhelming here and there. The only thing Nicole Reed wants is for her children to have a happy life. Unfortunately, her version of a happy life includes the perfect spouse, the perfect house, and babies.

I have none of the above.

With the newness of my and Devlyn's relationship, I don't assume to have any of the three in the near future. At this point in the game, I go with the flow. Marriage and picket fences and offspring don't necessarily equal a happy life. Happiness comes from a deeper place. One I have barely started to discover but am eager to explore.

From the moment I witnessed it on screen and read it in romance novels, there has only been one thing that matters when it comes to the future. Love. Deep, hungry, *I can't go a day without seeing you* love. One that steals the air from your lungs, whisks you off your feet and has your heart banging out of your chest.

Above everything else, I want that type of love. If the other things follow in love's wake, so be it. But without love, the other three don't matter.

Walking under the row of icicle lights, I step onto the porch and pause in front of the door. A fresh evergreen wreath with red berries hangs on a hook. My hand hovers over the knob as I inhale the earthy pine scent and let it relax me. "It's Christmas. Mom won't nag me. Not today," I mumble. I nod as if to reassure myself, then twist the knob and step inside.

Three things hit me at once. Deep, booming laughter, mouthwatering baked cheese, and the clanging of pans.

I toe off my shoes in the foyer, set my purse and bags down, and tiptoe toward the kitchen. Peering around the corner, I spy my dad and Peyton seated at the breakfast bar. Tears roll down Dad's cheeks as he presses a loose fist to his mouth. Peyton clamps down on her lips, her cheeks and neck blotchy, as she tries not to laugh.

Across from them, in the heart of the kitchen, are Mom and Micah. My dear, sweet, occasional pain in the ass brother is decked out in Mom's *I love to rub meat* apron. Mom is at his side, coaching him as he sautés carrots in one pan and stirs gravy in another. Sweat beads his forehead and temple. His tongue peeking out between his lips as he shifts his weight left then right.

To most, this sight would be endearing. A son helping his mother cook Christmas dinner. Lovable as the moment is, Dad's tumultuous laughter when I walked in the house now makes sense. Because Micah in the kitchen is equal parts frightening and hilarious. I love my brother, but his ability to cook is null. Mom refuses to give up on him, though. Has him over or goes to his house once a week and shows him something new. Before Peyton, Micah burned water. Now, he successfully cooks five full meals without supervision. This is the first holiday meal he has cooked, and I am proud of him.

"Look at you," I say as I enter the kitchen. "Keep this up and you'll be cooking all the holiday meals."

He shoots me with wide eyes and a slight shake of his head. "Ha ha. Best not push your luck."

Stepping around Micah, I hug Mom and kiss her cheek. Dad and Peyton slide off their stools and pull me in for hugs next. Since Micah is too focused on not burning dinner, I wrap my arms around him and squeeze until he taps my arm.

"You're doing great, big brother," I whisper so only he hears. "Proud of you."

He sets the spoon on the rest, spins around, and hugs me properly. "Thanks, Shell." He kisses my crown then releases me. "Means a lot."

The stove timer buzzes and he goes back to work. I fill a glass with sparkling cranberry-apple cider—a Reed family tradition—then join Dad and Peyton. Micah and Mom put the final touches on dinner while we all catch up. Mom declares dinner is ready and we all file into a line with plates in hand.

I pile my plate high with herb and citrus roasted duck, potato gratin, baked macaroni and cheese, sautéed carrots, cranberry-orange relish, balsamic Brussel sprouts, and a homemade roll. The next ten minutes pass in silence as we savor the meal.

"Starlight, this is the best yet." Peyton beams at Micah. "You might have to cook some of this again. Soon."

My brother glows from her compliment. And as if they were alone, he takes her elbow, tugs her closer, and kisses her. Not a sweet peck on the cheek. Nope, this is my brother we are talking about. He kisses his wife as if his parents and sister are nowhere in sight. When the kiss breaks, Peyton's cheeks pink.

I doubt her flush is darker than mine.

Public displays of affection don't bother or embarrass me. I adore seeing people so happy and in love. It reminds me true love exists. The heat on my cheeks comes more from picturing myself in a similar situation. Caring for someone—

Devlyn, perhaps—so deeply, I can't not kiss them. Regardless of who is around.

The last month plays like a movie in my head.

The night I took Devlyn's face in my hands and kissed him. What it felt like when he kissed me back. The splendor in that first kiss. How perfect the moment was. All the romance novels I'd read finally made sense. The rapid pulse and shortness of breath. It all made sense because I felt them too.

Until Devlyn pulled away. Until I saw the fear on his face. The dread. The regret. I now know why, I understand it, but it still hurts.

Fast forward two weeks later. The text. His appearance at my front door in the middle of the night. Hours of apologies and shared history and heartache spilled between us. In less than twenty-four hours, Devlyn and I had become somewhat inseparable. And over the last three weeks, our need to be with each other has magnified.

Now, we just need the balls to share our relationship with everyone else. We aren't intentionally hiding our relationship, are we? Maybe. I don't know.

A sharp sting on my shin snaps my eyes across the table. Micah winces, his silent apology for kicking my leg. "You okay?" he mouths.

I nod, subtly.

"Liar," he mouths before taking a bite.

*Great.*

It isn't a lie. I just haven't figured out how to tell him the truth. I have a boyfriend.

God, I feel his brotherly wrath and see his macho chest slaps already. Someone preemptively saves me from my brother.

We decide to save dessert for after gifts.

For the last five years, my parents have told us no gifts. Micah and I refuse to give them nothing. So, we coordinate. We both buy them a card and gift certificate for their favorite restaurant. The first year, they smiled and accepted the gift. Since then, they invite us out for dinner and take us to the restaurant. The first time they did this, Micah and I argued with them and tried to pay our part of the bill. We were unsuccessful. Now, we pick somewhere everyone likes and add more to the gift price, so we are still paying for ourselves.

Mom and Dad graciously thank us for the cards and gift certificates. Micah surprises Peyton with a photo album full of pictures of their first year and a half together. Since falling for Peyton, my brother has become such a romantic. He isn't all goo-goo eyes and flowers every week, but he is more affectionate than I have ever seen him. Hand-holding, whispering in her ear, subtle touches on her cheek, neck or shoulder. And the occasional flower delivery from Petal and Vine.

I envy what they share so openly. Fingers crossed, one day in the near future, that will be me. Giggly and doe eyed and curled into Devlyn's side while we spend time with loved ones.

"Here, Shelly," Mom says as she hands me a gift.

I take the large, thin rectangular package. As I peel back the paper, I wonder if my parents framed our family photo from last Christmas. Wouldn't be abnormal. With each passing year, my parents get more sentimental. Valuing time together and photographs over anything else.

I discard the paper and flip the frame over, prepared to plaster on my fake enthusiasm for an oversized family photo I won't hang. Instead, my jaw drops and my heart stammers.

"Wha-What is this?" I mumble as the backs of my eyes sting.

"Isn't it beautiful?" Mom asks as she leans into Dad. "A friend at work gave me the link to a local artist's website. She wouldn't shut up about his work. So, I went on and found this. The moment I saw it, I knew I had to get it. Like it was drawn for you."

*Not for me*, I want to tell her. *This* is *me*.

Framed in light oak is an up-close view of a woman's face. From just above the brow to the edge of the top lip, from the bridge of the nose to the lateral edge of the eye. The piece is in pencil with no color. Impeccable detail over every inch. A constellation mapped out in her eye.

The only pieces I have seen of Devlyn's are what he painted at the shop and those from the gallery—which were also me. Perhaps that is why he didn't let me into his studio while touring his house. Would it freak me out? Are there more images of my likeness in his studio? On his website? Something tells me there is a lot more where this came from.

"Let me see," Peyton says.

I close my eyes briefly and swallow. The second Peyton takes in the image, she lifts a hand to her mouth and gasps. Micah may not pick up on the connection as quickly as Peyton. He doesn't stare at his eyes like she does. Plus, Peyton was at the baby shower when I spilled my heart out about Devlyn.

"It's…" She pauses and bites her bottom lip a moment. "It's stunning."

I restrain the tears begging to roll down my cheeks. Last thing I need is for Mom to think I don't appreciate the gift. I do love it. More than any other gift I received.

Mom gifting this to me feels like another sign. A broadcast alert that my relationship with Devlyn is bigger than either of us realizes. How big exactly? I have no clue.

"It is," I garble out then clear my throat and look to my smiling parents. "Thank you, Mom, Dad."

Dessert goes by in a blur of apple pie and light chatter. The melodies and baritones of voices echo in my ears, but I miss everything said. My eyes continue to drift to the drawing in the oak frame.

*When did Devlyn draw it? How long would it take to draw something with this level of detail? Days, maybe weeks. Plus, listing it online, processing the sale, shipping. Did he draw this shortly after coming back to the shop? Are there more drawings or paintings of me in his studio?*

I shake my head to dispel the endless questions I have no way of answering. Instead, I zero back in on my family. Listen to Mom prattle on over the new client her firm attained. Listen to Dad tell tales of strange client stories as they buy an insurance policy. And listen to my brother and Peyton as they regale all the wonderful parts of married life.

Scooping apples, crust, and fresh whipped cream on my fork, I smile and respond and laugh at the appropriate times. Inside, I scream for the night to be over already. I pray to walk out the front door any second, so I can call the one person with the answers. And to ask Devlyn for a tour of his studio.

I'd rather go to Devlyn's house than Jonas and Autumn's. Less than forty-eight hours have passed since we were together, and every opportunity to see or speak with each other gets squashed by someone else. Not that I don't want to spend time with loved ones, but I want time with Devlyn too.

So I plaster on my best smile and trudge through each moment. Take deep breaths, remind myself to be grateful and that I will see Devlyn soon.

Our call when I left my parents' house was short lived due to his mother pestering him in the background. Plus, if I don't show at Friendsmas, my phone will blow up with unmerry threats and promises to come get me.

Over the last few hours, I've stared at the drawing gifted to me from my parents. Art with such precision and detail had to take Devlyn a while to draw. Weeks, possibly a month or more, to finish. The more I study it, the more intimate it feels. Like Devlyn spills his secrets through his art. The biggest secret of all… how he feels about me.

Artists don't paint or draw the same person over and over or with such delicacy without a reason. What is Devlyn's reason? When did I become his muse? Although it feels as if a lifetime has passed since October, our relationship beyond the friends stage is still so young. It's difficult to imagine him creating such a piece months ago. Is this—his art—it can't be… *love*.

Dizziness consumes me with the possibilities.

My heart has her hands in the air, hips swaying, as she screams *yes* at the top of her lungs. My head, on the other hand, has calculators and spreadsheets and pro/con lists out. A scale on the desk, weighing emotions versus life. And I hate that my brain steals this moment of joy.

With the purchase of Petal and Vine a year out, my focus has been prepping for the business handoff. Getting all my financial ducks in a row. Albeit a good one, Devlyn has been a distraction. The type of distraction I haven't had to deal with in the past. The type of distraction I need to learn how to balance in my life.

Hopping up from the couch, I take a few cleansing breaths. Close my eyes and hum with my inner zen master. Tell myself I am strong, I am capable, and I can accomplish anything I put my mind to. When I open my eyes, relief filters in.

*I got this.*

After a bite to eat and a shower, I dress in my comfiest jeans and long-sleeve V-neck pink sweater. I blow out my hair and dab on a light coat of natural makeup. Satisfied with my appearance, I slip on my matching pink Vans then grab my purse and gifts.

I arrive at Jonas and Autumn's just after five. Several cars are parked out front, but not everyone is here yet. Unbuckling, I exit the car and scramble to the passenger side. Snag the gifts from the seat and head for the door with full arms.

When we all asked to bring something for the food, Jonas and Autumn insisted we leave it to them. So, aside from gifting them a small houseplant and matching fuzzy socks for everyone, I got them a gift card for the grocery store. Seeing as they pay for the majority of our gatherings, this is my way of contributing. I told Cora my idea and she agreed to buy them one too.

Spartan greets me at the door with paws to the chest and attempts to lick my face. Jonas apologizes profusely and I laugh.

"For some reason, he's a little extra today. Probably because we spoiled him yesterday," he says as he hugs me around the gifts. "Let me take that off your hands." Jonas takes the gifts and parks them under the tree. He points a finger at Spartan. "Leave it."

Spartan grumbles then trots off in search of Clementine, who lets him get away with more.

"How was Christmas?" I ask.

He leads me to the kitchen where everyone lingers around the island. "Good. Spoiled my girls more than ever." The brightest smile lights his face. "How was dinner with the parents?"

"Good. Mom was less invasive than usual." I keep the news of the artwork gift to myself. Sidling up to Cora, I hug her side. "Hey, you. Merry Christmas."

She twists to face me head-on and hugs me tight. "Merry Christmas."

Her hug lingers longer than normal and I wonder if everything is okay. She releases me, but the soft sadness on her lips tells me she wanted to hold on longer. "What's wrong?" I ask.

The lines of her forehead deepen for a beat. Had I blinked, I would have missed it. Her eyes dart over my shoulder then back to mine. She either looked to my brother or Peyton. My guess… Peyton. And judging by her extended hug and careful attitude, she knows about Mom's gift last night.

*Really don't want to talk about Devlyn with everyone here.*

At the baby shower, I told every woman here that I was letting Devlyn go. Although I did when I sent the text, things are different now. And on Friendsmas, I get to bring them up to speed. No doubt the guys will overhear and jump in on the conversation.

*SOS. This gal needs help.*

"If you need to talk, I'm here."

Closing my eyes, I let out a huff. It's now or never. If I don't speak up and tell her Devlyn and I are no longer on the outs, Cora will be hurt I kept it secret. We share everything— even the painful stuff. For the longest time, I was her shoulder to cry on. Now, she wants to be mine. It would be wrong of me to let her believe I needed one.

"Thanks, but…" I throw her a look, one we have shared over the years. *There's more. Just wait a minute.* She nods subtly.

Once I give everyone a hug, I fill a plate with holiday-themed snack foods and a glass with wine. I sit in the end seat at the dining table and munch while I wait. Cranberry-peach glazed meatballs, cheesy-herb pull-apart bread, ham and Swiss pinwheels, four-cheese sausage quiche, and rosemary-garlic hasselback potatoes. There is plenty more I didn't grab, but I will save them for later.

The chairs closest to me drag against the floor and fill a moment later. Without looking, I know it is the ladies, each of them with a plate and drink of their own.

"Sorry," Cora mumbles, and I look up.

"No need. Never apologize for being thoughtful." I bring the glass to my lips and take a sip. "Things have changed since the shower."

"Changed how?" Cora asks before stuffing her mouth full of green beans and potato.

Looking around the room, I see everyone else chatting or otherwise occupied. After a deep breath, I explain what happened after I sent the infamous text to Devlyn. How twisted up I felt inside. How I couldn't sleep. And the fact that Devlyn was on my porch in the middle of the night. At this, Cora and Autumn gasp.

Then, without spilling the intricate details of Devlyn's past, I tell them about our talk. How Devlyn confided in me and explained why he shut down. The more I shared, the more my friends got dreamy eyed.

Did I tell them about the kiss? Of course, but more from a *it made me melt* point of view. They don't need all the dirty details.

I share how much time Devlyn and I have spent together these last three weeks. How wonderful it has been to get to know each other better. And for some reason, as the words leave my lips, my stomach twists in knots. Somehow, this moment reminds me of high school. How others teased me for not having a boyfriend. How hungry I was for the inside scoop on all the things boys, but never asked in fear of embarrassment. The girl of my youth rejoices that she is finally experiencing those moments. That she gets to brag to her friends. But the woman I am now wants to zip her lips and keep Devlyn to herself.

Cora rises from her chair and hugs the air from my lungs. "So glad you're happy. It's about damn time."

*Couldn't agree more.*

"When do we get to meet him?" Autumn chimes in just as Jonas sidles up to her and says it's time for gifts.

Halle-freaking-lujah!

The gift exchange goes down with much enthusiasm. Spartan and Clementine play with the packages and wrapping paper. Jonas and Autumn frown at the number of grocery gift cards we all gifted. Between everyone, they accumulated over three hundred dollars. Plants and ugly sweaters, gag gifts and graphic tees. Smiles and laughter abound in this more relaxed holiday celebration.

As I look around the room and take in this wonderful group of people that are the best family I know, my heart wobbles a little. So much has changed over the years, but we are still together. Through thick and thin. Our lives full and bountiful.

My only wish… for Devlyn to be here too.

Then I ask myself if he'd want to be here. Would he want to sit with this colossal group of people and share a piece of himself? Would he want to insert himself in my life, with my family? Devlyn belongs here. With me. With us. He may be timid and quirky, but I easily picture him fitting in with us all. I easily picture everyone loving him as much as I do.

It may be too soon, and I may have read too many romance novels, but I think I am in love with Devlyn. But how will I know if he is in love with me?

# twenty

## DEVLYN

Holidays and birthdays have never been big on my to-do list. Growing up, my mother turned every occasion into a lavish party. No matter the event, she was the center of attention— even when the party wasn't for her. Over time, I grew to despise celebrations. Avoided as many invites as possible.

Until now. Until today.

Spending New Year's Eve with Shelly sounds like the perfect way to kick off a new year. Considering I have never watched the ball drop or made a list of resolutions, I look forward to doing both with her.

Petal and Vine closes early today and doesn't reopen until January second. I get a full, uninterrupted day and a half with her, and I have never been this damn nervous in my life.

Last night, after she spent an hour in the kitchen making the most amazing pasta carbonara and garlic bread, I asked her to come to my place for New Year's. Without hesitation, she said yes. Then, as I fisted my napkin beneath the table, I asked her to stay the night.

Considering we have spent the night together a few times now, asking her shouldn't flip my stomach upside down. But the previous times we slept in the same space were different. The first was accidental. The second, we were both exhausted. But the third, and most recent, didn't happen from falling asleep on the couch or pure exhaustion. Shelly said she was tired, took my hand, and walked me to her room. The action felt so normal. A natural progression in our relationship.

That said, we haven't broached anything beyond spooning or kissing in bed. No bare flesh or fondling through clothes. To some, our relationship may appear clean or innocent, but the truth is we are both waiting for the right moment. That unspoken word to say we are ready for more, for the next step.

Me asking Shelly to stay over—preplanning a sleepover—carries the heaviest weight yet. Pushes us to the next level of seriousness in our relationship. A step I think we're ready for, but I don't want her to think I have assumptions about what will or won't happen.

My goal in asking her to stay isn't about sex. Not that my thoughts haven't drifted to the fantasy of what it'd be like to connect with Shelly in such a powerful way. More than any other reason, I asked Shelly to stay because I hate when she leaves. I love her in my space and in my arms. Her in both at the start of a new year… I can't think of anything more right.

Parking at the grocery store, where everyone and their mother is shopping for last-minute party goods, I head inside, grab a cart, and wind through the aisles. The plan for tonight is to cook instead of order takeout. A chef I am not, but I have some meals down to a science.

After I load the cart with ingredients for tonight, essentials, dessert, and movie snacks, I head for the checkout. Four brown bags and way too much money later, I pack the groceries in the back of the car and leave. Traffic is heavier than usual with people driving to parties or beachside hotels for the fireworks.

I make it home before Shelly arrives and put everything away except the ingredients for dinner. As I toss the chicken breasts in a resealable bag with marinade, there is a soft knock at the door.

*She's here.*

With a simple knock, I grow dizzy. My steps wobbly as I walk to the front door. Breath stuttering as I unbolt the lock and twist the handle. Heart hammering as I open the door and see my favorite smile. Skin dampening as I take in the larger than normal bag on her shoulder.

*This is really happening. Shelly is here and staying the night. In my house. In my bed.*

I swallow past the nervous lump in my throat. "Hey." Stepping back, I make room for her to enter then close the door.

"Hey," she says, voice softer than usual. "Where can I..." Her question trails off as she lifts the bag from her shoulder.

Taking the bag from her, she toes off her shoes before I slip my hand in hers and start for the bedroom.

When I gave Shelly a tour of the house on her first visit, there were two rooms I intentionally left out. The studio and my bedroom. The studio because I didn't want her to panic at how often she inspired my recent work. And my bedroom because I didn't want to insinuate something or make her more uncomfortable on her first visit. After all, we were just friends then. At least, that is what I told myself a thousand times a day.

The notion of *just friends* never really stuck.

I lead her into the bedroom and set her bag on the bed. As best I can, I hide the tremor in my limbs. With our romantic relationship still in the early stages, the last thing I want to do is give Shelly the wrong impression. That I only have one goal in mind. Sex. And although I want to experience everything with her, sex is not what drives me to be with her.

But I am a man.

More times than I care to admit, I've fantasized what it would be like to have Shelly beneath me. Aura a blazing red as my mouth devoured hers. Skin damp with sweat, her nails in my back. Heels digging into my ass as I rock my hips forward. My name whispered from her lips as we reached euphoria.

Needless to say, my soap supply has depleted much quicker since meeting Shelly.

But I won't pressure Shelly into anything she isn't ready for. This woman… she is worth waiting a lifetime for. I want every other part of her too, not just the physical. Her heart. Her trust. Her soul.

"Your room is not what I expected," she whispers into the dimly lit space.

I twist to face her. Take in her inquisitive eyes as they roam the space. "No?"

She shakes her head. "Don't laugh." Heat pinks her cheeks. "I expected to see more color. Paintings on the wall and sculptures on the dresser."

I bite the inside of my cheek and fight the smile on my lips. "Not laughing. Promise." I let my smile loose. "However, I do find it cute that you'd think my room would be vibrant."

Shelly shrugs. "You're a hard man to read sometimes."

Every now and then, I felt the same about her—that she was difficult to read. Simple things that made Shelly happy were easy to see—her love for minimalism and simplicity, her food and drink preferences, the way she regarded flowers as she placed them in paper or vases.

What I wanted to learn were the things that made this beautiful woman tick. Where to touch her with fingertips and lips that would make her back bow and lungs gasp. The sights that captivated her, so I could take her to each one and memorize the way her smile lit up the sky. What quenched her soul, so I could gift it to her more often than not.

I lace my fingers with hers. "You haven't seen it yet, but my studio is kind of chaotic. Organized chaos, if you will. Which is why my bedroom is the complete opposite." I stare around at the bare pewter-painted walls. Scan the pale oak dresser free of clutter. Glance at the two nightstands in the same pale oak; soft light glows from selenite lamps on both. Then I take in the king bed with cream bedding, four pillows and nothing more. "After spending all day in a kaleidoscope of color or deep in thought, I need a blank slate. A way to reset myself."

"Never thought of it like that, but it makes sense."

Walking toward the door, I lead us back out to the main part of the house. "C'mon. You can help me make dinner." Back in the kitchen, I set Shelly up to chop and assemble salad ingredients while I work on root vegetables for roasting.

By no means am I a pro in the kitchen, but I watched too many shows on Food Network in college and some of the easier meals stuck. Bless my dorm mates. At the time, I hated how often I heard about mincing garlic and dicing carrots. They used it as background noise while working on projects. And after weeks of it, I grew to love the channel too. Not just for the distractions I desperately needed, but also the skills it taught me.

We work in silence and it's as comfortable as every other

moment with Shelly. Every now and again, I glance her way and watch her work. Her precision with a knife reminds me of how intricately she assembles a vase of flowers. Arranging is her version of art, and it is so damn mesmerizing.

Once the chicken and vegetables are in the oven, I clean up. Shelly finishes the salad then pours the ingredients for a vinaigrette into a mason jar and shakes. While waiting for the food in the oven to finish, we head to the living room and set up the table and television.

When the timer buzzes, I remove dinner from the oven. After plating the chicken and vegetables, I carry the plates and salad bowls to the living room and we park ourselves on cushions on the floor. Food and wine and episodes of *Dark* on the screen. It all feels so natural and sublime and effortless.

When our plates and bowls are empty, I take them to the kitchen and leave them for later. On my return, I bring the wine bottle and two slices of black forest cake I snagged from the grocery store bakery.

"This looks so good," Shelly says as she twists the plate left and right to inspect the slice enough for two.

"Wasn't sure what you liked, but these looked too good to pass up."

She twists in her seat and gives me the smile I love too much. "Good choice."

We devour the cake in no time then move up to the couch and I flip off the light. Shelly curls into my side as we continue another episode. When this episode ends, the plan is to flip over to the broadcast of the ball drop.

The closer it gets to midnight, the louder the neighborhood gets with fireworks and party cheers. And the more my stomach wrings with nervous energy. A sensation that has become more familiar in recent weeks. A ball of chaotic energy just beneath my diaphragm that, if I tried to translate it on canvas, would look like a maddening swirl of blue and red and yellow. Bright and vibrant and begging for attention.

Shelly's breath heats the skin of my neck as the room goes black at the end of the episode. Much as I want to relish in the feel of her so close, I pick up the remote and switch the television to the channel broadcasting the festivities.

With less than a half hour to midnight, the crowd in Times Square is so boisterous I feel their excitement. For the first time, celebrating a holiday feels significant. All because of the woman in my arms.

"Hey," I whisper, unsure if Shelly is still awake. All I get is a low *hmm* in return. "I'm going to clean up in the kitchen. Need anything?"

Shelly uncurls herself from my side and I immediately miss her warmth and touch. She lifts a hand to cover her mouth as she yawns. "No. Might go splash my face so I don't fall asleep early."

With a light chuckle, I press my lips to her forehead. "Take your time."

While Shelly heads for the bathroom, I clean up in the kitchen. It doesn't take long to rinse the dishes, put them in the dishwasher and start the load. With a glance at the clock on the stove, I note it is seven minutes to midnight. Uncorking another bottle of wine, I wander back to the living room and stop when I reach the threshold.

In the corner of the couch, Shelly is curled up with the throw blanket, eyes closed and chest rising and falling at a slow rhythm. I take in the sight of her, inhale deeply, and tiptoe toward the couch. Setting the bottle on the table, I gingerly sit next to her, hoping not to disturb her from sleep.

But the moment my weight shifts the cushion, her eyes pop open.

"Did I miss it?" she asks, voice thick with exhaustion as she scoots up to a seat.

"No. A few minutes to go." I tuck a stray lock of hair behind her ear. "But we can head to bed."

She sits straighter and shakes her head. "It's almost time. No backing out now." Shelly drops her head to my shoulder. "Sorry I dozed off."

I weave my fingers with hers and rest my head on her crown. "Don't apologize. It's been a long day."

On the television, the crowd grows restless as midnight draws closer. The clock in the corner of the screen drops under the minute marker. I pour enough wine into our glasses to toast the new year and hand Shelly hers. Thousands of crystals and lights change color on the screen as the final ten seconds count down.

Cheers and fireworks erupt outside the moment midnight strikes. Shelly and I clink glasses and take a swig of wine as we stare at the countless people on the screen kissing. With each new camera shot, a new couple flashes their smiling faces together in a lip lock.

*Is this what couples do on New Year's to celebrate?* I wouldn't know. But without a second thought, I take Shelly's glass from her hand and set it on the table with mine.

"What are you—"

I frame her face in my palms and crash my lips to hers. Startled by the sudden gesture, she doesn't kiss me back immediately. When I pull her bottom lip between mine, though, she melts into me, fists the bottom hem of my shirt and returns the kiss with heat and intensity.

Time and noise vanish as our lips dance and tongues

tangle. Color dances behind my eyes as I taste the wine on her tongue and breathe in her sweet, earthy scent. When her nails graze my abdomen beneath my shirt, I drag in a sharp breath and inch back from her.

Her eyes flash open and lock on mine, worry etched in the lines of her forehead. "Sorry, I—"

I press a finger to her lips and shake my head. "Don't apologize." I wrap her hand in mine, rise from the couch and tug for her to follow. She untangles herself from the blanket and scoots off the couch. I guide her out of the living room, shutting off the television as we pass, and walk us to the bedroom.

It takes less than a minute to reach the bedroom, but my heart bangs in my rib cage the entire time. The moment we cross the threshold, Shelly grips my hand tighter. When we reach the foot of the bed, I stop and turn to face her.

*Damn, she steals the air from my lungs.*

Reaching up, I wrap a lock of her hair around my finger. "Hey," I whisper in the dimly lit space. Her eyes lift and rob me of my next breath. "If all you want to do is sleep, we sleep." I press my lips to her forehead. "More than anything, I just want you here with me. Okay?"

Her fingers curl in the cotton of my shirt again and drag me closer. Lips inches apart, she whispers, "Okay." Then she eliminates the remaining space between us, presses her lips to mine and picks up right where we left off in the living room.

My hands fall to her hips and hold her flush to my frame, the bulge in my pants undeniable. Her hands draw parallel lines up my torso, snake around my neck and skate up the base of my skull. Every impulse in my hormonal makeup fights the urge to strip her bare and mark her as mine. Fights the urge to be less than a gentleman and tender boyfriend.

Of the few times I had sex in the past, I never once was aggressive. Never once had the *impulse* to rip clothes and imprint skin with nails and teeth.

Right now, with Shelly flush against my erection and her lips ravaging me as if the opportunity won't come again, fighting my base instincts proves more difficult. I *want* to claw at her skin with nails and teeth. Taste every inch of her on my tongue. Inhale the perfume at her neck and the pheromones between her legs. Watch her body react as I tease her flesh with fingers and licks. Listen to her soft cries and throaty moans as I give her pleasure and drive her to ecstasy.

Her fingers tug at my hair, lips skirt along my jaw and teeth nip at my ear. My jaw falls slack as a gravelly moan escapes.

God, I want her. Desperately.

But physical intimacy with Shelly isn't just about what I want. She has to guide us along the path she wants us to take. Say when she wants more. Tell me when to stop. Because at this rate, I won't stop. Ever.

I drag my hands up the sides of her torso, beneath her shirt, along the warm curves of her body. At the base of her bra, I clutch her rib cage and drop my lips to her ear. "Shelly." My voice husky and foreign. "Tell me what you want." The tips of my fingers curl in slightly and dig at flesh and bone. My tongue darts out and I lick the shell of her ear. "Tell me."

She frees my hair, slides her palms down my chest and fists my shirt. I inch back and lock our gazes. Her eyes shine as they look up. All I see is every star in the night sky, burning hot and bright and intense. I lick my lips then swallow, on edge while waiting for her response.

Her lips part as she pushes up on her toes. "I want *you,*

Devlyn." Her eyes drop and trail the length of my body before they slowly make their way back up. "*All* of you."

My eyes drift shut as her words sink in. My grip on her tightens as I stroke beneath the base of her bra with my thumbs. I drag in a deep breath then drop my forehead to hers. "Are you sure?" The question a soft stutter on my lips. Subtly, she nods and my body sighs. I press my lips to hers and kiss her softly. "I want that too."

# twenty-one

## SHELLY

Heat blooms low in my belly at his whispered words on my lips. His next kiss is softer, more tender as his fingers knead my skin. Trace lines between my ribs. Unclasp the closure at the back of my bra. Free my breasts beneath my top.

I break my lips from his. Gasp as his hands roam the length of my spine without interruption. Slide my palms lower to his waist and dip them below his shirt. Close my eyes as my fingers trail over the ridges and valleys of his abdomen.

I may not have had sex, but I am not virginal in all things. My experience is minuscule, but I have gotten to second base with a few guys. Of course, they got a little too handsy when the kiss deepened, going from light, over-the-clothes petting to trying to strip me bare. Needless to say, I cut things off and never saw them again. If someone won't respect voiced boundaries, who knows what else they'd push past.

Right now, this moment, is different.

Tonight is the first time I want to explore and be explored beyond impassioned kisses and hands fondling parts through clothes. Tonight, I want to be more than the woman Devlyn can't take his eyes off of. More than the woman he holds in his arms. I want to be the woman he can't get enough of. The woman he never lets go of.

His kiss travels from my lips to the line of my jaw. Every press of his lips to my skin, along my jaw, down the column of my throat sends a ripple of heat and leaves an unfamiliar, but desirable tingle in its wake. Each kiss sears me, brands me, marks me in a new way. And I love every single one. Yearn for the next kiss he gives.

With a gentle tug, Devlyn inches up my top and bra, peels them away and drops them to the floor. My breath comes in short bursts as goose bumps blanket my exposed flesh. On instinct, I cross my arms over my chest. Hide my bare breasts as my line of sight drops to Devlyn's still clothed body.

He paints his fingers along my jaw then tips my chin up. Warm affection greets me in his gentle green eyes. "Please don't be embarrassed. Not with me." His lips press mine and vanish too soon. "You ravish me, Shelly." *Kiss.* "Rob me of sight and sound and thought." *Kiss.* "Inspire me more than anyone or anything." *Kiss.* "And as hard as I fought against this—against being yours, against you being mine…" *Kiss.* "Subconsciously, I knew we'd always be more than friends." *Kiss.* "So much more."

Fire licks my skin as my arms fall away. Devlyn steps closer, cups my cheeks in his palms, and kisses me slow and deep. As his tongue tastes mine, I take the hem of his shirt in my fists and slowly push the fabric up and over his head. The moment his chest is bare, he molds my body to his. Snakes an arm around my rib cage. Digs his fingers in my hair. Tilts my head and devours every whimper bubbling in my throat.

It's too much and not enough.

Devlyn drops his hands to my hips and guides me until my legs bump the mattress. I trace his hip bones with needy fingers. Move to the dip on either side of his spine just above his waistband. Journey up his back and memorize the corded muscles beneath my touch.

The kiss breaks as I drop to the bed. Eyes locked, I press my hands into the fluffy comforter and inch back on the bed. Beneath my breastbone, my heart rattles my rib cage while my lungs beg for air. Devlyn leans forward, his hands on either side of me on the bed as he kisses the curve of my neck.

"Beautiful," he whispers, breath hot on my skin.

His lips travel to the hollow of my throat, kissing me once, twice, three times before drifting lower. An arm comes around my waist, his palm in the middle of my spine, and then he leans into me more. Guides me to lie on the mattress. Shifts me up the bed and near the pillows. Crawls up my body and cages me in.

Then his lips drive me wild again.

My eyes drift closed as each sensation stirs new life in my veins. I fist his hair as he paints my skin with his lips. Kiss by kiss, his mouth deviates from my midline. Leaves a trail of tingles as he moves toward my left breast. A rush of adrenaline spikes my bloodstream as my heavy breaths fill the room. My fingers in his hair curl tighter.

"Breathe, Shelly." He inches up the bed and pins me with his gaze. One breath at a time, my breathing settles. His greens dart between my blues a moment before he swallows. "Didn't think it was possible, but I'm more lost in your starry eyes." Eyes wide open, he presses a heady kiss to my lips. "My Andromeda."

Caught off guard by the reference—or perhaps, nickname—I tilt my head and study him a beat. A smile kicks up the corners of my lips. "Ruler of man, huh?"

Devlyn shrugs as his own smile appears. "Ruler of man.

The only constellation I see when I look in your eyes." His face grows more serious. "Ruler of my heart."

"Devlyn…"

He captures my lips with his and rocks his hips against mine. "It's true," he says, cupping my cheek. "And I admit it without shame."

Heat radiates from the center of my chest as I lift off the mattress and kiss him. Trailing my fingers down his abdomen, I pause at his jeans. Trace the tip of my finger along the hemline, hip to hip. Relish in the shiver of his body and stutter in his breath at my touch.

Then I unbutton his jeans. Drag the slider down the teeth. Separate the fly and expose his cotton-covered bulge. Palm his thick erection, go wide eyed at the length and freeze.

Devlyn rears back enough to catch my gaze. "What's the matter?"

I shake my head. Embarrassment heating my cheeks as I bite back my words.

"If you want to stop…"

"No." My headshake grows panicky. "I want this. You. Us."

He presses a chaste kiss to my lips. "Please tell me what's wrong."

My pulse quickens for an entirely new reason. "It's just…" Devlyn doesn't push me to speak. Hovering above me, he gives me a moment to formulate the words to explain my suddenly tense muscles and obvious anxiety. I rotate my head slightly, enough to lose eye contact. "Nerves. It's just nerves." I swallow and close my eyes. "Then I… felt how big you are and I freaked out," I mutter in a rush.

The room goes quiet. Too quiet. Silence with Devlyn has always been comfortable. Soothing. A balm I never knew I needed. But now, his silence feels like a bomb ready to detonate. An explosion of disappointment and concern. Something I have never felt with anyone.

"Look at me, Shelly." I take a deep breath and roll my lips between my teeth. "Please." His voice barely audible.

On another deep breath, I open my eyes. He takes my chin in his fingers and brings me back to his line of sight. And what I see in his eyes is the complete opposite of what I expected.

Warmth and hope and something akin to love. I swallow and pray he doesn't hear the action.

"All of this is new for you." His knuckles graze my cheek. "Hell, it's practically new for me." I furrow my brow and a subtle smile pushes up his cheeks. "I may not be a virgin, but my experience is minuscule." He kisses the tip of my nose. "Is it weird that I kind of love how uncoordinated we'll be together?"

Out of nowhere, I laugh. And then Devlyn laughs.

"Seriously, Shelly. You have nothing to fear or be embarrassed about with me. Ever." His finger twirls in my hair. "I love that I get to be your first. Not because your virginity is a trophy or something to conquer. But because it means no one mattered before me. Even with my broken parts and odd view of the world, you chose me over everyone else."

"Wasn't really a choice," I say softly.

"Couldn't agree more." He lightly traces a finger along my jaw to my chin, his eyes following the movement. "So if you want to stop, I'll understand. I won't be upset. Promise."

I shake my head. "I don't want to stop."

He stares at my lips, hungry. "You're sure?"

"Yes."

"Thank God."

His lips crash on mine, kissing me like a starved man. With deft fingers, he unbuttons my jeans and parts the zipper. Tugs the snug denim at my hips and drags the material down my thighs, my calves, then tosses them on the floor. Crawling up my body, he stops when his eyes land on my panties and I internally berate myself.

I had no expectations of staying the night at Devlyn's house. Okay, that's a lie. I assumed we would probably fool around. Maybe grope each other under our clothes. Which is why it never crossed my mind to wear my prettier underwear. The baby-pink lacy thong and matching bra.

Instead, I wore the cotton thong with a hole near the hip and a fading floral print from too many washes. What bra had I even been wearing? The dingy white one. *Ugh. Kill me now.* I mentally slap my forehead.

I peer down at Devlyn as he hovers a place no one else has been. The longer he remains frozen, the more embarrassment claws at my insides.

Then his eyes track up my body until we connect. A subtle half smile kicks up his lips. "You know, I love these." I want to roll my eyes, but then he traces his fingertip above the waistband and I forget all thought. "That you didn't *dress* for the occasion." His finger dips below the elastic and brushes the thin strip of curls. "That I see you how you are naturally and not what you think I want to see."

His hands land on my hips. Fingers hook beneath the elastic. Slowly, ever so slowly, he peels the cotton down, down, down; eyes locked on mine the entire time.

When my panties join my jeans on the floor, he is back at my center. Breath hot on my skin. Thumbs drawing circles on my hips. Hovering. Waiting. Panting between my spread legs. I don't dare move. Don't dare say a word. I simply wait for his next move while reminding myself to breathe.

Devlyn runs the tip of his nose up my center and inhales deeply. Strengthens his grip on my hips. Kneads my flesh with his fingers. Breathes heavily over my mound for one, two, three breaths. Then his mouth meets my lower lips. A gentle, wet kiss. Followed by another. And another. Then his tongue darts out and flattens against my seam as he slowly licks up my center.

"Oh god," I moan out as I fist the comforter.

He groans at the junction of my thighs then releases my hips from his touch. In a swift move, he sweeps his arms under my legs and rests my thighs on his shoulders. His hands cup my butt and tug me closer. Bringing my center to his mouth. And then his tongue licks up my lips again. Tastes me with unmatched hunger. Flicks at the small bundle of nerves.

I squirm beneath him. Moan without restraint. Curl my fingers in his hair and tug when he hits *the spot* that has me begging for more. Grind against his mouth without shame as he inserts one finger then another and slowly pumps in and out of my core. Fist the comforter until my knuckles sting as fire and power and ecstasy swirl low in my belly and spill out of me in the form of euphoria.

Blinding light illuminates behind my closed eyes as I float in the heavens. And before my feet hit earth again, the mattress dips as Devlyn crawls up my body. His lips kiss a slow trail up my midline, stray left to suck my aching breast and pert nipple between his lips, followed by the right. Releasing my breast, he kisses and licks along my collarbone. Nips at the length of my shoulder, the curve of my neck, the column of my throat before sucking my earlobe between his teeth.

"Please tell me you're sure," he whispers in my ear then rubs his bare length along my center.

*When did he remove the last of his clothes?* Most likely when I was in a trance, blissed out by what he had done to my body.

"Yes, I'm sure." I lift my hips and rock against him. I don't miss the audible shake in his next breath. Or the way his fingers bruise my hip.

"Need to get a condom." Devlyn shifts his weight off me and reaches for one of the nightstand drawers. He fumbles with the box, still wrapped, and glances back with a wince. "Sorry."

I giggle under my breath. "The fact that you have to unwrap the box is more than okay." To some, this would kill the mood. Waiting while their partner fumbles with the cellophane and breaks into the box. But me? I find the action sexy. Yes, Devlyn said he hadn't been with anyone in years—not that his sexual history changes how I see him—but watching his dexterous fingers maul the box of condoms while he pins his lips between his teeth… I have a front-row seat to his inexperience. A fact that calms my jittery nerves a little more.

"Halle-freaking-lujah," he mutters as he takes a square from the box. I want to giggle again, but stop myself the moment our eyes connect.

In a microsecond, the seriousness of what is about to happen hits me full force. A fresh wave of anxiety blooms in my chest, kicks my heart into fifth gear, has my lungs begging for oxygen. Everything moves in slow motion as Devlyn tears the wrapper open, removes the condom, fumbles with it slightly then rolls it down his thick length.

*Holy shit!*

I shouldn't have looked. Shouldn't have watched.

Shouldn't have stared at the size of him. Because my anxiety amplifies tenfold. My skin feels tight on my body. A hand wraps around my heart and squeezes, tighter and tighter. And for the life of me, I can't remember how to breathe. My sight blurs as my ears fill with white noise.

What was I thinking? I thought I was ready. Thought I could go through with this. But right now, it feels like death is swallowing me whole. Death by embarrassment. Death by panic attack because this thirty-two-year-old woman is scared to have sex for the first time.

*What was I thinking?*

And then he is there. Devlyn. Body pressed to mine and face a breath away. Still blurry, but slowly coming into focus as he strokes my cheek. His lips move, but his words hit my ears in a garbled mess. Then he kisses me—my lips, my cheek, the spot beneath my ear.

"Breathe," he says, soft and slow. Another kiss heats the skin beneath my ear. "I've got you." He shifts to meet my gaze. "Just breathe."

Then I take the deepest breath of my life as Devlyn rocks his hips forward.

# twenty-two

## DEVLYN

I never want to let her go.

Forehead pressed to hers, I tighten my hold on Shelly. Our heavy breaths mingle in the air and further dampen our skin. Still inside her, I shift us onto our sides and band my arms around her more securely. Hold her impossibly closer and kiss her forehead, the tip of her nose, her cheek, her lips.

My fingers comb through her hair as our breathing settles and the room grows still. I close my eyes and bask in the hormonal high my body is on. Relish the heat and sensation of Shelly in my arms, bare and natural and uninhibited. Cherish the subtle touches she gives as her fingers paint small circles on my lower back.

"That was…"

"Incredible," I finish for her.

"Incredible," she repeats wistfully.

Sex—making love—with Shelly was more than incredible. Once I calmed her, once the sharp sting of my invasion faded, we fumbled with our rhythm. But it didn't take long for the lack of coordination to fall away. In its place, we figured out the perfect tempo. Learned when to rock our hips at the perfect time. Discovered which position or angle made each other moan. And then she let go.

Watching Shelly come undone beneath me is a sight I will never forget. A sight I will mentally revisit time and again. The moment her orgasm peaked, it was like watching the most beautiful flower open its petals and come to life. A magical sight to behold. Her skin blotched in various shades of pink and red. Shades I will only associate with her.

But making love was more than just a physical act with Shelly.

When her starry blues locked on mine as we let go, an inferno of emotion burned beneath my sternum. The shimmering stars in her eyes sucked me deeper. The connection we shared from the start tightened its grip around my heart. And it was in that singular moment, in that infinite blip of time, I knew I would never spend a day without Shelly in my life.

Is it too soon to confess such bold statements aloud?

Minute by minute, I grow more flaccid inside Shelly. Much as I don't want to break the physical connection, remaining like this isn't ideal. So I reluctantly withdraw from her. Press a kiss to her forehead and excuse myself to dispose of the condom.

When I crawl under the sheets, Shelly is softly snoring on my pillow. I don't wake or move her. Instead, I adjust myself to mold my body to her frame, wrap my arms around her waist, and whisper good night against the skin beneath her ear.

I wake to cold sheets where Shelly fell asleep in my arms only hours ago. The smell of bacon and fresh bread float through the house and my stomach grumbles in response. I press a palm to my stomach to quelch the feisty organ.

Arms above my head, I stretch the sleep from my muscles. As I scoot toward the edge of the bed, I pick up Shelly's scent on the pillow. I roll over, press my nose to the space she abandoned not long ago and inhale the scent distinctly Shelly—sweet and floral and earthy. Fisting the pillow, I smother myself with her perfume.

*How will I ever sleep without her in my bed again?*

Now is not the time for such questions or answers. I may want Shelly in my bed—not strictly for sex—every night going forward, but that doesn't mean she is ready for the same level of commitment. Last thing I need to do is scare her off. Doesn't mean I won't skirt the subject and put out feelers.

Out of bed, I dig a pair of sweatpants from the dresser, step into them, and presumptuously grab a condom from the nightstand and pocket it before wandering to the kitchen. At the end of the hall, the kitchen comes into view and I freeze. My breath catches in my throat as I take in the view.

*Screwed. I am so screwed when it comes to this woman. Without a doubt, my heart is hers.*

With her back to me, I survey the scene unannounced. Shelly has her toffee-blonde locks securely piled on her head; a few stragglers tickle the nape of her neck. She wears the shirt I wore last night, and only the shirt. Her bare legs go on for miles. I swallow and try to temper the thoughts causing my sweats to tent.

Moving away from the cutting board, she spots me in her periphery. A hand slaps her chest as she gasps. "Holy shit." I amble into the kitchen as she catches her breath. "You practically gave me a heart attack," she says, smacking my bare chest as I snake my arms around her waist.

I kiss her lips. "Sorry." *Am I, though?* "Actually, I'm not sorry. I rather enjoyed watching you a minute."

My favorite smile lights up her face. "Yeah, you do have a thing for watching me."

So she has noticed the way I can't look away from her. How *long* has she noticed?

"Is that so?"

"Mm-hmm." Her finger draws circles on my pec. "Don't think I didn't notice you at the shop. Or in the museum. Or the park." She licks her lips. "And every other time before we decided to be more than friends."

Part of me is embarrassed she noticed every time I studied her face longer than normal. No wonder she was confused. My words constantly told her one thing while my actions said the complete opposite. The other part of me is delighted that she read the signs the way she did. That she didn't shove me away, that she gave me room to breathe. To figure out how to move forward with her. To clear some of my past demons and make room for her light.

The back of my knuckles brush along her cheekbone. I kiss her forehead, the tip of her nose, her lips. Press my forehead to hers. "Glad I didn't scare you off." Another kiss to her lips; this one deeper, potent, ravaging.

"Never." Out of nowhere, she straightens her spine. "Shit," she hisses and breaks free of my arms. She bolts to the stove, fiddles with the knob, and stirs what I assume are eggs. "Oh, thank goodness."

I step up behind her and peer over her shoulder. "All good?" My lips drop to her neck.

"Yeah." She melts into my touch. "Breakfast will be done in a few, if you want to set up a place to eat."

I kiss her neck again. "On it."

The dining room rarely gets used, but today I want to sit with Shelly and share a meal at the table. Add touches of her to yet another room in the house. Maybe after breakfast, if I gather up enough nerve, I will walk her up the stairs and show her my studio. The only space she has yet to see, for good reason. Weeks ago, the sight of my studio—her face and likeness on several pieces of canvas and stock—may have sent Shelly running for the hills. Now, she may accept my obsession with more grace.

Shelly walks into the dining room with two loaded plates, sets them down, and turns back for the kitchen. Before I get the chance to ask if she needs help, she returns with two mugs of tea.

"This looks wonderful." I scan the plate of cheesy southwestern scrambled eggs, bacon, tangerine segments, and toast with sliced avocado. "Thank you for making breakfast."

Heat pinks her cheeks as she shrugs. "No big deal. Just wanted to do something nice for you." With both hands, she brings the mug to her lips and sips her tea. "Plus, I might be in love with your kitchen."

It is on the tip of my tongue to invite her to use my kitchen every day of the week. But jumping on that bandwagon prematurely probably isn't the best idea. Still, I open my mouth and abbreviate the idea.

"You're welcome to use it whenever you like."

Her eyes drop to her plate. *Shit.* Stepped over the line anyway. *Dammit.* But then I catch the corners of her mouth as they tip up. That small action steals every worry I felt seconds ago and fills me with jubilation.

I devour each bite, and it isn't long before I pat my stomach and push my plate away. "So good. If you're not careful, you'll cook all the meals."

Shelly rolls her eyes. "Ha ha." She sips her tea then sets her mug down. "Aside from the occasional *when will you get married and give me grandchildren* moments, my mom is pretty great. She's no kitchen guru but made sure we knew basics before moving out. Her lessons stuck with me, but not so much with my brother."

"So what you're saying is the kitchen is his archnemesis."

She laughs. "Once upon a time, yes. But since meeting his now wife, he's putting in the time and effort to learn."

We sit in silence for a beat, both of us letting our full bellies settle while we sip tea. And I can't help but think how much I love this. Sitting here, across the table from Shelly, eating breakfast, sipping tea, having casual conversation, enjoying each other's company. I also can't stop thinking about how I want this with her more often than not.

"I want to show you something," I say, eyes on hers.

"Okay. Just give me a minute to clean up."

"No." My chair legs scrape the wood floor as I rise to my feet. "Leave it. We'll clean up after."

I offer my hand and she takes it, standing from her seat. "O-okay."

With a deep breath, I walk to the left and up the staircase. There is only one room when you reach the top. My studio. And I am about to expose the biggest piece of myself to her. Something I have never done with another soul.

# twenty-three

## SHELLY

Slowly, we ascend the stairs. With each step up, Devlyn's breathing quickens. His grip on my hand tightens. This isn't just his studio he is leading me up to. This *is* Devlyn. The inner workings of his mind. Him expressing all the things he can't find a voice for.

We reach the landing and the massive space comes into view. There is no door to separate the studio from the stairwell. The only door to this room is at the other end of the stairs. To the right, a large window brightens the space naturally. A second smaller window sits on the opposite wall higher up. A skylight in the center of the ceiling.

My eyes dart in every direction as I absorb the chaos that is Devlyn's studio.

A closet with an open barn door is packed with canvases in various sizes. Some painted, others blank. One wall of the closet is lined with shelves. Implements and brushes, cleaning supplies and rags, pencils and more sit on the shelves—many of them unopened.

A bathroom with a stall shower, toilet, and double sink with a black countertop is brightened by a small window. Hand towels hang from the bar. A bottle of mineral oil and bar of soap sit between the sinks. The faint splatter of paint from washed hands in one of the bowls.

The main room of the studio has a drafting table at one end, a cart and shelves beside it. In the heart of the room is a large table covered in used rags, large coffee cans with brushes sticking out, various-sized glass jars with dripped paint on the glass, and an abundance of paint tubes in different states of use.

Canvases lean against walls and each other. Drawings lie scattered on the floor and pinned to the walls. Some in color, others monochrome. But there appears to be a theme with several of them. A theme that doesn't shock me after seeing Devlyn's work at the exhibition or the piece my parents gifted me for Christmas.

*Me*. I am the theme.

Considering our romantic relationship is fairly new, this should bother me. Shouldn't it? Some women might think an artist's obsession with one person—their muse—is awkward or disturbing. But as I scan the room and take in all the various ways Devlyn has reconstructed my image, a warmth builds in my chest.

Devlyn may have difficulty expressing himself with words, but the art in this room says more than any words ever will. *Devlyn is in love with me. Madly.*

"Wow," I breathe out.

I haven't met his gaze since we entered the room, but his eyes sear my profile. His silence begs for me to expand on my single-word response. To tell him if I love it or never plan to return.

"Is it weird that I love seeing myself in so many different

ways?" I ask this to lighten the tension rolling off him. And it works.

A soft chuckle leaves his lips, growing louder with each breath, and soon I join in. As our laughter fades, he gives my hand a squeeze.

"Does it freak you out?" He waves his hand around the room. "Seeing all this. Seeing how much you inspire me."

Turning to face him, I bring my body flush with his and lock my fingers behind his neck. His hands automatically find my hips. "Nope." I press my lips to his. "Maybe because of the images at the exhibition." Another kiss. "Or maybe because my parents bought one of your pieces and gifted it to me for Christmas."

Devlyn jerks his head back. "Really?"

I nod. "Mm-hmm."

"Was it the iris drawing?" I nod again. "Funny enough, I thought maybe it was someone related to you. But I'd never heard you mention a George."

"Ah. That would be my dad. Mom uses his cards to shop online."

"Gotcha." Devlyn brings his lips back to mine. "Seriously, though… you're not bothered by all this?"

I shake my head. "Is it weird that my face might be on someone's wall? Sure." I glance around the studio for a beat. "But I love that you can't get me out of your head."

His hands drop beneath the hemline and dip under the cotton of my shirt, inching up the material. One arm bands around my waist while his other hand traces up my spine.

"I don't sell paintings or drawings where the image is noticeably you. Those, I keep." Leaning in, he devours my lips. When the kiss breaks, fire and passion brew in his eyes. "Can I paint you?"

Confused by the question, considering he has painted me countless times, I narrow my eyes. "Um, yes."

The corner of his mouth kicks up and my stomach does somersaults. Before realization dawns on me, Devlyn is peeling the shirt over my head. Pushing my panties to the floor. Exposing me completely with a wicked grin on his face.

"Uh, Devlyn." The urge to slap an arm over my breasts and lady bits is strong. "I don't know if I'm okay with you putting my nude body on canvas."

His smile widens. "Good thing that's not what I'm doing." He takes my hand and walks me over to a metal stool, the seat splattered in every shade of the rainbow and more. "Sit here."

I park myself on the stool, shiver as the cool metal meets my skin, hide my breasts behind my forearms, and cross my legs. My heart pounds in my chest while Devlyn roams the studio, picks up a tube of blue paint, then pink, then yellow. I lose focus as he continues, oblivious to my mini panic attack.

I may not be the shyest woman in the room most days, but the idea of having my naked body on display—even if it never leaves this room—has me in crisis mode.

"Breathe," Devlyn says in my ear. His hands come up from behind and take hold of my biceps. He kisses along my shoulder, the curve of my neck, up my throat. "Trust me." His words hot and soft on my skin.

My entire frame sags as he peels my arms away and lets them fall to my sides. Stepping around the stool, he parts my legs and positions himself between them. With a finger under my chin, he tips my head back and presses his lips to mine. The kiss starts off slow and gentle with light pecks. But with each kiss, it grows more intense. Impassioned and hungry.

We roam each other's bodies with our hands. A moan spilling from my lips as a growl builds in his chest.

Something slick coats my skin when he palms my breast. I tear my lips away and look down. A hand-sized streak of magenta paint smears my skin. Adds a pop of contrast to my pale, bare flesh. And that is when it clicks.

*"Can I paint you?"*

Did Devlyn mean he wanted to put paint on my actual body? Not paint my likeness on canvas? By the questioning look in his glass-green eyes right now, I would say yes.

Off to the right, I stare at the tray of paints squeezed out. Dipping two fingers in the dark green, I swirl the paint onto my skin. Then I bring them to Devlyn's chest, look him square in the eyes, and streak his skin with the pigment.

Hunger and need darken Devlyn's green irises. Before I make a joke about him asking for it, he strips off his sweats. Kicks them aside. Grabs the paint tray from the table then wraps an arm around my waist and sits us both on the floor.

Time evades us with each laugh, moan and fondle as we paint each other. Our paint-coated fingers roam and clutch and bruise. Our mouths crash together while our lips and tongues taste. After the majority of our bodies are paint slicked, Devlyn pulls a condom from the pocket of his sweats, rolls it on, and eases his thick erection between my legs. I fist his hair as he clutches the nape of my neck. My legs wrap around his waist as his hips rock at a steady, delicious tempo. The paint on our skin swirls in a kaleidoscope of colors and it isn't long before my orgasm vibrates every nerve ending in my body. Then Devlyn is right behind me, jaw slack and body trembling in ecstasy.

Minutes pass and we don't move. Our breaths calm as Devlyn props himself up on his forearms, then kisses me deeply.

"Thank you for christening my studio. Work will never be dull again."

I slap his arm and laugh. "Painting me will never be dull."

The same hunger from earlier ignites his eyes. "If by painting you, you mean this"—he glances between our bodies—"damn right. Given the chance, I'd paint you every day."

Heat crawls up my neck to my cheeks, but the paint disguises most of it. "I'd like you to paint me every day. But only if I get to do the same."

Devlyn drops his lips to mine as his hips start to rock. I am about to mention something about the condom needing to be replaced when I hear a noise from downstairs.

Breaking the kiss, I ask, "Did you hear that?"

"Hear what?" He kisses my stained skin.

"Devlyn?" a woman calls from downstairs. "You home?"

Above me, Devlyn freezes and goes wide eyed. "Shit." His eyes slam shut. "Shit, shit, shit."

A new dose of panic floods my veins. "What's wrong? Who is that?"

"Devlyn? Are you upstairs?" The woman sounds closer than she did a moment ago.

Devlyn pulls out quickly and I wince. "Sorry." He fumbles for his sweats, my shirt, and panties. "Here." He hands me the garments with a pained look. "Give me a minute, Mother," he shouts. "I'll be right down."

*Oh. My. God. Oh my god!*

Devlyn's mom is here. Downstairs. Right now. There is no possible way for either of us to skirt past her without her seeing us. And with the paint covering both our bodies, literally, it won't be difficult to surmise what we were doing.

*Kill. Me. Now.*

He removes the condom, tosses it in the trash, then steps

into his sweats. I slip the shirt over my head and pull on my panties. As I straighten, he steps into me, frames my face with his hands, and presses a gentle kiss to my lips.

"Wait here a minute. I'll see if I can get her to leave."

I tuck my lips between my teeth and nod. "'Kay."

"Be right back."

Devlyn dashes down the stairs, paint smeared over ninety percent of his body, and greets his mother. I move closer to the landing and try to listen in on their conversation without being seen.

"What in the world, Devlyn?" Her tone blade sharp. "Why are you covered in paint?"

"Hello to you too, Mother."

"Don't be smart with me." Her shoes clap the floor and grow quieter as they move away.

Hesitantly, I go down a few stairs and listen for further movement.

"What brought you by?" Devlyn doesn't hide the curtness from his words. The sharp tone so different from what I am used to hearing from him.

Devlyn has told me about his parents, but not in in-depth detail. From what I do know, she sounds like a lot to handle. And by the way she speaks with Devlyn now, I don't disagree with that opinion.

"Well," she huffs out. "I came over to ask you to lunch, but with the state of your appearance, that isn't happening." Her shoes clap the floor again. This time, they grow louder and I panic. "Your father and I have planned a post-New Year's party at the house for next Saturday. It's more than enough—"

She stops speaking the moment my foot slips on the top stair and I fall on my butt.

"Shit," I whisper as I scurry up into the studio. There is nowhere to go, nowhere to hide. So, I dash over to the table and sit on the stool. At least I can hide my bare legs.

*Clap, clap, clap.*

With each step she takes up the stairs, my heart shrivels a little more. When she reaches the landing, looks around the room, and spots me, a snarl displays on her face. Albeit brief, I still catch it.

The woman eyes me with disgust as Devlyn darts past her and comes to my side.

"Devlyn, who is this girl?"

*Girl?*

"Mother." Devlyn wraps an arm around my waist then kisses my temple. "This is Shelly." His eyes home back in on her. "My girlfriend." She grinds her jaw. "Shelly, this is my mother, Karen Templar."

If the tension were any thicker in the room, we would all suffocate.

Without a word, she turns on her heel and stomps down the stairs like a pouty juvenile. When she reaches the bottom floor, she shouts up the stairwell. "Devlyn, a word downstairs. Now."

He doesn't answer her. He doesn't move from my side. Instead, he frames my face and holds my stare. "We'll talk when she leaves. But please, don't let her bother you." He kisses my lips, my nose, my forehead. "Let me get rid of her, then we can talk."

Speechless, I nod.

Devlyn darts down the stairs and I stay put on the stool. From my seat, I hoped to not hear what his mother would say next. Sadly, I hear every seething, ugly word.

"That girl will ruin your career. She will tarnish the

Templar name. I bet she only wants your money. Have you gotten a good look at her?"

All the ugly words twirl in my head like a cyclone gone astray. One by one, her words cripple me. Douse me in fear and hurt. Steal the happiness from my soul.

Then Devlyn pipes up. "Enough, Mother!" he booms. "Enough."

"Don't you dare—"

"No, Mother, it's my turn to speak. That *woman* upstairs is brilliant and wonderful and kind. More than I could ever ask for or deserve. Without hesitation, she gives me her heart. More than you ever have."

"I've heard enough."

"No, you haven't. Because you never listen." Her shoes clap the floor and get quieter. "She matters to me. A lot. And if you can't respect her or my feelings, I suggest you don't stop by unannounced. Ever."

My heart races in my chest. Tears well in my eyes. Not that no one has ever stood up for me, but this is different. This is someone I love putting me first. Over their family.

"How dare you speak to me with such disregard."

"How dare I? *How dare I?*" Devlyn laughs without humor. "I'm done, Mother. Done. Don't call or email. Don't reach out at all. I'll be changing the code to the door as soon as you leave."

"You can't just get rid of your mother, Devlyn. It doesn't work that way." The house goes eerily quiet a beat. "When that girl trashes your life, when you have nowhere left to turn, you'll beg for my forgiveness."

Dear god. What the hell is wrong with this woman? She obviously thinks of herself as holier than thou, while everyone at her feet is shit.

"Get out!" he screams. "Get out now!"

"How dare—"

"Now!"

A moment later, the door slams. Then Devlyn screams at the top of his lungs.

Immediately, I want to run down the stairs and go to him. Comfort him. See if he needs anything, even if it is time alone. But I also don't want to crowd him. Make him think he doesn't have the space or time to process what happened on his own. Be a nag or pest when what he needs is solitude and quiet.

I don't want him to think I'm like *her*.

Sliding off the stool, I tiptoe to the landing, then down the stairs. The house is quiet. Too quiet. When I reach the bottom floor, I peek around the doorway. No sign of Devlyn. I pad across the room, look left into the living room then right into the dining room. Still no Devlyn. I round the corner, walk past the kitchen, and step into the formal sitting room at the entrance of the house.

There, on the floor, near the front door, Devlyn is curled in on himself, back to the ceiling. Slowly, I pad across the room, come to his side and crouch down. I don't say a word. Instead, I gently rest a hand on his back. He startles at my touch. A breath passes between us and then he twists, wraps his arms around my waist, and clings to me as if I am the air he breathes.

His frame shakes as he sobs into my lap. I bend over him, blanket him with touch, and kiss along his spine. "I got you." I hug him tighter. "No matter what."

He grips me impossibly tighter, his fingers bruising my flesh. But I don't care. "I need you, Shelly. Always."

"You have me."

Wiggling free, he sits up and frames my face. "Promise?"

I lift my hand and stick out my pinkie. "Promise."

He hooks our pinkies then drags me onto his lap. "Never letting you go," he says before smashing my lips with his.

Good. Because there is nowhere else I want to be.

# twenty-four
## DEVLYN

Life has never been this exhausting.

When I cut ties with my mother two weeks ago, it felt like she sucked part of my soul out. Knowing her, she probably did.

Although life feels less weighted with her absence, my body is still recovering from our screaming match. Not just my physical self, but my mental and emotional self too. Dumping toxic people from your life, especially family, isn't as simple as saying goodbye. You don't just get to wave a hand and be done with it. Because, as expected, my mother has continuously tried to keep in contact. At this point, I am ready to block her. Put a ten-foot cinder block wall around my home and shut out the possibility of her knocking on my door again.

Thank goodness I have Shelly. The only light in my life. The sole reason I wake up each morning and roll out of bed. In the last two weeks, we haven't spent a night without each other. A couple of times, she has hung out with her friends after work. As soon as they all went separate ways, Shelly came to me.

"Ready?" she asks as she exits the bathroom.

With each night she stays in my home, she adds more pieces of herself. Occasionally, we stay at her apartment, but more often than not, she walks through my door. Cooks in my kitchen. Curls into me on my sofa. Eats meals at my table. Spoons with me in my bed.

And I don't want it any other way. Well, I would rather call them *ours* instead of mine, but that is a conversation for a different day.

"Yeah, I'm ready."

Tonight is a big deal. Tonight, I am meeting her friends at their weekly Sunday gathering. But not just her friends, I also get to meet her brother and sister-in-law. The whole situation has me sweaty and itchy.

From what little Shelly has told me about her brother, he sounds pretty protective of her. I mean, I get it. Shelly means everything to me, so I am pretty protective of her too. In a different way. But since Shelly asked me to join her at the Sunday night gathering, I haven't been able to shake the jitters from my limbs.

As if she senses my unease, Shelly wedges herself between my legs at the edge of the bed. Bringing a hand to my cheek, she wipes away any discomfort with the soft brush of her thumb.

"I know crowds aren't your thing, but I promise this is a low-key gathering. Just friends hanging out and catching up." I nod as my arms band around her waist and haul her closer. "It's usually a little odd when someone new comes, like when Micah brought Peyton the first time, but I promise everyone will resume normal conversation in no time."

Being the odd man out has never been something that bothered me. Throughout my middle and high school years, I had been the subject of bullies. People who thought I was weird because I didn't dress the same or socialize the same or join all the clicks. So, instead of getting to know me, they said hurtful things, threw food at me in the cafeteria, or rigged my locker. After a while, it simply became a part of who I was and I accepted it.

When Kelsey came along, I often questioned if she was truly interested or if befriending, then eventually dating me was a prank. It took months for me to believe she cared. When she ended our relationship, the questions came back again. Nothing but heartache came from our breakup, so I brushed the idea under the rug where it belonged.

"As long as you're there, it doesn't matter how strange everyone acts." I hug her to me, bury my nose in the hollow of her throat and inhale. "Meeting new people is always uncomfortable. But these people matter to you, so I want to know them too."

I hold on to Shelly for three breaths, then let her lead me from the bedroom. After we stop in the kitchen to grab the Crock-Pot of sweet-and-spicy meatballs, we get in my car and drive toward the party. On the drive over, Shelly gives me small tidbits about everyone who will be in attendance. When she starts talking about the seventh person, my mind goes numb.

*She said a lot of people would be there, but I didn't think it'd be more than a dozen. Jesus.*

My heart runs rampant as the whooshing of my pulse fills my ear. I take a deep breath. Then another. And just like she always has, Shelly settles the craziness inside. She grips my hand a little tighter. Rubs her thumb in small circles over my skin. Tells me everything will be okay, that she won't leave my side. Reminds me that everyone at the party is cool and fun and can't wait for us to arrive.

I steer the car into the neighborhood and take in the homes on the street. Most are two-story and look to be built in the last twenty to thirty years. Simple yet clean and elegant. Yards with tall trees and manicured landscapes. Flower beds and wind chimes and welcome signs. Strategically placed lights to illuminate sturdy magnolias and clustered palms.

I park on the street two houses down and take the Crock-Pot from Shelly when we exit the car. She laces her fingers with mine and guides us toward the house. "They'll love you," she says softly, kissing my cheek.

Not bothering to knock or ring the doorbell, Shelly twists the knob and walks us inside. Just as the door closes, a husky gallops around the corner with a little girl hot on its heels.

"Sparty!" she shouts over the music and chatter. "No, sir." The girl's bossy tone says she is not to be messed with. Before the dog collides with our legs, it screeches to a halt like a speed skater on ice.

Not releasing my hand, Shelly squats down and the dog steps up to lick her face. "Hey, Spartan. This is Devlyn."

*Woof, woof, woof.* He cocks his head while looking up and assessing me.

Shelly rises and ruffles the fur on his head. "Be a good boy."

The little girl reaches us and wraps her arms around Shelly's midsection. "Hi, Miss Shelly. Sorry if Sparty was a jerk."

With a laugh, Shelly says, "He's just being himself. Clementine, this is my boyfriend, Devlyn." Shelly wraps her free hand around my bicep and molds herself to my side. "Devlyn, this is Clementine, Autumn's daughter."

Autumn. She and Jonas own this house. They also are expecting a baby any day now.

I untwine my fingers from Shelly and offer Clementine my hand. "It's nice to meet you, Clementine." The girl looks at my hand as her forehead bunches into crooked lines.

About to ask Shelly if I did something wrong, Clementine wraps her arms around me as if we have been friends all her life. "Nice to meet you, Mr. Devlyn."

Shelly leans into my ear. "She's a hugger." I chuckle and return Clementine's brief hug.

Minus the unexpected hug, everyone else greets me with the same enthusiasm as we walk deeper into the house. One by one, I put faces to the names of people Shelly told me about. Some of them are how I pictured them in my mind's eye, others the complete opposite. When Shelly introduces me to her brother, Micah, and sister-in-law, Peyton, I half expect to get the big brother lecture. But Micah surprises us both with a brief hug and big smile.

As the night wears on, I learn why Shelly is so bonded with these people. Her people. Every person here has been kind and wonderful and accepting of me. They smile my way and spark up conversation as if we have been friends just as long as anyone else here. They ask about my work and I ask about theirs. The easiest conversations are with Rex and Reznor from the tattoo shop. They show me pictures of pieces they have done and I show them my art too.

And before the night ends, I feel as if I am just as much their family as everyone else in the room. It stirs new meaning to the term family in my life. Studying the face of each person, I home in on the connection they share that is nothing like what I have ever known as family. Love. Consideration. Tenderness. Friendship.

When it is time to say good night, every hug and promise to see them again is heartfelt and genuine. Nervous as I was before we arrived, every person here made me feel as if I belonged. As if I were their family.

We load into the car and I drive us home. Our fingers laced together and resting in her lap.

"Did you have a nice time?"

I lift her hand to my lips and kiss her knuckles. "I did. Thought I'd be more overwhelmed, but everyone was very welcoming."

She leans across the console and rests her head on my bicep. "See. I knew there was nothing to worry about."

The drive home is quick with less traffic on the roads. When I turn onto my street and spot the white SUV not far in the distance, I bring the car to a halt. Even from half a block away, I know who is parked in front of my house. The woman who just won't give up.

Shelly straightens in her seat. "What's wrong?" When I don't answer, she follows my line of sight. "Is that?"

"My mother?" My knuckles whiten on the steering wheel. "Yep."

"Turn around."

"What?" I twist in my seat to look at Shelly.

"Turn around and go to my apartment. She doesn't know where I live." Shelly lifts a hand to my cheek. "I don't want her to ruin our night."

I pull into the closest driveway, back out, and exit the neighborhood the way we came. The entire drive to Shelly's place, I mull over why my mother is so damn persistent with keeping me in her life if I am such a bother. The only answer I come up with is that she needs someone to step on so she can feel higher and mightier. So she has more people at her feet to kiss them.

In the last two weeks, so much has changed. Once you step out of the shadow of someone else's light, you see the world differently. Once that person no longer has the ability to squash you under their thumb, they come back with more persistence.

After hours of online research since I pushed her away, I concluded my mother is most definitely a narcissist. To what degree? I don't know, nor do I have the time or energy to figure it out. But the further I fell down the dark online hole, the deeper it sank into my bones. The more I realized that people like her will never be happy unless they have someone to belittle or trample.

I don't want to be that person for her. I can't be.

So if I want to break the cycle, if I want to have a healthy life and relationship with Shelly, I have to cut her off. Cut all direct ties. No matter the cost. No matter who I lose in the process. Because from what I've learned, if I don't make a clean break, my mother will slowly and intentionally ruin everything I love. Everything I hold close to my heart. As long as she comes out feeling mighty in the end, she won't care who she crushes along the way.

And I refuse to let her rob me of happiness.

Everyone is on edge.

Any day now, Autumn is due to deliver. Jonas started paternity leave days ago, in case Autumn went into labor early. Clementine hasn't allowed Autumn to do a thing on her own except use the bathroom. Even then, she hovers close by.

Although Autumn and Jonas aren't her children, Elizabeth is geared up for the next baby in our group to arrive. We won't be closing Petal and Vine like we did when Cora went into labor, but she is prepped and ready to let me leave the shop and deliver bundles of flowers.

More than ever, Devlyn is holed up in his studio. When I arrive at his house after work, more often than not, he is upstairs. Music echoes throughout the house while he works on commissioned pieces. I don't go up uninvited, not because he doesn't want me up there, but because I assume he needs the time to himself.

Since the unannounced visit from his mother and then seeing her car out front days later, Devlyn has turned inward slightly. He doesn't shut me out, but is selective with what he shares. His reservation doesn't hurt—I have always known

Devlyn's reticent nature—but it has me ready to go into protection mode. Not to protect me, but to safeguard him and his heart.

Art is how Devlyn processes life. How he expresses himself and unleashes what inhabits his thoughts. The good and the ugly. Whichever consumes him, he needs the time to get it out without guilt or interruption or influence.

Most nights, once I start cooking, he comes down. His warm arms band around my waist as he kisses my shoulder, as I melt into his frame and sigh. I love our new routine. Love how easily both of us have fallen into this way of life, without effort or hardship.

"Still no word?" Elizabeth asks as I fill the loose stems at the front of the shop.

I pull my phone from my pocket, tap the screen and find no new messages. "Nope." Just as I pocket my phone, it pings with a text.

JONAS

It's time!

I spin my phone around and show the message to Elizabeth. The biggest smile plumps her cheeks as she brings her hands to prayer at her lips. Then my phone blows up.

PENNY

On my way!

REZNOR

We'll head over when the shop closes.

GAVIN

Holy shit, man! Congrats!

> CORA
>
> As soon as we drop off Clara, we'll be there.
>
> REX
>
> Congrats, bro! Can't wait to meet the newest family member.
>
> MICAH
>
> Peyton and I will swing by in the morning. Congrats, man!
>
> ERIN
>
> Ahhh! Turning around now!

My fingers race over the keyboard in response.

> Aunt Shelly is on the way! Can't wait to meet him or her.

Then, I flip to my text history with Devlyn and type a quick message.

> Autumn's in labor. Headed to the hospital.

The small gray bubble dances at the bottom left of the screen a moment before Devlyn's response appears.

> Just left the park. Be there in a few and we can go together.

Since the incident with his mother, Devlyn spends most of his days at the park and evenings in the studio. Not sure if he draws or paints while at the park, but he appears calmer on the days he visits. As if he needs to sit on our bench while working. As if he needs the energy and serenity of the trees and air and wildlife. As if he needs to be in the same space we shared so many times before.

I fear the reason he leaves the house is on the off chance his mother will stop by unannounced, attempting to stir up more toxic drama. The thought rakes my nerves. No one should fear being home, in their personal space.

On the days a shadow glints Devlyn's gaze, he chauffeurs me to the shop. I don't question his heart or motives. Small as it may seem, I grant him this minute assurance, this form of armor. A way he can shield me from hurt, from his mother.

Yeah, that's perfect.

Shouldn't be long.

I fill a few more bins before ditching my shop apron and shouldering my purse. Elizabeth gives me a hug and tells me to send tons of pictures. I bolt out the back door with a small bouquet and hop in Devlyn's SUV, then we are off.

We arrive at the hospital and park in the visitor's lot. After weaving through the main lobby, we step inside the elevator and ascend to labor and delivery. The car comes to a stop and the doors whoosh open. The air hits my face as we step out and my stomach rolls a little at the scent of lemon-scented bleach. I take a deep breath, hold it to the count of ten then release it.

"Hey." Devlyn gives my hand a squeeze. "You okay?"

"Yeah," I say with a nod. "Never been a fan of bleach and it smelled especially strong when the elevator opened."

"Huh."

We steer into the waiting area for the floor, and I look to Devlyn. "What?"

He shrugs. "I barely smelled it is all. Maybe it's because

of the cleaning agents I use for my brushes. My nose is desensitized to the strong stuff."

The subject gets dropped when Penny, Cora, and Gavin approach. Cora wraps her arms around me and squeals a little too loudly in my ear. Gavin smiles brightly and says hello to Devlyn.

"How is everyone? Do we know if she's delivered yet?" I ask Cora, wanting to hold my next niece or nephew sooner rather than later.

"Jonas's mom came out just before you got here. They were going to have Autumn start pushing any minute."

I clap my fingers excitedly and smile so hard my cheeks sting. We settle into the chairs and place bets on if it is a boy or girl. It's three to two for a boy when Erin strolls in and evens the score. Before we get into a face-off about why each of our opinions is fact, Jonas's mom, Irene, walks out with a megawatt smile. The room goes quiet as we all rise and step closer.

"It's a boy!"

The room erupts in cheers. Irene tells us she will come get us once we are allowed to see Autumn, Jonas, and the baby. She disappears down the hall and it isn't long before she returns and invites us back to meet our newest family member.

One by one, we file into the hospital suite. The first thing I notice is how radiant Jonas is. Without question, he will be the best father. That man has the biggest heart and I have never seen it so full.

Like our last trip to the hospital when Cora had Clara, baby Ryker gets passed around for everyone to hold and coo. When I sit with him in the rocking chair, I tell him how lucky he is to have such wonderful parents and the best big sister in the world. And also the world's best aunt.

Baby Ryker has Autumn's dark hair and Jonas's hazel eyes. One thing is certain, this boy will break hearts over the years. Jonas and Autumn may have their hands full with Clementine, but Ryker will be right behind her.

I pass Ryker to Penny and squeeze between Devlyn and Cora.

"Guess you're next," Cora says with a laugh.

It's a joke. I know it is a joke. But I freeze. Not because I fear pregnancy or motherhood or permanency. I freeze because my romantic relationship with Devlyn is little more than a month old. Cora said the words in the moment because she recently had a baby. She'd probably say the same to Peyton if she and Micah hadn't openly told everyone they have no plans to have kids.

But there is another reason I freeze. Another reason my mind tailspins.

*When was my last period? Think, Reed. THINK.*

I search my mental calendar for my last period. It was before Christmas. A week before. Maybe two. I need my planner. Where the hell is my planner? *Oh god. Oh. God. No. No, no, no, no, no.* This cannot be happening. There is no possible chance I am… pregnant.

"Shelly?" Devlyn's lips are at my ear. "What's wrong? You're shaking. And you look… gray."

Oh god. I think I'm going to be sick. As the thought crosses my mind, my stomach rolls.

I drop Devlyn's hand, slap mine to my mouth, and dash out of the room. In the hall, a nurse smiles then frowns. A hand to the mouth is obviously the universal sign for "I'm going to puke" because the nurse rests a hand on my back and rushes me down the hall to the restrooms.

Bolting into the bathroom, I run for the stall, slam the door and lock it, then drop to my knees and expel the contents of my stomach. When my body finally relaxes, I ease up from the floor, flush the toilet, and step out of the stall. Erin stands next to the sink with concern marring her expression.

"Shell, are you okay? Jesus. You scared us all."

I turn on the faucet, splash my face with cold water and rinse out my mouth. "Yeah. Must've eaten something bad at lunch." The lie rolls off my tongue with too much ease.

She gives me a hug. "Long as you're okay." She releases me and hands me a wad of paper towels. "Devlyn's outside." She points to the door.

"Thanks. Will you tell him I'll be out in a minute?"

With a nod, she says, "No problem. Sure you're okay if I leave?"

I smile at my friend. "Promise I'm good." After another hug, she exits the bathroom.

Staring at myself in the mirror, I brace my hands on the sink and take several deep breaths. For the next minute, I have a heart-to-heart with myself.

I didn't eat anything bad in the last few hours—lunch was more than five hours ago. But the nausea could be from a number of things. The chemical smell of the hospital mixed with the adrenaline rush of being here plus not having much in my system. That has to be it.

"There's no way I'm pregnant," I whisper to my reflection. "We used protection. Every time."

But what do I know about condom usage? Other than the sex ed classes in school—more than fifteen years ago—I haven't had much experience or education in the department.

Sure, I know they aren't one-hundred-percent effective, but Devlyn would have said something if the condom broke.

Regardless, I need to exit the bathroom before Devlyn panics and waltzes in. After one last deep breath, I push off the sink and head for the door. Soon as I step out, Devlyn is inches from me, his hands framing my face, eyes studying every detail.

"Are you okay?" he asks, voice low and shaky.

Tears sting the backs of my eyes because I have no clue. For all I know, I could have a virus. It is the time of year for that. I shrug. "Yes. I think." He hugs me to him and I fist the back of his shirt.

A moment later, the same nurse who guided me to the bathroom steps up. "Sorry to intrude, sweetheart. Just wanted to check on you." Her smile is bright and warm.

"Might be a bug," I tell her.

"Why don't you come with me and we can have you checked out? Shouldn't take but a few minutes, if you'd like."

Might as well since I'm here. *Will they also test to see if I'm pregnant?* "Thank you. I appreciate the help."

She walks us to the elevator then takes us to another floor, this one more clinical and cold. Coughs and sneezes and grumbles echo from every direction. The bleach scent is ten times worse and I force myself to breathe through my mouth rather than my nose.

"Hey, Suzanne," a man says from behind the desk. "How can I help?"

"Paul, this young lady…" The nurse looks my direction.

"Shelly," I say.

"Shelly wasn't feeling well upstairs. Would you please run a virus panel?"

He smiles at Nurse Suzanne and nods. "Sure thing." Then

he looks in my direction. "I'll just need identification, Shelly, and some forms filled out."

I dig through my purse and hand over my identification. He hands me a clipboard and points to a group of chairs along the wall. While I fill out basic personal and health information, Devlyn wraps an arm around my shoulders and rubs small circles on my skin.

As I sign my name on the consent to treat line, Paul calls me to the counter and says he is ready. He escorts us to a small room with white walls and generic framed art across from the patient chair.

"We'll do a cheek swab and draw blood." He glances at his watch. "Results won't be available for another twelve or so hours. Will you still be in the hospital?"

I shake my head. "No. We're visiting a friend who had a baby."

He nods as he wraps and ties the tourniquet around my distal bicep. "Make a fist." He jiggles his gloved fingers over the veins at my elbow. "Nice veins." His smile makes me want to smile, but I can't muster the strength. "I'd recommend you don't return to see your friend until we know what this is. Don't want to expose the newborn."

Just before the needle pricks my skin, I look up at Devlyn. He lets me squeeze his hand while I breathe erratically.

"Almost done," he mouths.

The phlebotomist unties the elastic on my arms before easing the needle from my vein and bandaging me up. Next, he removes a long Q-Tip from a sealed tube, asks me to open my mouth and runs the cotton over the inside of my cheek. He places it back in the tube, seals it with a new sticker, then sets it next to the blood vials.

"All set," he says, peeling his gloves away and washing his hands. "Take your time getting up."

Back at the desk, he returns my identification and verifies my telephone number. "We'll give you a call in the morning. Is there a time that works better for you?"

"Any time is good. Thank you, Paul."

"You're welcome. Go home and get some rest. We'll talk in the morning."

And with that, Devlyn and I amble out of the hospital. Devlyn thinking I may have some sort of cold and me considering the possibility of being pregnant.

Devlyn just went through so much with his mother. I don't know if he is in the right headspace to discuss the likelihood of something other than the common cold. During the drive home, I keep the details of my late period to myself. More than pregnancy causes cycle disruption. Stress, diet, a change in sleep habits, physical exertion. No need to ratchet up his anxiety too.

It isn't long before Devlyn parks in his driveway, guides me inside, and tends to me like the most adoring boyfriend. He cooks and feeds me, helps me with a bath, then curls up behind me under the covers.

As my eyes grow heavy, he kisses my shoulder then whispers, "Love you, Shelly."

I tighten his grip around my belly, tears stinging the backs of my eyes. "I love you too."

# twenty-six

## DEVLYN

We startle awake to Shelly's phone ringing on the nightstand.

"Hello," she answers, voice thick with sleep. "This is Shelly Reed." She goes quiet while the person on the other end speaks. I toy with her hair and wait for her to tell me the news. "Yes, I heard you. Thank you for the update."

Shelly ends the call and stares at the ceiling with glassy eyes. Something twists in my gut. Something that says this isn't just a cold. Maybe it's something much worse. Cancer. Something with her heart. My mind races with various ailments I have heard of. Diseases that appear like common colds but are much worse.

I hate how quiet she is. I hate how scared she looks. More than anything, I hate that she won't look me in the eye. As if I won't like what she has to say.

Unable to deal with the silence any longer, I brush my knuckles over her cheek and swallow down my nerves. "You're scaring me," I mumble. A tear rolls down her temple. "Please talk to me, Shelly."

"I don't understand," she whispers to the ceiling. "How?"

"How what?" God, I want to shake the information from her brain and soothe away her fears.

Finally, she turns to meet my gaze. "I'm scared." Another tear spills and I am ready to crawl out of my skin.

"I can't help unless you tell me what's wrong."

"Please don't hate me."

This has me confused. Why would I hate Shelly for being sick? "No matter what it is, we'll get through this." I drop my lips to hers to seal the vow. "I love you, Shelly."

She closes her eyes, takes a deep breath, then opens them. "I don't have a viral infection."

Well, that is good news. I breathe easy for only a moment. Wait? Does that mean it is something worse? My mind automatically goes back to cancer or some inherited immune disorder her family doesn't know about.

"I don't know how, but I'm pregnant."

I inch back from her and take in her wince. "What?" My voice comes out louder than I intend it to.

"Oh god."

She pulls away from me, slides out of bed on the opposite side, and fumbles for her clothes. Meanwhile, I can't move. My body weighted with a ton of bricks. My limbs in a state of paralysis.

*How?*

Before I get another word in, before I get off the bed, she darts for the bathroom with her purse and starts opening cabinets and drawers. As she dashes out and heads for the closet, I finally snap out of my haze and dress.

"What are you doing?" She yanks shirts from hangers and shoves them in her bag. She attempts to push past me, but I grab her elbow. "Shelly, talk to me. Where are you going?"

"You're freaking out." She sniffles and wipes her cheeks with the back of her hand. "I see it in your eyes."

"Well, I'm in shock." I take a deep breath and speak as calmly as possible. "Please, don't go."

"Did you not hear what I said?" She hangs her head. "I'm pregnant." Her sobs grow louder and I pull her into my arms. She fights it at first, but caves. Then hollow laughter spills from her lips.

"Why are you laughing?" Nothing about this situation is funny. If anything, her laugh has the hairs on the back of my neck standing straight.

She leans back and looks me in the eye. "I heard your mother say I'd ruin your life. Never thought she'd be right."

My eyes go wide and I freeze for the second time in minutes. *Why would Shelly say something like that? Why would she believe a word that comes out of my mother's mouth?*

Shelly slips from my arms. The air around me grows thick and heavy and encapsulates me. Pulls me into a fog. My pulse soars in my ears and drowns out every noise in the house. Until I hear the front door slam. I shake my head and snap back to reality. Run for the door, burst outside and chase after her car as it backs out of the driveway.

"Shelly, no!" I scream after her, desperate for her to come back. For her to park in the driveway, get out of the car, and come back in the house so we can talk about this.

But she doesn't stop. She just keeps driving. Away from me. Away from us. Away from love. With our baby in her belly.

*You promised me. You promised that you'd stay.*

My knees buckle, and I fall to the pavement. Sharp pain radiates through my legs, and I accept every treacherous stab as I curl into a ball. In the middle of my driveway. For all to see.

A chill that has nothing to do with the January temperature blankets me head to toe. Seeps into my bones as numbness begins to wash over me. A numbness I know all too well.

*Shelly, please don't go. Please. You promised you'd never leave. Please... I need you.*

# Abstract Passion

BOOK TWO

*To those who choose to rise up in the toughest of times and fight for yourself, and love.*

# one

## SHELLY

A block from Devlyn's house, I pull over and throw the car in park. Tears spill from my eyes in a violent torrent of pain and confusion. Every muscle in me aches with agony.

*I'm pregnant. No. No, no, no. What the hell am I going to do? What the hell* am *I doing?*

I stare out the windshield with blurred vision and try to collect myself. Try to slow the tears and quiet my irrational mind. Try to stop the convulsive sobs crawling up my throat and spilling from my lips. I close my eyes and shut out the chaos whirling in my head. Eviscerate the words like *ruin* and *over*.

Swiping at my eyes, I wipe away the tears and look in the rearview mirror. Stare down the street behind me as a new version of panic squeezes my heart. As new found alarm constricts my airway.

*Devlyn.*

"What have I done?" I whisper in the cab of my car.

Understandably, he went into shock with the news. So did I. Where he went completely still and utterly speechless, I went into full-on hysteria. My brain short-circuited and I made irrational decisions in the heat of the moment, undoubt-edly hurting him.

*What have I done?*

I steer the Beetle into the next driveway, back out then drive back to Devlyn's house. The small neighborhood block feels miles long as I roll closer and closer. Two houses away, I swipe my cheeks dry and take a deep breath. When I pull into the driveway, I am definitely not prepared for what I see next. Devlyn curled into a tight ball, knees crushed to his chest, and head tucked as he rocks back and forth.

I press the heel of my palm to my chest as the pain beneath my breastbone kicks up to level ten.

Cutting the engine, I bolt from the car and run to his side. Drop down in front of him and gingerly lay a hand on his head. Lightly comb my fingers through his hair and hover over his bundled frame. "Devlyn," I whisper. His tempo and erratic rocking don't pause, so I try again and with more volume. "Devlyn."

He startles on the second call of his name. The constant shaking of his body stops. His head lifts and I am stabbed in the heart by the pain in his puffy, red eyes. The way he regards me, rakes his eyes over the lines of my face, it's as if he is unsure I am real or a figment of his imagination.

I add more weight to my touch on his head and in his hair. Slide my hand slowly down the side of his face. Wiggle my fingers in his hair and scratch them along his scalp. When my palm cups his cheek, he leans his weight into my hand. Closes his eyes. Inhales deeply and holds the breath in his lungs for three of my breaths.

When his eyes reopen, he scrambles forward and wraps me in his arms. "You can't go," he mumbles in my ear, voice strained and raw. "I need you." He hugs me tighter to his chest and kisses my neck. Takes another deep breath and sighs heavily. "Please stay."

My arms squeeze him impossibly tighter as my fingers roam his hair and my lips kiss his shoulder. "Let's go back inside." I lean back and frame his face in my hands. Hold his turbulent gaze as tears blur my vision. "I'm sorry. I wasn't thinking rationally." My lips press to his, again and again. "So, so sorry."

On unsteady legs, we rise from the pavement and wander back into the house. Devlyn's hand firmly holds mine as we wind our way to the living room and sit on the couch. He inches closer until it's difficult to tell where I end and he begins.

"Do you want a drink? Maybe some tea or water or juice," he suggests, tone antsy.

A fresh layer of guilt washes over me. I hate that my first instinct was to run away. To abandon Devlyn. What kind of person does that? *You were scared and so was he. And you both process fear differently.* Internally, I hang my head and berate myself.

"Some tea would be nice," I whisper, and he nods. Then he is off the couch and dashing to the kitchen.

While Devlyn prepares us drinks, I mull over what to say when he reenters the room. I feel the need to apologize until I lose my voice. My actions were spontaneous and foolish, but my head was—is—a scrambled mess. And when I said the words aloud—*I'm pregnant*—Devlyn froze, then thawed, only to freeze again. I went from panicked to unreasonably hysterical in a heartbeat.

So I bolted.

But I can't run away from this, from us. Devlyn or our unborn child. It may be unplanned, it may throw both of our worlds completely off-balance, but that doesn't change anything.

I lay a hand over my still flat belly, close my eyes and take a deep breath. Tell myself it will be okay. That it will all work out. That everything happens when it is meant to.

When my eyes open, I consider how to broach the conversation again. This time with calmer heads and less anxiety. Hopefully.

I am—we are—pregnant and we will be parents before the end of the year. A baby... Devlyn and I are going to have a baby. Another human to love and nurture.

Mentally, I laugh at myself. Leave it to us—the fumbling virgin and almost virgin—to mess up condom usage.

Regardless, it is done. Neither of us can change the past. All we can do now is prepare for the future. But what does that future look like?

Devlyn wanders back into the living room with a mug in each hand. He sets them both on the table, drops next to me on the couch, and wraps me in his arms again. Eliminates every ounce of space between us with a fierce hug. Holds me like he fears I will bolt for the door once more.

And I hate that I did this. Inflicted him with this level of fear. Fractured the trust he has in me. Created doubt that I will stay.

I want to stay. For as long as he will have me, I want to stay.

"Sorry I freaked out. Sorry I didn't say anything right away." He tugs me into his lap and shifts his hold. Shakes his head as he burrows into my chest. "Sorry I froze."

I lay my cheek on his head, close my eyes and comb my fingers through his dark locks. "This isn't all you, so don't you dare try to take all the blame." My arms circle his shoulders and head. Cradle him in my hold. "I'm just as guilty. I shouldn't have packed my bags and jumped in the car." My lips press to his hair. "But I wasn't thinking. Not clearly."

Nose buried in my hair, Devlyn inhales deeply. On the exhale, he leans back and frames my face in his hands. "This is scary, for both of us, but I know we'll get through it." He lowers my lips to his and kisses me with newfound tenderness. "I love you, Shelly."

Tears sting the backs of my eyes. An emotional ball grows thick in my throat. I lift my hands to his cheeks, cup either side of his jaw, and stroke his cheekbones with my thumbs. "I love you, too," I choke out.

Time creeps by, our tea cools on the table, but neither of us move. For now, I simply want to breathe him in. Want to let all the madness from earlier fall away. Want to feel his arms and warmth blanket me in love. Want to give the news of us becoming parents a moment to seep in.

Pregnant. Me. The woman that plans all the big moments in her life. The woman that makes five-year plans and intends to stick to them. I am pregnant. *We* are pregnant. This was definitely not in the five-year plan. Finding love was in the plan, but not becoming a mother.

My mind drifts to the piece of paper pinned to the wall in my apartment bedroom. My current five-year plan. The biggest thing on the list... purchasing Petal and Vine from Elizabeth.

*Oh, god.*

I close my eyes and sink deep inside myself. Try to steady my rapid-fire pulse with steady breaths. Clear the worrisome thoughts invading my head.

Elizabeth won't be upset about the pregnancy. Knowing her, she will rejoice at having another baby to spoil. Be excited that her own grandchild will soon have a playmate. But her happiness won't erase the guilt holding me hostage daily as I delay her retirement. Something she has looked forward to for the past two years.

Will I still be able to purchase Petal and Vine when the time comes? Will I be able to run a business with a newborn in my arms or on my hip? It's silly to think such things. Plenty of women and families manage this all the time. But maybe they planned ahead. Had all their ducks in a row before the pregnancy test came back positive.

Then my thoughts drift to Autumn and Clementine. Autumn's first pregnancy was a surprise. In a matter of months, she wasn't just a pregnant mother with an absentee father, she'd also been kicked out of her home. Abandoned in every way imaginable. Her family had been that cruel.

But she kept going. Never gave up. Moved forward and persevered. Found a place to live and got a job she loved. Thrived when some might fall. And if she can overcome such heavy obstacles—struggles much worse than the possible ones I will face—then I can do this. *We* can do this.

"You're so quiet," Devlyn whispers against my skin.

I shift off his lap, pick up my mug and sip the now cool tea, then take his hand. "Just thinking."

"About?"

Everything. "How much this will change our future."

He nods, then tucks a strand of hair behind my ear. "True." Glass-green irises lock on my blues while his thumb leisurely strokes my cheek. "But I know we'll make it work."

"How?"

For a beat, his eyes drop to my lips before meeting mine again. "I just know." He shrugs. "With you, I believe anything is possible." I raise my brows in question. "Shelly, I have been through hell. In more ways than one." He takes my hand in his, pulls it to his lap and strokes my skin. Slow and steady. His eyes on the movement. "The first round was young love gone astray. Although it sent me in a downward spiral, I'm grateful it happened. Without that loss, I wouldn't appreciate and love you the way I do."

"And the other?"

He sucks in a deep breath and speaks on the exhale. "That hell is still ongoing."

"Your mom?"

He nods. "Yeah. Not sure what to do about her." He shrugs and looks off in the distance. "Things with her... it's been brewing a long time." His chest expands as he takes a deep breath. "I don't want my past with her to affect our relationship or the baby." He trails the pad of his thumb over my knuckles. "Maybe I should talk to someone again. Get advice from a professional or someone who's been in a similar situation."

I squeeze his hand and he brings his attention back to me. "If that's what you want, what you need, I'll support you." I huff out a laugh. "Heck, maybe I should talk to someone." His eyes narrow. "About pregnancy. Motherhood. How to keep moving forward without feeling like I'm pulling everyone under."

"Shelly..."

The backs of my eyes sting and I hate how I am already so emotional. "Well, it's how I feel." I shrug. "Like I'm letting Elizabeth down." Tears well in my eyes. I take a deep breath and try to hold them at bay. "I'm supposed to buy the shop from her after this year." My jaw wobbles back and forth. "How will I be able to do that now? How will I run a business with a baby?"

"Hey," he says, voice barely above a whisper. "We'll figure it out. All of it." He chuckles and I look up. "Maybe I'll need to learn how to run a florist shop too." I furrow my brows. "So you're not doing it alone." He presses a chaste kiss to my lips. "Because you aren't alone, Shelly." Another kiss. "Ever."

"Aren't we just a hot mess," I say on a laugh.

"Wouldn't want to be in a hot mess with anyone else." Devlyn rises from the couch and extends his hand. "Come. Let's go make something for breakfast." His eyes drop to my belly. "Need to feed you two."

And in a blink, life returns to a seminormal state. We bring our mugs to the kitchen and add a touch of hot water. I scramble eggs and cook sausage while Devlyn cuts fresh fruit and toasts bread. We move around the kitchen as if we have done this for years. Been in a relationship. Existed in the same space. Loved each other.

Speaking of space… Suppose our living situation will be one of many conversations we share in the near future. A new knot forms beneath my diaphragm. Twisty and tight.

When the time comes, when we talk about housing and what will work best, I hope we are on the same page. *Please let us be on the same page.*

# *two*

## DEVLYN

Pregnant. Shelly is pregnant. *We* are pregnant. In the not-too-distant future, I will be a dad. Another human will depend on me to care for them. Raise them, feed them, nurture them. Turn them into a respectable human.

Is this within my power? Can I raise a child? Am I capable of molding a mini human into a decent person?

God, I hope so. Just the mere thought of letting someone down—my own child, no less—scares me to death. Has my limbs shaking and palms sweaty.

But Shelly and I will get through this. Together.

While Shelly showers and gets ready for work, I search the internet. One tab loads results of psychologists in the area. A second tab loads results of how condoms fail. And on the third tab is what steps to follow after learning you are pregnant. To some, tabs two and three may seem asinine. To me, I just want answers.

An idiot I am not. Since high school health class had a more than lackluster curriculum on sexual education, I did my own homework. At the time, I had no expectations with where my relationship with Kelsey would go, but I wanted to be prepared either way. Searching videos on how to properly roll on a condom at sixteen was awkward. After watching various oblong fruits and vegetables get sheathed, I considered myself knowledgeable enough. Kelsey never got pregnant, so I must have done something right.

Obviously that all went out the window when I rolled on condoms with Shelly. Either that or one of a handful of other factors came into play.

According to my brief research, the list of reasons why condoms fail is short. Poor manufacturing. Stored at the wrong temperature. Used after expiration date. Torn during removal from the wrapper. Wrong size. Not enough lubricant. Using the wrong lubricant, such as oil-based. The condom was rolled on incorrectly. Not pinching the tip before rolling it on. Snuggling after and going flaccid while still inside your partner.

Of all the reasons listed, two stand out the most. Two slap me in the face, hard. Snuggling and oil-based.

"Damnit," I whisper into the bedroom.

In no way am I upset with the pregnancy or Shelly. But as I read those two common reasons, I hang my head.

One—how am I *not* going to snuggle with Shelly after we have sex? Ever. After the most physically intimate moment, I will cuddle with the woman I love. Every. Damn. Time. Going forward—well, after the baby is born—cuddling will have to be after I pull out. We have time to sort out the finer details.

Two—the body painting. Although the paint never ended up between our legs, it coated my hands and pretty much every other part of our bodies. It's quite possible, I didn't clean everything off of my hands before I put the condom on.

It's quite possible, I sabotaged that moment and unintentionally put us in this situation.

"Everything okay?"

I look up from my phone to see Shelly dressed in a pink, long-sleeve V-neck, light-blue denim jeans and pink Vans. Her toffee locks hang in loose waves down her back, accented with a pink headband. Her face is free of makeup, twilight eyes sparkling as they roam my face, a slight flush on her cheeks.

Not sure how it's possible, but she is more beautiful than ever.

"Yeah," I croak out, then clear my throat. "Yes. Was just researching stuff online."

Her eyes drop to my phone, then lift back to mine. "Find anything noteworthy?"

Yes. No. I shrug. "A little. Wondering what we're supposed to do next."

In slow, measured steps, Shelly closes the distance and steps between my legs at the edge of the bed. Her fingers trail up my chest, my neck, then settle in my hair. My eyes roll back and close as I get lost in her touch. Lost in the whirlwind she stirs beneath my diaphragm. Lost in the new rhythm she sets for my pulse, my breathing.

My hands find her hips. Fingertips bearing down on her denim-clad soft skin. Without second thought, I drag her closer. Sweep the tip of my nose along the column of her throat. Inhale her earthy, sweet floral scent. Allow it to soothe me in the way nothing or no one else has.

Shelly is my solace. The sunshine after the storm. We may be headed into unfamiliar territory, but so long as I have her, everything will work out.

"My guess is we visit a doctor." I lean back and look up at

her. A soft smile tips up the corners of her mouth. "I know a few people to ask."

"Are you worried?"

*What a stupid fucking question.*

Her fingers comb through my hair as her eyes dart between mine. "Yes and no." I tilt my head in question. "It's a definite shock, but I'm surprisingly not worried about pregnancy. What I am worried about is how we'll balance our lives once the baby comes. Between the shop and your art, I worry we won't have the time or energy to do what we love."

I give her hips a gentle squeeze. "We'll find a way."

"How can you sound so sure?"

I laugh without humor. "There isn't much in life I'm sure of, Shelly. But when it comes to you, to us, I believe anything is possible."

A weighted sigh leaves her lips before she drops her forehead to rest on mine. For a moment, we just breathe each other in. Absorb this new path life has put us on. Settle into the realization that every day going forward, our lives will be forever changed. Entwined. Connected.

"I should head to work." She lifts her head and retreats a step. "Elizabeth was already worried when I messaged and said I'd be a little late."

Although I don't want her to go, I nod because she is right. This big news, this baby, will change everything we know, but we can't stop living life. And that includes going to work. "Let me walk you out."

It has only been a few hours since learning Shelly was pregnant, but it feels as if weeks have passed. Our minds are spinning, but we need to slow them as best we can. Try to focus on the day to day. Talk to those who can help us or tell us what to expect. Follow our current routines until we need to adjust them.

This may be new to us, but it's not new. With the countless number of people in Shelly's corner, we will have more support than imaginable. Support and love.

Shelly unlocks her car and slips in behind the steering wheel. She rolls down the window and I lean in to give her a kiss. "Come over after work?"

She nods. "Yeah. May be a little later. I should make up some of my missed time at the shop. Plus, I need more clothes."

"'Kay." I press my lips to hers once more. "Drive safe. See you tonight."

Shelly backs out of the driveway and waves as she drives off. This time I don't fear whether or not she will return. Don't crumble to the ground like a piece of my heart abandoned me. Deep in my bones, I know Shelly will always return. To me, to us.

I walk back into the house, wander to the living room and plop down on the couch. Pulling my phone from my pocket, I unlock it and go to the browser tab with the list of local psychologists. One by one, I click the links and read the doctor's credentials, what their area of focus is, and the frequently asked questions. In my notes app, I jot down the names and contact information of each that sounds like they may be a fit.

Visiting a psychologist is twofold. To face and conquer the demons of my past, and to make sure I don't pass my darkness on to my child. I accept that the darkness in my veins will never go away. It is part of who I am. But learning how to properly cope when it creeps in is essential. Learning how to not let the darkness win is mandatory.

Part of that darkness stems from my upbringing. The intricate ways my mother twisted my way of thinking. The type of love she taught me that wasn't love at all. I wasn't aware of her warped mindset years ago. Didn't know I was as much her pawn as anyone else.

It should hurt… the realization of who she is and what she has done. But it doesn't hurt. That part of me, the piece reserved for Karen Templar, is just numb.

Although I accept this, I want to move past the numbness. Not let her take up residence inside me any more than she already has. I want to let her go. Permanently. Not just for my own mental health, but so I can be the best version of myself for my child.

I refuse to let my past haunt my future.

The idea of my child not knowing part of their family hurts. But my family not assuming a role in this child's life is in the best interest of me, Shelly and our baby. Optimistically, I'd like to think becoming a grandparent may change my mother. That it could flip a switch inside her and she'd become a better person.

But I won't put my child in harm's way. Ever. My mother's poison slithered into my psyche for years. Her tainted words and cold actions deformed a piece of who I am. Skewed how I interpreted connections and life and love. Contributed to a mountain of untold damage. Damage I pray is reversible. Damage I hope to heal, on some level, before our baby is born.

My biggest fear is passing on the toxicity in my blood. The defect in my genetic makeup. Because like it or not, pieces of my mother live inside me. Like it or not, darkness taints my head and heart.

But Shelly… she is the one shining light in my darkness. The light leading me back to a place of love and hope. The light I refuse to let go of or lose.

Because without her light, I fear the darkness will take over. If that happens, I won't survive.

# *three*

## SHELLY

Today feels a week long and it is only noon.

On the way to work, I called Cora and asked if she had plans today. Relief relaxed my bones when she replied with a firm *nope*. But the second she asked if everything was okay, anxiety rippled through me head to toe. I played it off. Said everything was fine. Then asked her to come to the shop for lunch and to bring Clara.

The second I set foot in Petal and Vine, Elizabeth showered me with a barrage of questions. I wanted to answer each and every one of them, but remained tight lipped. Told her I invited Cora for lunch and would answer everything then. Since then, I have felt her concerned gaze on my profile. Have seen her lips part—questions written in the soft lines of her forehead—before she snaps her mouth shut.

It's been torture.

Any minute, my best friend will walk through the front door of Petal and Vine, pushing a stroller and cooing with her angelic daughter. And then, the three of us will dig in on lunch as I spill the beans about my accidental pregnancy.

Since calling her, I've mentally rehearsed more than a

dozen ways to say *I'm pregnant* without saying those two specific words. For some reason, saying more feels necessary.

I hate how I'm riddled with anxiety. About saying the words aloud. About telling my best friend and second mother news that will thrill them. Speaking the words to someone other than Devlyn makes it more real. Tangible. Legit.

Nerves aside, Cora and Elizabeth are the first two women I want to tell.

Mom will find out soon enough, but I need to be in the right headspace to share such big news with her. Hell, Mom doesn't even know about Devlyn. Doesn't know we have been in this weird friends-to-lovers relationship for months. Had she known, I would've heard an endless string of pleas from her. Daily texts asking for updates on my love life. Calls more than once a week, masked as her checking in but really searching for unspoken clues.

*Ugh.*

Sharing the news with Mom will be a blast—insert thick layer of sarcasm. I already hear the long list of questions on her roster.

*"Why didn't you tell me you were dating someone?"*

*"When can I meet him?"*

*"You found someone* and *you're pregnant?"*

*"Did you find a doctor yet?"*

*"Can I go to your appointments?"*

*"How long have you known?"*

*"Why didn't you tell me sooner?"*

*"When are you moving in together?"*

*"Are you planning to get married?"*

Of all the questions I picture my mother asking, the last is the one I fear most. Deep down, Mom only wants the best for me and Micah. But I am fully aware that, in her mind, love equals marriage and babies. If the solid relationship my parents have isn't proof enough, her reasons for starting family dinners more than a year ago is definitely hard evidence.

I love my mother. Love her big heart and desire to see everyone happy. Love that dreamy look she gives Dad. I only wish she understood happiness comes in different forms.

When Micah and Peyton announced they wouldn't start a family, Mom all but lost her shit. She didn't understand how or why they didn't want children. Because Nicole Reed doesn't look beyond her own experiences. Can't fathom anything other than her own way of life being great. With Micah and Peyton not wanting children, I pray her perspective changes.

The bell over the front door jingles. I plaster on a big smile and mentally prepare myself for the most adult conversation I've had in years. Then sag against the arrangement table when a man steps around the pails of loose flowers.

He holds up two large paper bags. "Delivery from See Ew Thai."

I step around the table, dig into the pocket of my apron, hand him a cash tip then take the bags. "Thank you."

"Have a great day, miss."

As the man exits the shop, Cora walks in with baby Clara in her beast of a stroller.

*Oh god. Something else to worry over. All the gadgets and gizmos we will need for a baby.*

"Auntie Shelly must have big news if she's sweet-talking Mommy with Asian food," Cora coos at Clara as she sidles up to the arrangement table. Eyes wide, Clara slaps at a toy dangling inches from her face.

"Guilty," I say, bending over the stroller and lightly

pinching Clara's toes. "How's my favorite niece today? Is Mommy spoiling you rotten?"

Clara makes an unintelligible noise and we both laugh. Elizabeth exits the storage room and gives Cora a warm, welcoming hug before removing her granddaughter from the stroller.

For a moment, I watch the three of them. Revel in their smiles and sweet talk. Relish the ease of this new change in their lives. Envy how simple Cora makes motherhood look, although I've heard the struggles she experienced.

My best friend may be new to parenting, but she does it like a pro. She isn't back to working full-time, but has taken a couple of small, scenic jobs this month. Her way of easing back into the norm at her own pace. Outdoor photo shoots of places and not people. That way, she can bring Clara along and not worry.

"It's not ideal, but I'd like to have lunch with all of us. At least for a few minutes," I say as I start carrying the bags to the back. Cora and Elizabeth exchange a look of concern. "I'll set things up at the table. We should be able to hear the bell if anyone comes in."

Before either of them gets a word in, I step into the office-slash-break room and set the bags down. One by one, I pull out the food boxes and set them on the table. Get everything in place. Ready for them to stuff their mouths while I confess my pregnancy and beg for advice.

I peek my head around the doorframe and spot Cora and Elizabeth fawning over Clara. Warmth spreads in my chest at the sight.

*Later this year, that will be me and Devlyn.*

Tears sting the backs of my eyes, but I blink them away before they well and fall. I inhale deeply in an attempt to settle the nerves fluttering in my belly. "Ready when you are," I say.

Cora parks Clara back in the stroller before she and Elizabeth wander into the break room. I point out their places at the table on either side of mine. We take our seats and open the boxes. Elizabeth dives into her pad thai while Cora bites down on a spring roll. The moment their mouths are full, I open mine.

"I'm pregnant," I blurt out.

To no surprise, both of them go into coughing fits. Okay, so waiting until they had their mouths full was a *bad* idea. I thought it would be a great way to keep them from screaming or squealing or blurting out words I'm not prepared to hear. Obviously, the method to madness is actual madness. Oops.

After a few hard slaps to the chest and half a bottle of water later, Cora's skin looks a little less red and blotchy. Elizabeth continues to cough, but at least it's calming down.

"Sorry," I say on a wince.

Cora lays a hand on mine and shakes her head. "Don't apologize," she croaks out, then coughs to clear her throat more. "I knew something was up, but I didn't think it was that."

"But you said…" I furrow my brows. "At the hospital yesterday…" I drop my gaze to her box of garlic tofu. "You were joking…"

Why the hell can I not finish a damn thought aloud?

"Shell, it *was* a joke." She squeezes my hand and I lift my line of sight back to hers. "With Clara born only months ago, Ryker yesterday… I would've said it to Peyton, but I know she and Micah aren't planning to have kids." She shakes her head subtly. "Shell, I didn't mean anything by it." Concern mars her forehead. "Is that why you ran from the room? Why you disappeared?"

"Not just from what you said." I shake my head. "But it kind of sent me into a thought spiral. Before I knew it, I felt nauseous. So I ran for the bathroom."

The three of us sit at the table as I recant the rest of the evening and earlier this morning. My initial shocked state and Devlyn's after the call from the hospital. My moment of panic when Devlyn froze. How I thought that he didn't want to do this, that he couldn't do this. Be together. Have a baby. Any of it.

And then I tell them when the moment of realization hit. While I sat on the side of the road and cried until it struck me what I'd done. That I just got in my car and left. That I ignored Devlyn as he hollered for me to stay. Then when I turned around and drove back, how I found him in the drive-way. Cold and shaking and in full crisis mode.

That was the second time I found Devlyn curled in on himself. I pray it is the last.

He looked so scared. In pain. And in that moment, I hated the spontaneous choice I'd made. Getting in my car and leaving had been irrational and juvenile. To just walk away without talking more, without listening…

I will never do that again. To him or us.

The bell rings out front and Elizabeth rises from her chair. "I'll be back." She bends and kisses my crown. "Keep talking, sweetheart."

Not a second after Elizabeth leaves the room, Cora rises from her chair, yanks me from mine, and pulls me into the tightest hug. "I don't know how you expect me to feel, Shell." She loosens her hold and inches back to look me in the eye. "But I'm happy for you." The corners of her lips turn up as she smiles brightly. "Things may be crazy for a bit, but you will be an amazing mother."

I purse my lips as my brows shoot up. "You say that now, but this gal"—I point to myself—"is freaking out. A lot."

She drops her hold on me and we park ourselves back in the chairs. Cora spears a piece of broccoli and tofu while I stab curried chicken. For a moment, we sit in amicable silence. We eat lunch like we would any other day. Me and Cora. Two best friends spending time together.

"I freaked out too," Cora says after a few bites. "Ask Gavin. We'd been back together barely two years. Irrational as it was, I thought he might leave again." She laughs without humor. "Although we were happy—are happy—I thought an unplanned pregnancy would send him away." She shakes her head, her eyes glassy. "But it didn't, Shell. He was so happy. So damn happy. I'd never seen him light up like that. It was that look, that one moment… I knew we'd be okay." Setting her fork down, she reaches for my hand again. "And you will be too."

I tighten my hold on her hand. "How can you be so sure?" I whisper-ask.

Her smile brightens the room. "Because he chased after you. Asked you not to leave. Cried in the driveway when you left. Then he opened his arms up again when you returned. He took you into the house and you talked. You made breakfast and plans."

For the umpteenth time today, my eyes burn with the promise of tears. When I walked out Devlyn's front door in a fit of anxiety, I was one step closer to messing all of this up. Ready to throw in the towel without giving him a chance. I didn't get far, thank goodness. It's almost as if fate intervened.

As if something bigger than me stopped me from making a huge mistake.

"What do I do now?"

Cora points to my lunch. "Eat." She laughs. "Take a minute to breathe and soak it all in. Yes, it's big. Huge. Life changing." She picks up her own fork and takes a bite. "But it's also incredible, Shell." She looks over at Clara sleeping in her stroller. "There's good and bad days. And yours will be different than mine." Her eyes find mine again. "But it's all worth it. My first piece of advice—the only one I'll give today—is to talk to your gynecologist. If they're an OB-GYN, you're golden. If not, they'll direct you where to go next." She sips her water. "And the rest of us will always be here. You have us. And Devlyn."

For a first-time mother of an infant, Cora is giving me a confidence boost. She and Gavin still navigate being new parents, but her calm reassurances settle some of the anxiety. Instinct told me she and Elizabeth were the right people to tell first. And who knows, I may wait until after my first official doctor's appointment to mention anything to Mom. That will give Devlyn and I time to adjust a little more before Mom shrieks in joy and asks unnerving questions.

"Thank you," I say. "Somehow, I knew you'd alleviate some of my worry."

"You never have to thank me, Shell. That's what best friends are for. You'd do the same for me in a heartbeat." It's true, I would. "So, when are you telling Mama Reed?"

I wince. "Uh, not for a bit. I want to see the doctor first. Give myself and Devlyn a little more time to process this before the big reveal." I shake my head on a laugh. "Mom doesn't even know we're dating. Doesn't know Devlyn exists. So, not only will I be saying, '*hey Mom, meet my boyfriend,*

*Devlyn.'* I will also be saying, *'and by the way, we're preg-nant. Woo!'* I close my eyes and take a deep breath. "Swear to god, if the first thing out of her mouth is wanting to know when we'll get married, I will lose my shit." I startle and look to Clara. "I mean cool. Lose my cool."

Cora laughs. "Shell, it's okay. Clara has no clue what we're saying right now. Down the road, yes, the alternate swear words will be in full force. For now, you're fine." She scoops up another bite. "And I promise not to say anything to anyone else. Not until you give the green light."

Elizabeth walks back into the room and joins us at the table. "What'd I miss?"

Over noodles, rice and veggies, I share with Elizabeth everything I did with Cora. She, too, promises not to say anything until I give the go-ahead. Then she hugs me, tighter and harder than ever. She assures me everything will be fine. She tells me not to worry about the shop, that she will be here until I am ready and able to handle the change. Of course, I cry. Because today is the day to cry until my eyes puff like clouds.

And when lunch ends, I feel lighter and more stable on my feet.

After the call this morning, it felt like someone had grabbed me by the ankles and held me upside down. Now, I feel strong enough to walk. To move forward. To handle this big change in my life with more confidence.

# *four*
## DEVLYN

"How does that make you feel?"

I love and loathe therapy. Getting in my car twice a week to drive to an office across town to talk about my feelings, about my past, about what makes my blood boil and my mind abandon reality is just… awkward and relieving and unnerving.

I thoroughly enjoy the opportunity to vent. To expel the darkness that has plagued me longer than I allowed myself to realize. To shed weight I didn't realize I carried.

What I don't like is the aftermath. The emotions stirred up during each session. Emotions I walk out the door with and sort through in the days between sessions. Emotions I must process, but don't want to expose to Shelly.

The first session after my consultation, I left the office in a mass of confusion. We'd barely scratched the surface, but my mother had been a huge topic of discussion. It *hurt* to talk about her. Not just my head, but also my heart. Because the more I talk about her, the more it registers how much she *doesn't* love me. Her definition of love is warped. Whatever makes her feel important, puts her in the spotlight, has people fawning over her… that is her version of love. For Karen Templar, love has a price tag.

How sick and twisted. And sad.

During our first session, after my need to pause and take several deep breaths, Dr. Prince had said, *"You can't move past this if you don't process it."* I have to let in the feelings I concealed for years. Unearth all the memories that once seemed loving and innocent, so I can dissect and process them with a fresh perspective.

So that is what I have been doing. Processing.

And processing hurts. Profusely.

"Afraid," I answer.

Dr. Prince tilts his head and reads my expression a moment before jotting something on the notepad in his lap. "Can you elaborate? Share why you feel afraid."

Elaborate. I don't *want* to elaborate. But I *need* to open up and expand. Spread my wings. Peel back the layers and expose my heart. Let the poison spill from my veins so I can move on, move past my fears. Move forward.

My eyes shift to the window, to the somber gray sky through the cracked wooden blinds. To the semibare branches of a tree. The day as moody as I feel. For two deep breaths, I close my eyes. Give in to my fears and let them take over. Give myself permission to voice the thoughts haunting me since learning Shelly was pregnant.

*I am safe here.*

"What if I become her?" I open my eyes and meet Dr. Prince's gaze. My fingers toy with the bottom of my hoodie while my leg bounces uncontrollably. "What if I do to my own child what my mother has done to me? Suppress them.

Make them feel less important, less than human. Worthless. Trivial."

Dr. Prince scribbles on his notepad. "Tell me an occasion when you felt suppressed or worthless."

A fist wraps around my heart. Squeezes the pounding organ until it quivers, until it begs for relief. I rock slowly in place on the sofa. Take a deep breath. Then another.

I hate this. Digging up my demons and letting them trample over my soul. Letting them sink their claws a little deeper. Chip away at what heart I have left before I vanquish them.

I get it. The process is a necessary evil. But *fuck*... it rips me apart.

"When I was eight, my school hosted an art fair for students in third through fifth grade. We'd been working on a special project since the start of the school year. Each student drew a word from a hat and was told to create something that made them think of that word. We could draw or paint or paste magazine clippings. Whatever we had access to. Whatever called to us. My word, ironically, was love."

I clamp my lips between my teeth, take a deep breath then continue.

"Love means something different to each of us. My eight-year-old brain had difficulty processing the term. Had difficulty explaining love in the form of art. Even at that age, art was the one thing I loved most." The backs of my eyes sting. "I don't think I really knew human love. I had a warped perception of it."

Leaning forward, I swipe my bottled water from the table and take a sip. "On the night of the art fair, I was giddy for my mother to see my artwork. Far back as I can recall, she's worked in museums. Art existed in her life each day. I'd been so proud of my mixed-medium painting. The clipping of two people smiling at each other. I'd added various shades of red. Painted over the magazine page around the people." I laugh without humor. "For my age, it was remarkable. My teacher raved over the piece and instilled me with so much hope. Told me how talented I was. That I'd be an incredible artist one day. Have my work on display for the masses." I tip my head back and blink a few times before leveling my gaze. "That teacher made me feel loved. More than my own mother."

I lift my hand to my hoodie strings and fiddle with the strands. "We made our way around the room and my mother criticized each piece harshly. As if children should be perfectionists. As if children shouldn't create art unless it will win awards and sell for thousands of dollars." My vision glazes over. "She didn't even know she was degrading my piece until she finished speaking."

The only words I remember hearing that night were trash and sloppy and hideous.

"When her eyes dropped to the small paper placard and she saw my name, I'd never seen my mother so disgusted. Her lip curled as she looked down on my wilting frame. She said, *'I'm disappointed, Devlyn. I expected better from you. You know what real art looks like. I never want to see such trash again. It's embarrassing. You're a Templar. Remember that next time you pick up a brush or pencil. Don't throw my name in the garbage.'"*

The first round of tears this session spills down my cheeks. The salty drops sear my skin as they trail to my chin. I swipe them away and shift my gaze to the window again. To the gloomy sky that matches my mood. Mercurial and lusterless and meh.

"I know sharing that moment wasn't easy, Devlyn. Thank you for being brave enough to share it with me." I nod and swing my gaze back to him. "Processing years of pain will take time. But each time you choose to come here and speak with me, it's a step forward. One step closer to healing." His pen scratches against the pad of paper. "How've things been with Shelly?"

My soul sighs and breathes easier with the subject change. The heavy thoughts from a moment ago drift off. Fade to background. Make room for the light to enter. My peace. My heart.

"Great." My cheeks sting as my lips stretch into a wide smile. "We have our first appointment with the doctor today."

"That's wonderful, Devlyn. Have you and Shelly talked further about the future? What either of you want it to look like?"

At the end of my Thursday session last week, Dr. Prince gave me a *homework assignment*. To sit down with Shelly and talk about my feelings. Not just the way I feel about her, but how I feel about all the changes happening in both our lives.

He also asked me to voice my desires. What I want my future with Shelly to look like.

Three months have passed since Shelly and I officially started dating. The two months prior were a bit rocky. Unstable due to my uncertainty more than hers. But in the past five months, I have never been more in tune with someone. More certain of what I want. More confident of the path I want to walk in life, with Shelly at my side every step of the way.

What I don't know is if Shelly is ready to walk the same path.

"Yes and no." When I don't expand, Dr. Prince asks me to

elaborate. Secretly, I think *elaborate* is his favorite word. "I told her I want to be involved during the pregnancy. That I want to be there for her. The things left unsaid, well… I fear she may panic if I say them aloud."

"Like what?"

My fingers toy with my hoodie strings once more. "Am I crazy for wanting to ask her to move in? Is it too soon in our relationship?" I zero in on the fraying end of the string and sigh. "I don't want her to think the only reason I'm asking is because she's carrying our baby." I drop my chin to my chest and close my eyes. "It's not the only reason."

As many notes as Dr. Prince writes during our sessions, he'll undoubtedly have a novel before the end of the year. His notes are a point of reference, a way to chart my growth. I know this. He told me this. But sometimes I wonder if he takes medication after our sessions. If my long list of issues is too much for even him. He never seems put off or out of sorts, but I still wonder how he manages to breathe after such intense talks.

"First of all, not all relationships evolve at the same pace. Some couples wait years before living together. Some want to marry beforehand. And others move in together and get married in under six months. No two relationships are the same, Devlyn. There is no rule book on when to take the next step. Whether it's sex or cohabitating or nuptials. You and Shelly have to go at the pace that feels right for you both. In order to know the pace, you have to communicate." He glances at his watch and notes we only have another five minutes. "Before our next session, I'd like you to talk more with Shelly. Voice your fears with her. As many as you feel comfortable sharing. Then ease into the conversation about where you want your future to go with her."

*Expose my fears and tell Shelly I want her to move in.*

Nausea rolls in my stomach. My mind screams to back down. My heart begs me to wait. To hit pause. Because the last time I was so utterly vulnerable to someone I loved, they squashed me with pointy heels.

"I'll do my best," I say with a nod, as if to assure myself.

"There's no pressure, Devlyn." He sets the pen and pad of paper on the table. "If you go to bring up the future, but the timing doesn't feel right, drop it. This isn't a race. There's no prize for reaching the finish line before others. This is about progress. About letting go of what doesn't serve you and making room for what you want in your life. It won't happen overnight. And you shouldn't expect it to."

*Let go of what doesn't serve me.* I never thought about anything that way, but I like how it sounds.

"Thanks, Dr. Prince."

We both rise from our seats and he walks me out. "See you in a few days, Devlyn."

I unlock the car, slip into the driver's seat and crank the engine. While the cab warms, I recall Dr. Prince's words. *"This is about progress. About letting go of what doesn't serve you and making room for what you want in your life."*

To let go of my mother and all the subliminal pain she inflicted over the years, I need to rehash the memories that hold me prisoner. The memories that diminish and suffocate. The memories that make me feel less than worthy. That makes me feel undeserving. That hinder me from moving forward, from growing.

I need to let her go so I can let Shelly in fully. Let her shine her love and light on all the dark places. Cast away the demons and shadows. Replace the hurt with affection and passion. Help me heal and grow and move forward.

And if I am lucky enough, Shelly will say yes. When I ask her to move in, she will agree with my favorite smile and a resounding yes.

# *five*

SHELLY

Think I'm going to be sick.

I pause at the entrance of the doctor's office. Brace my hand on the wall. Take a deep, cleansing breath. Then another. Close my eyes and allow the cool air to settle the chaos in my stomach. After a third deep breath, the nausea subsides. A little. Enough for me to stand straighter and trudge forward.

Do all medical facilities use the same lemon-scented bleach?

*Ugh.* This is going to be a long, *however many months I have left* pregnancy.

At least I haven't thrown up since the day at the hospital. Puking is the worst. The. Worst. Need someone to hold your hair while you hurl into the porcelain throne? I am *not* the gal to ask. Don't care how tight we are, don't care how many years we have known each other, if you bow to the porcelain throne, I will run the other direction.

I check in at the reception desk and am handed several pages on a clipboard with a pen.

When I called to set the appointment with my regular gynecologist—who also specializes in obstetrics, lucky me—

the woman on the phone told me new paperwork is necessary. Standard form updates plus new documents for the pregnancy appointments and a more thorough family history.

I'd rather fill out new paperwork than have to visit a new doctor.

Halfway down the first page, the door to the office opens and Devlyn walks in. The remaining bit of my nausea vanishes at the sight of him.

Slipping off his sunglasses, our gazes lock. A brilliant smile lights his face as he walks in my direction. Warmth embraces me in an everlasting hug. He takes the seat next to mine. Curls his fingers around my elbow, leans in and presses his lips to mine.

Damn, I will never tire of him. Not the smile he reserves only for me. Not his gaze that heats my blood. Nor the simple yet potent way he caresses my skin with his masterful hands.

Not sure if I can pinpoint what it is about Devlyn that calls to my soul, but he quiets the noise. Grants a sense of peace I didn't know existed until him. Bestows me with love I hoped was possible, but never experienced until he entered my world. And he just makes me feel… alive.

"Am I late?"

I shake my head as I work to calm my heart. "No. I got here a few minutes early to fill out paperwork." I hold up the clipboard. "Should finish before they call us back."

"Need help?"

"Maybe with health questions when I get to the family history section." He nods, then sits back and wraps an arm around my shoulders. His thumb paints small circles on my upper arm, distracting me from my task.

*Devlyn is my favorite distraction.*

I trudge through most of the paperwork on my own. When

I reach the family history page, Devlyn chimes in with what he knows about his family. High blood pressure on his father's side. Ovarian cancer on his mother's side. For the most part, my family history is boring. Grandma Reed had diabetes, but not until later in life. Other than that, our slate is pretty clean.

"Shelly," a female voice calls out. I peer up from the clipboard to see a nurse at the doorway leading to the patient rooms. "Come on back." Devlyn and I rise from the seats and walk toward the nurse hand in hand. She steps aside to let us pass, then closes the door behind us. "Hi Shelly, I'm Ramona. Don't think we've met yet." She extends her hand to me, then Devlyn. Next, she hands me a small plastic cup with a sealed lid. "We need to collect a sample before heading back."

This part of the visit isn't new.

I take the cup from Ramona, ask Devlyn to hold my purse, then enter the restroom to the right. Once the cup is full and the lid secured, I set the sample in the pass-through box in the room, wash up and exit.

Outside the restroom, Ramona has me step on a scale, measuring my weight and height. After noting the numbers in my chart, she walks us to the patient room and closes the door behind us. Paper crinkling echoes in the room as I sit on the exam table. Devlyn parks himself in the extra seat off to the side while Ramona sits on a wheeled stool after washing her hands.

"How has your health been since your last visit, Shelly?" Ramona asks as she wraps a blood pressure cuff around my bicep.

"Good. No changes. Except the obvious," I say on a nervous laugh.

She peels the cuff away and jots numbers down in my

chart. "Blood pressure looks good." Grabbing the thermometer from the counter, she holds it a couple inches from my forehead until it beeps. "Temp is normal."

Her warm gaze lifts from the stack of papers in my file and meets mine. Over the next few minutes, Ramona asks a series of questions. Most of which I am used to answering at my regular checkups. Today, though, new questions get added to the mix. Questions about sexual partners and methods of protection and what changes I have noticed in diet, sleep and mood. The questions aren't awkward or uncomfortable. Devlyn knows the answers as much as I do.

Ramona rises from the stool and tucks my chart under her arm. "Dr. Webster will be in shortly." Then she exits the room.

Wood squeaks against the linoleum as Devlyn scoots his chair closer to the exam table. He wraps my hand in his, then lifts it to his lips. "Doing okay?"

My blues lock onto his greens as a small smile plumps my cheeks. My shoulders lift in a half shrug. "Yeah. It's just a lot." I lift my free hand to cup his cheek and he leans into my touch. "But we got this."

He rotates his head and kisses the inside of my palm. "We do."

A soft knock on the door interrupts our quiet moment. Dr. Webster enters the room with a cheery smile on her face. Not a single visit to her office goes by without her beaming disposition.

Before I found Dr. Webster, I'd visited a couple other gynecologists in the area. Of the three doctors, Dr. Marianne Webster made me the most comfortable. Her office and staff were warm, inviting and relaxed yet still professional. Every time I walked through the doors, I never felt like a number or just another patient to cash in on. And that stood out the most.

"Hi, Shelly." She smiles brighter then shifts her attention to Devlyn. "And you must be Dad. I'm Dr. Webster." She extends her hand and Devlyn freezes for two breaths before taking it.

*Dad. She just called him Dad. Cue the waterworks.*

"Devlyn," he chokes out before clearing his throat. "Excuse me. Devlyn. It's nice to meet you."

The next thirty minutes are filled with more questions— from Dr. Webster and us—answers and too much information. Of all the details she shares, one piece sticks out the most. Roots itself deep in my memory. Imprints itself on my heart. My expected due date.

*September twenty-first.*

The moment Dr. Webster says the date, Devlyn squeezes my hand a little tighter and we share similar smiles.

Dr. Webster tells us the date can change from one appointment to the next, but based on dates in my paperwork, September twenty-first falls in line. Next, she goes over what to expect in the coming months. The number of appointments and what to expect during visits at specific week markers. When she will order the first ultrasound. Changes I will experience, if I haven't already, physically as well as emotionally and mentally. She discusses diet and exercise and creating healthy habits now. Vitamins and changes I should experience in the first trimester.

Information overload is an understatement, yet I feel as if I need more.

She removes a gown from the cabinet, asks me to dress down for a pelvic exam and excuses herself from the room. While I disrobe, Devlyn looks at his fumbling hands in his lap. Although we've had sex several times, his timidity as I peel off my clothes in the doctor's office comes as a surprise.

Back on the table, I reach for his hand and lace our fingers together. "Doing okay?"

He nods and gives my fingers a gentle squeeze. "Yeah. Just trying to remember everything she said." His eyes widen for a beat. "It's a lot of information."

I chuckle and he joins in. "Agreed. Lucky for us, we'll walk out with a folder full of brochures."

Leaning forward, Devlyn kisses my temple. "Love you."

I tighten my hold on him as his words wrap around my heart. "Love you, too."

Dr. Webster performs a routine pelvic exam and Pap smear since my last appointment was more than six months ago. Since I had a blood panel done at the hospital and provided a copy with my paperwork, I luckily get to bypass more needle sticks.

Just when I think Dr. Webster is going to exit the room and let me redress, she rolls a cart closer to the exam table and grabs a tube of gel.

"Seeing as you're roughly five to six weeks, I don't want to set any expectations." My brows pinch together as she holds the gel tube over my abdomen. "Going to see if we can hear a heartbeat yet."

My own pulse kicks up a notch and whooshes behind my ears. In my periphery, Devlyn rises from his seat and inches closer to the exam table. His hand seeks mine once more and clutches it tightly.

*This is really happening. I'm pregnant. With Devlyn's baby. Our baby. And we may hear a heartbeat.*

"Just relax," Dr. Webster says, and I take a deep breath. "This might be a little chilly."

She squeezes a dollop of gel onto my lower abdomen and I startle. Devlyn strokes his thumb over my knuckles. Back and forth. Again and again. Settling my nerves and steadying my heart.

Dr. Webster picks up a wand attached to the machine on the cart and presses it to the gel on my belly. For three breaths, the room falls completely silent. Not a peep as the goop smears my belly. And then a strange but quiet, pulsing sound filters through the air.

*Whoosh. Whoosh. Whoosh.*

Such a strange sound. Like the rapid push and pull of water.

I look up at Dr. Webster in question. Her beaming smile is all the answer I need. The whooshing sound…

"Is that?" My gaze shifts to Devlyn and I see the same question in his eyes.

"Your baby's heartbeat?" Dr. Webster finishes and we both nod. "It is." She moves the wand and the sound intensifies. "Definitely six to seven weeks along." Then the sound vanishes as she removes the wand. She wipes the gel from my belly and closes the front of the gown. "I'll step out and let you change. Then we'll go over what to expect at your next appointment before you leave."

After I redress, she comes back in with a large envelope filled with brochures and resources. She shares what to expect at my next appointment in a month. And before she steps away from the checkout area, she gives me a brief hug and congratulates us once more.

With my next appointment scheduled, Devlyn and I exit the office hand in hand. He walks me to my car and pauses near the driver's side door.

"Hungry?"

My stomach grumbles as I say, "Yes."

"Why don't you head to the house and I'll stop at the store. Any requests?"

I shake my head. "Surprise me."

Devlyn dips down and presses his lips to mine. "I'll be quick."

As I settle in the driver's seat, Devlyn jogs to his car. I wave to him as he drives off. And then, for a moment, I sit in the parking lot and absorb the reality of today.

Yes, I knew I was pregnant. But after hearing the heartbeat… the reality of it *really* sank in.

"I'm going to be a mom," I whisper to myself. My hands settle on my lower abdomen and cradle the still flat area. I breathe deeply and close my eyes. "Wow."

Then, my little bliss bubble pops.

Time to buck up and tell Mom. *Please… someone save me.*

# *Six*

## DEVLYN

"I'm sorry, what?"

A loud clang vibrates the air as Shelly's fork falls to her plate. Her brows pinch at the middle and eyes narrow as she regards me across the table. My heart beats a vicious rhythm while I internally cringe.

I set my fork down, take a deep breath and lift my line of sight to hers.

*Remember Dr. Prince's suggestion. Talk with Shelly. Share my fears. Tell her my desires for the future.*

"I'd like us to move in together," I say, my voice quieter. Smaller. Meek. My palms damp and fingers twitchy as I swipe them over my denim-clad thighs.

The room fills with eerie silence. Across the table, Shelly sits frozen in place. No shift in posture or facial expression. Her eyes still on mine, but unmoving. Unyielding. I don't sense anger—which settles my anxiety a degree or two—but, for the life of me, I can't pick up what exactly she *is* feeling. Her stillness, her voicelessness, the uneasy energy around her… it has me concerned. Off balance. Scared. Lost.

If I were in my studio upstairs, painting her in this very

moment, she'd be haloed in burnt orange—a color I don't typically associate with Shelly. Not due to indignation. No, the color would represent the disorientation pulsing off her. And perhaps a hint of fear.

*It's okay. I'm afraid too.*

"Please say something," I say just above a whisper.

Her chest rises and falls as she inhales a deep breath. She licks her lips, traps them between her teeth a moment, then releases them on a swallow.

"Devlyn, I…" Her eyes lose focus for two breaths before she blinks a few times. "Isn't it too soon?"

I twist my hands in my lap beneath the table and ask myself the same question for the hundredth time since learning Shelly was pregnant. *How soon is too soon to live together?* Dr. Prince said there are no written guides to dictate when couples take the next step. Only we determine our time line. Our future.

My shoulders rise and fall. "It doesn't feel wrong."

Wanting Shelly in every aspect of my life has never felt so *right*. Is moving in together after dating three months a premature decision? Probably. Considering I let no one in for four years after Kelsey, this change may be deemed irrational and foolish and swift. A decision made in the heat of the moment. An open invitation to doom our relationship.

But I don't care what other people think. I only care what Shelly thinks. What she wants.

"Can I think about it?"

Every joy-filled cell in my body plummets. Wilts. Turns cold. "Yeah. Sure. Of course."

What else can I say? Shelly is her own person. Makes her own decisions. I need to let her make this decision as well. Having a baby together doesn't automatically equal cohabita tion. It doesn't mean our romantic relationship will last forever.

But I want it all with her.

Taking a deep breath, I remind myself that she loves me and I love her. Her asking for time to make a decision is better than her shooting the idea down immediately. Not like I haven't mulled over the idea for days. Only fair that I let her do the same.

*She could've said no and walked out the door. Give her time.*

After a beat of silence, she picks up her fork and I mimic the action. We eat dinner in companionable silence for a few bites. In my periphery, she sips her water, then gingerly sets down the glass. Her fingertips swirl over condensation droplets, her eyes zeroed in on the action.

"While I consider the idea of moving in" —I lock onto her mesmerizing eyes and stop chewing— "will you think about meeting my parents?"

The bite of chicken in my mouth lodges in my throat. I smack my chest and cough violently. My face and neck and chest go hot as I attempt to dislodge the food from the wrong pipe.

"Oh god."

Shelly evacuates her chair and dashes to my side. *Whack.* Her palm smacks between my shoulder blades with force. *Whack. Whack.* I cough harder and the food clears my windpipe.

"Are you okay?"

I nod as my lungs burn and beg for air. Grabbing her hand, I bring it to my lips and kiss her between coughs. "I'm—" *Cough, cough.* "Fine." Tears spill down my cheeks as I hold up a finger, asking her to give me a moment.

Her hand rubs small circles between my shoulder blades. The gentle motion calming, soothing. And soon, my lungs settle. My throat stills. I take a sip of water. Then another.

"Better?"

I nod. "Yeah." My voice like froggy sandpaper. I swallow a bigger gulp of water. "Much."

Shelly settles back in her chair and shakes her head. "I seem to have a talent for saying things at the wrong time." I cock my head as my brows scrunch together. "When I told Cora and Elizabeth I was pregnant, they both nearly choked on their lunch." She rolls her eyes and laughs under her breath. "Really should work on *when* to say certain things."

Setting my glass down, I lay a hand on the table, palm up. She places hers atop mine and I sigh.

My skin warms and tingles at the point of contact. Our connection a live wire. Buzzing. Sparking. White hot and a constant burst of light.

The pulse never dulls. The magnitude never fades or shrinks. If anything, what I feel for Shelly, the connection we share, it continually expands. Like the birth of a new galaxy. Mighty and endless.

This… her hand in mine… this is all I need.

"It's okay. Maybe next time, ease into it." We laugh until the reason I started choking circles back. "I'd love to meet your parents, Shelly. Whenever you're ready. Wish mine were worth meeting," I say with a hint of solemnity.

Shelly squeezes my hand and my eyes dart to hers. "Me too."

We finish dinner and talk about the first of many visits to the doctor's office. After I clear the table, Shelly and I snuggle on the couch and watch television. Her head on my shoulder, it isn't long before she falls asleep and I carry her to bed.

As she sleeps in my arms, I lie in the dark and mentally paint a picture of what our life will be like. When the baby comes and the years that follow.

I see it all so clearly. As if it already exists, but I have yet to live it.

Shelly and I existing in the same space. Living together. Loving each other. I see her brilliant smile and flushed cheeks as we hold our child for the first time. How she will turn my house into a home. Paint the walls with her warmth. Add small touches of joy and hope. Introduce a level of love that only exists within her. Love I want, crave, live for each day.

The mental picture soothes my soul in an unfamiliar way. Settles the unease I have over Shelly not instantly agreeing to move in together.

And as I drift off to sleep, one thought plays on repeat. I will do whatever it takes to make the image in my head a reality.

Whatever it takes.

# seven

## SHELLY

Why does it feel like every day something major happens? Where the hell did all the simple days go? Get up, go to work, eat, sleep, rinse, repeat—plus time with friends and Devlyn.

Since the day my phone rang and the nurse from the hospital told me I was pregnant, every day is filled with some form of chaos.

Okay, not exactly chaos. But is there an actual term for the craziness scale? Lunacy level. Madness meter. Deranged degree. Psycho scale. There is probably some technical term, but I have no clue what it is.

Most of my life, I have been in the chill zone. Low key. Easy, peasy, lemon squeezy. But now... now everything is pure madness. Constantly midscale or higher.

Tonight, life is reaching the high end of the scale. And I'm not sure how much more crazy I can handle. Tonight is dinner night with the family. With my *when will you get married and have two-point-five kids* mom and my dad that looks at her as if she does no wrong.

Someone... *please* help me. Help us.

Poor Devlyn is sweaty and pale, and it's maybe sixty

degrees on my parents' front porch as we hesitate to step inside. Thank god, Micah and Peyton are already here. Although neither of them know about the pregnancy, at least they have met Devlyn. Not everything will be a complete shock with them.

I lace my fingers with Devlyn's and inhale deeply as I glance up at him. "You ready for this?"

His eyes meet mine as he squeezes my fingers tighter. "Yes. No." He pinches his eyes tight for a beat. "Yes. Your parents are a million times better than mine. Guess I'm just worried about your dad or brother choking me after the news." He gives me a sheepish smile.

Pushing up on my tiptoes, I kiss his cheek. "I'll keep you safe." A promise I plan to always keep.

"Pinkie promise?" He offers me his little finger.

Without hesitation, I hook my pinkie with his. "Promise."

Devlyn has yet to divulge all the secrets of his past. Can't say I blame him. It's a lot for him to unpack, to relive. But he has shared bits and pieces, and that is enough. The strength it must take to share such truths... his bravery astounds me daily.

In twenty-two years, he has endured a lifetime of heartache. Most of which occurred in the four walls he called home. The saddest part of all, he didn't comprehend how catastrophic his homelife had been until he left for college. Until he lived in and experienced the world. Gained new peers that came from loving homes. Met friends' parents and professors that never said an untoward or demeaning statement.

Devlyn had been hurt in ways I will never fathom. I don't know and couldn't possibly understand the hardships he experienced. With all he's dealt with, I also refuse to pressure him to share. In his own time, when he feels safe doing so, he will give me those pieces of him. And until that day arrives, I will stand by his side. Be a pillar of strength when he needs someone to hold him upright. Give him time and space when his mind won't quiet. Hug him impossibly tight for hours when it all feels too much. Lend an ear and a shoulder when he chooses to spill his bottled-up pain.

Digging up demons is no easy feat. Fighting those same demons alone is your worst nightmare times a hundred.

He won't fight his demons alone. I refuse to allow it. Not now. Not ever.

As my hand reaches for the handle, Devlyn lifts his free hand to my cheek. His thumb strokes my cheekbone and I sigh, leaning into his touch. He leans in closer and I breathe him in. Inhale the earthy scent on his skin that reminds me of his studio, his drawings, the way he sees me. Then his lips are on mine. Slow and steady, soft and warm, bestowing me with unrivaled comfort and peace.

"Love you, my Andromeda," he whispers on my lips.

"Love you too." I take a deep breath. "Here we go."

I open the front door and lead us inside. As we toe off our shoes, a pungent smell hits my nose and my stomach rolls. My eyes fall shut as I inhale deeply and exhale slowly. Again and again.

Devlyn takes my elbow in his hand and brings his lips to my ear. "What's wrong?" Concern evident in his whispered tone.

I straighten and lift a hand to cover my nose and mouth. *Jesus. What the hell is for dinner?* Please do not let pregnancy ruin all the foods I love.

"Just the smell," I say as I drop my hand. "I'll be okay in a minute. I hope."

Thankfully, no one has caught wind of our entrance. We

stand by the door as I take more breaths to settle my stomach. The nausea subsides for the most part. I slide my hand into Devlyn's and lace our fingers in a silent ready signal.

Now that my stomach is calmer, I zero in on the chatter and laughter spilling from the kitchen. No doubt, Mom has Micah cooking again while Dad and Peyton watch the show.

My brother has been such a trooper through it all. A year ago, he would have burned the house down making dinner for the family. But through his persistence and desire to be a better man for Peyton, he learned to navigate the kitchen like a certified chef. Mom was on standby, in case he needed help, but mostly stood there with a smile on her face. Pride in her eyes as she watched her son accomplish a task he never cared for until he met his wife.

On quiet feet, Devlyn and I round the kitchen island near Dad and Peyton. Peyton spots us first and spins on her stool, a warm and welcoming smile on her face.

"You haven't missed much of the show," she says as she slides off her stool and pulls us in for a hug.

"Good. I need these moments for posterity," I say on a laugh.

Peyton hugs Devlyn briefly before everyone catches on to our arrival. "Nice to see you again," she tells him. "No need to be nervous. Promise."

My favorite smile softens Devlyn's face as he thanks Peyton. Then Mom and Dad are footsteps away. Dad appears cool and collected. Mom, on the other hand, looks as if she is about to squeal like a tween at a boy band concert.

*Please, I beg you, universe, don't let Mom scare Devlyn.*

"Mom, Dad, this is Devlyn." I gesture to Devlyn, his arm snugly hooked in mine. "Devlyn, these are my parents, Nicole and George Reed."

Dad offers a warm smile and extends his hand. "Nice to meet you, Devlyn."

"You too, sir." Devlyn takes his offered hand and shakes.

Before their hands separate, Mom steps in and wraps her arms around Devlyn. My eyes widen more than Devlyn's as he looks to me for help. He doesn't *not* hug her back, but the embrace looks awkward from where I stand.

"Mom," I admonish. "Please don't frighten Devlyn."

It's a half joke. A way to lighten the mood, but also tell my mother to take her enthusiasm down a notch. She just met him for crying out loud. Yes, my mother is an exuberant woman, but I damn well know she doesn't hug strangers like this. Devlyn may not be a stranger to me, but he is to them.

She drops her arms and takes a step back. Then another. "I'm so sorry, Devlyn. Where are my manners?" Pink stains her cheeks. "Please, excuse my outburst. It's just—"

"Nicole," Dad says, resting a hand on Mom's shoulder. "Give the guy a moment to breathe."

"Yes, of course." She winces. "Sorry."

Well, well, well. The hug could have been predicted, but the embarrassment and apology, not so much. Not that Mom doesn't apologize when necessary, she does. In this circumstance, though, I expected her to wave it off like it was no big deal. To throw out some excuse as to why it'd be acceptable to embrace Devlyn so fiercely.

Hmm. How intriguing.

Stirring a pot on the stove, Micah glances over his shoulder and smiles at Devlyn. "Hey, man. Good to see you again."

Devlyn nods. "You too."

Mom resumes her spot in the kitchen near Micah while Dad and Peyton return to their stools. Devlyn pulls out the one beside Peyton and gestures for me to sit. After I do, he steps up behind me, wraps his arms around my waist, rests his chin on my crown and sighs. I rest my hands over his and give him a gentle squeeze, silently asking if he is okay. He answers by hugging my middle tighter and kissing my crown.

"What's for dinner?" I ask Peyton.

"With St. Patty's around the corner, Momma Reed thought corned beef and cabbage were a good idea. We're also having roasted carrots and potatoes."

Sautéed cabbage. That must have been what I smelled when we walked in the house.

Don't get me wrong, I love cabbage. Coleslaw, in salads, cooked. To be honest, I love most foods. But something about the cabbage scent when we walked in… it was foul. Maybe they added different seasoning to it.

It isn't long before Micah pulls the corned beef and roasted vegetables from the oven. Mom sets the serving dishes on the dining room table as Dad, Peyton, Devlyn and I rise from the stools.

The six of us sit around the table. Mom and Dad in their usual seats. Micah and I on the same side we've sat on since childhood, only now with someone special next to us.

As we fill our plates, I bypass the cabbage and pray it finds a resting place far from my seat.

"So, Devlyn," Mom starts. "What do you do for work?"

*This is not an interrogation. This is my family getting to know Devlyn.*

"Artwork. Oil painting, pencil drawings, charcoal. Whatever calls to me for the piece."

A flicker crosses Mom's face before her eyes widen. She stares at him for two breaths before her eyes dart between the two of us. "Oh my goodness." She sets her fork down and brings her hands to her lips in prayer. "Are you Devlyn Templar?" she asks, her tone filled with awe.

Devlyn spears a potato and nods, acting as if her local celebrity moment is no big deal. "Yes, ma'am."

Mom's eyes dart to me, then back to Devlyn. This happens three times before she finds her words again. "How long have you been dating?"

I know why she asks this question. The drawing she gifted to me for Christmas. She bought it off a local artist's website. My reaction to the piece. Peyton's reaction. The pieces are slowly clicking into place in her mind.

*Please don't let her give me grief for not broadcasting my relationship sooner.*

"Since early December," I answer. "But we met back in October." My gaze shifts to Devlyn as I lay my hand on his thigh beneath the table. "He did some artwork at Petal and Vine."

For a split second, Mom's face falls at the time line. It doesn't take a genius to do the math. Devlyn and I have dated nearly three months. Have known each other five. That isn't what makes her face temporarily wilt. She doesn't have to say it, but I know it's because I didn't share the news sooner.

The Reed family isn't big on secrets. We share important details about our lives on a regular basis. But just as my brother didn't come right out in the beginning and tell our parents he and Peyton were dating, I followed suit. Not to hurt my parents. More to give myself time to adjust to the change. To see where our relationship went.

After what happened in my apartment the night of Devlyn's art show, had I told my mother sooner about a potential relationship, the update of our weeks apart would've been harder. Mom would have brought Devlyn up more often than not. Asked questions I wasn't prepared to hear or answer.

And my heart would have snapped sooner.

I love my mother, but she can be a handful at times.

"Oh." Two letters. One word. That is all she says as she picks up her fork. Then she blinks a few times and swallows. Pierces the beef on her plate and cuts off a smaller piece. "And the drawing we gave you at Christmas…" She doesn't finish her question before she shoves the fork in her mouth and meets my eyes that match hers. A coincidence she probably never considered when the art was purchased.

I squeeze Devlyn's thigh as he sits quietly at my side. "That's me," I say with a little too much exuberance, then laugh under my breath. "Well, it's mostly my eye. But you know what I mean." Across the table, Micah bites back a smile at my rushed words while Peyton's eyes drop to her plate. "What're you smiling at, *starlight*?" I tease my brother with an arched brow.

"Starlight?" Dad chimes in. "What the hell does that mean?"

Peyton and I burst out laughing while Micah and Devlyn pick at their dinner and my parents sit in a cloud of confusion.

"Dad, you of all people should understand. Between Micah's nickname and the drawing with the constellation in the iris." I gesture toward Mom. "Have you not noticed how identical my and Micah's eyes are to Mom's?"

Dad stares at Mom across the length of the table for two breaths. Then a soft smile plumps his cheeks. "Her eyes always remind me of the nights we used to camp in the woods. When there wasn't a light for miles. All you could see were thousands of stars." His eyes glaze over as his memories flood in from years past. "She's always been my favorite starry night."

My heart melts as I listen to Dad speak with so much love for Mom. After more than thirty-five years, they are just as in love today as they were back in their teens. If not more. And it is a beautiful and envious thing.

Dinner continues with less intense conversation. Talk about Micah and Peyton and business at Roar. Dad mentions his time line for selling the insurance firm in the next three to five years. He has an eye on the market and wants to make sure he sells before a downshift. Mom talks about trends she has noticed in marketing and the shift on how to advertise. She mentions helping me when I take over Petal and Vine at the start of next year.

At this, Devlyn fidgets in his seat. His leg bouncing beneath my hand.

Mom and Dad clear the table and suggest we head into the living room for dessert. While they are in the kitchen, we meander to the living room and sit on the love seat.

"What's going on?" Micah whisper-shouts from his seat on the couch.

Leave it to my brother to detect the blip in my radar. He may not be the most intuitive person on the planet, but when it comes to me, he knows when something is off.

"I'll explain when Mom and Dad come back." His eyes narrow. "Micah, please," I plead with him.

Devlyn wraps his arm around my shoulder and kisses my temple. "Deep breaths," he whispers in my ear. Inhaling deeply, I rest my head on Devlyn's shoulder, eyes still on Micah.

"Please," I whisper.

Mom and Dad enter the room with a loaded tray. Small portions of peach cobbler and a scoop of vanilla ice cream. They hand out dessert and spoons, then take their seat on the couch.

*It's now or never. Devlyn's here. You can do this.*

I set my bowl down on the table, not a bite taken. Mom looks at me with a furrowed brow and questions on the tip of her tongue.

"Mom, Dad." My eyes shift from them to Micah and Peyton then back. "Devlyn and I have some news." Unlike the last few times I announced something important, I wait until no one has food in their mouth.

"What is it, sweetheart?" Dad asks as he sets his bowl on the table.

I *feel* Micah's intense laser focus on me, but ignore it and push forward. Taking Devlyn's hand, I intertwine our fingers and form an invisible barrier to keep us strong.

"I'm pregnant."

The room goes silent. Scary silent. No one moves. No one says a word. But four sets of eyes *stare* at us. Hard. As if searching for answers as to how and when and why.

I understand why they're in shock. Hell, we were in shock too. But I at least expected Mom to be a bit more vocal and bouncy. How long has she been harping me and Micah for grandchildren? Close to two years.

My eyes land on her face and all I see is confusion and emptiness. And it is so disconcerting.

"Someone please say something," I whisper, although it filters through as a scream.

Of all the people I expected to speak up first, it wasn't Peyton. "Congratulations." She rises from her seat, sets her bowl on the table and walks across the room. Bending at the waist, she hugs me and Devlyn in turn. "Just give them a minute," she whispers between us and I nod.

The second she lands in her seat, it is as if a switch flipped. Micah pipes up next, his eyes glassy as he searches mine. "Are you happy?"

I love that this is his only concern. After all our conversations about relationships, my virginity, and how we both felt about the future, neither of us spoke deeply on the topic of children. Before Peyton, both of us were unsure. Once he and Peyton were serious, they'd decided to forgo starting a family. I fully supported my brother and Peyton's decision. Mom was harder to convince.

Last Micah knew, though, I was a virgin. Devlyn and I had been dating, but my brother knew I wouldn't take that major step easily. So this news also tells him how deeply I care for Devlyn. That he is much more than just another guy to date. After several conversations about my love life, or lack thereof, he knew no one fit the bill. Made a big enough impact for me to want more. My brother knew I'd been waiting for the right person.

"Yeah, big brother." I twist and lock onto my favorite shade of green. Lift Devlyn's hand to my lips and kiss his fingers. "I am."

"You know I had to ask."

I face him and smile. "I know."

"Are you getting married?"

Beside me, Devlyn stiffens. Can't say I blame him. If I were in his shoes, I would too. Mentally, I was prepared for such radical questions. Mom had peppered me and Micah with them for years. But I didn't quite prepare Devlyn, and that is on me.

"Nicole!" Dad shakes his head as his eyes widen at her. "Not the time."

Thanks for the rescue, Dad.

I lean into Devlyn and wait for his frame to relax. One, two, three breaths pass before his muscles soften beneath my touch.

"Better?" I whisper and he hums. "No offense, Mom, but Devlyn and I have more important priorities to consider right now." My tone is gentle and nonconfrontational. "We're still adjusting to the news ourselves."

"Have you been to the doctor?" she asks, her eyes softening at the edges.

This we can handle. Simple conversations about the pregnancy. Without asking, my parents have to know I am not that far along. Even if Devlyn and I had gotten pregnant early in December, I'd only be a few weeks further into pregnancy. Not enough for the naked eye to notice.

For the next hour, we finish our dessert, discuss doctor's appointments, and how pregnancy was for Mom. My pregnancy may be completely different from Mom's, but knowing her experiences gives me insight on how mine may go. After all, I favor her more than Dad.

When it's time to exchange hugs and goodnights, Mom makes me promise to check in after each appointment. She also tells me to update her more often. She won't admit it outright, but the double whammy tonight—meeting Devlyn and learning about the baby—caught her off guard. Probably bruised her heart.

My intention wasn't to hurt her. I wanted to wait until the time felt right for me and Devlyn. In this one thing, I should get to be a little selfish. Devlyn too.

After an endless hug from both my parents at the same

time, the four of us head for our cars. We stop between the two cars and fumble over what to say next. Surprisingly, Devlyn is the first to break the silence.

"You should both come over for dinner one night."

Micah looks at me for a split second. Questions and emotions flit his expression. Although he won't come out and ask right now, I know he wants to ask if we are living together. Months have passed since the two of us last sat down for lunch and sibling catch-up. After tonight, it wouldn't shock me if he texts and sets up a brother-sister date.

"Sounds nice." A smile brightens Micah's face as he wraps an arm around Peyton's shoulders. "Just let us know when. Shell knows our schedule."

"Wonderful."

Devlyn's shoulders round as he visibly relaxes next to me. I hate how stressful this night must have been for him. Nervousness over meeting my parents. Worry over whether or not they'd like him as a person and approve of him to date their daughter. Unriddled anxiety over sharing news about the baby.

It had to have been a lot for him. He hid the tense moments well.

We exchange hugs one last time, get in our cars and go our separate ways.

I lace my fingers with Devlyn's and hold his hand the entire drive to the house. Keep my eyes on his profile and watch him as the streetlights zip past. Breathe in his earthy scent that has quickly become my favorite comfort. And fall for this beautiful man a little harder.

It may be too soon, but my answer is yes. Yes to moving in with Devlyn. Yes to sharing a home and life with him. Yes to everything us and our future.

But first, I need a minute. A little time to sort things out. To talk with Elizabeth about the shop and new time line for the sale. Talk with the apartment complex manager, seeing as I renewed my lease six months ago. And maybe I should talk with myself. Mull over what this next step means, not just for me but also Devlyn.

I just need a minute to breathe. Because this baby… they will change everything.

# eight

## DEVLYN

"Can we stop at the store?"

I lift Shelly's hand to my lips and kiss her knuckles. "Of course. What do we need?"

"Antacids and more dessert."

Chuckling, I shake my head. "Sounds like a winning combination."

I steer the car into the grocery store parking lot and park in a spot near the front. With the lot almost empty, Sunday evenings at the supermarket look to be the best time for shopping. Good to know.

We hop out of the car and walk to the door hand in hand. The automatic doors whoosh open and I pick up a handbasket from the stack. Shelly guides us to the healthcare aisle first, grabbing the largest container of Tums from the shelf and tossing them in the basket.

She shrugs. "Probably going to need them all." I wouldn't care if she threw ten bottles in the basket. If she needs them, I will buy them.

"Any dessert in particular?"

"Maybe peanut butter cups and ice cream."

We stop in the aisle loaded with candy and chips next. I stand back and observe as Shelly eyes the Snickers and Reese's and Baby Ruth bars. She taps a finger against her lips. Darts her eyes from one to the other over and over. And when she finally decides, I laugh because she puts all three in the basket with a radiant smile on her face.

The ice cream aisle carries the same level of indecision. But after I add a pint of cookie dough in the basket, she reaches into the case and fetches a tub of the nondairy Ben and Jerry's P.B. & Cookies. I sense of trend. Lots of peanuts or peanut butter.

It's cute.

She is cute.

Damn, but I got lucky with Shelly. Our relationship could have ventured so many different directions from the path it took. But it didn't and I thank my lucky stars every day.

After experiencing heartbreak, I never pictured myself in this place. Happy. Excited about life. Eager to spend each day with another person. Loving someone again. Yearning for the future.

But here I am, ready for it all. Ready to share my future with someone I love. And I have never felt better.

With our dessert loaded into the basket, Shelly and I stroll hand in hand toward the checkout. We round the end of the ice cream aisle and I skid to a stop after one step. Shelly jerks back and looks at me over her shoulder.

She tugs on my hand. "Dev?" Her fingers squeeze mine tighter. "Are you okay?" I'd answer, but my lips won't move. My tongue refuses to form words. My voice box forgets how to vibrate the proper sounds. Shelly steps into me, frames my face with her hands, and looks me square in the eyes. "Devlyn," she whispers, a breath from my lips. "You're scaring me. What's wrong?"

After a beat, I blink. Take a slow, methodical breath. Swallow past the bubbling anxiety clawing its way up my throat. Shift my gaze and lock onto Shelly's starry-blue irises. Eyes that soothe me in ways nothing else does.

"My mother is here," I whisper almost inaudibly. Shelly starts to turn her head, but I grab her elbow. Switch her focus back to mine. "Please don't turn around." A surge of fear spreads through my bones and rattles me head to toe. The need to protect Shelly from her floods my veins.

"Where is she?" Shelly whispers.

"Two aisles down." I shake almost imperceptibly. "Don't think she saw us, but can't be sure." I close my eyes for two breaths. *Why is she here? She doesn't live on this side of the bay. So why is she shopping* here? "Just please... please wait a minute. I'm sure she'll—"

My words get cut off as my mother sidles up to us. "Dev-lyn, what on earth?"

Hours of therapy turns to dust in my head as my mother stares down at me with black eyes. In a blink, all rational thought leaves my body. And in its place... the scared little boy living inside me emerges. I don't speak. Don't know the first response to the situation. All I know is, I don't want to be here. I don't want to exist in the same space as her. Don't want to breathe the same air as her.

I need to leave. *We* need to leave. Now.

When I don't respond, she tackles me verbally. "I have been calling and texting and stopping by the house. What is the matter with you?" While she babbles on about how my lack of contact bothers her, I take note that she has yet to acknowledge Shelly. "Your father and I have been worried sick. Your behavior has made me absolutely sick."

I tighten my hold on Shelly and nudge forward, hoping she catches my signal to leave. I take a step and Shelly falls in line beside me. Then, she is the one tugging us faster to the check-out. As if she senses my absolute need to leave. To get out of this store and away from my mother, sooner rather than later.

All the while, my mother is on our heels, berating me loud enough for the entire grocery store to hear.

"You will not walk away from me, young man."

Shelly and I dart into the express line, toss our snacks on the belt and face the cashier with pained smiles.

"Look at me when I speak to you," she demands, but I don't comply.

Per Dr. Prince's advice, I carry on and try to push past the cold demands. Ignore the words that are meant to sound sad, but are actually a ploy to crush me with her pointy, overpriced heels.

The cashier scans our groceries and bags them quickly. *Thank you.* I slip my card into the reader and press the appropriate buttons to pay the bill. As soon as the receipt is in the bag, I swipe it from the counter, take Shelly's hand and dart for the exit.

"She'll leave you. Just like the last one did. Who will be there when she abandons you?"

I freeze just before the door. Close my eyes and grind my molars. Remind myself to breathe. Remind myself that she will use whatever manipulation tactic necessary to keep me exactly where she wants me. Alone and at her mercy.

Never again.

Shelly squeezes my hand. Snaps me back to the here and

now. Reminds me of why I need to make a change. Why I need to vanquish the pain and hurt and misguidance of my past. For her. For our baby. A baby my mother will never know about. Ever.

"Let's go." Shelly's thumb strokes the top of my hand. "I got you." Without a backward glance, Shelly and I exit the store. When we reach the car, she makes me sit in the passenger seat. "It's better if you don't drive right now. You need a minute."

Behind the wheel, she cranks the engine, clicks her seat belt into place and throws the car in reverse. We zip out of the lot and drive slightly over the speed limit the entire way home. If we get pulled over, I'll gladly pay the fine to avoid one more second in the same space as Karen Templar.

Shelly parks the car in the driveway. And it's not until we are in the house, door locked and alarm set, that I finally take a full breath. Finally let everything that just happened sink in. I shiver from head to toe. Shelly drops the groceries at her feet and wraps her arms around my chest. She hauls me forward until not a breath of air resides between us. Then she hugs me with unimaginable force. It isn't strength. More like warmth and love and a promise to always pick me up when I fall.

Right there, near the entrance of the kitchen, I hold on to her as if my life depends on it. I hug her and cry into the crook of her neck. Sob and shake as years of pain and hurt spill from my body, from my soul.

"Let it all out." One of her hands is in my hair, the other squeezing my middle. "I got you." She kisses my shoulder. "I always have you."

When my tears slow, I lean back and cup Shelly's cheeks with my palms. "Love you so much." I press my lips to hers.

Kiss her with unimaginable tenderness. "Don't know what I'd do without you."

A soft smile dons her lips and lifts the corners of her eyes. "Good thing you'll never find out." She kisses me chastely. "I love you more."

*I highly doubt that.*

# nine

## SHELLY

The bell jingles over the front door of Petal and Vine. I peek up from the arrangement in front of me to see an older couple. "Good afternoon," I greet them and lift my hand to wave.

They return the greeting with bright smiles, then wander the perimeter of the store. The woman runs her aged fingertips over the dried flowers and wispy grasses. Her eyes scan the bins before she leans forward and inhales the dried lavender, followed by the eucalyptus. The man with her follows two steps behind, hands clasped behind his back, eyes on her. A small smile highlights his weathered skin as he watches her with love in his eyes.

My first thought is that may be Devlyn and me one day. Meandering a store, one of us shopping while the other observes in companionable silence. Simply happy because we exist in the same space.

Then I shake off the errant thought.

My relationship with Devlyn hasn't broached six months yet. Although things are progressing quicker than imaginable, thinking about us together with gray hair and a hobble in our step is a bit of stretch. Although I don't foresee a day without

Devlyn in my life, flashing forward to our retirement years isn't ideal.

While the couple scans the flower selection near the meadow painting, I covertly—at least I hope it's covertly—watch them. Watch the way she plucks stems from the pails and lifts them to smell before deciding whether to put it back or hold on to it for purchase. Then I shift my gaze to him. Watch the way he stands just a step back and off to the side. Watch the way he studies her every move with a keen eye and slightly leans in her direction. The longer I stare, the more my heart melts at the sight.

I *do* want that. The simple happiness of existing in the same space as someone you love. To find joy in the small things, like the way they look at a flower or brush the hair from their face.

"Brought you lunch."

I jump back, slap a hand to my chest and nearly knock over the vase of flowers I'd been working on. "Holy sh—" I pivot and catch sight of Devlyn. "Jesus. Make noise or something." Planting my palms on the table, I take a deep breath and give him my sharpest side-eye. "Scared the sh— crap out of me."

He leans in and kisses my temple. "To be fair, I did call your name. Twice, actually." His gaze drifts to the older couple. "But you were preoccupied."

"You did?"

A soft smile turns up the corners of his mouth as he notices what had my attention. "I did." His eyes drift back to mine as his smile deepens. "But I see why you were distracted. They're adorable to watch."

"That they are." I twist to face him fully. "You brought me lunch?"

He holds up a white paper bag. "Yes. Sandwiches from the deli. Hope that's good."

I nod as my stomach groans in agreement. "Let me go find Elizabeth so we can take lunch."

"Already done." Devlyn leans his hip on the heavy arrangement table. "When she let me in through the back, she said to give her a minute."

The words leave his lips just as Elizabeth enters the shop from the storage room. Sidling up to me, she lays a hand on my shoulder. "Go enjoy your lunch." I start to argue about not finishing the arrangement, but she sweeps it from the table and stows it in the storage cooler. "It'll be here when you're done. Now go."

Is this how it will be throughout pregnancy? Being parented, but not, all over again. Family and friends treating me as if I am fragile. Earlier, I went to pick up a box and Elizabeth rushed to my side. Told me not to lift it. The box weighed maybe seven pounds, which is nothing. Hell, most babies weigh that much when they are born.

I wish everyone wouldn't handle me as if I am breakable. Yes, I carry precious cargo, but my body is quite capable of physical activity. And while it's still possible, I'd like to do what my body will allow.

In the pamphlets I'd read, exercise and routine fitness are encouraged during pregnancy. Obviously certain movements and higher weights are off-limits, but lifting is permissible unless otherwise instructed by the doctor.

Inhaling deeply, I move past the notion that everyone will treat me with kid gloves. I remind myself they are looking out for me and the well-being of the baby. Their actions aren't meant to offend or suggest I am incapable. They love me and want the pregnancy to progress without hiccups.

"Got you the same sandwich as last time," Devlyn says as he pulls the food from the bag.

"Sounds perfect."

We take our seats and peel back the butcher paper around the sandwiches. Take the lid off the fruit cups. Dive into our sandwiches and enjoy the first bite as the flavors hit our tongues.

Except mine doesn't taste right. Or smell right.

I swallow the bite as my nose bunches. Slowly, I lift the sandwich to my nose and sniff. An odd tang hits my nasal cavity and I push away the offending scent. Set the sandwich on the butcher paper and peel back the bread. Inspect the cheese as if it were a suspect in a murder investigation. Narrow my eyes at the offensive smell.

"What's the matter?"

"The cheese smells off."

Devlyn sets his sandwich down and picks mine up. Lifting it to his nose, he inhales the unpleasant odor, only he doesn't seem as perturbed. He sniffs it again. Then again. No wince or offensive look. No puckered nose indicating disgust. Devlyn just appears… normal.

*Damnit.*

Please, please, please tell me this is not a pregnancy thing. Because not being able to eat the foods I love is unacceptable. I love cheese. All the cheeses.

"Smells okay to me," Devlyn says with an edge of uncertainty in his voice. "Want mine?"

I stare at his Cuban sandwich and my stomach grumbles. They have never been my thing, but maybe because I haven't tried one in years. Plus, Devlyn takes off the mustard and pickles. A win, if you ask me.

"I'll give it a try, but only if you don't mind."

Devlyn lifts his hand to my cheek, sliding it down until he pinches my chin between his thumb and finger. "Wouldn't offer otherwise."

We switch sandwiches and I take a hesitant bite. Worried the cheese from the Cuban will offend too. But as I chew the bite, as all the flavors hit my tongue, I moan. Then I take another bite, close my eyes and savor the taste. Dare I say, I love this sandwich more than my favorite.

"Better?"

I nod with a little too much enthusiasm. "Much, thank you."

"Think it's pregnancy related?"

Setting my sandwich down, I eat some of the fruit. "Probably." I swallow a bite of strawberry. "I read in one of the brochures that diet changes are different for each expecting mother. Some women don't experience any, with the exception of eating more. Other women crave foods they hated and dislike foods they've loved." I pierce another strawberry and blueberry and point to the sandwich in Devlyn's hands. "Hope that's the only issue."

"Me too."

Most of lunch goes by in relative silence. A little more than a week has passed since the Karen incident at the grocery store. The first two days post-Karen were iffy. I kept an eye on Devlyn every minute humanly possible. Watched for signs of detachment. Held him often so he didn't shut down and curl in on himself.

But being with him twenty-four seven is impossible. Life and work continue to demand our time.

Thank goodness he had an appointment scheduled with Dr. Prince two days later.

Although I want Devlyn to share everything with me, I

know he needs someone else's guidance when it comes to this piece of his past. One day, when he is in a better place with it all, he will share.

Until his appointment, Devlyn and I spent every available minute together. When I worked, he was in the studio. Loud, angry music vibrated the walls when I walked through the front door every evening. The music wasn't offensive, but more like a key to his mood. A glimpse at what I was walking into each day. And with each passing day, the music became less harsh. Less *I want to throw shit at the wall* sounding.

I want to smack Karen Templar. Dig my nails in her skin and listen to her cries. Get in her face and scream obscenities. Tell her she doesn't deserve to have someone as wonderful and extraordinary as Devlyn in her life. Make her feel an inkling of the pain she inflicted on her son.

But I won't do any of the above. Physical altercations and acts of violence wouldn't help. Not me or Devlyn or the situation as a whole.

This is Devlyn's battle. One I will help him with, whatever that looks like, but only as he needs me to. I need to be strong for him. Hold him up when his knees buckle. Tell him how much I love him. How I will be there for him always. And if he needs me to step up to the plate, if he needs me to be his voice or his shield, I will do exactly that.

The butcher paper crinkles as we finish lunch and toss our trash in the bin. We tidy up the table and meander back out to the main room of the shop. The older couple from earlier is long gone. A man lingers near the cooler of prearranged vases while a woman wanders near the loose flowers in the customer walk-in.

"See you after work?" Devlyn leans his hip on the

arrangement table, his eyes wandering the lines of my profile, heating my skin.

I nod. "Yeah. After I stop by the apartment first."

He straightens, then leans into me. Presses his lips to my temple. Drops his lips to my ear. "Love you, Andromeda." He tugs the loose length of my hair. "See you in a bit."

I reach out, pinch the bottom hem of his shirt as I twist to face him, and kiss him for all to see. The kiss isn't obscene, but the gentle press of my lips to his lingers. The moment his lips leave mine, I want to dive back in for another. But I resist the urge. Remind myself there is plenty of time for that later. After work.

"Love you too. I'll text when I'm on my way."

With one last kiss, Devlyn weaves his way through the back of the shop and out the employee door. I miss him the second the door clicks shut. But his earthy scent and the tingle from his kiss remains. For now, it will have to do.

Elizabeth takes lunch while I man the shop. I wrap a mix of flowers in brown paper and tie them with twine for the woman. She pays and exits the shop.

I snag the arrangement I worked on before lunch and pick up where I left off.

As I finish up the bouquet, the man steps up to the table and asks for help. He wants to send flowers to a friend who lost a loved one. Sifting through the available options, I opt for a small bundle of lilies, add them to a vase with some greenery and give him a small card to fill out for the bouquet. After he pays and exits, the shop is quiet. Too quiet.

I start a new arrangement. Grab a fresh vase and an array of colorful flowers. Add a handful of stems, various greenery and some baby's breath. As I place it in the prearranged cooler, the bell over the door jingles. Tipping up the corners of my mouth, I pivot on my heel and open my mouth to greet the next customer.

But no words leave my lips. My whole frame stiffens and I forget how to speak.

Twenty feet from where I stand, not facing me head on, is Devlyn's mother.

*What the hell?*

Much as I'd love to give this woman a piece of my mind, much as I'd love to shove her out the front door and tell her to never return, my lips refuse to move. Words refuse to form on my tongue.

And before she sees me, I spin around. My feet trek across the floor and toward the break room. Elizabeth hasn't been back here but maybe ten to fifteen minutes, and I hate that I will interrupt her time. But I swear to make it up to her. Give her extra time, let her come in later on a different day. Whatever she wants.

Anything but be in the same room as Karen Templar, forced to interact with her. Not on my own. Not anytime soon.

"I need a favor," I say as I enter the room.

Elizabeth looks up from her book, finishes chewing and swallows. "What's the matter?"

I pick at the pocket of my apron. Twist my lips between my teeth. "Devlyn's mother is out front." Elizabeth's brows pinch at the middle. It isn't my place to share Devlyn's past, but I need to give Elizabeth something. Some indication as to why I refuse to be in the same room as her. "It's a sticky situation." That's putting it lightly. "Things aren't good with Devlyn and his parents, and we bumped into her the other night. It was bad."

Tucking her bookmark between the pages, Elizabeth rises from the table and wipes her mouth with a napkin. "Say no more." She sidles up to me and rests a hand on my shoulder. "Stay back here. I'll come back when she leaves."

My entire body deflates. "Thank you."

Not a minute after Elizabeth exits the room, my stomach starts to roll. *Nerves or morning sickness?* It's long past morning, but I read the nausea happens at all hours. Most women just happen to get it in the morning.

I lock myself in the bathroom, crank the cold-water knob on the faucet and soak a paper towel. Then I park myself on the lidded toilet and dab my cheeks, forehead and neck with the towel. Bend at the waist and tuck my head between my knees.

As a child, I passed out quite often. My blood sugar and iron levels were never where they were supposed to be. At an early age, I learned the signs leading up to a fainting spell. The doctors told me if I felt that same woozy feeling, felt like the world was too wobbly beneath my feet, I needed to sit in a chair or on the floor. Somewhere safe. That I should tuck my head between my knees and take slow, deep breaths. In through the nose, out through the mouth. Help the blood and oxygen flow to my head. It wasn't an immediate fix, but it helped.

After the third deep breath, I slowly sit straighter. Open my eyes. Focus my thoughts on something calming.

*Nights snuggled with Devlyn on the couch. Just me, him, good food and whatever show we're currently watching. His warm arms around my waist. The stroke of his fingers on my skin.*

Another deep breath and the nausea passes. "I got this," I whisper with renewed confidence.

A knock on the door startles my peace. "Shelly? Everything alright?"

I rise from the toilet and toss the paper towel in the bin. Twisting the handle, I open the door to see Elizabeth, her face etched with concern.

"All good. Felt sick for a moment, but it passed."

She rubs my back between my shoulders as I walk out. "Glad it's better. May need to keep some ginger ale and saltines on hand." A gentle smile dons her face. "Just in case."

"Not a bad idea." My eyes dart to the doorway, then back to Elizabeth. "Did she... uh..."

"She left. Didn't buy anything, actually. She wandered the shop for a few minutes, then started asking questions."

"About the shop?"

Elizabeth shakes her head. "Not one. She asked questions about Devlyn." She pauses to swallow. "And you."

*Shit.* I hoped she wouldn't remember my face from the shop. She'd only been in here the one time, well over a year ago. I wasn't even the one to help her.

Obviously, Karen Templar has a fantastic memory. One I'd like her to forget.

"What did she ask?"

I hate that Elizabeth is suddenly in the middle of our mess. It isn't fair to her.

"At first, she asked about the new piece on the inside wall. The meadow." *My meadow.* "Asked if Devlyn had painted it." My eyes widen. "And when he was here last." A light layer of sweat dampens my skin as the nausea starts to make a comeback. "Since I hadn't seen her in a while, I told her Devlyn painted the inside when he'd done the exterior more than a year ago."

Thank god.

The last thing I need is this woman constantly snooping

around the shop. Barging in at any given moment and pestering me or waiting for Devlyn to show.

"What did she ask about me?"

An audible exhale leaves her lips as Elizabeth takes my hands in hers. In that small touch, I feel every ounce of her love and concern. "Please tell me you are safe, Shelly." Her gaze pierces mine with a fierce level of protectiveness. "If that woman is harassing you…"

"For now, everything is okay." I nod imperceptibly. "There's just been some recent events with her and Devlyn." My eyes fall to our joined hands. "Wish I could share more, but it's not my place."

"I know, sweetheart. Just promise me one thing." I lift my eyes back to hers. "If it gets too bad, if you or Devlyn are in harm's way, don't keep this secret." Her gaze drops to my belly briefly. "It's not just the two of you anymore." Her eyes dart between mine. "It's okay to ask for help. Especially with this."

"I promise," I whisper.

Elizabeth's shoulders visibly relax. "She asked if the young blonde girl still worked here. I didn't answer. Just deterred her and asked how I could help. The way she left…" She shakes her head. "I don't think she'll return."

I pray she is right. The last thing any of us needs is to be on the receiving end of Karen Templar's wrath.

"Thank you." I pull Elizabeth into a hug and hold on tight. She squeezes me until I have to tap out of the embrace. "Sorry I interrupted your lunch." I point to the table where her sandwich sits. "Take all the time you need."

Before she rebuts my courtesy, I dart from the room.

The last few hours of the day go by uneventfully. But as I compile online orders and start arrangements for deliveries, the thought of that woman in here, in *my* shop, gazing at *my* meadow, eats away at my happiness.

She may not have said one word to me, but her presence alone sucked the life from one of my happy places. And I intend to get it back.

I will not let her stomp all over me or Devlyn. Will not let her ruin the love and joy we have found together. And I downright refuse to be bullied and squashed by anyone, especially that wicked woman.

Not today. Not tomorrow. Not ever.

# ten

## DEVLYN

Difficult as it is, I try not to spend most days hating my mother. Dr. Prince says I should focus on how to relieve myself of the trauma. Find new ways to dispel the pieces of my past that affect my present and possibly my future. That I should forgive my younger self for not knowing or understanding the influence my parents had on me at such a vulnerable age.

It is okay to forgive past me. It is okay to let go of things I had no control over.

Forgiving and letting go of the past opens up space for the future. Is silent permission to love without fear of repercussion. To hope for the things I want in my life. To experience happiness without apprehension.

In order to move forward, in order to work through all the parts that eat away at my soul, I have to learn to forgive. And forgiving the woman who should have loved me more than anyone, but didn't, is difficult.

I *want* her love. I *want* her approval.

Knowing I will never have either is the hardest part. But knowing I will never have either also helps.

When I argued with Dr. Prince, told him I didn't have the energy to forgive my parents, he countered my rebuff. Said forgiveness and release don't need to be done face-to-face. It's more about letting go of the piece of them that still takes up residence inside me. It's about discovering a way to dig up the painful parts, dissect each moment on its own, make peace with the hurt, and then let that piece of the past go.

Weeks ago, he'd said, "Mental and emotional trauma leaves invisible scars. Healing those scars will take time. It's not something that can be rushed. We all heal at our own pace and in our own way. Grant yourself the time your mind needs. Be open to expelling the past and making room for the future."

So, one session at a time, one relived memory at a time, I learn how to forgive and let go of my parents.

During an early session, I argued with Dr. Prince that my father was not to blame. He'd never said an unkind word. Never raised his hand in physical threat. Never belittled me in private or public. It had always been my mother who'd done those things. My mother was the villain.

After my counterstatement, Dr. Prince asked how my father acted while my mother behaved in this manner. For minutes, I stared out the window of his office. Watched the birds flutter around the tree branches and chase one another. Got lost in the fluffy white clouds as they floated in the Mayan-blue sky. Drifted away mentally with the breeze, wishing it was easier to escape the disasters of my past.

It was then that I realized what he'd meant when he said my father had also been part of the problem. Because James Templar never did a damn thing. Not to help me, anyway.

He'd coddled my mother. Admonished me for upsetting

her. Told me to be on my best behavior. All with a pained look on his face.

To this day, I don't know if that pained look was because my mother was upset. Or because he suffered her wrath as well.

The more I dug into my past, the more I paid attention to the little moments over the years, the more I saw it. Although my father was a victim, it wasn't the same. He *chose* to stay. He *chose* to elevate my mother. To put her on the pedestal that slowly lifted her higher and higher with each passing day.

My father fed—feeds—my mother's narcissism. He fuels her by never telling her the words she speaks or actions she takes are harmful. And together, they buried me in hurt and confusion and emotional detachment.

"Is she still attempting contact?" Dr. Prince asks from his plush leather chair.

Three months have passed since my first session. In those three months, a lot has been brought to light. A lot has been picked apart and evaluated with a new lens. But with each session, life moves forward rather than backward. With each session, I learn how to heal.

Not long after seeing my mother in the store, when she blew up and made a scene, she stopped by Petal and Vine. She'd missed me by mere minutes. Thankfully, Shelly escaped to the back and avoided another interaction unscathed. My mother probed Elizabeth with questions, but got no answers.

Surprisingly, it has been quiet since.

No constant calls or voice mails. No text messages. No incessant emails.

Almost as if Karen Templar vanished without a trace. And that has me on edge.

"No." I shake my head as I scoot to sit straighter in my seat. "Is it weird for me to be worried by her silence?"

Dr. Prince scratches a note down on his pad of paper. "Not weird at all. Oftentimes, in situations such as yours, it's alarming to feel free after years under someone's thumb."

"I just know my mother." I laugh without humor and drop my gaze to my lap. "She never lets anything go. She always has a plan. A way to come out the *winner*, whatever that looks like in her eyes." I lift my gaze and lock on Dr. Prince's steely irises. "My mother isn't the type to throw in the towel. Walking away isn't her style."

"What do you worry about most when it comes to her silence?"

I don't hesitate. "Shelly."

"Can you be more specific?"

Weeks of silence from my mother bother me more than her deranged display at the store. Since that night, I have agonized over Shelly's safety, and the baby. After days of deep breathing and mental reflection, I can't dislodge the twisted feeling in my gut. That the worst is yet to come.

"I worry Shelly will get caught in the cross fire. That my mother will do something unpredictable and Shelly will be hurt physically. And so will the baby."

"Do you believe your mother is capable of physically harming others?"

I shake my head and laugh again. "At this point, I believe my mother is capable of just about anything. She may not wield that weapon, but she is the one responsible."

Dr. Prince sips his water, then jots more notes on his pad of paper.

God, he has to have a ream's worth of paper in my file by now. Not sure if that is good or bad. Maybe a bit of both.

At least I have an outlet for my thoughts and emotions. A safe place to get everything off my chest. A safe person to help me make sense of it all so I can grow past it.

But how does this man sleep at night after hearing such stories?

"Has Shelly responded to your request for her to move in?"

Another item on the list that has me restless.

Months have passed since I asked Shelly to move in. I haven't pressed her for an answer and she hasn't hinted one way or the other. Yes, my asking was premature in our relationship and during a sensitive time. But I meant every word. Wanting Shelly in my home, at my side more often than not, hadn't been an irrational idea. I still want us to live together. Still want a future with her.

I mean, she practically lives in my house already. With each passing week, more of Shelly's belongings find a new home in my house. Small touches of her invade each room.

Her clothes hang in the closet and fill the drawers of the dresser, adding softer tones and a splash of pink. The little bit of makeup she uses lies on the vanity in the master bathroom. Her sweet but earthy floral scent is now a permanent fixture in the bedroom. *Our bedroom.* Her favorite throw blanket, the one she had draped over the couch in her apartment, now lies over the back of my couch. *Our couch.* She even brought over the container she keeps on her kitchen counter with all her favorite teas.

Whether Shelly realizes it or not, we live together. It just isn't official.

She still pays rent on the space she doesn't frequent often. A space now filled with barely used furniture, slowly emptying cabinets and less of Shelly's personal possessions.

In the past two months, she has added life to my home—*our home*—as her old apartment becomes a vacant shell.

"Not yet." I pick at my cuticles, then force myself to stop. "I want to ask again, but I don't want to upset her."

"Why do you think asking would upset her?"

*Great question.*

Anymore, I feel like I don't have answers to any questions. That I am just going through the motions most days. Trapping myself in the studio and mood painting. Impatiently waiting for Shelly to walk through the front door with a smile on her face and arms spread wide. To bring me further into her light.

"A lot has happened in such a short period. I often question if my intentions *are* out of impulse. I wonder if she thinks I'm only asking because she's pregnant."

"Are you?"

"Am I what?"

"Asking Shelly to move in because she's pregnant?"

Guess I shoved myself into this corner.

The baby isn't the chief reason I asked Shelly to move in. I asked because I love her. I asked because she matters more than anyone. Is the baby a secondary factor? One hundred percent, yes.

I don't doubt Shelly's ability to handle herself. She is incredible and strong and lovable. But she is not alone. Not in life or love, and definitely not when it comes to the baby. *Our baby.*

"No. With or without the pregnancy, I would've eventually asked her to live together. We just click. Can't put it into words, but there's something about her that I connect with on a base level." Long before we were together, Shelly had been my muse. When I saw her again after nearly a year, she reignited that spark inside me. "When we're together, it all just locks in place. Flows smoother."

With Shelly, life isn't a chore. I look forward to each day. To seeing her, holding her, being with her. She breathes life into my soul and elevates me in an incomprehensible way.

Dr. Prince glances down at his wrist. "Homework time," he says with a hint of laughter. The homework term has become a little joke with us. Don't know if he uses the same word with his other patients, but we laugh at it. Make it lighter and less about actual work.

"Ask Shelly again?" He nods and scribbles on the notepad. "Will do."

"Remember Devlyn, asking for what you want shouldn't be a chore. Don't treat it as such. It's normal to ask for what you want. The delivery is what makes all the difference." He rises from his seat and I follow suit. "Mull it over before you ask. Think of how you want the question to come across—out of a place of love and not need—and practice how you think that should sound. When it feels right, ask."

He makes the task sound so simple. Like taking a breath or painting what I feel. If only.

I don't fear Shelly. I don't fear the love she has for me, for us. What I *do* fear is rejection. Especially from her.

For years, I handed out rejection like Halloween candy. Hell, I rejected Shelly's and my own feelings for weeks. Shoved her away after the kiss on the exhibition night. Subjected us both to suffering so *she* wouldn't hurt *me* the way I'd been hurt before.

I'd still hurt, but at least it was my own doing. At least I was in control.

But now, I need to be brave. I need to step up and ask for

what I want. I need to stow my insecurities and be a little self-ish. Not just with Shelly, but also in life.

I love her. I want her. And I shouldn't feel shame in that.

She makes my life better, brighter. Wraps me in her arms and warmth and heart. Gives me more love than imaginable. Soothes the pain of the past without effort and replaces it with hope and passion and conviction. Shelly gives me purpose. A reason to wake up and keep going.

"Thanks, Doc." I extend my hand and we shake. "See you in a few days."

"Take care, Devlyn."

I exit the office and head for my car. Unlocking it, I slip behind the wheel and press the ignition. For a beat, I sit idle in the lot. Stare out the window at nothing in particular. Let my eyes lose focus and my mind drift off with the clouds.

*Shelly is not Kelsey. Shelly won't reject me. She won't throw me away.*

I repeat this again and again. Let the words seep into my bones. Chant them like a mantra until I believe them into existence.

*The past will not repeat itself. Shelly is* not *Kelsey.*

Shelly's hesitation to move in is because we have dated such a short time. But Dr. Prince says no one person determines when to take the next step in a relationship. There is no handbook for love. No guide for relationships. We set the pace. We say what comes next.

Our relationship cannot be compared to anyone else's relationship. Sure, we may have similar circumstances, but our relationship otherwise is different. Because *we* are different.

Over dinner, I will ask again. Ask Shelly to move in. I just need to find the right words. Pregnancy or not, Shelly doesn't need additional stress or pressure. But I'd like to know if she has given the idea any merit.

I won't force an answer from her lips, but I would like to know if there's a chance she will say yes.

Now… time to butter her up. Thankfully, I know the way to her heart.

# eleven

## SHELLY

I just landed in heaven.

The moment I walk through Devlyn's front door, the delicious scent of bulgogi hits my nose. Savory with a hint of spice. My mouth waters instantly. *Damn, that smells good. Thank god.*

After the cheese incident, I worried what else would turn up my nose and have me queasy. I'd cry if my favorites made me cringe. To date, cheese and cabbage are the only items on the naughty list. Everything else has been ten times better.

I toss my purse on the chair in the sitting room and toe off my shoes. Winding my way through the house, I slow my pace as I approach the living room. Rounding the corner, I spot Devlyn with his back to me. He removes boxes and tubs from a brown bag and sets them on the table. And for a moment, I stand silently in place and watch him move around the room. Watch him organize dinner and set up the room for a perfect date night in.

The bag crinkles as he flattens it. Then he spins around and spots me at the edge of the room. A small smile pushes up his cheeks and I melt at the sight.

"Didn't hear you come in." He saunters across the room, steps into my space, wraps his arms around my waist and crushes my lips with his.

*Damn.*

Every day should be this incredible. Every day *can* be this incredible. If I let it be.

When he breaks the kiss, I peer up at him. Stare at the darker shade of green rimming his glass-green irises. Swallow at the smolder in his gaze. At the love this man gives only to me.

*Damn*, I mentally repeat.

"Wasn't purposely quiet," I say. "Just saw you setting up dinner and didn't want to interrupt." I kiss the tip of his chin. "Smells so good."

He kisses the tip of my nose as he unravels his arms. "Sit. I was going for drinks." Before I offer to help, he steps around me and heads for the kitchen.

A few shifts on the floor pillow later, Devlyn walks back in with water and hot tea. Setting them on the table, he situates himself next to me between the couch and table on the floor. We tear open disposable chopsticks and break the sticks apart. And as Devlyn hits play on the remote, I dive into the bulgogi.

An unladylike moan exits my lips and Devlyn laughs.

"Good?"

"So damn good." I savor the bite. Let the umami roll over my tongue. "I'll admit, I was worried." His brows pinch at the middle. "That I wouldn't be able to enjoy it. After the whole cheese thing, I wondered what other foods would gross me out."

"And?"

I shrug. "Just the cheese." I clamp down on another piece

of beef, then point my loaded chopsticks at him. "Actually, most of the dairy has made me queasy."

"At least you didn't eat or drink a lot before."

"True." I pop the beef in my mouth and close my eyes. *Thank you*, I say to the pregnancy gods. At least I still have this.

The rest of dinner goes by in quiet bliss as we watch *Dark*. This show really swirls my mind into a blur. But in a good way. Romance is my bread and butter, but this multilayered mystery is a close competitor.

When the boxes empty, we pause the show, take the trash to the kitchen, and grab dessert. Curled up on the couch, I lay my head on Devlyn's shoulder while I spoon ice cream into my mouth.

"Can I ask you something?" Devlyn asks as the end credits flit across the screen.

"You know you can." I wrap my hands around his bicep.

Three breaths pass before his voice fills the room again, so soft and quiet I almost don't hear him. "Is there a reason you haven't agreed to move in?"

Feels like a lifetime has passed since Devlyn asked me to move in with him. I'd told him I needed to think about it. He granted me the time and I have mulled it over, but I have yet to answer him. Is it too early to blame that on pregnancy brain?

I lift my head and rest my chin on his shoulder before kissing it and sitting up straighter. Glance into his glassy, soulful eyes. Eyes that question if I love him enough to want this. To be with him full time. To share the same space as him. To cohabitate.

And the uncertainty in his head and heart, that is on me. Too many days have passed since he asked. Too many days have passed without me answering. God, his mind must be in overdrive. Crazy with assumptions.

How unfair of me to make him wait, considering I decided not long after he asked. I assumed my actions made my answer evident. But Devlyn needs to hear the words. With all the hurt in his past, he needs to hear the answers. When it comes to Devlyn, I should never assume.

"It's not that I don't want to move in."

He shifts in his seat to face me more easily. Arm resting on the back of the couch, his fingers toy with the loose strands of my hair. Twirl and lightly tug. "Then what's holding you back?" His knuckles graze the angle of my jaw and I lean into his touch. Let my eyes fall shut and my body relax. "So beautiful," he whispers.

The backs of my eyes sting as I swallow down his words. God, I love this man. This beautifully broken man.

"I'm scared," I say, my eyes still closed. "I'm scared to give in." Slowly, I open my eyes. "Scared to fall harder and lose you."

His other hand cups my cheek, his thumb stroking beneath my lashes. "You'll never lose me, Shelly. Never."

"How can you be so sure?" I fist the hem of my shirt and tug it over my swelling belly. "What if having the baby puts a wedge between us? What if I move in and things become too much? Right now, everything is new and happy. But what if that changes when the baby comes?"

Leaning forward, Devlyn kisses my forehead. His lips linger for three breaths before he resumes his previous position. Warmth spreads from the spot he kissed to my heart. I take a deep breath and hold his vibrant greens.

"I don't doubt things will change when the baby comes." His fingers go back to the loose strands of my hair. "But we control how they change. Yes, the baby will throw a glitch into the life we currently know, but we have the ability to shape how we want the future."

Since Devlyn started therapy, we haven't had many serious, in-depth conversations. I don't ask how his sessions go. I don't mention his mother or parents. Not from lack of curiosity, but more because I don't want to invade that area of his privacy. I don't want to rehash possibly upsetting moments. More than anything, I want to respect his boundaries.

With unparalleled patience, I wait for him to broach the heavy subjects. Wait for him to spark those weighted conversations. Because they aren't mine to bring up. They aren't my stories to tell when ready.

The strength in his words as we talk about our future tells me therapy has been beneficial. Has given him the opportunity to look at life through a new lens. With new perspective. With a positive outlook.

"I just don't want you to grow tired of me," I huff out. "Then we're both stuck in a crazy situation." I lift my hand to his jaw and trace my finger to his chin before letting it fall away. "Don't want you to feel pressured to keep me around if something changes."

"One… not going to happen." I open my mouth to rebut and he holds up a hand to stop me. "Yes, all couples experience the bad. Moments when they don't get along. It's inevitable." He takes my hand, brings it to his lips, and kisses each knuckle in turn. "But I'll never wish you away, Shelly Reed. All of my good days involve you."

He takes a deep breath and I don't interrupt. "Shelly, you are the only shining light in my life. My life preserver. The sunshine after the rain. The one person I can count on. No matter how shitty my day has been, no matter how poorly I behave, all the bad vanishes because I have you. And I realize how unhealthy and codependent that sounds. It's something I've been working on with Dr. Prince." He closes his eyes briefly. "But I also know those deep, deep feelings are genuine. They aren't misguided sentiments from a broken boy."

He presses the heel of his palm to the center of his chest. "You are here. Rooted so deep." His eyes glaze over. "I think you were here long before either of us knew. Because damn, I feel so much for you. So damn much. At times, I question my own sanity, my own mental health. But every time I do, I come up with the same result."

"What's that?" I whisper-ask.

His eyes roll closed for one, two, three beats. "That I've never loved anyone the way I love you. At times, the depth of that loves scares the shit out of me. Because I've only truly loved one other and that ended in devastation." He shakes his head as light laughter leaves his lips. "I fought this" —he gestures between us with his hand— "for so long. Tried to keep you in the friend zone. But fate knew better and I caved." He leans in and presses a chaste kiss to my lips. "Loving you was inevitable, Shelly Reed. And I will keep you forever, if you let me."

The backs of my eyes burn as tears blur my vision and emotion clogs my throat. I don't know what to say. How to react. What to do after Devlyn just spilled his whole heart at my feet.

Every truth that left his lips wrapped itself around my heart and hugged me fiercely. I will keep those truths tucked safely in my heart for the rest of my life. His sacred, vulnerable truths. His love. Him.

Concerned as I've been, I knew weeks ago I would say

yes to him. I will always say yes. Not to please Devlyn, but because he will never intentionally put me in an uncomfortable situation. He will never intentionally hurt me.

More than any other person, I know Devlyn. Know his heart. Know his softness and the pieces he keeps hidden from the rest of the world. His softness is one of my favorite parts. A part he reserves only for me.

"Yes."

His eyes narrow as they study my expression, flit over the angles of my nose and jaw, home in on my eyes and lips. "Yes?" A layer of uncertainty laces his voice.

"I'll move in," I whisper, the words floating softly from my lips to his ears.

The moment they hit, the moment they truly sink in, his whole body shifts. Lights up. Comes alive.

His hands frame my face, thumbs brush my cheeks. Inch by inch, he eviscerates the space between us. Vivid green irises hold my sparkly dark blues. His breath warm on my lips.

I fist the cotton of his shirt at the heart and tug him forward until our lips meet in the middle. Soft and warm, Devlyn kisses me with unprecedented tenderness. Once, twice, his lips sweep over mine reverently. Then his tongue paints my bottom lip and I gasp. Invite him in. Taste him on my tongue. Melt into him.

Crawling into his lap, we shift until his back presses against the cushions and I straddle his hips. His fingers curl at my waist as mine lace behind his neck. The kiss deepens as his hands shift and trail up my spine beneath my shirt. My fingers finding their way into his long, thick strands.

"Love you, Shelly." His lips kiss along my jaw, down the column of my neck, across my collarbone.

I curl my fingers in his hair, scrape my nails over his scalp. "Love you, Dev."

Over the next several hours, until the faint light of dawn filters through the windows, we love each other. With lips and fingers. Light touches and whispered words. Occasional scratches and bite marks. Skin on sweat-slicked skin. Linked and bonded through the most pivotal, base connection. The most real and raw and undeniable connection. His body and mine.

Until my heart no longer beats, until my lungs no longer fill with air, I will love this man. Will share my heart with him. Will let him hold it close to his own. Let him care for me —for us—in a way no one else ever will.

Because Devlyn isn't just a boyfriend. He isn't just the father of the baby growing in my womb. This man is my heart. This man is my soul. More than anything, this man is my life. Where I am meant to be. In his arms, every day of forever.

# twelve

## DEVLYN

"Put that down," I shout across the living room of Shelly's apartment. She narrows her eyes. "Please," I say a bit softer. "You shouldn't be lifting anything that heavy."

Bending at the knees, Shelly sets the box on the floor and I breathe easier. "It's not even heavy." She rests fists on her hips. "Maybe ten pounds. Knickknacks from the kitchen junk drawer and the stuff I had on the fridge." Her eyes drop to said box. "Heck, it's probably not even five pounds."

Last week, Shelly had a checkup and the doctor said all looked great with the baby. We got our first baby picture with the ultrasound. Dr. Webster said the baby is roughly the size of a sweet potato, which I thought was odd as a visual reference but it works.

She asked if we wanted to know the gender of the baby. We declined, opting for the surprise.

During that same visit, Dr. Webster noted Shelly's elevated blood pressure and ordered she take it easy. Rest as much as possible. Not strain herself or lift anything too heavy.

Packing up her apartment and moving her into the house have made this directive difficult.

Shelly spoke with her landlord at the start of the week and since she only has two months left on her lease, they agreed to let her break it. Granted, she won't get her deposit back, but the money doesn't concern me more than her well-being.

One step forward, then another, I hold her at arm's length. "This sucks, I get it. But you heard what Dr. Webster said. You need to take it easy. Pack up the boxes and I'll carry them."

Her eyes fall shut as she takes a deep breath and sighs. "Ugh. I hate this." She shakes her head. "Feels like I'm help-less. Incapable."

I wrap my arms around her waist and draw her close. Press my lips to her cheek. "You aren't and you know it. Pregnancy won't last forever. We're almost halfway there." I kiss her other cheek. "It's a big adjustment, but if it keeps you both safe, then it's what matters most."

Warm arms tighten their hold on my waist. "I know." She kisses my neck, then takes a step back. "I'll go work on filling the boxes in the bedroom."

Hours pass as Shelly and I fill boxes with clothes and books, dishes and small appliances. I carry them out, one by one, and load them in my car or hers. When not an inch of empty space is visible in either of our cars, we lock up the apartment and drive across town to the house.

We park in the driveway and I start unloading both our cars. Pile the boxes in the empty space near the sliding glass doors. Do my best to separate the box stacks by room to make the next step less stressful. When all the boxes are in the house, I help unpack, but let Shelly place her things where she'd like them.

"Is everyone getting together tomorrow?"

Weeks have passed since we last hung out with her friends. Not because we haven't wanted to; life has just been busy for us all.

"Yeah. Cora messaged earlier and asked if we'd be there."

I peel newspaper off a plate and hand it to her. "Did you answer?"

Shelly spent so much time with her friends before our relationship blossomed. Now, she sees them less often. Not because of our relationship and the pregnancy, thank goodness. I'd be upset if I were the reason. Between love and marriage and babies, everyone else's lives have changed too. Both Cora and Autumn have newborns. Cora and Gavin, as well as Micah and Peyton, are still in the honeymoon phase.

She nods. "Mm-hmm. Told her we'd bring potato salad." Her eyes find mine. "Hope that's okay."

I shrug. "Potato salad's fine. Kind of prefer macaroni salad, but it's cool."

She knocks my arm with her shoulder. "I meant me responding without checking with you, not the potato salad." A soft chuckle leaves her lips and I love hearing the gentle laughter.

Setting the dish in my hand down, I take her chin in my fingers and press a kiss to her lips. "More than okay. It'll be nice to see everyone."

Sunshine lights her face in the form of a smile and I question the last time I saw her so bright. It's been too long.

Right here, right now, I vow to make Shelly smile more often. Recent worries had stolen her smiles. Worry over herself, the baby, the move. I need to be better. Do better. Take some of that stress off her shoulders. Carry the burden and help her relax.

I flatten the empty boxes and take them to the recycling bin. Shelly and I cook dinner, then settle in front of the television to eat. When the episode ends, I carry our dishes to the kitchen and tidy up.

Back in the living room, Shelly sits curled in the corner of the couch with a book. I pad across the room, take her book, mark the page, and set it on the table. Slip my hand around hers, help her stand, then escort her up the stairs to my studio.

"What're you up to?" she asks, brow arched.

When we reach the landing, I spin around to face her and walk backward until we reach the middle of the room. I frame her face in my hands and crush my lips to hers. She fists my shirt at either hip and draws me in until no space exists between us. It is just her and me and our personal bubble of bliss.

Our tongues tangle. Hands skim arms and waists. I graze the length of her spine as she kneads the sides of my neck. Fingers fist hair and tug. The kiss morphing from gentle to hungry in seconds. And when she tips her head back and gasps, I kiss my way down her neck and drag my tongue along her collarbone.

"I want to paint you," I say against the hollow of her throat. "But not like before."

Her fingers tighten in my hair and pull my lips from her skin. "How?"

I nip at her chin. "On canvas. Just you." I tug at the bottom hem of her shirt and lift up. My fingers skim down her sternum, over the center of her bra, over her belly that is slowly swelling with our child. "No barriers."

"Devlyn, I…"

"Abstract," I answer quickly. "Or not. I leave it up to you." My palm flattens on her lower abdomen and I splay my fingers. "So beautiful." I drop to my knees, my eyes peering up at Shelly as my lips press to the skin beneath her navel. "Please."

Gentle fingers comb through my unruly hair as she holds my gaze. Neither of us says a word for several heartbeats. And then her head slowly moves up and down.

"Okay," she whispers into our bubble. "You can paint me." She takes a deep breath. "However you're inspired to."

Once again, this woman astounds. Her love and bravery and confidence. Without much negotiation, she handed over an incomparable level of trust. Laid it in my hands, certain I would keep it, and her, safe. Something I will never abuse or take for granted.

I shift a few things around in the studio, run downstairs to grab several pillows and blankets, and set up a comfortable space for her to lie. As she disrobes, I prop a blank canvas on the easel and shift its position, grab my paints and brushes, and take a seat on my stool.

Shelly lies down on the pillows and shifts until she finds a comfortable position on her side.

"If you need a break," I say, "just tell me. It's late, so I promise not to keep us up here long."

Shelly folds a pillow in half and stuffs it between her head and arm. "How long will the painting take?"

My head teeters left and right. "Several hours." I lick my lips and swallow as my eyes trail over her curves. Take in her creamy, bare skin. "If we're up here daily, a couple hours each time, maybe two weeks. Or less." I trace a finger over my upper lip. "Also depends on how I paint you. The heavier the details, the longer it'll take."

She inhales deeply and swallows on the exhale. "Okay."

Then she closes her eyes and her entire frame relaxes. Not a hint of resistance or timidity dons her expression.

*Damn, she is beautiful. Too beautiful.*

Over the next four hours, my eyes flit between Shelly and the canvas. The bristles of my brushes dip in various shades of pigment as I take in the bow of her lips, the slope of her nose, the swell of her breasts and arch of her hip. Blending. Shaping. Contouring. One stroke at a time, I bring this incredible woman to life on canvas in an unfamiliar way.

Abstract art has never been my style. I appreciate the style, but feel odd painting it. As if I'm misrepresenting the subject. Much of my art resembles the muse. Clean lines and sharp detail. When you study the piece, you see my muse.

With this, though…

Shelly bares herself to me fully, and not just her flesh. Just out of reach, she exposes every piece of herself and grants me permission to portray her beauty and vulnerability in my artwork. Allows me the opportunity to uncover an unseen layer of her charm and magnificence. Paint her nude heart and impassioned aura.

I have no plans for anyone else to see this painting. This piece is personal. The most intimate art I will create.

But accidents happen. And although I'd never intentionally betray Shelly or her trust, I can't take the risk.

So this piece will be as complex and stunning as the woman herself.

Splashes of color in a display unlike any other. Short, blotchy strokes of my brush on the canvas. Bursts of bright pigment to offset the occasional shadows.

And when she and I see it, we will know. We will see what no one else sees. We will remember the nights and hours we spent in this studio. The way her breaths evened out as she fell asleep. The way I bit the end of my brush as I looked from her to the canvas, then smiled.

We will remember, and that is all that matters.

Her love. My love. Us.

I set my brush down and open my mouth to call it a night, but snap it shut when I see her closed eyes. Her slightly parted lips. Hear her soft snores as her chest rises and falls steadily.

On and off during the session, her eyes drifted closed, but her body never fully relaxed. Not like it is now.

Quietly, I clean up what I need to. Then I tiptoe over to where she sleeps, wrap her body in the blanket, and scoop her up into my arms. Halfway down the stairs, her eyes flutter open and she curls into my chest.

"Sorry I fell asleep," she mumbles into my neck.

I press a kiss to her forehead and hug her closer. "Sleep, my Andromeda. Sleep."

In the bedroom, I lay her on the bed, but she gets up and shuffles toward the bathroom. After a moment to herself, she tugs one of my shirts over her head and slips on a pair of boy shorts. We crawl under the covers and I press my front to her back, slipping one arm under her pillow and laying the other over her belly.

"Love you," she whispers into the darkness as she scoots closer.

I kiss her hair. "Love you."

She drifts back to sleep within seconds. For hour-long minutes, I lie awake and listen to her soft snores. Stroke my fingers over her belly, over our baby, and I send a thank you to the universe.

*Thank you for bringing this brave, strong woman into my life. Thank you for gifting me with her heart. Thank you for giving me the chance to find love, real love, with her.*

As long as there is breath in my lungs and blood in my veins, I will protect her, her heart and our baby. I will love them. Unconditionally and without fear. Always.

After one last kiss to her hair, I drift off to sleep. My entire world wrapped in my arms.

# *thirteen*

## SHELLY

Something isn't right.

I take a deep breath. Then another. And another.

My heart pounds viciously in my chest. The beat hard and heavy. An uncomfortable throb beneath my sternum.

I close my eyes and try to calm the worry flooding my thoughts. Breathe deeply and picture my heart settling.

*Deep breaths. Slow and steady. In through the nose. Out through the mouth.*

Minutes pass and the bang, bang, banging of my heart settles a fraction. I kick my feet out from beneath the blanket and welcome the cool air. After a few more deep breaths, my throbbing heart calms further.

Devlyn shifts behind me, his fingers tracing small lines over my belly.

"Morning," he says with a rasp I've grown to love more each time I hear it.

"Morning."

His lips trail kisses down the side of my neck and along the ridge of my shoulder. His hand glides over my belly and up my body until he palms my breast. I arch my back and fill his hand further.

Rolling onto my back, I bring my lips to his. Weave my fingers in his dark, wayward strands. My heart beats a brutal rhythm, but it's nothing like the pounding from minutes ago. This rhythm is one I know, one I feel head to toe.

I peel my shirt off and strip out of my panties as Devlyn shoves his briefs down and tosses them to the floor. His lips dance over each collarbone, my sternum and breasts, down my midline until he lands beneath my navel. For a beat, he stares at my belly and caresses it with such delicacy. He kisses the slight swell, then lifts his gaze.

Tears brim his green eyes and it steals my breath. Freezes me on the spot. Thickens an emotional ball in my throat.

"Love you, Shell."

My eyes sting as I look down at him, as I stroke his cheek with my knuckles. "Love you, Dev."

His head dips beneath the sheet as his palms trail up the sides of my torso. His tongue paints the flesh between my thighs. Flicks my clit and licks up my center. Consumes me while his fingers toy with my nipples until I writhe beneath his talented tongue.

With my orgasm on his tongue and lips, he kisses his way up my body. Positions himself in the cradle of my hips. Crashes his lips to mine and kisses me fiercely. Rocks his hips forward and fills me fully. Our shared gasps echo off the walls.

And then our eyes lock. For a beat, we simply breathe each other in. Connect in the most primal way. He kisses me once, twice, three times before sucking my bottom lip between his. The simmering fire in his green irises burns brighter. Hotter. Fire that ignites every inch of my soul. Fire that arouses and stokes my love for this man.

Our bodies move in a synchronized rhythm. An incomparable rhythm. A rhythm that is only ours.

My legs hug his waist, ankles lock at his lower back. As he thrusts forward, my heels dig into his muscled glutes and drive him deeper. Harder. With each rock of his hips, I climb back up that peak. With each stroke of his bare cock, I cry out for more.

His hand drifts down the curve of my breast, my waist, my hip, then dips between us. Slowly, his thumb paints small circles over my clit.

My jaw slackens as my breaths stutter from my lips. One delicious stroke after another, he summons my orgasm from somewhere deep. His tongue traces my lower lip. Teeth nip my chin and along my jaw. He sucks my earlobe between his lips. Kisses and nibbles down the column of my throat. Wraps his lips around the flesh at my shoulder and sucks. Bites. Ravages. Hard and fast and desperate.

And it's all too much.

A harsh growl spills from my lips as heat spreads up my chest, over my breasts and throat before hitting my cheeks. My legs shake as my body hugs Devlyn everywhere. And with one more rock of his hips, his orgasm fills me.

Sweat slicks our skin as our heavy breaths float through the room. His pulse pounds in his chest to the same beat as my own. My fingers trail up and down the sides of his spine before threading in his hair.

His lips kiss the spot on my shoulder where he sank his teeth in and imprinted my skin. One kiss at a time, he works his way to my lips. Our tongues twist and tangle and taste. Say I love you in ways our voices never will.

I will never get enough of his kisses. Never get enough of him.

He breaks the kiss and lifts slightly, bracketing me with his forearms. His fingers toy with strands of my hair as his greens lock onto my blues. One inhale after another, he breathes me in while I do the same.

I hadn't anticipated how emotional sex would be. How all-consuming the act would feel. Sure, I expected it to be more than just a physical act—hence why I waited—but I never imagined feeling so much, so deeply, all at once.

With Devlyn, sex isn't just something that happens with genitalia and lips and hands. It isn't just something we do to reach physical euphoria. We make love with our bodies and hearts and souls. Connect on a deeper, more profound level. Give in to our deepest desires and share a piece of ourselves no one else will have.

Until him, I never understood the bond Cora and Gavin shared. Couldn't grasp the devotion Jonas and Autumn felt. Was confounded by Micah and Peyton's love after such a rocky history. And although I'd read countless romance novels, the concept of sex being more than a physical act left me baffled.

But I get it now. I understand.

Sex is more than a means to an end with Devlyn. I won't deny loving the bliss of orgasm. Surely, Devlyn wouldn't either. But it's more than that.

It's the way his fingers caress my body. The way his breath heats my skin. The way he whispers in my ear and tells me he loves me. More than that, it's how his eyes lock with mine as our bodies come together. How his gaze penetrates deeper and captures my soul. Pumps the fist-sized organ in my chest and floods my veins with unconditional love.

Devlyn owns my heart, is the protector of my soul, and I wouldn't want it any other way.

I comb my fingers through his damp strands and lift off the pillow to kiss him.

"Hungry?" he asks and I nod. "Take your time getting up. I'll make breakfast." He rocks back and I immediately miss the weight of him.

He kisses my forehead, then rises from the bed and grabs a pair of sweatpants. I stare after him without shame. Push up on my elbows and ogle his body as he slips on the pants. Watch his every movement as he pads across the room. Salivate as his muscles bunch and flex with each step. Clamp my thighs together as he ruffles his hair with his fingers. Lick and bite my bottom lip as a smile kicks up the corner of his lips.

He disappears into the bathroom to clean up and brush his teeth. I fall back onto the mattress, close my eyes, and breathe in the moment. Breathe in the scent of him and sex and love.

After a beat, he reappears and presses another kiss to my forehead. "Any requests?"

Countless breakfast foods flit through my head, but one continues to circle back. "French toast, please."

"Powdered sugar?"

"Is that a serious question?"

He chuckles. "Powdered sugar it is. Bacon or sausage?"

"Bacon. Oh, and the leftover eggs from dipping the French toast, add extra cinnamon."

Walking out of the bedroom backward, he blows me a kiss. "Extra cinnamon. Check."

Pans and bowls clang outside the bedroom as I slowly slip out from under the covers. As I enter the bathroom, my pulse mimics the same turbulent beating from earlier. My heart feels bigger, heavier, almost painful. Every other beat, I gasp for air, but it doesn't fill my lungs. Not fully.

I plop down on the toilet, grip my knees, and close my eyes. Bend at the waist and drop my head. Inhale deeply and hold it until my lungs burn.

Several breaths pass before my pulse returns to normal and the pain in my chest subsides. Slowly, I sit up and open my eyes. Rub the center of my chest with the heel of my palm. The backs of my eyes sting as worry seeps in.

*What is happening? Maybe this is a normal side effect of pregnancy. Should ask Cora and Autumn tonight.*

After I use the toilet, brush my teeth, and untangle the bird's nest on top of my head, I tug on one of Devlyn's T-shirts and a pair of sleep pants.

The scent of maple and cinnamon and butter fills my nose as I head for the kitchen. The worry from minutes ago fades to the background. My stomach growls and I press a hand to the beast, muttering, "Almost time."

Before long, Devlyn piles two thick slices of French toast, scrambled eggs, several strips of bacon, and mixed fresh berries on plates. He dusts the French toast with powdered sugar, then fills glasses with orange juice. He delivers it all to the dining room table and waves me off when I try to help.

I pour a generous helping of real maple syrup—not that sugary brown goop—and dive in, moaning around my fork. Devlyn smiles in satisfaction as he lifts scrambled eggs to his lips.

"Maybe we should have breakfast for all the meals," he suggests.

Holding up a finger, I mumble around the bite. "I'd vote yes, but there're too many other good things to eat."

His smile widens. "True, but breakfast seems to be your favorite."

It is definitely a top contender. I point my fork at Devlyn. "Anything you make is my favorite."

A brow arches on his handsome face. "I'll have to remember that."

Why do I feel like I just walked myself into a corner? *Because you did.* Oh well, too late now.

We park at Jonas and Autumn's house just before seven. Two cars other than theirs are here—Gavin's SUV and Micah's truck. I scoop up the bag on the floorboard between my feet and Devlyn reaches for it.

"No." I hold it just out of reach. "I know I shouldn't be lifting anything heavy, but this is like three pounds max. It's freaking side salads."

"Shell..." Devlyn looks out the windshield and sighs. "Just trying to help," he mumbles.

My hand rests on his forearm as I wait for his eyes to meet mine. "I know you are and I love you for that." I take his hand in mine, lift it to my lips, and kiss the top. "But I'm not helpless. I can still do some things myself. Yes, I need to be cautious. But that doesn't mean I stop living." Holding up the bag, I say, "I got this." He nods as his lips fumble between his teeth. "And if I need help, I promise to ask."

"It's just..." He breathes heavily. "I worry."

I graze his cheek with my fingertips and his eyes close briefly. "Me too. But we're doing everything according to plan." I lean in and press my lips to his. Let the warmth of his touch and breath comfort me. "For now, let's try not to worry. Let's try to not stress ourselves over the what-ifs."

For a moment, we just stare at each other. Neither of us says a word. Then subtly, he nods. "I'll try."

We amble to the door, hand in hand, and are greeted by Clementine and Spartan first. Hugs are exchanged with everyone and it isn't long before I get pulled away by Cora and Autumn. Clementine watches over Clara and Ryker while we catch up for a few.

Two songs later, the house is bustling with all of our friends.

Laughter floats through the room and outside on the back patio. Hickory and the scent of grilled meats and shish kebabbed vegetables fill the air. Old-school rock plays from speakers mounted on the back of the house while fire lights tiki torches around the yard.

Devlyn chats with some of the guys while I sit with Cora and Autumn on the lounger.

The more Devlyn and I join everyone on Sundays, the more he steps out of his shell. The more he smiles and laughs and comes alive. Opens up a little more. This family... we balance in ways genetic families don't. We provide love and advice and comfort. We avoid judgment and hurt.

I love how easily Devlyn fits in our circle. How everyone accepted him without hesitation. He needed us as much as we needed him. And damn am I lucky that I get to call him mine.

Zoning out, I stare at the fire. Think back to this morning and the vicious pounding in my chest. Take a deep breath and blink away the fog. "Can I ask you guys something?" I ask Cora and Autumn.

"Always," Cora says as Autumn answers, "Of course."

"It's a pregnancy question." I toy with the bottom hem of

my shirt. "I haven't said anything to Devlyn because I don't want him to freak out. Especially if it's a normal thing."

When I don't continue, Cora lays her hand over mine in my lap. "Shell, what is it?"

"A couple times now, I've had this heavy feeling in my chest." I press my palm to my heart. "Like a strange heartbeat. It doesn't *hurt*, per se, but it makes me breathless." I look to Cora then Autumn. "Did either of you have that?"

The twist in my belly sinks deep when both of them shake their head.

*Not good.*

"No two pregnancies are the same," Autumn says. "Clementine was a wild child in the womb and Ryker just chilled for the most part. But I never had chest pains." She winces. "Probably a good idea to talk with your doctor."

"I'll second that," Cora adds. "Clara was a little gymnast during the last trimester, and I had the occasional bout of heartburn, but nothing like what you're describing."

*Great.* This is what I feared. This is why I also haven't said anything to Devlyn yet.

As it is, he doesn't want me to do anything besides relax. Which, in theory, is nice, but spending every day on the couch with my feet up isn't realistic. I have a business to run, and eventually take over. There is so much to prepare for with the baby. Classes to attend. New mother skills to learn. Labor breathing and learning how to breastfeed.

The pounding in my chest kicks in and I press the heel of my palm to my sternum as I inhale deeply.

Cora leans closer and whispers in my ear, "Is it happening now?" I nod. "What were you just thinking about? Right before it happened."

I close my eyes and pinch them tightly. Breathe through

the pain in my chest. "Everything that's to come. With the pregnancy, motherhood." My eyes open and I glance up at my best friend. "The shop. How this baby changes everything I thought I knew. How it disrupts so many lives, not just mine."

Cora wraps an arm around my shoulders and pulls me into her side. Autumn scoots closer and leans her weight into my other side. On a sigh, I absorb their comfort. Let it fill the cracks of doubt. Let it ease my worry about the future and motherhood and new responsibilities.

"First of all, I felt everything you're feeling," Cora admits. "Gavin and I hadn't been back together long before we got pregnant." She shifts to look me square in the eye, her gaze never more serious. "I was scared, Shell. Scared we weren't ready. Scared I'd lose him again. Scared we wouldn't be *us* with a baby." The corners of her mouth tip up in a small, soft smile. "But my fear was for nothing. Just past pain haunting my present."

"How did you let go of the fear?"

She tips her head to the side. "It never fades. Not fully. But it lessens with each passing day. With each assurance that I'm not in this parenting gig alone." She looks across the patio. Her eyes land on Gavin, baby Clara cradled in his arms while he chats with a few of the guys. Jonas is there too, Ryker bundled in a blanket and snug against his chest. They talk and joke and laugh, all while doing the dad thing. "You aren't doing this alone, Shell."

"Not for a second," Autumn adds. "After everything with Clementine's father, I worried about Jonas's reaction to the pregnancy." She lays a hand on mine. "But then I reminded myself that Jonas is a different man. He walked through hell alongside me as I fought for Clementine, for our livelihood."

"Jonas has a heart of gold," I tell her.

Her eyes find his across the patio and his entire frame lights up. "That he does." Then she shifts in her seat to face me more. "What about Devlyn? How's his heart?"

God, what a loaded question. Not one I can answer simply. Not one I can answer fully without sharing secrets he isn't ready for the world to know.

"When it comes to me, to us, he has the biggest heart."

Cora's brows scrunch together. "Why do I feel like there's more to the story?"

Because there is. Because Devlyn has demons to face, to conquer, to let go. "There is more." I look to Cora, then to Autumn, before my eyes land on Devlyn, a brilliant, genuine smile on his lips. "But his story isn't mine to tell. All I will say is he came from a past none of us can comprehend. Not fully. But he's working on it. For me, for us, for the baby."

Cora rubs small circles on my shoulder. "It's silly, but I have to ask."

"What?"

"You're safe, right?" If I thought she looked serious minutes ago, I was dead wrong. My best friend has never been more somber than she is now. "Please tell me you are."

I take her free hand and Autumn's in both of mine. My eyes darting between the two of them. "I swear to you, I am safe. And if that ever changes—for any of us—we tell each other." They both nod. "No matter what."

"No matter what," they say in unison.

After a squeeze of my hand, Cora releases mine from her grasp. "Enough of the heavy talk." Autumn nods in agreement. "Please call your doctor in the morning." She points a finger at me and narrows her eyes like a stern mother. "And tell Devlyn. I understand you not wanting to worry him, especially if it's nothing, but he deserves to know. This is his baby too."

I love and hate that she is right. But this is why I talk with my best friends. They look at my situation from a different angle, with a fresh perspective.

"I will. Promise."

The last hour at Jonas and Autumn's house goes by a bit lighter. Devlyn curls me into his side as we sit by the fire bowl and chat with our friends. By the time we exchange hugs and goodnights, I breathe easier.

Tomorrow, I will call Dr. Webster and set an appointment. Tomorrow, I will tell Devlyn what I felt earlier. Tell him about the pain in my chest. That is what partners in committed relationships do; we share everything. No matter the outcome.

# fourteen

## DEVLYN

My phone rings on the drafting table, inches from where I'm sketching a new piece. A drawing requested by a new client. A portrait of the woman's grandchildren, their adorable smiles —one of which is missing a front tooth—glowing in the photo she sent.

I set my pencil down and swipe my phone off the table to see Shelly's name on the screen. I tap the green phone icon and smile as I say, "Hello."

"Hi," she replies, her voice a breath over a whisper. "Do you have a minute?"

My muscles tense up at her question. Why would she ask that? Of the two of us, my schedule is nothing but flexible. "Of course. What's wrong?"

"I, uh…" She goes quiet, but I still hear noises in the background. Then she exhales audibly. "I had to set a new doctor's appointment with Dr. Webster."

Metal scrapes wood as I rise from my stool. My vision blurs and stomach twists as my mind conjures up countless reasons why Shelly would need to see Dr. Webster sooner than her next appointment. Unable to be still, I pace the length of the room. Take a deep breath and inhale the scents of the studio. Allow the earthy smells to ground me as I grow more frantic with each breath.

"Why?"

"I, uh…"

Shelly goes quiet again. I picture her fidgeting with her apron strings as she works up the nerve to answer. Why is she so hesitant? Did something happen to her? Is the baby okay? The longer she remains silent, the longer my list of worse-case scenarios gets.

After what feels like a week, she speaks again. "I've been having pains," she says a breath above a whisper.

As I reach the landing for the stairs, instead of spinning around to pace the room again, I take the stairs two at a time. Reach the bottom floor before the next words leave my lips. "What kind of pains? Is it the baby?"

I dash to the bedroom, put the phone on speaker and strip out of my clothes. I grab a clean pair of jeans and a fresh shirt, slipping them on as she talks.

"No. I don't know. I-I don't think so." Her voice stutters. "It's in my chest, near my heart."

My hands freeze as I slip on socks. *Her heart. No. No, no, no.* I take a deep breath and beg my mind to not travel down the road of misdiagnoses. Not to think of things such as heart failure or angina or embolisms. Shelly is too young for heart problems, isn't she? *Stay calm. You can't help her if you're freaking the fuck out.*

"When is your appointment?" My voice cracks at the end.

"Today at four."

"I'll pick you up."

"Dev, no." She huffs on the other end as I pick up the

phone and take it off speaker. "My car is here. I'll meet you there."

My eyes close and I clamp them tightly. Let the discomfort distract me momentarily. Tell myself to take another breath and not force my insistence upon her. We don't know what the problem is. It could be something minor. Completely normal. I need to let her make decisions. I need to not steal her choices like my mother did for me.

Unless the doctor says otherwise.

"Okay, I'll be there." I wander out of the bedroom and into the kitchen. Stare blankly at the counters and cabinets and appliances, unsure what to do next. "Do you need anything until then?"

The clock on the stove reads just after two. I inhale deeply and twist the phone up on the exhale. Close my eyes and focus on what I *can* control. In less than two hours, I will see her. In less than two hours, we will figure out why she is having chest pains. *Shelly will be okay. The baby will be okay.*

"No, thank you," she says softly, a smile in her voice.

"Take it easy until you leave. Please." I don't care if I come across as desperate. I *am* desperate.

She chuckles. "I will. Elizabeth won't let me do anything except arrange. Not even paperwork. She says it'll stress me out too much."

Light laughter spills from my lips, although I feel anything but weightless. *Thank you, Elizabeth.* "I need to send that woman a fruit basket or something. Gift her art for her birthday."

"She won't say no."

"I love you, Shell," I say, my tone more somber. "So much."

"Love you too, Dev. See you soon."

"Soon."

The call disconnects, but I don't lower the phone from my ear. My limbs remain frozen while my mind continually whirls from the news.

I don't know what is happening with Shelly, what has her heart in literal pain, but I swear to do whatever it takes to keep her safe. To keep the baby safe. She may not like what happens next, what treatment the doctor prescribes and how fragilely I tend to her every need, but I can't lose her. I *won't* lose her. Not now, not ever.

I *need* her. More than the air I breathe, more than the life force that keeps my heart beating, I need Shelly. And nothing will take her from me.

With each symptom Shelly tells Dr. Webster she experienced recently, I bite down harder on the inside of my cheek and curl my fingers tighter. Taste iron on my tongue as I break the skin. Feel the sting in my palms as my nails dig deeper.

These aren't minor issues. Chest pain that occasionally gets better with deep breathing, but not always. Tingling in the chest. Problems breathing and tightness in the chest. Profuse sweating and random dizziness. The more symptoms she rattles off, the more it sounds like signs of a heart attack.

Why didn't she tell me about this? I love her pride and independence, but this is different. This is serious. This not only affects Shelly, it also affects the baby.

*You know why*, my mind mocks. Because I would have rushed her to the emergency room. Would have begged her to stop working. Would have strongly encouraged her to sit on the couch all day and not lift a finger. All for something her regular doctor can easily help with.

Still… Shelly not speaking up and sharing this vital information makes me question her trust in me, in us. And that hurts the most.

Dr. Webster jots notes in Shelly's file, then looks up with a soft, but serious expression. "From everything you've shared, it sounds as if you're suffering from panic attacks. This isn't abnormal for new mothers or parents." She rolls herself closer to us on the stool. "But this is your body telling you that you need to relax more. Physically and mentally." She lays a hand on Shelly's forearm. "It's okay to let go of some control right now. It's okay to let others help."

Paper crinkles as Shelly drops her head back on the exam table. "Feels like I've already given up so much."

"And you may have. Just remind yourself why you're giving up these tasks. Temporarily." She scoots the stool back and stands. "When the little one arrives, life will slowly go back to normal. Well, the new normal." Dr. Webster shifts her gaze my way. "Let Dad help out. Anything heavy or stressful, let him carry some of the weight."

Pushing up on her elbows, Shelly moves to a seated position. "What about work?" She tugs her top back in position. "I need to work." Desperation licks her tone, pleading with Dr. Webster to not take work away from her.

"You're still at the florist shop?" Shelly nods. "Work is fine." Shelly sags in relief just as Dr. Webster points a finger. "But no picking up boxes or bending at the waist. Simpler tasks only. Desk work or flower arrangements. I don't foresee many disgruntled customers."

Except maybe another visit from my mother. *Please, no. No more visits from Karen Templar.*

"I know giving up some of your freedoms isn't easy, but it's not just about you anymore."

"You're right." Shelly sighs. "It's just… how will I know what's too strenuous until I do it?"

Dr. Webster chats with us a few more minutes before escorting us to the checkout desk. She mentions how panic attacks could elevate blood pressure. And uncontrolled blood pressure may equal bed rest, something Shelly definitely does not want. Before she walks off, she reminds Shelly one last time to go slow, to take her time. She suggests pregnancy yoga and meditation and more walks at the park.

We wander out the door and head for our cars. I hate that we are leaving in separate vehicles, especially after this visit, but thankfully the drive home is short. And then I will cater to Shelly while she relaxes.

The situation isn't what either of us expected or wanted, but we have to adjust accordingly. Remind ourselves this modification in our daily routine is temporary. Remind ourselves why this change is necessary.

Sidling up to Shelly at her car, I press my lips to her forehead. "See you at home."

She nods, her eyes glazed over slightly. "At home."

As she drives away, a weight forms in my stomach. A weight I cannot shake. A weight that tells me there is more to come. And honestly, I'm not sure how much more I can handle.

# fifteen

## SHELLY

The next four months are going to be the death of me.

Am I being a bit dramatic? Probably, but I don't care. I have earned the right to be a drama queen. When you have done everything on your own for decades, being told you can't sucks. Losing any semblance of your independence sucks. Feeling helpless sucks.

Not a minute passes where I regret this pregnancy. If anything, I consider myself lucky to have found Devlyn, to have fallen in love with him, to start the next phase of life with him.

But so much has changed in such a short period. In the process, part of me feels as if I have lost myself. Lost the woman I was before Devlyn and pregnancy. Lost the time I once had with friends and family.

Again, I have zero regrets about my relationship with Devlyn. I love him. More than I thought I could love another person. I don't regret the baby either. It's just… I wish our time line was different. I wish Devlyn and I would've had more time together first. To explore life and love, just the two of us, before going from zero to one-hundred in the blink of an eye.

All of it happened so quickly. Us evolving from *just friends* to boyfriend and girlfriend to living together with a baby on the way. In less than six months, we went from nothing to everything.

Much as I wanted a relationship like those in my romance novels, I didn't expect to get the whole shebang all at once. The guy, the house, the baby. Fingers crossed, I get the happily ever after too.

Two weeks ago, Dr. Webster said I'd suffered from panic attacks. The most unfathomable part of her diagnosis was that I'd never experienced anxiety prior to pregnancy. Not once. Perhaps it takes a momentous occasion to trigger anxiety or depression. Or maybe it's part of our genetic makeup and remains dormant in some until the match is struck.

Hopefully my lessened activity and new meditative regimen helps reduce the attacks. Hopefully they vanish altogether, otherwise there will be medication and the possibility of bed rest. I'd like to avoid both.

"That's stunning," Elizabeth says as she returns from lunch.

I eye the bouquet on the arrangement table, twisting the vase left then right as a smile plumps my cheeks. "Thank you."

The plethora of pink flowers is at the request of one of our regular customers. His wife adores pink—she obviously has good taste—and he ordered the arrangement for their twenty-fifth wedding anniversary. After a hefty payment, he gave us free rein to choose the flowers and greenery. His only request… *"It needs a lot of pink."*

"How many stems have you added?"

I lean back and look for any *empty* spots in the bouquet. "Thirty." I twist my lips in concentration. "I'd like to get a full three dozen."

Elizabeth pats my shoulder. "You will." A soft smile on her lips as she wanders off. "I'll be in the back unpacking the delivery. Holler if you need me."

"Will do."

I go back to the bouquet and zone out as I add the last remaining stems to the vase. Satisfied with the bouquet, I take it into the cooler where we stash orders waiting to be delivered. As I exit, I spot a man in the store near the meadow mural.

"Good afternoon," I greet him. "Is there anything I can help you with today?"

For two breaths, he doesn't acknowledge my presence. Doesn't speak a word. He simply stares at the painting on the wall.

Queasiness twists my stomach. Has me inching away from this stranger. My eyes fall shut as I inhale deeply and tell my body and mind to relax. Tell myself to not get worked up over nothing. He could simply be admiring the work, nothing more.

Cool and a bit more collected, my eyes open as I put on my best work smile. I open my mouth to tell the man I will leave him to browse and check back with him shortly, but he speaks up first.

"Beautiful piece," he states. The soft timbre of his voice is vaguely familiar. Though I have never met this man, something about him screams recognition. My brows pinch together as I study him from the corner of my eye.

"Um, thank you." I wipe my hands on the apron at my waist. "A local artist painted the mural for the shop."

The man shoves his hands in the pockets of his dress slacks, rocks back on his heels once, then nods. "I'm familiar with his work."

Never said the artist was a man. The queasiness in my belly builds as bile climbs up my throat.

*Who is this man? And why the hell does he make me uncomfortable?*

Taking a step back, then another, I separate myself from the wobbly energy he exudes. "Well, if you need—"

"Are you Shelly?"

Every instinct in me screams to not answer him. Is he some kind of stalker? It wouldn't be the first time a customer obsessed over the way I arrange flowers. Odd as it is, it has happened. To both me and Elizabeth.

"Uh…"

The man twists to face me head on and extends a hand my way. "Sorry. James Templar."

*For the love of all that is holy in this world. Someone, please rescue me from the never-ending surprises.*

James Templar… for a beat, I take him in. Brown locks trimmed neat and close to his scalp. Familiar angular jawline. Same height. Same build. Same glass-green irises. Without question, this man is Devlyn's father.

But why is he here?

Reluctantly, I place my hand in his and shake. "Shelly. But you already knew that somehow." I quickly withdraw my hand.

His hand goes back to his pocket and he takes a step back, granting me room to breathe. Time ticks by and neither of us says a word. And in this momentary blip of time, I acknowledge that James Templar is nothing like his wife. Quite the opposite, actually. While she demands attention, he seems content with disappearing. She is the spotlight and he is the shadow. How odd.

So why is he married to her? Why does he allow her to verbally and emotionally abuse their only child?

"Is there something you needed?" I ask, my tone as neutral as possible. Although this man has not garnered my respect, my parents would berate me for weeks if I spoke to a stranger without courtesy.

"I, uh…" He glances back to the mural before meeting my eyes once more. "It's not my place or position to do so, but I came here to apologize."

My forehead tightens as my brows drop. "Apologize?"

The only person who should apologize is Karen Templar. She has inflicted one wound after another. This man, Devlyn's father, has not slighted me. As for Devlyn… I don't know their history or how often he speaks with his dad. I honestly can't recall a time when Devlyn mentioned his father.

He swallows, then nods. "Yes. For how Devlyn's mother has behaved recently."

*Seriously?*

Not sure what it is, but this man driving an hour to come apologize for his wife's actions pisses me off. Try as I might, calming my rising blood pressure proves challenging. But with each throb and whoosh of my pulse, I remind myself I need to find my zen. I need to relax. If not for me, for the baby.

But I swear, as soon as this baby is born, these people will hear my wrath.

"Why?"

He tilts his head and eyes me for a beat. "Why?" he asks and I nod. "Shelly, I don't know you. Don't know anything about you, but you seem like a nice person." He smiles and it instantly makes me think of Devlyn and the identical smile he doesn't grant many or often. "For Devlyn to be so taken by you…" His eyes avert to the mural for a breath. "With his past, it must mean you matter to him. Very much."

"So, you're apologizing because Devlyn and I are together and I seem like a nice person?"

What a strange reason.

First off, he shouldn't *have* to apologize for his wife. She should apologize. Not that I'd listen after her degradation. That woman believes she is the epitome of perfection, when in truth, she wouldn't know real courtesy if it slapped her in the face.

Second, and still, why? Why is he here? What has he heard in regard to our recent interactions with his wife?

Last, and probably most importantly, why does this feel like a bandage over something that requires surgery to fix?

This whole interaction feels like one big clusterfuck of confusion. Maybe James Templar usually skirts around the truth. Maybe he is always the fixer-upper. The one that steps in after hurricane Karen wreaks havoc on whatever upsets her and rebuilds the broken structures.

I don't get it. Why he is here and what he hopes to resolve with this conversation. But if he doesn't get to the point soon, I may just ask him to leave and walk away.

On an audible exhale, he shakes his head. "Not just that." His head hangs forward, his eyes on his dress shoes. "I haven't spoken with Devlyn for months." Slowly, he lifts his head and our eyes meet. "Our relationship, mine with Devlyn, isn't the same as with his mother. Since he left for college, we talked less. That's just our personalities. But we always talked. At least every couple of weeks, if only for a few minutes over the phone." He works his jaw in a nervous jitter.

His eyes crinkling at the corners slightly. "I haven't spoken with him since November. Not since the day before the art exhibition."

*More than six months. Didn't he spend time with them during Christmas?* Maybe his father wasn't there. Devlyn attended a holiday party his mother hosted, but perhaps it was more of a schmoozing event than actual time spent with family.

Did Devlyn cut his father off because of his mother? Because of me?

"I'm not sure what to say."

It's the truth. I have no clue what to tell this man. I don't make decisions for Devlyn. And from what he has told me about his parents, he didn't really make his own decisions until he left home. Even then, his mother still directed part of the narrative.

But I won't do that. Ever. Nor will I let his parents disrupt all the progress he has made with countless hours of therapy. Therapy no person should have to endure. Not for this.

"You don't need to say anything." He rocks back on his heels again and I realize this must be a nervous action for him. "I truly am sorry for how Devlyn's mother has behaved. Toward him and you."

"All due respect, Mr. Templar, you shouldn't be apologizing for her." I give him a tight, uncomfortable smile. "And I'm not sure if an apology will ever make up for the damage she has done."

An odd flutter erupts in my belly and, without thinking, I lay a hand on my lower abdomen. The second I do, his eyes drop and land on my hand. Immediately, I shift and tuck my hands in my back pockets.

But it is too late. The deed is done. I see it in the widening of his eyes. Hear it in his loud swallow.

His eyes lift to mine and I watch as they glass over. As recognition truly sets in. As this man realizes I am carrying his grandchild, someone he may never meet because of his wife.

"It's not your place, Shelly, but will you please ask Devlyn to call or text me?" He blinks back the tears rimming his eyes. "I won't say anything" —his eyes drift to my belly for a breath— "to his mother about…" *the baby*. I see the words in his eyes. A proclamation he won't voice, maybe to protect the baby and Devlyn.

"I will make mention, but not any promises." My eyes hold his. "Devlyn makes his own choices. If he wants to speak with you, that is his decision to make. His voice has been stolen from him for too many years. I won't do the same."

James nods as he rolls his lips between his teeth. "Thank you, Shelly." He takes a step back and removes his hands from his pockets. "For what it's worth, I hope to know you one day. From what I can tell, you're a good person. I'm happy my son has you."

Every cell in my body wants to thank this man for the kind sentiment, but I stop myself. Clamp my lips tight and refuse to grant him gratitude. Not when he has enabled his wife's cruelty toward Devlyn his entire life. Thanking this man wipes away all the harm he caused by not stepping up for his own child. Thanking this man would imply compliments and recognition diminish the pain his wife—and by proxy, him—inflicted.

I won't grant him such kindness. Not because I, too, am cruel. But because I love Devlyn. Unconditionally. I stand by him, through the hurt and happiness. Through the tears and laughter.

When it dawns on James I have nothing more to say, he nods, takes a step back, pivots away, and ambles toward the door. "Hope we meet again, Shelly." He glances one last time at my belly, gives me a pained smile, then leaves.

I wander to the door and stare out the glass to watch him drive away. He slips behind the wheel of a white BMW sedan, lifts a hand when he notices me watching, then backs out.

My hand goes to my ponytail, my fingers toying with the strands as I continue to look outside. Watching. Waiting. Praying for no more surprises. Although this one isn't half as bad as the previous surprises, it still unsettles me.

James Templar may be nothing like his wife, but he still hurt his son. Making up for all he and his wife have done will take a heck of a lot more than one conversation in Petal and Vine. It will take drastic measures. A larger-than-life change.

For Devlyn's sake, I hope he gets to keep at least one parent. Without the influence of his wife, James Templar may be a good man. A man worthy of being a grandfather to our child. A man Devlyn might look up to in the future.

# sixteen

## DEVLYN

"Your dad stopped by the shop today."

My fork hovers between my plate and mouth as I process what Shelly just said. Slowly, I set my fork down and swallow. Let her words sink in.

*My father was in Petal and Vine today.*

Why?

"Are you okay?" I don't need my father stirring up my mother's wasp nest of activity and upsetting Shelly.

"Yeah," she says on a nod. "He was kind."

This doesn't come as a surprise. My father never had a mean bone in his body. He also lost his backbone standing beside my mother.

"What did he want?"

"To meet me, and to ask me to ask you if you'd call or text him."

Shelly says the words so casually. Not an ounce of concern in her tone. Which is a tremendous relief.

My father may not be barbaric like my mother, but he disregards her words and actions as if they mean nothing. As if they harm no one. Recently, I learned his behavior was unacceptable. I learned his actions were equally as damaging as saying and doing the acts themselves.

Shelly reaches across the table and lays her hand over mine. "He was kind," she repeats. "I made him no promises. That I'd tell you or that you'd follow through." Her shimmery blues lock with my greens. "Reaching out is your choice." She gives my hand a gentle squeeze. "Also..."

My eyes dart between hers as I wait for her to finish. "Also, what?"

"I think he surmised I'm pregnant." *Shit.* "I felt this flutter and my hand automatically went to my belly."

I don't curse Shelly for inadvertently letting my father know about the baby. I curse that he may say something to my mother. Which may trigger another visit. A visit we do not need.

"Devlyn, I don't know the first thing about your father, but he seems to genuinely miss you. Or at least the conversations you shared."

James Templar is a good man that has done countless good deeds for others. He never speaks ill of anyone, ever—including my mother, which is part of the problem. He may be a good man, but he doesn't know how to be strong—for himself or others.

If he has a good heart, is it possible to fix his broken pieces? Several hours per month, I work to mend my own broken parts. Perhaps he can do the same. I like to think it is possible, but as long as he stands beside my mother, I won't take unnecessary or foolish risks.

"I'll reach out to him." I pick my fork back up and lift the bite to my mouth. "How was the rest of your day?"

Over the rest of dinner, Shelly recants her day at work. Although she dislikes all the physical adjustments she's had to make, I see the impact. In the rosy blush on her cheeks and endless vibrant smile. In her twilight irises as they twinkle and shimmer. In the radiant light of her aura as she stands in my presence.

It is all I need. Her. Her smile. The peace she provides. The love she gives.

Just Shelly.

~

Bristles stroke the canvas as I paint Shelly in various swirls of pink. A splash of fiery rose. A sweep of delicate blush. A swish of addictive taffy.

Painting this piece without her here isn't the same. This interpretation is new. Poles apart from my usual pieces. An unrealistic portrayal of the woman I have come to love so profoundly.

I see her so clearly when I close my eyes. Her curvaceous breasts and hips. The hollow of her throat and contour of her collarbones. Wisps of hair on her cheek as she lies on the pillows and blankets. The parting of her lips and glimmer in her eyes as I leer around the canvas with the brush between my teeth.

The more pigment I add, the more abstract the painting becomes. As it evolves, I fall harder for my muse. *My Andromeda.*

More often than not, my art is realistic. I paint and draw objects and people as I see them with the naked eye. Maybe tweak the color or shading or position, but not much else.

This painting is unlike every other I have created. This painting is unrestrained passion.

Every tinge of red coats the canvas. From borderline

black to muted pink. Because Shelly *is* the whole spectrum. She is red and pink and every tint and shade between. She is passion and love. Soft and pure. The gentlest caress and fiercest protector. She is the light to my dark. My North Star.

In my periphery, my phone lies on the table beside my easel. Taunting me. Provoking me. My hand freezes, the brush an inch from the canvas as I stare at the annoying piece of technology.

Computers and tablets and cell phones have existed in my life as long as I can remember. They were tools in school and distractions at home. Although I appreciate the ways technology has saved lives, I hate how some innovations have robbed people of their lives.

I may have grown up in the internet era, but I wish it didn't exist.

It sucks the joy from my soul and gifts anxiety in return. The pressure to always be available. Emails and text messages and calling you wherever and whenever. While people become addicted to apps and social media, I work harder to disconnect from it all. If a website wasn't essential for business, I would let it go.

My eyes shift to the table again and the urge to throw my cell phone in the garbage skyrockets. Only because my father wants to speak, wants me to call or text him.

"Should just get it over with," I mumble as I set down the paintbrush.

From everything Shelly told me three nights ago, my father was nothing but cordial and kind while he spoke with her in Petal and Vine. She said he'd even looked a bit sad.

Dad always had a forlorn look about him, but I never asked why. Was I the reason for his sadness? We hadn't spoken in so long, but it's not as if we had profound conversations. Or is it Mom who has made him unhappy?

As years passed, and I put more distance between myself and my parents, I often wondered if Dad was happy with Mom. On any level. She had always been equally wicked and degrading toward him. Criticizing him harshly and not strictly behind closed doors.

Why did he put up with it? Did he not think himself worthy of more? It boggles me how someone could be with a person who treated them as if they didn't matter, as if everything they did wasn't good enough. Even in love, a person should only tolerate so much. How did Dad love her, or even like her, when she treated him like garbage?

But asking myself these questions will get me nowhere. The only person that can answer them is him.

I need to call him. I need to talk with him. Both I have avoided, but can't put off any longer.

Swiping my phone from the table, I rise from the stool and step away from the painting. Regardless of the direction this call takes, I don't want negative energy tainting this piece. Not Shelly.

I trek down the stairs and head for the kitchen. With Shelly at work, the house is quiet. Too quiet. Months ago, the stillness of my house, my space, was something I craved. Solace in solitude. Peace among the chaos. An abrupt shift from my busy art mind.

Now, the silence makes my skin crawl. I don't like when Shelly leaves. Although her earthy floral scent lingers and I see her touch in every room, I miss her energy. Miss her sweet voice and soft words. The way she brightens a room without effort.

Her absence is why I seclude myself in the studio all day. When she works, so do I.

I fill a glass with water and reheat leftovers for lunch. As the microwave counts down to zero, I unlock my phone, press my father's contact in the list, and stare at the screen.

*He isn't as bad as her, yet he is.*

A shrill beep snaps my attention from my phone. I carry lunch to the dining room table and sit in my usual seat. At the heart of the table sits a small vase of peonies. Fresh flowers are a simple touch Shelly has added to almost every room in the house.

I ignore lunch to stare at the delicate pink petals for a beat. So soft, so elegant. Quintessential and very much Shelly. Even in her absence, she is here—her warmth and heart—swathing me in strength and support and love.

Unlocking my phone again, my finger hovers the phone icon as I pick at the pasta primavera.

*Now or never. Just get it over with.*

Before I lose the nerve, I press the icon and lift the phone to my ear. With it being the middle of the day, Dad should be at work and nowhere near Mom. The phone rings once, twice, then he answers.

"Devlyn?"

"Hey, Dad."

Silence stretches between us, but it doesn't unnerve me, not like with Mom. Dad and I have always had this unspoken language. A side effect of our reticent nature. Neither of us feels the need to fill every second with unnecessary speech. Sometimes, the most profound things come about in silence.

"How are you?" His question not abnormal, but his tone is hesitant. Unsure. Troubled.

I stab a piece of pasta and carrot. "Good. You?"

Shelly said Dad pieced together she was pregnant, but never stated as much before leaving the shop. Until he says or asks, I won't touch the topic. Until I know where Dad's head is, I will keep all things Shelly related in the background. To protect her and the baby.

"Could be better." His heavy sigh reaches me through the phone. Tugs at the sympathetic heartstrings I have for him. "Devlyn, I…" He goes silent for a moment, but I don't interject. Don't butt into the words he wants to say, but has difficulty vocalizing. While he thinks, I eat. "I have some news." The lack of inflection in his voice gives nothing away.

"Okay," I drawl out the word.

"I asked your mother for a divorce."

The bite in my mouth goes down the wrong pipe as I go into a coughing fit. I pull the phone away from my ear, beat a fist to my sternum, and cough until the stray noodle dislodges.

When I bring the phone back to my ear, he asks, "Are you okay?" True concern laces his voice.

I cough again, then sip my water. "Fine," I croak out. "What brought this on? The divorce, I mean."

While Dad sits quiet on the other end, I drink more water. I push the food away with the intent to hear him out and not go into another choking fit. Who knows what other surprises he will hit me with.

"It's been a long time coming," he finally says, a hint of relief in his words. "When your mother and I met, life was different. *We* were different." He audibly exhales. "She changed after we said I do. I'd been so in love with her at the time that I didn't give attention to the little signs. When we found out she was pregnant, those little signs got bigger, but I blamed them on hormones. I blamed it on the worry that comes with impending parenthood." He goes silent and I picture him hanging his head. "But it wasn't that at all. As much as I wanted to leave then, I couldn't. I wouldn't abandon you and let you suffer alone."

Dad stayed married to Mom more than half his adult life… for me. Wow. Just… wow. I don't know whether to thank him or slap him.

Both of our lives could have been polar opposites of what they are today. It is quite possible neither of us would feel emotionally annihilated had he left sooner. Yes, most courts side with the mother in custody cases. But I question whether or not my mother would've wanted me without my father. Sure, she may have molded me more in her likeness had he not been around, but I can't picture her *wanting* me around. Period. Unless she had something to gain.

"Dad… why didn't you say something sooner?"

"Son, it's not your burden to bear." He takes a breath. "After the incident in the grocery store not long ago, which I cringed at when your mother told me, I knew it was time. Way past time. Since you moved out and we moved to Tampa, your mother has been on some kick. I thought it'd taper off, but it's only gotten worse."

*Great. My mother losing her shit more often is* not *what I need. Not what any of us needs.*

"When I asked why she'd been in the grocery store an hour from home, she struck me. Told me it was none of my business. That she was working." He audibly exhales. "But it was a lie. Her work never puts her near you. So, I started monitoring her closer. Tracking where she was and her phone activity." He laughs without humor. "Sounds creepy, but I was worried about you."

"You were?"

"Always, Devlyn. I took the brunt of your mother's

attacks over the years… to protect you. As much as I could, anyway." He pauses a beat. "I learned your mother had been following you and your girlfriend. More often than I care to admit. When I called her out on it, she lost it. Said you were ruining your life." He sighs heavily and I picture him tracing his brows with his thumb and finger. "I don't want to rehash the horrible things she said, but in that moment, I no longer wanted to sit idle. No longer wanted either of us to be subject to her terror. So, I've spent weeks speaking with an attorney. A lot of things are tied to your mother's name, including parts of your life. I want both of us to come out as clean as possible when it ends."

White noise fizzles around me as I mull over this new information.

*Dad is divorcing Mom.*

*He is leaving her.*

*For himself, but also for me.*

Although I wish it would have happened earlier, I can't fault him for his decisions. James Templar is not brainless. For years, I questioned how he loved my mother. How he loved someone so manipulative and brutal and poisonous. But he'd hid what lay beneath the surface of his relationship with her. He buried his suffering to keep me close.

Much as I wish he'd made a change years ago, I understand his reasons for staying.

"What happens now?"

Not much of my mother is entwined in my life. Her name carried weight in the art community and opened doors for me in the past, but it no longer bears the same influence. Yes, the Templar name has significance in the area, but I tip the scales more than her now. My art speaks volumes and I no longer need the influence of Karen Templar.

The only thing I question now is my house. Mom insisted on helping out when purchasing the house after college. Seeing as I had minimal credit and was just building my savings, I didn't deny her.

When was the last time I looked at my mortgage statement? Months, perhaps. And how had the deed been titled when the sale of the house finalized? My name was on the deed, but it hadn't been the only name printed. Did half of my house belong to her? *Oh, god.* Bile rises in my throat at the idea of my safe space—the house I invited Shelly into, the place where our child will grow and learn and laugh—is possibly tainted and at risk.

*Shit.*

"I hear your mind spinning from here. Devlyn, everything will be fine."

"What about my house?" The words a squeaky whisper on my tongue.

If her name is on this house, I will move us out. Find us a new home, far from here. Last thing I or Shelly need is my mother's torment because her life is upside down. I won't put Shelly or the baby in harm's way. I won't allow my mother to ruin either of them the way she did me and Dad.

"Your house is yours, son."

"Isn't she—"

"No. She's not on the deed or the loan. I am, which I'll happily change, if you wish."

*Thank the powers that be.*

Dad and I talk another twenty minutes before he says goodbye. But before he hangs up, he asks to have dinner with me and Shelly sometime soon. That and he wants more calls or texts, even if there is nothing notable to talk about.

When the call disconnects, a tremendous weight lifts from

my shoulders. Not all of it is gone, but it feels more bearable. Manageable. Less pained and more healing.

It feels like my life is finally heading in a positive direction in every way. Something I need—not just for myself, but also for Shelly and our future.

For the first time in my adult life, I breathe and it hurts less.

# seventeen

## SHELLY

I might die from this incessant heat.

Far back as I remember, I have loved living the Florida life. Sunshine year round. Blue skies with the occasional fluffy cloud or two. Countless outdoor activities. Theme parks and festivals and concerts. The beach, the sand, the warmth.

But right now, in this paralyzing summer weather, my ankles are swollen. My fingers look more like small sausages than tools to write and eat and function. Sweat slicks my skin in the most awkward places. My clothes are itchy and tight and annoying. And this new ache formed in my lower back.

I am not okay with this. Not at all.

With each passing month, my body changes more and more. I get it. Really, I do. I am cooking a human.

Some of the changes aren't so bad. Nausea—gone. Me and all the cheeses are good friends again. Hallelujah. Body swelling… unacceptable. Wasting money on maternity clothes… unacceptable. Instead, I wear Devlyn's T-shirts and loose shorts or lounge pants. Hell, I will wear a robe all day if need be. Back pain… also unacceptable.

Dr. Webster recommended pregnancy massage for the

back pain. I jumped on that bandwagon immediately. She also said the swelling is perfectly normal, especially in the hotter months. She recommended less salt in my diet, more water, walking daily, and the usual rest and relaxation with my feet elevated.

I feel like an elephant. Maybe a hippo. No offense to the elephant or hippo population. But if I swell anymore, I will undoubtedly resemble Violet Beauregarde from *Willy Wonka and the Chocolate Factory* after she blows up—minus purple skin, of course.

"Why don't you relax while I start dinner," Devlyn suggests as we come in from a stroll around the neighborhood.

Tonight, Devlyn's dad is coming over for dinner. When Devlyn ran the idea past me weeks ago, my blood pressure spiked. So, he pushed it off. Told his father we needed more time.

In the last month, Devlyn has spoken with his dad at least three times a week. Gotten to know the man James really is versus the man he thought he knew. During those conversations, Devlyn found a new level of comfort with his father. A bond they should have had years ago. And when his father agreed two weeks ago to have joint therapy sessions with Devlyn, some of my own worry eased.

I want our baby to be surrounded by as much love as possible. Having at least one person from Devlyn's family present would be wonderful. Devlyn deserves love too. A love he wanted for years, but didn't realize how much he'd been deprived of until recently.

"I'd like to help," I say, toeing off my shoes.

We wander to the kitchen and Devlyn starts pulling food

from the cabinets and fridge. I lean my hip against the counter and watch as he moves around the kitchen.

"Kick your feet up for a few. I'll do the tedious stuff, then come get you for the rest. Deal?"

I huff under my breath. *Really hate feeling like a useless child.* Not overexerting myself is good for me and the baby, deep down I know this. But when I am used to doing it all, sitting on my butt while others wait on me, hand and foot, makes me feel like a nuisance. Like I don't contribute in any way.

That stings the most.

Sticking out my pinkie, I wait for Devlyn to hook his with mine. Two steps in my direction, he latches our pinkies as his lips kick up in a half smile. "Promise."

Making my way to the living room, I plop down on the couch and scroll through the shows. I land on *The Vampire Diaries* and hit play. It's been a while since I binged this show.

Halfway through the episode, Devlyn wanders into the living room and parks next to me on the couch. He lays his head on my shoulder and stares at the screen. Minutes of the show carry on, neither of us speaking. And it is moments like this that calm every woe. Moments like this that make all the craziness—family and pregnancy and our fast-paced relationship—worthwhile.

For years, I wanted this. Someone to love me without effort. Someone that connected with me on an unprecedented level. Someone that will stick with me through the good and not so good.

The start of our love story may be muddled with indecision and chaos, but I wouldn't change it or us. Devlyn wouldn't be who he is today without his past, and neither would I. Our love wouldn't be what it is without it either.

"Ready to cook?" he whispers when the episode ends.

"Yes."

As if we have done it years, Devlyn and I move around the kitchen with ease as we prepare dinner. Minutes before the timer goes off for the oven, the doorbell chimes.

*Here we go.*

Devlyn sets the spoon on the rest. With his hand on my lower back, he kisses my temple. "Be right back."

"'Kay," I breathe out.

He pads off to answer the door and I stir the couscous with more gusto than necessary. Sweat dampens my skin as I hear the dead bolt disengage and the door open before mumbled hellos filter in.

*This is it.* I take a deep breath and check on the chicken in the oven. *Devlyn's father is* not *his mother. This dinner will end in smiles.*

A moment later, Devlyn reenters the kitchen with his father in tow. A loud beep fills the room as the timer on the range goes off. I turn it off, along with the burner for the couscous, top the pot with a lid and remove it from the heat.

Jitters flow through my limbs as I spin around to face Devlyn and James. Two breaths pass and my nerves settle a little as I stare at the two of them. Looking at James is like looking into the future. Devlyn is definitely his father's son. If James's appearance is any indication, Devlyn will age well.

The room is filled with awkward tension as the three of us stand there, unspeaking. After a beat, James breaks the silence. "Nice to see you again, Shelly." James offers his hand.

*Devlyn's father is not his mother.*

I take his hand and note how similar yet different his grip is from Devlyn's. Devlyn has soft hands with the occasional callous. His fingers are thin and long. His touch gentle yet strong. James harbors a different type of strength. One built from years of labor and life. The skin where his fingers meet his hand is rougher. Yet I still feel a gentleness in his touch.

"Nice to meet you officially," I say.

Our hands break apart and Devlyn offers his father a drink. The two men open a beer while I fill a glass with sparkling cider. While I fetch plates, Devlyn takes the chicken from the oven. We dish the meal onto plates and make our way into the dining room.

James's gaze drifts around the room as if seeing it with new eyes. *How long has it been since he has set foot in this house?* Until meeting James in Petal and Vine last month, I'd never seen him. It was always Devlyn's mother that made an appearance. And until last month, Devlyn hadn't spoken to James since late November.

I watch as his eyes take in all the new additions to the house. A short vase of flowers at the heart of the table. Art on two of the three dining room walls—Devlyn's art, of course. Large candles on either side of the vase that Devlyn lit when I wasn't looking. A soft rug beneath the table and chairs. And that is just this room.

Devlyn lived a monochromatic life filled with occasional color before we met. My life had been the opposite. Now we balance each other. Spark new life where things once faded away.

"I love the changes you've made," James says, eyes darting from me to Devlyn. "Feels more like a home."

"I'll give you an updated tour after dinner," Devlyn suggests.

Wrinkles form at the corners of James's mouth and eyes as an all too familiar smile dons his face. "I'd love that very much."

*Thank goodness his genetics overpowered hers.*

Dinner carries on with timid conversation. James asks Devlyn about his recent artwork and me about the flower shop. Neither of us dives in deep at first, but the more we chat, the more comfortable we all become. We have yet to discuss anything about the baby, but hiding my growing belly becomes harder with each passing day.

When our plates clear, I offer to do dishes so Devlyn can show his father around the house.

Not much of the house has changed from my moving in. Not needing the furniture, I sold all but a few smaller items. The small space between the kitchen and doors to the patio had been empty prior to me moving in. Now, my small sofa, end and coffee table, and bookshelf fill the space and look out the sliding glass doors to the backyard. The small change doesn't overwhelm the nook, but makes it a cozy place to read a book or have additional seating if and when we have guests over.

As I load the last of the dishes into the washer, Devlyn and James enter the kitchen. Both wear matching smiles and carry a new sense of ease.

Devlyn needed this. They both did. The last several months have been a challenge for us both, but more for Devlyn. So much of his life has changed. He saw a new side to his mother, one he'd been willfully blind to for years, and disconnected her from his life. In doing so, pieces of his past flooded in and knocked the air from his lungs. Everything he thought he knew as a child and young man had been blanketed with falsehoods and manipulation. Although his parents, more so his mother, had twisted his mind, he has slowly found a way to unravel all the hurt and heartache and influence.

Now he has the chance at a new life with his father. One filled with love and compassion and trust—over time. And this small token warms my heart. That he gets to keep one parent. That he doesn't feel completely abandoned.

"So," James speaks up as we walk to the sitting room. "I don't know how to broach the subject..." Devlyn and I sit on the love seat as James sits in one of the chairs across from us. "Or if I should." He picks at the knee of his slacks.

"We won't know unless you do," Devlyn states with a chuckle.

I love how light and carefree he is at my side. How warm and comfortable he is as the evening progresses. Not that Devlyn has never displayed such qualities. Just wasn't sure what his reaction would be having his father nearby after a long absence.

A soft smile pushes up the corners of James's lips. "I'd like to talk about..." He pauses, his jaw working left and right, his lips clamped between his teeth. "About the baby," he says after a moment.

It wasn't a question of *if* the subject would come up before James left, it was a question of *when*. Honestly, it surprises me it didn't come up sooner.

Devlyn wraps an arm around my shoulders, tucks me into his side, and lays his free hand on my lap. If that doesn't scream his need to protect me and the baby, not much else would in this moment.

"Okay," Devlyn says, but doesn't expand further.

Tonight is more about Devlyn reconnecting with his dad than about me getting to know James. Devlyn needs this—

they both do—but his instinct to shield me from the toxicity of his past far outweighs his need to connect.

Every word and action from James this evening has been nothing short of kind and caring. Not once has he been cruel. Nor has he belittled Devlyn. The entire evening felt *normal*. And we can use all the normal we can get.

That said, this man also spent more than two decades of his life with Karen Templar—a woman I will never trust.

Tension thickens the air in the room as we all wait for what happens next. Wait for what will be said or asked. As prescribed by Dr. Webster, I do my best to not let the stress of the moment consume my thoughts.

As if he senses my semifrazzled state, Devlyn's thumb draws small circles on my shoulder. I focus my attention on his light touch. Focus on the solace it provides. Count in my head with each circuit his thumb makes.

"It will take time for us to be in a better place, I know," James says with a subtle nod. "But I want to be part of my grandchild's life. In whatever way you feel is best."

"Dad, I..." Devlyn pauses and shifts his greens to my blues. "We will need to talk about it." His eyes go back to his father. "A lot has changed. With us all." Devlyn's grip on my shoulder tightens slightly. "But more will need to change before Shelly and I consider the possibility."

Across from us, James nods as he hangs his head a little. "I can't fault either of you in this. All I ask is that you give it consideration." James looks at Devlyn for a beat before his eyes find mine. "Whatever you need of me—joint therapy sessions, time, specific actions—I will do it. Just please, don't shut me out."

I feel for this man. Truly.

James, too, has been through hell. Stuck in a loveless

marriage for decades just so he knew his son was safe. To some degree, anyway.

"We will," I affirm. My eyes drop as my hand comes to my belly. "This baby will be loved like no other. I'd like them to be surrounded by as much as possible." I lift my gaze as a smile lights James's expression. "But... I don't know you. Not really." I flash him a sad smile. "Your wife made one heck of a first impression. Sorry to say, but it automatically made one for you too."

"I get it."

"All I ask for is time," I tell him. "Time for me to get to know you. And time with Devlyn." I look at the man holding me close, a small smile curving my lips. "In whichever way he needs it. If it's therapy, a night out together or space without you, you need to respect and grant it."

Devlyn hugs me closer and kisses my temple.

It isn't my intention to speak for Devlyn. In the eight months we have known each other, Devlyn isn't one to always speak his mind. Scared to hurt himself or the feelings of another, he shelters his emotions more often than not. I won't speak for him, but I will speak up for him. In his twenty-three years of life, not many have. Going forward, that will change.

"Promise, I will." James checks his watch. "I should get going."

James slips on his shoes. Devlyn and I walk him to his car and share hugs and goodbyes. A minute later, we wave him off as he backs out of the driveway and drives off.

Back in the house, we wander to the living room hand in hand and plop down on the couch. Minutes of silence pass as we curl into each other and breathe through the tail end of our night.

"Was really nice seeing him again," Devlyn whispers against my shoulder. "He's so… different."

I rest my head on his. "How so?"

Devlyn traces his fingers over my own, then up my hand and forearm before drifting back down. I close my eyes and absorb his touch. Allow it to warm my skin.

"He's always been calm. Laid back. But now…" Devlyn sits up to look me in the eye. Tenderness softens his expression. "I can't remember the last time he smiled. Like a genuine smile. And tonight, he gave so many."

That he did. James's smiles varied from brilliant to subtle, but they were pleasant all the same.

"I hope he finds happiness," I say softly.

Devlyn lays his head back on my shoulder. "Me too. Although he hasn't made the best decisions, he deserves happiness. And the opportunity to change."

I wholeheartedly agree. My only hope is, after so many years under Karen's thumb, James is capable of change.

# eighteen

## DEVLYN

Keeping secrets from Shelly is not my strong suit. But this secret must be kept.

Better to deal with only her wrath than the wrath of everyone else.

"Breakfast out was the best idea," she says as she wipes her mouth with a paper napkin. "And this café," —her eyes drift around the bustling restaurant— "how did I not know about this place?"

I shrug and give her a half smile. "Good ole Google found it for me, so…"

She waves me off. "Give yourself some of the credit. The thought crossed your mind. That's what matters most."

"Always finding the bright side." My smile widens.

An hour ago, we left the house under the guise of me not wanting to cook. Forty-five minutes ago, several of our friends pulled up to the house, went inside, and got to work. Decorations and food and whatever else happens at fun-filled adult birthday parties.

More than a week ago, Micah sent me a text message. He mentioned Shelly's upcoming birthday and how everyone wanted to throw her a party. He promised it wouldn't be much different from Sunday night get-togethers. The only difference will be decorations, cake and more time together.

I'd stared at the screen several minutes before responding. Too stunned because I didn't know Shelly's birth date, which is partially my fault. I hadn't offered mine three months ago. Had I asked hers, she'd have felt bad for missing mine.

I answered the message and soon learned it was a group text. My phone blew up for hours. One idea after another filled the gray bubbles. Party GIFs and a slew of emojis filled the screen. I'd been thankful it was the middle of the day and Shelly was at work. Half a day and an insane number of messages later, a plan was devised. A plan for a surprise party. At our house.

My responsibility for the day… don't mention birthdays or our friends and keep Shelly away from home until I get the all-clear message. Cora and Autumn estimated two hours for party setup.

So I planned breakfast out with Shelly. Although it is for her birthday, she thinks it's just because. When we leave the restaurant, the plan is to drive to a bookstore so we can walk around in air conditioning while she picks out a few new books.

She shrugs. "We should come here more. The eggs benedict was excellent, and I saw a dozen other things I'd like to try."

The server steps up and clears our plates from the table. She asks if there is anything else she can get us—offering the restaurant's award-winning pie before ten in the morning—and Shelly's eyes light up. With a laugh, I gesture to the pie menu.

One slice of key lime and peanut butter pie later, I settle

the bill and we leave. A mile up the road, I turn into the plaza with the bookstore and park the car.

Shelly unbuckles her belt and shifts to face me in her seat. Her eyes narrow as she studies me intently.

*She knows that I know it's her birthday. Shit. Either that or she suspects I know. Play it cool.*

"Why are we here?" she asks, a hint of suspicion in her tone.

*She doesn't know. She can't. Play. It. Cool.*

"You haven't gotten a new book recently. When we drove past on the way to breakfast, I thought maybe you might like to look at what's new." I shrug, hoping to come across as nonchalant. "Plus, I wanted to look at baby books for dads."

Her eyes soften around the edges. "Okay," she acquiesces without an ounce of fight.

The part about looking for a book for new dads isn't a fib. Sure, I could talk to Jonas or Gavin about first-time father-hood and what to expect. But I'd also like a resource on hand, just in case something comes up neither of them has dealt with yet.

We wander the bookstore with no set path. Eventually, Shelly will make her way to the romance section, but she steers us toward the baby and parenting books first. I let her lead, but plan to keep us in the store until I get a thumbs-up text.

After discovering two great parenting books, Shelly leads us to her favorite part of the store. I sit on a chair randomly set up in the aisle while she peruses the titles. My phone vibrates in my pocket and, with as much discretion as possible, I remove it to look at the notification. A text from Micah with a thumbs-up and nothing more. I pocket my phone and wait until Shelly finishes browsing.

A hundred dollars later, we walk out of the bookstore and I drive us home.

"Did you find some good ones?" I ask.

Shelly nods. "Yeah. A few I'd heard other book friends online rave about and one by an author I read regularly."

"Good. Glad you found some pleasure reads. The baby books are nice, but you need books for you too."

"Do you pleasure read?" she asks as I turn into the neighborhood.

I shrug. "Not in years."

"What did you like reading when you did?"

"Mostly mysteries and thrillers." I glance over at her. "But I'll give anything a try."

As we approach the house, I note the absence of everyone's cars. Also part of the plan. To make everything look normal. Once everything was set up, all cars were to be moved a street over. The cars may not be out front, but everyone is inside. Once the surprise happens, the cars will be driven back to the house.

I fetch the bag from the back seat after parking in the driveway. Shelly and I slip out and walk leisurely to the door. She keys in her code, then swings the door wide. From the foyer, the house looks the same. But I know the second we round the wall dividing the dining and living room from the kitchen and sitting room, a burst of surprise will echo around us.

We toe off our shoes and I set the bag of books down on the chair nearby.

"Want to binge that show you were watching the other day?" I ask, knowing it will lead us to where everyone waits.

She hooks my arm in hers. "Sounds great. Maybe I'll start one of my books after."

I lead her to the living room. Just as we breach the entrance to the space, a booming "Surprise!" fills the air. Shelly slaps a hand to her chest as everyone steps up to her and wraps her in a huge embrace. Individual hugs and happy birthday wishes are given. And when Shelly sidles up to me again, her eyes are rimmed in tears.

"Did you do this?" she whisper-asks as she takes in all of our friends.

"Not just me." Micah approaches us. "Your brother actually reached out."

"He did?" I nod and she swipes a hand over her cheeks. "Oh my god."

"Hey, sis." Micah pulls Shelly in for a hug. "Happy birthday. Hope this is okay."

She sniffles. "More than okay, big brother."

The remainder of the day goes by in good conversation, hearty laughter, great food—with cake, of course—and time well spent with people we care about. As the sun sets, we congregate outside and lounge in the back. Since Shelly moved in, we have slowly added more to the backyard. More seating and plants. A firepit and grill. A wooden fence around the perimeter for privacy. An array of colorful flowers near the swing under the large oak.

One day at a time, Shelly turns this house into a home. A place I want to share with her always. A place where our child will grow and laugh and wonder. Color with crayons and paper. Play hide-and-seek. Bring more definition to our lives.

"Have you picked a date for the baby shower yet?" Cora asks Shelly.

Shelly tucks her feet beneath her butt and leans into my side. "Not yet. Should I?"

"When are you due?"

"The date changes with every appointment." I *hear* Shelly's eyes roll and I bite my cheek to resist laughing. She isn't wrong, though. "Basically, anytime between September twenty-first and October eighth. Your guess is as good as mine."

Autumn chuckles. "Clementine's due date changed seven times. Inevitably, she arrived on the original date the doctor said." She smiles at Shelly, then me. "But they come out when they're ready." Autumn looks over at Jonas, who is chatting with Gavin and Micah. "Take advantage of your free time now. You'll wish for more after the baby is here." Autumn shifts her gaze to Cora. "Maybe we should plan the shower for her?"

"You don't have—"

Cora cuts me off. "Count me in." My best friend meets my gaze with softened eyes. "Let us do this for you, Shell." Her hands come together in prayer, inches from her lips. "Let us take this on. It'll be fun. And zero stress for you."

"We won't take no for an answer," Autumn adds.

Beside me, Shelly fidgets. But not so much anyone looking would take notice. I feel the slight tremble in her limbs, though.

I kiss her hair. "Your choice, but I think they would enjoy doing this for you."

Her frame relaxes into me more. "I swear I'm not a control freak." She laughs without humor. "But after giving up so much, it's hard to give up more."

"Wish I could relieve that burden for you. I would, if possible." I kiss her hair again. "A little more than three months. And then, once you're cleared, you can do everything and I'll sit back with the baby and relax."

"Ha ha." She shakes her head. "Fine," she huffs out like

an annoyed teen. "You can plan the party." Cora and Autumn clap as giddy smiles stretch their cheeks. "But…" Shelly adds. "I want in on the plans too. I don't want it to be some big secret that I walk in on" —she waves her hand around us— "like today. If you promise to keep me in the loop, you have my permission."

"Done," Cora says at the same time Autumn says, "You got it."

Jonas comes up behind Autumn and rests his hands on her shoulders. "We should head out. Let Mom and Dad get home."

Babysitters. Another thing we should look into—although I am positive Shelly's mom will want every possible minute with the baby. With my flexible schedule, a babysitter will only be necessary when we want or need alone time.

If we are lucky, it won't just be Shelly's family and our friends who will watch the baby for an hour or two. Maybe, hopefully, my dad will be in the mix too. Only time will tell.

# nineteen

## SHELLY

"Ready for the next photo session, Mom and Dad?"

I lie back on the exam table for my twenty-eight-week appointment. Inching my shirt up, I suck in a deep breath and prepare for the cold gel to hit my belly.

"Yes," Devlyn and I say simultaneously, then smile at each other.

Dr. Webster told us ultrasounds aren't done as frequently during normal pregnancies, but because of my blood pressure changes and increased anxiety, she added two more to the schedule. One today and another at week thirty-two. Either way, I get another snapshot of our little one to add to the album.

The gel hits my belly and I squeeze Devlyn's hand. He squeezes back. Then Dr. Webster presses the wand to my gel-coated skin and moves it around. Three sets of eyes fixate on the monitor as the blurry image becomes slightly sharper. Head, body, and four little limbs.

My vision blurs as tears flood my eyes. Devlyn tightens his hold on my hand. The room utterly silent except for the fluttering sound of a rapid heartbeat through the ultrasound machine.

"Spine looks good." Dr. Webster traces her finger over the screen. "Everything looks on track." She presses a button on the machine and snaps the image. Her gaze meets mine, then Devlyn's. "Still don't want to know the sex."

I shake my head and Devlyn does the same.

"Okay." Her smile widens as if she has the answer on the tip of her tongue. "Just going to take a few measurements."

She shifts the wand over my round belly and pauses when she has a better view of the baby's head. She clicks a few buttons and moves on. All too soon, she removes the wand, cleans it and my belly, then makes notes in my chart before handing over our new photo.

"Everything looks great. Keep up with your vitamins and relaxation." She sets the chart on the counter and washes her hands. "Have you been experiencing any cramps, pain, nausea, shortness of breath?"

I shake my head as I tug my shirt back into place. "No."

Drying her hands, she resumes her spot on her stool. "Cramps and tightness are normal. How's the swelling been?"

"Better." Devlyn's been a trooper, making sure we walk each night, if only to the end of the street and back.

"And the baby's been as active or more?"

I rub a hand over my belly. "Yes." I peer up at Devlyn. "Our little water aerobics instructor."

Dr. Webster laughs. "That's a new one, but cute." She offers her hand and I take it. Devlyn places one on my back and helps ease me upright. "If you notice any changes that aren't normal or just feel off, call the office. But with everything we saw today, your little water aerobics instructor looks healthy and fit and right where they should be."

At the reception desk, I double-check the next appointment date and time. We exit the office, slip into the car, and buckle our belts. Devlyn cranks the engine, then looks at me over the console.

"I have an idea, if you're up for it."

I arch a brow at him. "Will there be food?"

He looks up, left then right, before meeting my eyes. "Kind of," he says on a laugh.

"Count me in."

# twenty

DEVLYN

Maybe this wasn't such a great idea.

I love color. I love seeing a wide palette of colors. But this… this is too much.

Every shade of pink—although I have a new appreciation for the color since Shelly—and blue, green and yellow, gray and khaki. Bolds and neutrals. Onesies and jumpers. Pajamas and long shirts. Pants with snaps from heel to crotch on both legs. Lace and frill. Sports logos and popular cartoon characters. Farm animals as well as sea creatures.

The baby and children's section in Target is bigger than any other section. Well, unless you go to toys. It has every possible thing you may need for a baby. Bibs and diapers. Clothing and bedding. Strollers and bouncy seats. Training potties and bathtubs. Bottles and nipples. Who knew there were so many types of nipples? *Jesus.*

And then I laugh. Shelly looks at me with pinched brows. "What's so funny?"

"Have you ever had the urge to scream *nipples* in the baby section? Like it's a eureka moment."

Shelly snorts, then stops and presses her legs together. "Stop it." She slaps my arm. "You'll make me pee."

"We wouldn't get in trouble. If a worker said anything, I'd act like we'd been looking for them and I found them before you."

"Devlyn," she says, laughing harder. "Seriously, stop."

"Fine," I huff out. "Party pooper."

I follow Shelly up and down the aisles. We stare at hundreds of baby products and read the packages of the ones we have no clue what their purpose is. Then I remember something Cora said.

"Hey, shouldn't we start a registry for the shower?"

Shelly pulls out her phone. "Oh, yeah." She pulls up the Target app and taps a few times until she reaches the registry she set up earlier. "All we need to do is scan things and add them to our wish list."

For whatever reason, I don't feel the need to add an over-abundance of items. Just necessities. Then again, this is a wish list and what the hell do I know when it comes to babies. Maybe we will need the wipes warmer and double electric breast pump. Maybe we need the video baby monitor that connects to our phone and the ultrasonic humidifier. Hell if I know.

My vision grows hazy as Shelly wanders and scans items on the shelves. Bottles and nipples. Diapers and burp cloths. Tubs and toiletries. Toys and clothes. Once she has half the baby department logged on the registry, she stows her phone in her purse and hooks my arm with hers.

"I want to buy something for the baby." She rubs a hand over her belly as her sparkly blues meet my greens. "The baby will get a ton of gifts from other people, but I want them to have something just from us. Doesn't have to be big. A small toy or their first book."

Twisting to face Shelly, I frame her face with my hands and pull her in for a kiss. Not a juicy public display, but a sweet kiss that tells her I love the idea.

"Anything in mind?" I ask.

"No. Let's wander a little more. Maybe something will stand out."

We weave through the department again, but this time with new eyes. On the hunt for the perfect first gift for our upcoming little one. Hands laced, we wander with no destination. Shelly picks up a small puppy dog toy. Black and white and red. Parts of it soft while other parts crinkle or rattle. The tag says it is perfect for sensory stimulation.

"How about this?" she asks. "It's cute and functional."

"And is gender neutral, which is good for us."

We both smile and stare down at the bright and bold puppy toy. Awe hits me square in the chest. Obviously, I *know* we are having a baby. Purchasing our first baby item... it's a whole new level of reality. It has my stomach flipping and fluttering. Adds a new dose of thrill and eagerness.

I hope the baby has Shelly's dazzling eyes and cute nose, as well as her kind heart and brilliance. More than anything, I just want our child to be healthy and happy.

Hand in hand, we wind our way out of the baby maze and make our way to the checkout. Shelly leans into me and I give her hand a light squeeze. As we round the end of the aisle near the registers, my feet stick to the floor and my legs lock in place.

*Can life quit throwing curveballs?*

I don't know what the hell I did, but I swear I will make up for it. Whatever *it* is.

Less than ten feet in front of us, Kelsey stands in the checkout line with a small basket in her hand. Maybe I can steer us right and she won't see me. But just as I shift us and point to a register with a shorter line, I hear my name.

"Devlyn? Is that you?"

*Someone, anyone, send help.*

Had she not spoken loud enough for Shelly to hear, I would have ignored her. But Shelly perked up at my name. I spin us slightly and meet the eyes of my first love. The girl who pulverized my heart five years ago. Someone I planned to never see again.

But the universe is intent on torturing me for some reason.

My hold on Shelly tightens as I say, "Hey, Kelsey."

Shelly jolts beside me. "*Kelsey,* Kelsey?" Shelly whisper-asks.

I give her hand a squeeze. A small assurance that everything will be fine. "Mm-hmm."

"How've you been?" Kelsey asks with too much excitement in her voice. "It's been what… five years?"

If my life could be summarized into one word this past year, it would be perplexing. Every sordid moment of my past has made some strange appearance. Like the universe is testing me on every level. Seeing if I am worthy and capable and strong enough to move forward. Not just on my own, but with Shelly and the baby.

*Dear Universe, you can stop now. I swear, I'm good.*

"Yep. Five years." I turn to look at Shelly and smile. "And life is incredible." For a moment, I lose myself in my Shelly bliss bubble. Stare at her shimmering twilight eyes and forget we are in the middle of Target and Kelsey is less than five feet away.

"Um, that's… I… that's great, Devlyn."

I kiss Shelly's temple before returning my attention to Kelsey. She shifts from foot to foot. Her eyes dart from me to Shelly and back. And for the first time in years, I don't open my mouth to try and appease someone else. Don't say anything to steer the awkward tension away from her. Because for too many years, I have always done things to make other people happy, but not myself. That time is over.

Except when it comes to Shelly. Her happiness is my happiness because she doesn't hold expectations over my head like a weapon. She loves me unconditionally.

"Well, we need to go," I say and start to turn us away.

"Was good seeing you, Devlyn."

I nod and lift a hand. "Bye, Kelsey."

Yes, I realize my response sounds cold and heartless, but I don't care. I owe that woman nothing. In another life, Kelsey meant everything to me. I would have done anything and everything for her. She took advantage of my selfless heart and broke it like I didn't matter. My curtness was me being nice, mature.

We go through the checkout and pay for the baby's first toy. Shelly and I wander to the exit, arms hooked at the elbows. If I were with any other person, I would have been bombarded with questions the second we stepped away from Kelsey.

But Shelly isn't like anyone else.

Inevitably, she will speak up. Curiosity will outweigh contemplation. But she will wait an appropriate amount of time to ask the most significant question. She won't drown me in an endless interrogation. Not Shelly. She will pick one question, just one, and ask without jealousy or guilt.

I crank the engine and let the air conditioning cool the cab before we back out. Shelly removes the toy from the bag and crinkles the floppy ears. Her eyes laser-focused on the little stuffed dog as she remains deep in thought.

I reach over the console and rest a hand on her thigh. In a flash, her eyes meet mine. And I see the question already forming on her lips.

"Are you okay?"

Of all the questions Shelly could have asked, of all the terse words she could have said, this was not what I expected. Not by a long shot.

Shelly has a big heart and a beautiful soul. The fact she is more worried about how I feel speaks volumes. She could have gone into a tizzy. Spewed words of jealousy or mistrust. Pushed away from me after dealing with yet another demon of my past.

But that isn't her style. Shelly has more class and is wise beyond her years.

"Yeah, I'm good." I shrug. "Honestly, I thought I'd feel different."

"How so?"

Months after our breakup, I often wondered what it would be like to see Kelsey again. Would it be tense and awkward or fueled by anger? Would I hate the sight of her or secretly wish to wrap her in my arms? With each passing year, the same unanswered questions lingered. Took up residence in my head.

Until Shelly.

In no time, everything I'd felt for Kelsey—the good and bad—vanished. For years, the sadness over losing one girl fueled a lot of my darker pieces. She'd blackened my young, impressionable heart.

The moment I saw Shelly, Kelsey became a ghost. I no longer saw or felt her. While the scars of what she'd done remained, her hold on me evaporated. Kelsey had been a placeholder until Shelly's path collided with mine.

"Long before you and I met, I pictured what it'd be like seeing Kelsey again. Considering her parents live in the area, the chances were likely. I'd always seen it as this big deal. Me being excited or angry when it finally happened."

"And how was it?"

My thumb strokes over her thigh and I watch the action for a beat. "Lackluster," I say on a laugh. "No anger, but there was a hint of happiness." Shelly tenses under my touch. "But not for the reason you think." My eyes lift to hers. "I'm happy because I've moved on. I'm happy because I have you." I suck in a deep breath. "Although what she did was horrible, although it sent me to a dark place for so long, had she not done it, I wouldn't be here with you."

Tears rim her eyes and add a new luster to the gold flecks.

"I love you, Shelly Reed. You." I lift my hand and rest it on her rounding belly. "I love everything about us. What we are and what we will become."

"I love you, Devlyn Templar." A tear falls down her cheek. "And I can't wait to see where we go from here." She holds up her pointer finger. "But first… can we stop bumping into the past?" she asks on a laugh.

I join in on her laughter. "Would be nice. I'm over this trip down memory lane."

Really, there is only one demon of my past left to conquer. Once that dragon is slayed, life will be as it should—happy and peaceful and full of love.

But I have a feeling that last demon won't go quietly. Let's hope I am wrong.

# twenty-one

## SHELLY

This is why I haven't been here more often. This is why I haven't answered my phone every time it rings. Nicole Reed may be the death of me. Not literally, but pretty damn close.

"Why don't you want to know the sex of the baby? How are we supposed to plan? How can you decorate the nursery without knowing?"

*Jesus, take the wheel. I love my mother. I love my mother. I love my mother.*

"And why haven't you been answering my calls? This is one of the biggest times in your life. A time when you need as much love and support as possible." Eyes that match my own lock me in place. "Family matters, Shelly."

Deep breaths. In and out.

*Tell her how you feel. Best to do it now than drag it out.*

"Mom, please." I pause and take another deep breath. "First of all, I'm a grown woman. I make my own decisions. Second, Dr. Webster put me on a strict health regimen. Low to no stress." My lips flatten into a straight line for two breaths. "And you stress me out." I shrug.

I will not apologize for giving myself air and room. I will

not apologize for eliminating the stressors in my life, even if it is someone I love. It may not be what she wants to hear, but this isn't just about her. Not anymore.

"Shelly, I—"

My mother speechless is new. Is it wrong of me to be proud I put her in this state? If so, oh well.

How many times did Micah and I sit at the dining room table and listen to her drone on about how she wishes we'd find love and start a family? Far too many. And now that I have done both—not that the family part was planned—she complains I don't spend enough time with her. She complains I am not doing this parenting thing the "right" way, because it is not how she did it.

And I am done. Done.

My mother has good intentions, but there is more than one way to love and parent. Her method worked for her, but it doesn't make it the best way.

"Devlyn and I decided we don't want to know the gender because it doesn't matter." I rub a hand over my belly, which seems to have grown another few inches in the last two weeks. "We want to give our child everything they need, but most importantly, we want them to feel loved. They won't care what color the bedroom walls are painted. They won't care if they're wearing dresses or sports shirts. The only ones who care are the parents."

Her brows knit together. No matter how many times Micah and I have told Mom that our version of happy is not the same as hers, it hasn't clicked. And I think it may be slowly sinking in now. A little.

"I just..." Lines crinkle her forehead. "I don't get it." Her eyes hold mine. "But I'm trying. Promise."

"Thank you."

A gentle smile softens her features. "Do you have plans for the nursery?"

I wince on a shrug. "Yes and no. We're leaving the room the same gray color. And I liked the black and white animal theme Autumn and Jonas did, so we're going with a similar vibe. Except Devlyn is painting the animals and trees and whatnot on the walls."

"That sounds lovely."

"He's excited to start." I adjust my seat on her couch and reach for my glass of water. Each week, it gets harder to move like a nonpregnant woman. "We're waiting to buy furniture until after the shower."

Devlyn and I make zero assumptions about what will be gifted to us at the baby shower next weekend. The registry list has doubled since our trip to Target. Cora told me I could add things from the website that might not be available in the store. My fingers are calloused from the new additions and the registry is jam-packed with everything a baby, infant or toddler may need for the first two years of life.

We agreed to stash money and buy whatever necessities we don't get at the shower. Furniture being the most expensive, we saved enough for those big-ticket items.

"And you're having men at the shower too?"

*Dear god, mother. Just quit with the gender nonsense.*

"Yes," I say and purse my lips. "If you haven't figured it out yet, I'm a little over the whole traditional way of doing things." Mom opens her mouth, ready to cast her opinion on me, but I hold up a hand. "Devlyn and I have been through a lot. He has dealt with things you couldn't fathom. I won't make him or his father feel like outcasts because of some ridiculous, asinine tradition someone started long before I was born." I take a deep breath and settle my rising blood pressure. "Baby showers should be about celebrating new life… by everyone in that life's world. No matter what's between their legs."

"Shelly," Mom admonishes me as if I am a child.

"No," I say sternly. "No," I repeat for emphasis. "I get it. You want me and Micah to fit some mold that society created centuries ago." I shake my head. "But even when those ideals were created, people snuck around and did what felt natural and right for them." I look Mom square in the eyes. "Love isn't black and white, and neither is life. Both are full of color and wonder without borders. And I wish you'd see that."

The baby sticks a limb in my ribs and I suck in a breath.

Mom scoots closer, concern etched in the lines of her face. "Oh my goodness, Shelly. Are you alright?"

I sit on the edge of the couch, raise my arms, and take in a lungful of air and nod. "Yep." I lower a hand to rub my belly. "Just the baby giving a fist pump."

*That's right. You tell grandma that Mommy is right.*

With too much effort, I slowly rise from the couch. "I need to head home. Devlyn's father is coming over for dinner and I need to help prep."

Mom opens her mouth to say something, but snaps it shut.

It has been a monumental day. Nicole Reed speechless more than once is something worth noting. The shock on her face is priceless. If only Micah were here to see me standing tall. Well, as tall as a pregnant woman with a hot-air balloon belly can stand.

Mom walks me to the door and helps me with my shoes. I shoulder my purse and give her a hug.

"Love you, Mom. See you at the shower."

She nods with red-rimmed eyes. "I love you, Shelly. Your father and I wouldn't miss it for the world."

I walk to the car with a slight waddle and slowly lower myself into the driver's seat. Something else I will have to give up soon—driving. My belly is getting too big to reach the wheel and pedals comfortably. Plus, the stress of traffic is too much.

With one last look at my mother, I put the car in reverse, wave to her, and back out of the driveway feeling much lighter than when I arrived.

Today, I think it really hit her. Today, I think Mom finally realized that my life, and Micah's life, will be what we make it, not what she wants to shape it as. I don't doubt my brother still gets lectured on not having children. But maybe after today, maybe after the baby shower, Mom will learn to love how we live *our* lives. Maybe she will learn to love that we are happy like this.

# twenty-two

## DEVLYN

Thank god we don't know the gender. I might have lost it if the house was a blue or pink vomitfest. Although Shelly has given me a new appreciation for pink, having it plastered in every nook and cranny would have been nauseating.

My eyes roam over the decorations strung up and laid out in every imaginable place. Banners and balloons. Confetti in the shape of bottles and pacifiers and diapers scattered on every available surface. *At least it's recycled paper and not plastic or glitter.* Stacks of paper plates and cups and napkins. A box of biodegradable cutlery. Food, lots and lots of food. And a cupcake tower with enough for triple the number of people attending.

I haven't seen the games yet, but I bet they are equally overwhelming.

Sitting on the couch, I watch as Cora, Autumn, and Elizabeth move around the house. They work in tandem as if able to read each others' minds and know what else needs to be done. Shelly loiters in the kitchen, picking at the trays of food and making space for the last few dishes expected as others arrive.

When Cora and Autumn set out to organize the shower, they asked if there'd been anything Shelly wasn't eating during pregnancy and what she'd been craving. The only enemy had been the cheese, but that phase passed. Now Shelly craves and loves her favorite foods more.

There is no shortage of variety on the shower menu. Had it been any other party, the crowd would question the assortment.

I wander into the kitchen, lean a hip on the counter next to Shelly and snag a chocolate-covered fruit skewer.

*Excellent decision adding these to the menu.*

"Nervous?" I ask before biting off a piece of pineapple.

She plucks a finger sandwich from the tray beside her—sliced banana, nut butter and chocolate peeking out from the slices. "Kind of." She takes a bite as her eyes scan the room and beyond. "I'm excited to celebrate the baby and get the room put together." She pops the last of the finger sandwich in her mouth and shifts her attention to me. "Don't really want to be fawned over, though."

My beautiful Shelly. The brightest star in the night sky, yet she doesn't want all the attention. Doesn't want all eyes on her. Soon, real soon, a lot of that attention will shift.

Shelly will always be my center, my point of gravity, the person who brings balance to my world. But it won't be long before we both learn how to love each other and love someone new.

I lift my hand and cup her cheek. Slowly stroke her soft skin with my thumb. Stare into her starry eyes as her body relaxes. She leans into my touch, shuffles closer, and wraps her arms around my neck. Buries her face in the crook of my neck and breathes deeply.

Hugs are much different now. With her belly growing

bigger every day, Shelly has learned new ways to do everyday activities. I won't say it aloud, but I love painting her toenails. I love massaging her feet every night before bed. And I love the way her eyes light up with both. It relaxes her and makes her smile. It also connects us in a new way. In a way more intimate than lips and tongues and sex.

Don't get me wrong, we still make out like lusty teenagers. Our sex life has never been more incredible. The hormonal changes have not only amplified her drive, but also cemented our emotional bond. Sex during pregnancy is… hot. Like *really* hot. And although we've had to learn new positions so Shelly is comfortable, it has also added a new level of spice to the bedroom.

"Won't be too long. Think of it like the normal Sunday gathering, plus some additional people and lots of baby gifts," I say.

"You're right." Her brows knit together as she clutches her belly. Before I open my mouth to ask if she is okay, she reaches for my hand and places it on the left side of her belly. "Wait for it." She shifts my hand a little lower and presses it more firmly into her belly. A second later, something jabs my hand. "Did you feel that?" she asks, eyes shimmering as they stare into mine.

"Yeah," I say in wonderment. "Is that a kick?"

She moves my hand again. "Or an elbow. Maybe a fist pump. Possibly a knee."

We laugh a moment, then fall silent as we wait for the next jab. Another two stretch her belly before the baby settles.

One hand on her belly, I cup her cheek with the other, lean forward and kiss her. The kiss is far from sweet as I haul her closer and trace the seam of her lips with my tongue. Public displays are not typical for us. Mini make-out sessions in front of people almost never happen.

But these aren't just *any people*. Every person here is family. With kindness and embraces and inclusion, these people have shown me more love than any person with my DNA. They accept me for who I am and not what I can do for them. They care for me because I care for Shelly and vice versa. And they will never say an unkind word to either of us. Doesn't mean they won't tease us later.

Slowly letting each of them into my life has been a gift I never expected. A gift I wouldn't have without this incredible woman in my arms.

"Our little water aerobics instructor," I say, pressing my forehead to hers. "Can't wait to meet them."

"Same. Won't be long."

The party is in full swing and it isn't as overwhelming as originally expected. It's like Sunday nights mixed with a birthday party. Kind of. If an actual itinerary for this shindig exists, I'd be shocked. So far, we have mingled and eaten food. I suspect gifts and games and cake will happen soon.

"Can I have everyone's attention," Cora yells over the chatter. She sidles up to Shelly and conversations quiet as all eyes turn her way. "Thank you." She smiles, then wraps an arm around Shelly's shoulders. "Today we're here to celebrate this awesome chicky." Cora presses a kiss to Shelly's cheek. "And her and Devlyn's impending arrival."

Hoots and hollers and applause fill the room. Shelly's cheeks pinken and I stare a little too hard at her heated skin.

How long has it been since a blush stained her cheeks? Far too long. I'll need to remedy that in the near future.

Cora guides Shelly to a comfortable chair at the far end of the room that was decorated to mirror a throne. Once seated, Cora places a crown on Shelly's head decorated with mini plastic babies. I open the camera app on my phone and snap a picture.

"Gifts first," Cora says. "Then we'll do some corny games. And since the guys are here, us ladies should sit back and watch as they embarrass themselves." A chuckle leaves her lips.

Another chair is moved next to Shelly's and Cora gestures for me to sit.

Small boxes and big boxes. Jumbo bags and miniature bags. One by one, gifts are handed to Shelly to unwrap. After the first gift is revealed—an overflowing box of onesies and sleep shirts and jumpers—Shelly suggests we open everything together. That the day isn't really about her, but about us and the baby.

Wrapping paper tears and crumples. Tissue paper gets tossed to the side. The black trash bag at my right gets fuller with each unwrapped gift.

With each new present, shock and awe spread from my heart to my lips, tipping them up in an impossible smile. These people, our friends and family… they are the true gift. At this point, I don't think Shelly and I will need to buy much else. Their generosity is the biggest hug around my heart.

A bassinet with sheets and blankets. A crib that converts to a toddler bed and, one day, to a twin bed frame with more sheets. Clothes for home and outside the house for the next year. Bottles and nipples and cleaning kits. Baby bathtub and toiletries and cute hooded towels. Socks and mittens. Enough diapers and wipes to last us for several months—although, I hear you need more than you think—and so much more.

They thought of everything. Not just the items Shelly and I added to our registry list.

The backs of my eyes sting at their love and support and big, big hearts. Warmth floods my veins as tightness wraps my chest.

How many years have I wanted this? Love from others without conditions. Before Shelly, I thought I'd missed out on my chance at happiness and love. That my opportunity came and went after high school.

But I was wrong.

Shelly gifted me this. All of this. Love, life, a future.

Had I not been brave enough to take the leap, I don't think either of us would be here. I fought it for so long. Discounted my worth. Dismissed that love was possible again. Suppressed my feelings in fear of getting hurt.

Then, in a blink, I grew tired of fighting what my heart wanted. Grew tired of denying myself. And little by little, I opened up to her and to myself. I let myself feel, *really feel*, for the first time in years. And it was… sensational.

*Shelly* is sensational.

If not for this incredible woman, I wouldn't know happiness. I wouldn't know love. Wouldn't wake each day with a smile on my face and warmth wrapped around my heart. Damn, am I lucky. And I will never take Shelly or our love for granted.

I turn and see the tears ready to spill down her cheeks. Hormones aside, she would have cried at the level of love gifted today. Wrapping her hand in mine, I give a gentle squeeze. The tears brimming her eyes make the gold flecks sparkle brilliantly against her twilight irises and we stare wordlessly at each other. *I know*, I mouth.

The road of our relationship has been bumpy. Between my initial resistance and the sporadic roadblocks, it felt like we were driving the wrong way at every turn. That something bigger than us was intervening and steering us toward a dead end.

We didn't let them win, though. We never will. Our love is too strong.

"Alright, party people. Time for the good stuff," Cora shouts.

Autumn switches the music and an upbeat tempo fills the room. Gavin, Jonas and my father grab boxes and start hauling them to the nursery. I fill my arms and follow in their wake. By the time we have all the gifts moved, Autumn, Cora, Peyton and Penny are organizing something at the dining room table. Elizabeth and Nicole laugh at the display, and nervous energy floods my veins.

I don't know much about baby showers except for food and gifts. Shelly tried to warn me about the games. *"Some of them are just gross,"* she'd said. Time to pull up my big boy pants and do this. Enjoy the moment and suffer through the grossness with a smile on my face.

More than an hour later, we wrap up the last of the games. *Halle-freaking-lujah.*

Changing "dirty" diapers on baby dolls. Tootsie Rolls and soft fudge will never exist in my life again. Ever. Bobbing for pacifiers sounded like fun at first. Lies. All lies. Blindfolded while tasting baby food. This one wasn't as horrendous as I expected. I blame it on the organic jarred foods that were purchased.

Those were the more outlandish games. The rest I enjoyed.

Everyone was given a piece of stock paper along with pencils and crayons and asked to draw a picture for the baby. Didn't need to be pretty. Just something to look back on years later and smile over.

Next, we were all given two index cards. On one, we were asked to write names for a girl and on the other, names for a boy. Shelly and I had briefly scoured the internet for baby names, but nothing had stuck yet. This game was the perfect way to come up with fresh ideas.

The last game—although not really a game—everyone was given a small card, blank on the inside. We were tasked with writing a note or letter to the baby. Nothing specific. Whatever was in our heart.

And when I put pen to paper and slowly wrote a letter to my unborn child, I couldn't hold back the tears. I didn't sob, but the tears came and I let them flow freely as I wrote. One drop, then another, splattered on the card, but I didn't wipe them away. I left them right where they were. Exactly where they belonged.

"We'll help clean up and get out of your hair," Gavin tells me and Shelly.

"You don't need to," Shelly offers. "We can clean up."

Cora sidles up the Gavin. "Uh, no you won't. You just sit there and watch. Tell me what leftovers you want and which we should divvy."

"Fine," Shelly grumbles.

When Dr. Webster first put Shelly on light activities only, she protested with every breath she took. But as her health became more of a risk to the baby, she conceded. Although she grumbles still, I know she doesn't mind the help.

With each passing day, the circles beneath her eyes grow a touch darker. Her belly more round and body more uncomfortable. Her willingness to give up tasks she once argued to do on her own has grown tenfold. Her grumbles are more for show now.

We wave everyone off as they leave and go back inside to a quieter yet fuller house. But not as full as it will be in the next eight to ten weeks. Before long, our house will be filled with more love than imaginable. It will be chaotic in the beginning, but beautiful chaos. The thought thrills and terrifies me equally.

My inner pessimist says it is too good to be true. My inner pessimist says nothing this wonderful ever lasts.

I do my damnedest to shove that negative beast down. To smother it with all the good. To suffocate it with love. To extinguish its existence.

Maybe it is time to up my visits with Dr. Prince. Maybe it is time I ask Shelly to come with me.

# twenty-three

## SHELLY

I stare at the beige walls, lightly decorated with colorful framed art prints, and wonder how many secrets have bled into the drywall.

Spilling my past or how I feel doesn't make me uncomfortable. I have nothing to hide.

Guess I wonder how a person can listen to other people's problems all day, every day, and not feel overwhelmed or ready to crawl out of their skin. How do they sleep at night after digesting all the trauma or heartache?

They are saviors. True miracle workers.

On the couch beside me, Devlyn bounces his knee uncontrollably. His fingers pick at the exposed threads in the distressed part of his jeans. Every few seconds, his eyes land on the edge of my profile.

His nervous energy is palpable, comprehensible. Although we are honest with each other, tonight, in this place, sharing himself with me is different. A new level of vulnerability for us both. Devlyn is familiar with Dr. Prince. Has shared countless secrets with him. More than likely, secrets he has yet to share with me. That fact doesn't hurt. My hope is that after today—and future sessions—Devlyn won't feel uncomfortable sharing painful parts of the past with me. That I gain a new level of trust with Devlyn. Strong enough for him to consider me his safe space in all matters.

Arm extended across the table, Dr. Prince offers me his hand. "Nice to finally meet you, Shelly." His smile is kind, warm, sincere. His expression gentle and soothing as he waits for me to take his hand.

Placing my hand in his, we shake. His grip is firm yet soft. Solid yet gentle. "You as well. Devlyn speaks highly of you."

We sit back in our seats. I rest a hand on Devlyn's leg and he takes my hand in his, lacing our fingers as his bouncing knee settles. Dr. Prince takes a sip of water, then picks up a notepad and a pen. He scribbles on the paper for a moment, his eyes occasionally peeking up at us. Observing us. Making note of Devlyn's reaction to me and mine with him.

His observation doesn't unsettle me. This is part of his job, not just to listen but to also survey. I will say his perception of us has me curious.

"How've things been since our last appointment, Devlyn?"

I turn my head slightly, enough to get a better view of him but not look at him directly. He nibbles at his lips as he mulls over his answer.

"Good." He shrugs. "The baby shower was this past weekend." He looks at me briefly and gives my hand a squeeze. "Was nice, but overwhelming."

"Overwhelming how?"

His knee starts to bounce again. I stroke my thumb in a slow rhythm over his hand and, after a beat, his leg calms. Dr. Prince jots something on the notepad then meets my eyes, smiles, and returns his attention to Devlyn.

Devlyn laughs under his breath. "Not like I didn't know the baby was coming, but after the party, it just felt more real. Y'know?" His fingers toy with mine. "Plus, we got so many gifts for the baby." Green irises meet mine for a breath. A nervous smile on his lips. "I didn't expect that much… love."

I watch as Devlyn's brows pinch together, his eyes narrowing as he drops them to stare at his lap.

In this very moment, I see so much, but one thing stands out the most. Devlyn feels undeserving of this level of love. He feels unworthy of affection from other people.

And it pisses me off.

As if sensing my irritation, Dr. Prince directs his focus my way. "Shelly, tell me what you're thinking right now."

Spotlight, party of one.

My eyes linger on Devlyn's profile a moment before I turn to look across the table. I lick my lips, swallow past the anxiety ball in my throat, and tighten my hold on Devlyn. "I hate that she did this to him."

Dr. Prince tilts his head. "His mother?" I nod. "Take a deep breath and let the anger pass. Then, when you're ready, I want you to expand on that."

I do as he suggests and take a deep breath. Then another. And another. One breath at a time, I feel my pulse settle and the pang in my chest dissipate. "When it comes to Karen Templar, I can't seem to keep my emotions at bay. I apologize."

"No need to apologize. There is no judgment here."

With one last deep breath, I continue. "Devlyn and I became friends in October. We'd met in passing a year earlier through work, but it wasn't until this past October that we spoke and interacted." I grab my water bottle, twist the lid off and take a sip. "It took time and effort for Devlyn to open himself up. To let me in. Partly due to a past relationship gone sour." I turn to lock on Devlyn's soft green eyes. "But another piece was because he'd never really been shown love. Not real love." I return my gaze to Dr. Prince and press the heel of my hand to my chest. "And that hurts on so many levels."

The backs of my eyes sting as the words leave my lips. But I bite them back. I don't know if my body is overreacting because my hormones are out of whack or if I'd feel the urge to cry normally. Right now, all my body wants is to release. Heartache. Pain. Love. All for the man at my side that holds my hand like a life preserver.

"Shelly, your feelings toward Devlyn's mother are natural and reasonable." Dr. Prince shifts his attention to Devlyn, but continues to speak to me. "I don't know how much Devlyn has told you about his mother, but we have been working through the harder parts of his past." His gentle eyes meet mine again. "It will take time, but I hope the both of you are able to heal from this. That one day, you'll be able to not give so much of your energy to someone undeserving."

For the remainder of the hour, we discuss how the healing process is going with Devlyn and his father, and what my feelings are in relation to James. With each new interaction, I grow fonder of James. He hasn't told me his entire story, but from what he has shared and what Devlyn has told me, he felt trapped for years. Not because of Devlyn, but because he didn't trust his wife to raise Devlyn without him present. He wanted to escape with Devlyn, but didn't know how to safely.

But James smiles more now. The gentleness in Devlyn is equally visible in James. Excitement vibrates off James as each day passes and we get closer to the arrival of his first grandchild.

I trust the Templar men will slowly heal and become

whole again. Put the harsh years of the past behind them and move forward. Both have so much love in their hearts and it'd be a shame for them not to share it with others.

Minutes before the session ends, Dr. Prince gives us homework. Before the next appointment, which I have been asked to attend, Devlyn and I are to spend time in the nursery. Whether it is unpackaging gifts and finding them a new home or building the crib or just sitting in the room. We are to spend time in the room and just feel. Fill the room with love. Talk to the baby while in the room. Get used to the idea of having more than just the two of us in the house.

After handshakes and goodbyes, Devlyn and I leave the office. And it isn't until we are in the car and driving down the road that I feel it. A newfound level of relief. A comfort that had been missing. I didn't know it was something I needed, but now that I have it, I am grateful.

# twenty-four

## DEVLYN

Is it weird for me to be turned on right now?

Having Shelly at my appointment was beyond therapeutic. A buzz coursed through my veins. Perspiration dampened my skin. And the pain of the past was slowly released from my bones. For the first time in years, it feels as if I can draw in a full, deep breath.

And damn, it feels spectacular.

I don't keep secrets from Shelly—well, unless you count surprise parties—but I haven't unpacked all of my past with her. Not yet. Not because I don't want to, not because I don't trust her, but more because it is a lot to take on and I have no idea where to begin.

Insert Dr. Prince.

This man has been a godsend. He doesn't look at me like I have two heads. He doesn't call me crazy or judge how I feel about my mother. No, he listens, digests, then helps me look at each point in time from a different angle. One memory at a time, he guides me down the road to resolution. Shows me how to let go of the bad and find ways to forgive the guilt I feel. Teaches me how to move forward and love myself first without fear of repercussion.

When the holidays roll around this year, I plan to get Dr. Prince something to show my appreciation. He will decline and tell me gifts are unnecessary, but I beg to differ. Without his counsel, my life would still be a mess.

I park in the driveway and dash to the passenger door to help Shelly out. Early in the pregnancy, she'd wave me off. Tell me she was capable of getting out on her own. But as her belly rounds more, she waits for my hand. Allows me to take on more of the load. Smiles or kisses my cheek when I suggest she rest.

With Shelly less than ten weeks from delivering, Elizabeth insists on her working less hours. Instead of forty to forty-five, she now works closer to twenty. In a few weeks, depending on how she feels, Shelly plans to start maternity leave. Originally, she wanted to work until her water broke. With her belly rounding faster, her ankles and fingers swelling more, plus the general discomfort of being on her feet all day, she conceded on the idea. Confessing she will likely start leave a week or two before the baby arrives. Which is right around the corner.

To say I am relieved would be an understatement.

"Should we start on our homework assignment now?" she asks, humor lacing her voice as we toe off our shoes near the door.

I remember the first homework assignment from Dr. Prince. How ridiculous it felt to have *homework*. But I followed through. Completed each task without argument. And now, I have grown to like the assignments. Grown more comfortable with the familiar activities that aid my peace.

"Yes and no."

"Yes and no?"

I nod. "Mm-hmm." I lace my fingers with hers, spin to face her, and walk us down the hall. She starts to pull us toward the nursery, but I tug us in the opposite direction. Toward the bedroom. Our bedroom.

"Want to change?" she asks as her brows knit together.

I shake my head as my legs bump the foot of the bed. I lift my free hand to her cheek and stroke her soft skin with my thumb. Leaning forward, I press my lips to hers. Brush her lips with mine slowly. Paint the seam of her lips with my tongue until they part and let me in.

In two rapid heartbeats, the kiss evolves from sweet to hungry.

Her fingers curl into fists and cling to the cotton of my shirt. She tugs me closer. Drags her hands up my torso and along my shoulders before wrapping them around my neck. The kiss turns frantic as our tongues tangle and hands grope.

I break the kiss, reach back for the collar of my shirt and yank the cotton over my head before tossing it to the floor. Shelly fumbles to tug her shirt free. "Let me," I say as I reach for the hem and slowly pull it up and off her body.

Not a breath passes before I drop to my knees. Inches from my face, her belly button pokes out. Pink and brown marks highlight her belly. Marks she isn't fond of, but I find sexy as hell. Those marks are evidence my baby—our baby —grows in her womb. Can't think of anything more beautiful.

"Gorgeous," I whisper as I lean in and press my lips to her belly. I lift one hand and rest it on her belly, then the other. Tipping my head back, my eyes trail up her midline until I reach her starry blues. "The most beautiful, remarkable, astonishing woman I know."

Pink floods her cheeks as she combs her fingers through my hair. "Make love to me," she says with fierce boldness.

The further into pregnancy Shelly is, the more challenging sex becomes. It took several nights to find the most comfortable position for her, but neither of us complained.

Her shorts and mine land in the same pile as our shirts, followed by her bra and panties. I help her onto the bed, add a second pillow beneath her head, then crawl up beside her. Plant my hands on either side of her. Feather kisses over her skin. Along her jaw and neck. The curve of her shoulder and length of her collarbone. Over one breast, sucking her nipple between my lips before trailing over to the other. Inch by inch, I kiss my way down her belly, whispering words of love—for her and our baby. Then I dip lower. Drop between her thighs and lick up her seam.

She gasps and reaches for me, clutching my hair in her fist. "So good."

Her moans fill the room while I feast on her body. Her fingers in my hair tug harder. Nails digging into my scalp as her thighs tremble and tighten around my head. On the brink of her orgasm, I insert two fingers and pump at the slow rhythm she begs for every time. With one last flick and pump, her body constricts around my fingers as a guttural moan spills from her lips.

Before she comes down from her high, I crawl up the bed and kiss her deeply. Her hands roam from my face to neck and down my upper back. Moving to her side, she shifts the second pillow to the side and rolls onto hers. I brush her blonde locks aside and kiss the back of her neck and over her spine between her shoulder blades. She lays a hand over mine on her hip, lacing our fingers and encouraging me to paint her skin with my touch.

Shelly hasn't stated as much, but I get the impression she feels less attractive as her belly grows. The dramatic changes to her body have darkened her mood some days. Stolen her sunshine. And on those days, I hold her more. Closer. Tighter. Longer.

Each day of this journey... I have loved them all. The light and dark. The highs and lows. They give me perspective. Allow me to appreciate life and love and us in unimaginable ways.

She may not enjoy the changes to her body, but I love her more because of them. Love what those changes represent. Our connection. Our love. Strength and bravery and hope. The future.

Tracing my hand along the curves and dips of her torso, she releases my fingers when I reach her breast. I palm one in my hand. Massage and pinch and tease. A moan floats through the air as she grinds her butt against my erection.

I want to be inside her, desperately, but I take my time. Tease her body with lips and fingers and insatiable hunger. Make her comfortable. Make her feel good. Make her as equally desperate for me as I am her. Let her know that I love her and her body at every stage of life.

Sex with Shelly isn't just about getting off—both of us could do that easily. Sex with Shelly is uninhibited intimacy. Deep and pure and indestructible. A physical act to show her just how much I want her, need her, can't be without her. A way to show her she is still who I want, always. That when I look at her, heat floods my veins, my heart, every cell in my body.

"Devlyn," she whisper-moans as I pinch her nipple harder. She pushes her breast into my touch. "Please," she begs as moisture coats the tip of my erection.

I release her nipple and trail my fingers down her body, over the curve of her ass, and dip down between her thighs. Two fingers trace her seam and she shivers. Up and down. Up and down. I slick my fingers in her juices before pushing them inside.

Her gasp fills the air as I slowly pump two fingers inside her, over and over. She grips my forearm, her nails biting my flesh. This pain is one I have come to love, one I look forward to feeling, receiving.

My fingers pump faster, harder as her breaths come in quick, shallow pants. She rocks her hips harder against my touch, grinding, and I know she is close. I slip my fingers out and circle her clit once, twice, three times before dipping back inside. Pin her back to my front with my other arm. Circle her clit again and close my eyes as her body catapults once more.

She rides out her high with my fingers still inside her. As her body comes down, I pull my slick fingers out and paint her orgasm on my cock. Positioning my tip at her entrance and hand on her hip, I kiss her shoulder. "Love you, Andromeda."

She brings a hand to my hair and fists the locks, pinning me to the crook of her neck. "Love you, too."

With a slow rock of my hips, I fill her fully. We moan in unison. Her grip on my hair tightens as she grinds back against me. Inch by thick inch, I pull out to the tip before plunging forward. The first few rocks of my hips are slow, methodical, premeditated. I bask in every little whimper that leaves her lips. Relish every move her body makes as she silently begs for more.

And then, we are anything but slow and steady.

In a blink, the beast inside me claws its way to the surface and growls. My hips piston faster as my touch digs and bruises her hip and breast. I strengthen my hold on her frame and pump a vicious, hungry, punishing rhythm with my cock.

Her sweet cries of pleasure fill my ears. Her sweat slicks my skin and hers. And it isn't long before her body lets go and she moans my name. I bite the curve of her neck as I come undone inside her, my hold on her never more fierce.

Nothing compares to this. Shelly in my arms. Our bodies connected in every possible way. Both of us in a state of euphoria. Our connection isn't purely sexual, but the sex is explosive.

Shelly and I were lucky. We connected as friends before becoming lovers. Formed a bond I never thought possible. Discovered love slowly and together. Constructed an unbreakable connection.

In less than a year, Shelly and I have experienced so much together. Good and bad. Had we not faced the hardships and heartache, our love may not be what it is today. In our small blip of time together, we have been through a lot. Although there was hurt, I wouldn't change any of it. Although I almost lost her, and myself, we found our way back to each other.

My arms band around her body—one above her belly, one below—and hug her closer. I pepper her skin with kisses from her neck to the edge of her shoulder. Breathe her in and bask in the taste and touch and scent of her.

"Love you so much, Shell," I whisper against the back of her neck. "So much." My hands shift and embrace her expanding belly. Our baby.

She lays her arms over mine and squeezes me to her. "Love you more, Dev."

Not possible. Not by a long shot.

A chuckle slips from her lips as her body shakes. "Should we do our homework now?"

I join her light laughter. "Yeah. In a minute. Just want to lie here a little longer." And never let go.

# twenty-five

SHELLY

I wake drenched in sweat, the covers tossed from my body hours ago. The ceiling fan whirs above as the air conditioning blows cool air from the vent. Yet, I look like I just stepped out of the shower.

Looking to Devlyn's side of the bed, I find it empty. The cotton sheets cool.

Pushing up on my elbows, I peer around the darkened room, Devlyn nowhere to be found. I inch up to a sitting position, scoot to the edge of the mattress and let the cool air chill my heated skin. Easing off the bed, I peel my top over my head and toss it in the hamper before grabbing a dry shirt.

I tiptoe out of the room, the house alight with the rising sun coming in through the windows on the back of the house. Wandering down the hall, I listen for any indication as to where Devlyn might be. But I hear nothing. No clanking utensils in pans or food sizzling on the stove. No muted sounds from the television. Nothing.

Just as I consider climbing the stairs to his studio, I stop between the kitchen and living room.

In my periphery, I spy Devlyn out back on the patio. A

canvas on his easel, paint palette on one hand while a brush rests in the other and paints in varying shades of pink and red on the canvas.

As if he might hear me, I tiptoe toward the sliding glass doors and loiter just out of view. But not far enough that I can't watch him while he works.

In seconds, I realize the painting on the easel is the nude of me he started before my belly was so round. The full canvas isn't visible from my vantage point, but I see the length of my legs and curve of my hip. Scattered in the image are various flowers and a winding length of green vines. Looking at the canvas, I *know* the image is me. But from an outsider's perspective, someone who isn't familiar with me or us, no one would know who the woman is in the flowers.

The sun slowly rises in the eastern sky, but the pergola covering the patio keeps some of the sunbeams out of Devlyn's line of sight. Leaning on the frame, I watch him a little longer. Absorb the serenity he bleeds as he puts paint on the canvas. Breathe deeper as I watch the muscles of his back flex as he paints a new likeness of his favorite person—his words, not mine. Rub my swollen belly as I stare at the man I love.

My stomach grumbles and I decide to leave Devlyn to his solitude while I make us breakfast.

The buzzer for the turkey bacon sounds as Devlyn pads into the kitchen and leans against the counter. Sliding on a hot mitt, I open the oven and take out the pan, setting it on a trivet.

"I would've made breakfast had I known you were up," he says as I add shredded cheese to scrambled eggs on the stovetop.

Setting the package next to him, I stir the cheesy eggs and turn off the burner.

"Didn't want to disturb you." My lips curve up slightly. "You looked so peaceful and in your element."

He fetches plates as I start toasting slices of bread. "Still too hot to be outside after the early hours. I try not to wake you when I'm up at dark thirty."

Plates piled high with cheesy eggs, turkey bacon, fresh fruit and toast, Devlyn carries them to the dining room. I park myself in the chair as he wanders back to the kitchen.

"Tea, water, juice, chocolate milk?"

On the last one, the baby gives me a swift kick to the lungs. I gasp, then settle my breath. "Junior wants chocolate milk," I say on a laugh.

"Oh yeah?"

"Yep. Soon as you said it, they kicked."

"Chocolate milk it is."

The first several bites go by in relative silence. After I down half the glass of chocolaty goodness, I point my fork over my shoulder. "How's the painting coming along?"

Devlyn finishes his bite. "Almost done." He pushes around a slice of watermelon with his fork. "Maybe a few more sessions on the stool."

Next week, I officially start maternity leave from Petal and Vine. Although I am not due for another month, minimum, standing and walking all day is becoming more difficult and uncomfortable. It isn't that I *can't* do it. More like it exhausts me to be on my feet more than an hour.

Weeks ago, Elizabeth made me sit down every so often. *"I've been there, sweetheart. You will thank me later for the stool," she'd said.* And she was right, of course. Parking my butt on the stool helped some with the swelling, but so did walking. If I was arranging flowers, my instructions were to be on that stool.

And I definitely didn't want to be in trouble with Momma Davies.

Working less hours had been a big adjustment. So was learning to give up my independence. Not that I gave it up fully. Some tasks I still manage on my own just fine. But driving and setting up the nursery are not on the "Shelly is allowed to do these alone" list.

With me home full time soon, part of me feels as if I am stealing Devlyn's time from him.

For years, he was used to his solitude. He was used to climbing those stairs and getting lost for hours or days in his art. And now, it feels as if I rob him of it all.

"Why don't you spend more time on it today," I suggest as he eats his last bite of toast.

Cocking his head to the side, he narrows his eyes. "Thought we were finishing up the nursery today. Or trying to, at least. I need to put the final touches on the mural."

I swallow down the last of my chocolate milk. "But if you want to paint more of something else, you can. I can unbox the diapers then fold the washed baby clothes and put them away."

The nursery is practically finished. Some bigger items still needed to be assembled, but the crib and bassinet are done. The baby swing and items the baby won't use right away are still in the box. They don't concern me, though I know Devlyn will assemble them sooner rather than later.

"Maybe for a little bit," he concedes.

A tension I didn't realize was in my shoulders relaxes. Parenthood is a big change for us both, but I don't want either of us to forget who we are and what we love. Devlyn should still get to spend time in his studio. Although I may need him to watch over me for a short time around the birth, I don't want him to feel trapped or bogged down.

"Good, because I want to see the finished product. Please and thank you."

Wood scrapes wood as he scoots his chair back, rises from his chair and laughs. "Yes, ma'am." He picks up my empty plate and his. "I'll get the dishes since you cooked. You do what you need to do and I'll meet you in the nursery in a bit."

I brace my hands on the chair and table and push up. Following him to the kitchen, I kiss his cheek. "Take your time."

I sway back and forth in the rocking chair near the window. My eyes on the tree just outside the baby's bedroom on the side of the house, watching the wind rustle the leaves as birds flit to and fro. My hand rubs small circles over my swollen belly as I talk to the baby.

"Mommy and Daddy should put a bird feeder in the tree. Maybe treats for the squirrels too. Then we can watch them while we rock in the chair together." My eyes fall to my belly. "Definitely need to add some more color. A flowering shrub, so you always have something beautiful to look at. What do you think?"

A knee or elbow or foot protrudes to the left of my navel as the baby stretches. I consider it an agreement to my idea. "Glad you think so too."

Laying my head against the back of the chair, I close my eyes and continue to sway. Minutes pass before I hear Devlyn pad into the room. He doesn't say a word, but I sense him close by.

Slowly, I open my eyes and scan the room. Just out of reach, he leans against the wall, arms crossed in front of him. His expression soft as he regards me in the rocking chair. The corners of his mouth tip up.

"Didn't mean to disturb you."

"You didn't." My eyes drop to his bare chest where random streaks of paint stain his skin. Heat floods my cheeks as the memory of us painting each other comes to the fore-front. "Was just relaxing after putting things away."

In two long strides, he reaches the front of the rocker and squats down. His hands come to my knees and slowly drift up my thighs. "What were you just thinking?"

"What?"

His thumbs draw small circles on either leg. "Just now, you looked at me and blushed. What were you thinking?"

Will I ever not blush around Devlyn?

Devlyn is the only man to stir up such desirous feelings and thoughts. Enough to heat every cell in my body and pink my skin. In the beginning, I was embarrassed by my reaction. Now, I embrace the way my body responds to his proximity, his words, him.

Licking my lips, I swallow and point to his chest. "Saw the paint on you and thought about the morning when we… uh… painted each other." Heat floods my cheeks anew.

His hands trail from my thighs to my round belly, his thumbs and fingers lightly massaging the stretched skin. And damn, does that feel good. So good.

"Definitely need to do that again," he says as he leans in and presses a kiss to my belly. "Maybe before you arrive into the world, little one," he whispers to my belly. Then he lifts his gaze, his eyes a shade darker. "Maybe now."

Heat spreads throughout my body for a wholly new reason. Hunger and love rise to the surface. My relaxed state from moments ago morphs into something new, something primal. Although my body wants to rest, my mind and heart scream to get out of this chair and follow Devlyn up the stairs to his studio. To squeeze colored pigment from tubes and paint him with my own abstract passion.

"Yes," I whisper. "Now."

Not needing reassurances, Devlyn rises to his full height and offers me his hand. My warm fingers slip into his hand as I stand from the rocker. Without a word, we weave our way through the house and climb the stairs to his studio. He parks me on the stool near his easel. While he sets everything up, I stare at the painting of me he has worked diligently on.

I have no words.

The piece so different from his others. A mess of pinks and reds layer the canvas. Some spots thicker with paint and in harsh yet soft lines. My face is almost absent of detail… except for my eyes. My nose is a simple streak and change in color. My unshapely lips a deep, rich red. But my eyes… I should expect nothing less from Devlyn. They pop on the canvas. Dark blue with gold flecks, naturally. Strands of hair fan over my cheek and down my shoulder to my breast.

My eyes drift along the canvas and take in the curves of my breasts, the dark pink of my nipples. The brush strokes on my body softer. Smoother. Gentle. He painted my belly—our baby —with even more tenderness. My hand splayed beneath my navel, and his hand added in and next to mine, forming a cradle.

The backs of my eyes burn with unshed tears.

The depth of this man's heart is unparalleled. He loves me in a way no one ever has. In a way no one ever will. He brought a new gentleness into my life and I showed him what real love looks and feels like. Our love is pure and breathtaking and everything I wanted in my life.

A sudden rush of images flash before my eyes. Mental snapshots of our past. Assumed depictions of our future. And it is so odd, the clarity of those pictures. Especially those yet to come. But I see it all.

Devlyn with our little one bundled in his arms. His eyes glassy with unshed tears as he stares down at them. And the way he holds my gaze when he looks up at me in pure awe. Delight. Brilliance.

Then the images flash forward to years from now. Devlyn and I swinging our mini between us as we walk down the beach along the surf. A sweet voice begging us to swing them higher. Soft giggles and shrieks of joy.

Tears spill down my cheeks without effort as my mind comes back to the present. The beautiful painting a blurry mess of reds and pinks as I swipe my cheeks and eyes. Devlyn catches the movement out of the corner of his eye and spins to face me.

"What's wrong?" A whack fills the air as he drops the supplies from his hands and strides across the room. He cradles my face in his hands and brushes away the wetness with his thumbs. "Tell me. Please," he whispers.

I lick my lips and swallow as I point a finger at the canvas. "This is the first time I've really seen the painting. It's just…" My blues dart between his greens. "It's so beautiful." I shrug. "Guess it overwhelmed me." I shake my head on a chuckle. "Damn hormones."

Devlyn leans in, kissing each tear trail on my cheeks

before pressing his lips to mine. The kiss is sweet and gentle, and ends far too soon.

"You're beautiful." His thumbs stroke my cheeks again. "The most beautiful creature I know."

"For now," I mutter as my eyes fall between us.

"Hey." One hand drifts to my chin and tips it up so I look him in the eye. "No." He shakes his head. "No, Shelly," he repeats.

One of my creeping insecurities rises to the surface. Maybe because I am overwhelmed with seeing the painting. Maybe because there isn't a lot of time of just me and Devlyn left. Whatever the reason, my secret spills from my lips with too much ease.

"When the baby comes, things will change." My vision blurs for a new reason. "They'll easily be more beautiful."

"Not possible." I open my mouth to rebut his words and he shakes his head. "Not. Possible." He presses another kiss to my lips. "Yes, we will love this baby. So much." His hand falls to my belly and rubs the outer swell. "But that won't change how I love you. Ever."

"You don't know that," I whisper-choke.

"I do." Soft, warm lips press mine. "Shelly, I will never love anyone the way I love you. Will I love our baby with unmatched affection? Absolutely. But my love for them will be new. A love neither of us will understand until it hits."

As his words sink in, as they resonate in my bones, I believe them more. The love for our child will be phenomenal. Otherworldly. Surreal. But loving them will be different than loving Devlyn.

I nod. "I love you."

His fingers twirl a strand of my hair as he drops his forehead to mine. "Love you, Shell." After another chaste kiss,

Devlyn straightens to his full height. "Come." He offers his hand. "Time to paint."

The corners of my mouth tip up as I take his hand. "As you wish."

Hours pass without care as I paint every line, curve and valley on Devlyn's body. And he paints mine as if it is the most precious thing his hands have touched.

# twenty-six

## DEVLYN

Shelly shifts on the bed for the umpteenth time. I curl into her frame, my front to her back, and try to calm her.

But she isn't sleeping.

Her hand takes mine and squeezes. Just as I open my mouth to ask if she is okay, her body tightens. Her breathing pauses a beat before she grunts softly.

"What's wrong?" I whisper-ask and kiss her shoulder.

I feel her head shake in the dark. "Can't get comfortable. And my stomach…"

When she doesn't elaborate, I prop myself up on my elbow and look at her profile. "Your stomach what?"

"It's just tight. Like painfully tight."

Without a word, I whip the covers off my body and slip out of bed. Circling the bed, I stand in front of Shelly. "Close your eyes. I'm turning on the lamp." I give her a moment, then flip the switch. We squint into the lit room until our eyes adjust. I hold out my hand. "Let's try to walk a minute. See if that helps."

She takes my hand without argument. I help her off the bed and guide her out of the bedroom. We take slow steps through the house. To the kitchen, then the living room before sliding the glass doors open and stepping outside.

Minutes pass as we wander through the yard barefoot. Shelly appears more relaxed than when we left the bed. Just as we turn to head back for the house, she stops. I take in her profile and see her brows knitted together.

*Something's wrong.*

*Is it time?*

It can't be time. The due date isn't for a few more weeks. Early October. Right?

My brain scrambles back to all the doctor's appointments, trying to recall the dozen different dates Dr. Webster told us. And then it hits. A couple months back, when the number of appointments increased and we visited every other week, then every week. At one of those appointments, Dr. Webster said the baby may come sooner. That it wasn't abnormal. But as long as Shelly was in the last four weeks, it was safe.

Is that what this is? Shelly going into labor.

We hadn't attended classes like most normal new parents. With all the mothers surrounding us—Elizabeth, Nicole, Cora, and Autumn—we'd been coached on all things birth and baby related. Shelly had found several Lamaze breathing videos online and opted to do those instead of in-person classes. They made her more comfortable and we did them on our schedule.

What did those videos say? For the life of me, I can't seem to remember a damn thing about the breathing right now.

And what about the books I'd read? They talked about what happens when labor starts. But it also stated no two labors are alike. So what good is that information?

*Damnit.*

"Talk to me," I tell Shelly. "Do you think it's time?"

Her free hand goes to her belly and rubs circles. Over and over. Again and again. From the expression on her face, she doesn't appear to be in pain. But maybe it isn't *pain*. Maybe she is super uncomfortable. Neither of us knows what to expect with labor, least of all me.

"It just feels tight." She looks up at me, unable to straighten to her full height. "Like my skin is being stretched." Her brows pinch at the middle. "Shit."

"What?"

"Need to pee. Now."

Quickly as possible, I guide us inside and to the bathroom. I stand outside the open door while Shelly does her business. I do my best not to stare or appear overbearing, but I worry. Maybe we should hop in the car and drive to the hospital. I glance across the bedroom to the alarm clock and note the time: 3:55.

The doctor's office doesn't open for another three and a half hours.

Do we wait? Give it time and see if it passes?

I should make her something to drink. Something soothing. A mug of hot cocoa.

Shelly flushes the toilet and washes her hands. "God, it feels like I need to pee constantly, but barely anything came out."

I take her hand and walk us toward the kitchen. "How about some tea or cocoa? Maybe it'll settle whatever this is." And while she drinks, I will search the internet and the stack of baby books for answers.

A smile tips up her lips as she curls into my side. "Cocoa would be great."

With measured steps, Shelly paces the kitchen while I heat

the oat milk. I scoop two spoonfuls of her favorite cocoa mix into her favorite mug and add the warmed milk.

Guiding us out of the kitchen, I park us on her old couch in our reading area. While she sips her cocoa, I Google what labor pains feel like. Thousands of results fill the screen and overwhelm me with all the possibilities.

Some articles indicate true labor starts when the water breaks. Others say labor begins when contractions start, that sometimes the water doesn't break on its own. Either way, Shelly's water hasn't broken yet. So I move on to another article. This one talks about painful contractions and the need to push. Shelly hasn't mentioned the desire to push, just the need to pee. Again, I move forward.

The next article has me blinking, again and again.

The article states some labor starts with a general pressure, low in the belly. The mother may feel like her skin is stretched to extremes—very tight. The need to use the bathroom often may be present, without much of a release. I continue reading down the page. The more I read, the more I am convinced it is time.

But the article also points out it may be false labor. That the baby may be shifting and moving into position for the big day. The article goes on and says to time how long the sensations last and how far apart they are.

Not wanting to alarm Shelly, I speak in mellow tones and relay what I just read. Surprisingly, she appears quite calm when I finish.

"I wondered as much," she says. "Right now, it isn't so bad. Like a barely noticeable ache." Her hand paints small circles over her belly while she sips her drink. "This has helped."

"Then I guess we wait." I shrug. "If it starts back up, we

time it and make note." I lay my hand over hers on her belly. Lace our fingers together and help soothe her discomfort. "Until then, maybe we just take it easy. Sit on the couch, under the blanket, and watch a movie in the dark." I kiss her cheek. "In a few hours, I'll make breakfast. Sound good?"

"Perfect."

~

I add eggs to each of our plates already filled with sausage, hash browns, and toast. Setting forks on each plate, I carry them to the living room and hand one to Shelly, who has made a makeshift table with a throw pillow on her belly.

We dive into our breakfast while a Passionflix movie plays on the television.

When Shelly added the Passionflix app to the Apple TV, I asked what the channel was all about. She'd said, *"It's all my favorite romance books coming to life."*

I have yet to read any of the countless romance books on her shelf, but perhaps I should check them out. See what all the fuss is about. The movies have been interesting and lovely, but the book is always better.

Over the last few hours, nothing new has happened. No more tightness. No urgent need for the bathroom. So, we have taken it easy. Rested in each other's arms and occasionally drifted off. Perhaps it was false labor. Books state false labor —Braxton-Hicks contractions—is one way the body prepares for the big day. Kind of like a delivery practice drill.

Whatever it is, I hope it passes until the real time occurs. Last thing we need is a scare after things have been so good.

When our plates empty, I take them to the kitchen and clean up. Just as I place the last pan into the dishwasher,

Shelly wanders in. I open my mouth to tell her I was on my way back. That she could have waited and I would have gotten whatever she needs.

But I don't say a word. Not when I scan her head to toe and take all of her in.

One hand braces the edge of the kitchen counter while the other rubs back and forth in rapid strokes on her belly. Her lips trapped between her teeth as her jaw works back and forth. The space between her brows wrinkled and tight.

And I know this is it.

Earlier was a drill. Like a like tremor before an earthquake. Like the warning winds and rain before the hurricane makes landfall.

But this is no longer a drill. It's go time.

"Talk to me, Shell."

"It's like before." She closes her eyes for a breath then holds my greens captive. "But stronger. Tighter. More intense."

"Did it just start?"

She nods. "A minute after you walked out of the room."

"Okay," I say, calmer than I feel. "Let's get the hospital bag and leave."

In the bedroom, Shelly puts on a pair of pajama pants before grabbing her phone from the charger. I trade my sweats for jeans and tug a shirt over my head. I grab us each socks from the dresser. We slip on socks and shoes at the door. Shelly fetches her purse from the hook while I shoulder the hospital bag.

Slowly, we make our way to the car. A minute later, I pull out of the neighborhood and aim the car west toward the hospital. Traffic isn't too bad yet, but may pick up the longer we're on the road.

At a red light, I turn to face Shelly. Her eyes forward as she takes slow, measured breaths. Her hands massage her belly from back to front, occasionally switching positions.

"Doing okay?" I ask, feeling like a fool the moment the words hit the air. *What a stupid question.* Of course, she isn't okay. The baby is trying to evacuate the womb. No way she isn't in some kind of pain. I sure as hell would be.

"Okay," she says between breaths. "But it's becoming more intense."

Sweat licks my temples as she says the words. I did this. I put her in this position. It is me who is responsible for her pain. Me, not her.

*Give her pain to me.*

If only it were so simple.

The city passes in a blur of fast-driving cars and a blend of residential and commercial buildings. Now isn't the time to take in scenery. Now isn't the time to observe sights and smells and places to visit in the future.

I flip on the blinker and zip into a turn lane. Tap the steering wheel as I wait for the light to turn green. An older man strolls leisurely in the crosswalk in front of us. Bass thumps from a car nearby. Sirens wail in the distance. But all of it vanishes as the light turns green.

And Shelly's water breaks.

"Oh god," she whispers. "Oh god."

*Fuck.* I smash the pedal to the floorboard and whip down the road. *We're almost there.*

# twenty-seven

SHELLY

Pain. Excruciating, inexplicable pain. It is all I feel. All I hear. All I see. Pain… it is everywhere. Everything.

I clutch my belly and bend slightly in the seat. "Ow. Ow, ow, ow!"

The car picks up speed as Devlyn takes the next right. I fist the handle above the window and hug my belly tighter.

"Sorry," he mutters. "Just trying to get us there."

"I…" Another stab of pain tears through my belly. I suck in a deep breath, hold it and count to three, then exhale. "I know. Just be careful."

Not a minute later, Devlyn whips into the hospital parking lot. He drives to the drop-off spot near the doors, jumps out and jogs to my side of the car. Flinging my door open, he helps me step out, kisses my forehead, and tells me he will be right back. From my spot near the entrance, I watch as he finds the closest parking spot to the entrance before bolting from the vehicle and running to me, hospital bag slung over his shoulder.

From there, everything but the pain is a blur.

Arm around my waist, Devlyn holds on to me as if my

knees will buckle. Which is smart, because I may give up any minute.

Elevator doors whoosh open and the familiar view of the labor and delivery floor comes into view. Today, I won't be twiddling my thumbs in a hard chair in the waiting area. For the first time, I will be in the hospital bed, cursing out people left and right as I push our baby into the world.

As we reach the nurses' station, Devlyn explains the past few hours and my water breaking in the car. As the words leave his lips, another contraction rips through my lower abdomen.

"Argh!" I bite out, bending slightly and clutching my belly.

Before the contraction ends, warm hands guide me to sit in a wheelchair. A nurse steers me down the hall like she drag races cars for pleasure. Three deep breaths later, the wheelchair is parked next to a hospital bed and I am ushered onto the mattress.

"We'll need you to change," the nurse says, offering me a sympathetic smile and a hospital gown. "Or, if you'd prefer, just strip down and slip under the sheet. If you choose to wear the gown, leave the front open." Then, she steps out of the room.

"Do you want the gown?" Devlyn pulls back the top sheet on the bed.

I shake my head. "Just want to ditch the wet clothes."

Devlyn helps with my bottoms and underwear. As I lift my shirt over my head, another contraction hits. While I clutch my belly and breathe through the pain, Devlyn wiggles off my top. He situates me on the bed and covers me with the sheet.

"What can I do?"

I hold up my hand. "Just be here."

He laces his fingers with mine, leans in and kisses my forehead. "Nowhere else I want to be."

The contraction settles and realization strikes. "We didn't call anyone." Our family and friends will lose their shit if we don't let them know I am in labor.

Devlyn releases my hand, pulls his phone from his back pocket, and taps on the screen. A moment later, he locks the device and stows it once more. From my spot on the bed, I hear the repeated vibration of responses, but Devlyn doesn't answer any of them. Instead, he takes my hand again and kisses my knuckles in turn.

It isn't long before nurses flood the room. A thick band gets strapped around my belly and the nurses adjust my position in the bed. Ice chips, water, and a cup are brought in and set up on the rolling table behind Devlyn. Dr. Webster walks in decked out in scrubs with a bright smile on her face. A nurse holds a glove open for her and she slips her hand in one, then another.

She steps closer to the foot of the bed, between my feet in the stirrups. "How you doing, Mom? Dad?" Her smile intensifies. "I hear this little cutie is ready to meet everyone?"

Devlyn remains a quiet beacon of strength at my side as I relay how I feel. The pressure from earlier, the cramping, and then the pain once my water broke in the car.

"Everything sounds on track and normal. Let's have a look and check your dilation."

Once upon a time, I reddened with embarrassment even thinking about my appointments at the lady doctor. Now, I don't care. All the people in this room are trained medical professionals. They have probably delivered hundreds, if not thousands, of babies. Nudity doesn't shock them. No doubt, they have seen it all. And in this moment, I honestly don't give a damn who sees what.

*Just get this damn baby out of my body.*

Dr. Webster recovers my knees and removes the gloves from her hands as she stands from the stool. Tossing the gloves in the biohazard trash bin, she turns on the faucet and washes her hands.

"Dilated to seven. Shouldn't be long now." Her glowing smile makes another appearance. "I'll be back to check on you soon. In the meantime, keep breathing and resting as much as you can." Her eyes go to Devlyn. "Dad, you're in charge of keeping her as calm as possible. Water and ice chips may help. But not too much."

All but one nurse leaves the room. He pulls things out of cabinets and sets up items on counters and trays and carts. I close my eyes and listen to the machine as it registers my heartbeat, the baby's heartbeat, and contractions. I let it soothe me as I rest against pillows softer than I imagined for the hospital.

Devlyn traces my fingers and hand with his. And right now, everything is calm and normal.

But that all vanishes a second later as another contraction stretches and pulls and rips at my abdomen. Devlyn kisses my temple and encourages me to take deep breaths. I squeeze his hand hard enough to detach it from his arm, but he doesn't complain.

When the pain eases, Devlyn offers me ice chips and pours water in a cup with a straw.

Not a minute later, another contraction hits. This one like a knife to my insides. Stabbing. Painful. Burning. Before I get the chance to voice my pain, the monitor off to the side wails loudly. Too loudly.

In an instant, the room overflows with medical personnel. One silences the machine, while Dr. Webster gloves up. Her smile from earlier gone. Her demeanor and body language more serious as she reads the numbers on the monitor.

She lifts the sheet away and exposes me fully. "Shelly, are you in pain?" She surveys between my thighs. "More than the previous contractions," she clarifies.

"Yes. What's wrong?"

She feels around my lower abdomen, near my pelvic bone, and presses hard in a few spots. "Does this hurt?" I suck in a sharp breath and nod. Her eyes drift to a nurse in light-blue scrubs and she gives a subtle nod. The nurse blurs out of sight and starts grabbing more items from cabinets and drawers. "I don't want to alarm you, but it seems as if this little one isn't getting enough oxygen. Your body isn't ready to push yet, so we need to do an emergency C-section."

Tears rim my eyes, blur my vision and spill down my cheeks. "Oh god."

"This isn't abnormal, Shelly. But we can't wait."

A nurse comes to Devlyn's side, hands him a pile of green scrubs, and tells him he needs to change before the surgery starts.

He kisses my forehead. "Be right back." And then he dashes into the en suite bathroom.

I cry harder the second he steps away. Dr. Webster continues to assure me everything will be fine, but I tune out her voice. I tune out every sound in the room. Because this just feels like another snapped tree in the road. Another major obstacle to challenge me. To challenge us.

And damn it. I am so fucking tired of this. So tired of having to fight. So tired.

Once I have the scrubs on and the booties over my shoes, I exit the bathroom. The room is abuzz, and not in a good way. When I look to Shelly, I notice her eyes are closed. My initial thought is she is relaxing between contractions.

As everyone moves rapidly around the room, a curtain is erected to hide the lower half of her body from sight. I go back to my position next to Shelly and scoop up her hand, lacing my fingers in hers. But she doesn't curl her fingers.

In fact, her arm is deadweight.

"Something's wrong," I say, but no one pays me attention. So, I repeat myself, louder this time. "Something is wrong." Dr. Webster peers around the curtain, mask covering her face. "She's limp," I choke out.

If I thought the room was chaos moments ago, I was dead wrong.

Dr. Webster shouts orders, but none of them makes sense to me. Then a nurse is at my side, taking my arm and guiding me out of the room.

"Everything will be fine, Devlyn. Just let us work and

we'll be out to get you in a minute," Dr. Webster says, calmer than she lets on.

"What's wrong with her? Is Shelly okay? The baby?"

"A nurse will be out to speak with you in a moment."

And then, the door is closed.

I have no idea what is happening, but it can't be good. At all.

First the baby is in distress. Then Shelly passes out. This isn't normal. Not by a long shot. Worst of all, I have no idea what is happening on the other side of the door. No idea if I am losing Shelly. Or if we are losing the baby.

Or both.

I fall to my knees. The linoleum smacks my bones hard, but I welcome the pain. I welcome every ounce. Because it is nothing compared to what is happening to my heart.

I can't lose Shelly. Or the baby.

Losing either of them isn't an option. Not even close.

Everything is foggy. The air, my thoughts. It feels as if I am floating. Lingering. Not really here or there.

What the hell is happening?

My eyes feel puffy and weighted. Heavy. Unable to open.

My throat is swollen and scratchy. Abrasive like sandpaper. My lungs dry and burning. I will myself to swallow to moisten my throat. But nothing happens. No relief comes. I try to take a deep breath, but my lungs won't fill fully.

Again, I try to open my eyes and take in my surroundings. Open my mouth and say something. Anything. Again, I fail.

What the hell is going on?

And where is Devlyn?

I don't sense him nearby. Not the smell of his addictive, earthy scent. Not his warm, charismatic energy. Not his whispered words of reassurance or the weight of his hand in mine.

*Where is he?*

My brain tells my muscles to move, tells my mouth to open and my voice to work, but nothing happens. I want to scream for help. Want to ask what is wrong with me. Want to ask if the baby is okay.

But none of it happens. Nothing works.

The thick fog returns. Clouds around me and pull me down, down, down. Without effort, I drift further into the darkness.

In the darkness, life feels peaceful.

In the darkness, everything feels safe.

In the darkness, the weight of the past falls away.

And now I understand. I get it. Why Devlyn liked the darkness for so long. It's like a warm hug after a long day. A welcome home when you have been away for days or weeks.

In the darkness, there is no pain. Just relief. And I welcome the repose.

# thirty

## DEVLYN

The past ten hours have aged me ten years.

Shelly lies in the hospital bed. Still. Silent. Except for the beat of her heart through the monitor. The room dimly lit by a lamp off to the side. The baby in the hospital nursery being monitored by nurses and the doctor.

And me… I stand on the edge of a cliff, head tipped back as I scream at the heavens.

This doesn't feel like another test. Another measure of my strength. No, this feels like the end. The end of a long obstacle course. One I didn't choose, but one I can't seem to escape.

Dr. Webster says Shelly will wake up soon. That her body is exhausted and needs the rest. Her vitals are perfect. It's just a matter of the anesthesia leaving her system and her mind waking up. Dr. Webster says there is no need to worry.

But worrying is all I can do. It is all I know.

With Shelly's hand sandwiched between mine, I give her a gentle squeeze. Paint lines my fingertips over each finger, each knuckle. I press my lips to the top of her hand on either side of the IV line.

"I need you to wake up, Andromeda," I whisper against

her skin. The backs of my eyes sting as tears surface and well. I don't fight the tears. Don't try to shove them down. No, I let them spill. Let them paint my cheeks. Let them fall from my chin to her hand. "I need you, Shell. Forever. Please," I choke out.

I close my eyes and lay my head on her fingers. Pray to whatever force, whatever deity is willing to listen. Beg them to help her wake. Open her eyes. Squeeze my hand. Whisper my name. Something. *Anything.*

Whispering voices in the room startle me from sleep. But I don't lift my head and greet them. Without seeing, I know it is Nicole and George Reed. They have been in the room almost as much as I since Dr. Webster allowed us. More than once, they suggested I get food or a drink or take a walk down the hall. That they would be here with Shelly and let me know if anything changed.

But I refuse to leave her side. Not for a minute. Food and drinks and walks can wait.

Shelly needs me more than I need anything else right now. Leaving her isn't an option. I fear what may happen if I leave this room. One step out, one minute away, and everything could change.

"We need to do something, George," Nicole whispers to her husband. Her voice scratchy and tired. "I can't stand this. The waiting." She sniffles. "What kind of doctor tells a mother to be patient while her only daughter lies in a coma? Does the woman *have* children? Does she have an inkling of what this feels like?" With each word she speaks, her voice escalates in volume.

George shushes her. "Everything will be fine, Nicole."

"You don't know that," she rebuts with a sharp edge to her words. "You can't be positive."

He audibly exhales. "You're right, I don't know what will happen. But I choose to believe she will wake up any minute. I choose to believe everything will be okay. Is it easy? No." At this, I twist my head and peek at the two of them on the couch in the room. George points a finger toward the bed and Shelly, but his eyes remain on his wife. "But I won't give an ounce of my energy to negative thoughts. Not when it comes to our children. Or our grandchild." He lowers his hand. "She will wake up." Rising from the couch, he stares down at Nicole for a beat. "I'm going to stretch my legs and get something for us all from the cafeteria."

Then he storms to the door and leaves without another word.

Although my mind drifts so easily into the dark, I side with Mr. Reed and silently vow to Shelly I will only think positive thoughts. I won't give in to the darkness that has come to me with such ease in the past.

Shelly will wake up. She will. She has to.

I lift my head and shift in the chair that now has a permanent mold of my body. Nicole catches the movement and swipes at her cheeks.

"Sorry if we woke you."

"Don't apologize," I tell her. "We're all on edge right now."

She rises from the couch and shoulders her purse. "I'll go update whoever is still here. Maybe walk the halls for a bit. Clear my head."

I nod. "Okay."

The door quietly clicks shut and it's just me and Shelly and silence. On a normal day, I love the silence we share. It isn't awkward or uncomfortable. Many of my favorite moments with Shelly didn't involve a single word spoken.

But this silence… I never want this type of silence again.

I kiss the back of her hand and stand from the chair. Twisting left and right, forward and backward, I stretch my stiff muscles. I lift my arms over my head and roll my neck. Shake my legs and wiggle my toes. Work my body from head to toe and get my blood flowing.

While her parents are away, I step into the en suite bathroom, leaving the door wide open, and relieve my bladder. Hands soaped up, I run them under the water and rinse away the suds. As I fetch a paper towel from the holder, my ears perk up.

The monitor beeps a different rhythm. Faster. Seemingly louder.

I drop the paper towels in the direction of the bin and dash out of the bathroom. Sidling up to the bed, I take Shelly's hand in mine and lean over her.

"Shell? Can you hear me?"

Her eyelids tighten briefly. Her fingers twitch in my hold.

Leaning in closer, I press my lips to her forehead. Then drop them to her ear and whisper, "I'm here, Shell."

Her fingers curl and wrap around my own. A low groan echoes from her throat.

Hovering inches from her face, I wait for her eyes to open. Wait for her sparkling blues to meet my faded greens. It hasn't been a full day, but I miss the hell out of those eyes.

Slowly, her lids lift. She blinks and blinks and blinks. Her tongue darts out to wet her lips and she groans. She lifts her free hand and taps her throat.

"I'll get you water." I kiss her forehead before untwining my fingers from hers. I pour water from a pitcher into a cup with a straw on the rolling table. Bringing it to her, I bend the straw and press it to her lips. "Small, slow sips."

She takes one, then another. Licks her lips. Swallows. Parts her lips in a silent request for more. After a few more sips, she releases the straw and nods. I set the cup down and take her hand in mine once more.

"How do you feel?" I whisper-ask as I brush stray hairs from her face. My knuckles graze her cheek and her eyes roll shut as she leans into my touch, a low hum in her throat.

Her eyes open and lock on mine. "Tired," she says, her voice raw. "Pain." She inhales deeply before her face morphs. Deep lines mar her forehead. The skin between her brows bunches and tightens. "Where…" Her eyes dart around the room, then circle back to mine. "The baby?"

And for the first time in what feels like forever, I smile. "She's in the nursery." My thumb strokes her cheekbone. "Healthy and perfect." I press the button on the bed and call for the nurse. "When you're ready, they'll bring her in."

Tears rim Shelly's lower lids before they spill down her cheeks. "She?" I nod and wipe the tears away. "A little girl," she whispers.

Nurse Tracy wanders into the room. "Did you—" Her eyes dart to Shelly and she smiles. "Glad to see you're awake, Ms. Reed." She steps up to the bed and looks over the monitor. "How are you feeling?"

"Tired." She swallows. "Some pain."

Nurse Tracy checks the saline bag and IV line. "That's to be expected." A soft smile lifts the corners of her lips. "Your body went through a lot today. Let's raise you up." She presses a button on the arm of the bed and the bed slowly scoots up. When Shelly is sitting up, but still leaning back slightly, she stops. "Let's adjust those pillows and get you water."

Once Shelly is a touch more comfortable and a little more

hydrated, Nurse Tracy gives us each a smile, tells us she will page Dr. Webster, and then be back with our baby girl.

I sit on the edge of the bed near Shelly's legs and retrieve my phone from my back pocket. "Everyone's been on edge, waiting for you to wake up." I unlock my phone and open the group chat.

Shelly lays her hand on my thigh as her eyes roll shut for a beat. "They're probably all freaking out," she chokes out.

There is no sugarcoating the situation. When I was kicked out of the room as they performed emergency surgery, I sat in front of the door for quite some time. Eventually, I ambled down to the waiting room and spoke with everyone. The shock was evident on each family member and friend's face, but no one lost it more than Micah.

I'd never seen a man so distraught, but I knew exactly how he felt in the moment. Frightened beyond words. Terrified of what might happen. Helpless because it was out of our hands.

I won't stress Shelly with all of that right now, but I will tell her. When she has her strength back. When we are home and she has a moment to rest and feel more at ease.

"Yes, they are, but they'll feel a million times better knowing you're awake and okay now." Her hand tightens on my thigh as I type out a text.

> Shelly is awake. Waiting for the doctor to arrive. More details soon.

And as suspected before I hit send, my phone blows up with one text after another.

> MICAH
>
> Thank fuck.

CORA

Give her our love until we see her.

AUTUMN

Oh, thank goodness.

NICOLE

On our way back.

One after another, the texts keep coming. I hold up my phone and Shelly stares at the screen, a small smile forming on her lips. I ignore the messages, lock my phone, and stow it back in my pocket.

And for the next few minutes, while we have alone time, I press my forehead to hers. Breathe her in. Feel her breath on my lips. Feel the weight and heat of her fingers and hand on my leg. I press a gentle kiss to her lips. Then another. Tears blur my vision as I hold her gaze. Emotion clogs my throat.

"I love you, Shelly Reed." My lips press hers again. "And I never want a day without you."

Tears roll down her cheeks as she tips her head and kisses me with desperation. "I love you, Devlyn Templar. Always."

And until Nurse Tracy reenters the room with our baby girl, we don't move an inch. Don't take our eyes off each other.

Desirée Rose.

God, she is beautiful. The most perfect thing I have seen in my life. Her plump little cheeks. A full head of brown hair. Eyes a hint lighter than my own, although Dr. Webster says both her hair and eyes may change color. Either way, she is flawless. A little piece of me and Devlyn in the sweetest package.

I stare down at our little girl as she suckles my breast and lays her hand on my skin. Soft sounds vibrate from her lips to my skin. Devlyn sits beside me on the hospital bed, his head on my shoulder as he watches her, watches us. Every few seconds, he twists to kiss my shoulder.

"God, how is it possible to love her so much already?" he whispers.

His question resonates deep in my bones because I wonder the same. How it is possible to love someone you just met. And not just love… no, it is much more complex than that. Not something I know how to define. Incomprehensible love.

"Not sure." I tilt my head and rest it on Devlyn's. "But I feel it too."

After four days in the hospital, we finally get to go home today. Of course, we will have a caravan. Since not everyone had the opportunity to come see us in the hospital, and because my labor circumstances were not what anyone expected, we will have visitors at the house on and off for the next few days. Mom already stated she will be at the house more often than not.

For once, I don't mind. I look forward to having her help. May even ask her to stay the night once or twice. While I feel less mentally foggy, my body still needs more time to recover. Until I heal fully, I can't lift anything more than one to two pounds, including the baby. Which means, to nurse her, I have to get situated before someone hands her to me.

Dr. Webster assures me I should be better in the next two weeks, then reminds me that everyone heals at different speeds.

Desirée falls asleep with her lips wrapped around my nipple. Slowly, I lower her and Devlyn fixes my gown. Then he drapes a cloth over his shoulder, scoops her up from my arms, rests her against his chest, and bops her up and down as he lightly pats her little back.

I love every side of Devlyn. The quiet and reserved. The passionate and hungry. The gentle and sweet. But seeing this side, watching him hold our daughter, care for her with such tenderness… renders me breathless.

After a soft burp leaves her lips, he carries her to the plastic bassinet and lays her down. He tightens the blanket around her tiny frame before leaning down and kissing her forehead. He whispers something to her, his voice too soft for me to hear, and I don't ask what. It's something for just the two of them. A shared moment.

Devlyn helps me up from the bed and leads me to the

bathroom. Peeling away the gown and my underwear, he helps me bathe with a small tub of warm water, a cloth and soap that smells sterile like the hospital. He dries me off and helps me into my clothes. Then he brushes my hair and secures it with a hair band. After I brush my teeth, we exit the bathroom and I slip on shoes.

Dr. Webster makes one last stop in the room and reviews our appointments over the next few weeks—for me and the baby. She gives us each a hug and walks out with us after Devlyn secures Desirée in the stroller. The moment we exit the hospital, I stop and take a deep breath.

"You okay?" Devlyn takes my hand in his.

"Yes," I say on a nod. "Just happy to leave." Out of nowhere, tears flood my eyes and stream down my face.

Devlyn steers us toward a bench, lowers us to sit, and parks the stroller in front of us. His hands cup my cheeks in an instant. His eyes lock with mine as he searches for the reason for my tears.

"I've got you." His thumbs stroke my cheeks. Scooting closer, he leans in and kisses me chastely. A breath later, he cocoons me in his arms and hugs me tight to his chest. "Always."

My fingers curl around the cotton of his shirt and ball into tight fists. "I was so scared," I admit, whispering into the crook of his neck. "It was so dark. At first, I enjoyed the peace that came with the darkness. But after a while…" I shake my head over and over. "I felt empty. Lost." I sob into the collar of his shirt. "I-I couldn't find you." My arms squeeze him impossibly tighter to my frame. "Couldn't see or hear or smell you."

"Shh, shh, shh." One arm tugs me closer. Squishes me to his chest. His other hand strokes my hair, my neck, my back in an effort to soothe the fear in my veins. "It's over now. You're here. I've got you." I don't miss his hushed sniffles and tears on my shoulder. "I was scared too. So scared," he confesses in a whisper. "Never been more scared in my life." He leans back and frames my face. His eyes red and veiny and laced with unspoken pain. "If I lost you…" His eyes fall shut as he shakes his head. I wait for him to finish, but he doesn't.

I press my lips to his. Taste his salty tears on my lips. Breathe in his faded, earthy scent as our lips part. Loosen my hold on him and take a deep breath. I trace the line of his jaw with shaky fingers. The scruff on his jawline the longest I have seen it. The dark half-moons below his eyes less prominent today, but still noticeable.

"Let's go home," I whisper.

It isn't only me that needs to escape the memories of this place over the last few days. I may need to heal physically, but Devlyn needs to heal too. Needs to know I am safe. That Desirée is safe.

And home… home is safe.

Much as I want time alone with Devlyn and Desirée, I have never been more appreciative of having so many wonderful people in my life.

For the last week, Mom has been a constant presence in the house. Dad practically shoved her through the front door and dropped her bag in the foyer. It didn't really happen that way, but he didn't hang out long on the first night.

Part of me thinks Dad is as exhausted as us. Sleep hasn't been easy to come by since I went into labor. But another part of me thinks Dad just needed time to himself. Time to mull over everything that happened in the hospital. Between Mom and Dad, he is the more sensitive and reserved person. Less likely to share his feelings. And seeing me in the hospital bed, completely out of it, probably took its toll on him.

With time, he will be okay.

Aside from Mom helping me with Desirée, she has also been a saint with housework and cooking. Taking on the tasks we sometimes take for granted. Not having to wash dishes every time we eat or drink has been a relief. Not having to worry over cooking or grocery shopping or general errands has been a tremendous help.

Occasionally, Devlyn goes into his studio and works. For the most part, though, he sits with me and the baby. On the couch while a movie plays softly in the background. On the back patio, when the sun begins to set and the heat is milder. We just sit together and hold Desirée and bond more.

"How's she doing?" Mom whispers as she enters the living room.

I peer down my chest and see a sleeping Desirée. My fingers gently stroke her hair. "Fast asleep."

"Want me to put her down?"

Since I still have at least another week—hopefully not more—before I am allowed to carry her on my own, Mom has helped with putting Desirée down in her crib or bassinet while Devlyn works.

"That'd be great. Thank you."

As Mom reaches for Desirée, Devlyn pads down the stairs and enters the room. He sidles up to Mom, leans in and presses a kiss to Desirée's crown. Devlyn drops on the couch beside me as Mom walks off. But the second Mom is out of sight, the doorbell rings.

"I'll get it," Devlyn says loud enough for Mom to hear, but not loud enough to wake the baby.

Devlyn starts for the door. Scooting to the edge of the couch, I gingerly stand and follow. With our friends on a daily rotation of stopping by to check on us and the baby, Devlyn doesn't think twice before unlocking the dead bolt. He doesn't hesitate before twisting the knob. He doesn't consider, not for a second, to check the peephole or peer out through the blinds.

But I wish he would have.

The door swings open and I freeze on the opposite side of the sitting room, near the kitchen. Because standing at the door, with a wicked grin on her lips, is Karen Templar. And something about her expression twists a knife in my already tender womb.

Why won't this woman just leave us be? Why won't this woman leave Devlyn alone?

*Let him be happy. Without you.*

Because if she isn't happy, she has to bring everyone else down. And people like Karen Templar will never be happy. Not until the entire ship sinks.

"I hear congratulations are in order," my mother says with disgust on her tongue. "You can imagine how upset I was to have heard I am a grandmother through a gossip circle." She curls her lip as her head tilts. "Don't be rude. Invite your mother inside."

I peer over my shoulder at Shelly and give her what I hope is an apologetic smile. "Be back in a second." Her eyes widen. "I'll be okay. Just stay in the house. Please."

She nods and walks toward the hallway. Toward her mother and the nursery.

I step out the front door and close it, but don't take another step. Crossing my arms over my chest and widening my stance, I form a barricade in front of the door. A barrier. A way to shield my home from this woman and the negativity she carries like a handbag.

"What do you want, Mother?"

She straightens her spine and rests her hands on her hips. "Has that girl drained you of intelligence and manners?" She shakes her head, her lips flattening for a beat. "I came to see my grandchild," she states, talking to me like an insolent child.

I take a deep breath and prepare myself for battle. I knew this day was inevitable, but hoped I wouldn't have to fight so soon. Dr. Prince's voice rings in my head as if he were here.

*"You will never be able to move forward until you deal with your past. Don't let your past set the tone for your future. Sharing genetics doesn't give someone power over you. It doesn't give them the right to harm you—physically, mentally or emotionally. It is one-hundred-percent acceptable to sever ties with relatives so you may live a happy, healthy life."*

"You don't have a grandchild," I say with more strength than I feel. But I refuse to back down. I refuse to give in. I refuse to let her hurt me or Shelly or our daughter. Not now. Not any day moving forward.

She rears back as if I slapped her. Disdain oozing from her every pore as she stares me in the eye. With a shift of her weight, her head tilts the opposite direction.

"What was that? I swear I misheard you."

"You didn't mishear a word." I harden my gaze. Inhale deeply and dig for the courage and strength Shelly has given me over time. Straighten my spine and square my shoulders as I speak with a firmer voice. "*You* are not a grandparent. My child is not some trophy you can parade around to get attention." I crack my neck left then right and roll my shoulders. "And I am not your son. Not anymore. You lost that privilege."

Loud laughter rips from her lips as she tips her head back. The sound and her action remind me of every on-screen villain. Heartless and maniacal. It sends a shiver down my spine and makes me nauseous. But I refuse to give in to her.

Refuse to back down. Refuse to let this vicious woman squash me with her thumb. Never again.

"You can't just get *rid* of your parents, Devlyn. It doesn't work that way."

I smirk. "Parent," I correct. "Just you."

Her lip curls as her eyes narrow. "This is your father. Feeding you bullshit stories and pegging you against me."

"No," I shout. Her eyes widen, but I don't care. I am sick and tired of this woman trying to use and abuse me for her own benefit. Sick. And. Tired. "You need to leave. Now." She opens her mouth to speak, but I cut her off. "Do not return. Ever. Stay away from me and Shelly and our family. Do not look for or follow us. No calls or texts or letters. Nothing. Not one single thing." I take a breath. "I will not be your punching bag. I will not be your scapegoat." I point a finger toward her. "And if I ever see you again or if you do anything to bother us, I will file a restraining order. I will take legal action." Taking a step toward her, I extend my finger farther. "Now get the hell off my property before I call the police."

Anger flames her cheeks and burns hot in her eyes. But I don't give a damn. I am done. More than done. And I will not subject my daughter to this woman. Not for a single second.

She storms down the walkway and gets in her car. A minute later, she drives away and I breathe deeply for the first time in minutes.

*Please let this be the end of her. Please.*

I walk inside and see Shelly lingering at the edge of the hallway. No doubt she heard everything. Which is good because I don't really want to repeat any of it.

In three strides, she closes the space between us, wraps me in her arms and hugs me with her fierce love.

It is in this moment that I feel a shift. Like the closing of a long and horrible chapter. Like the start of a new chapter—perhaps a new story.

The story of Shelly and Devlyn. The story of our life. The story where we both learned how to love.

Life has been peaceful. More peaceful than I imagined it could be.

Baby Desirée has been sleeping through the night more often than not. According to Mom, this is a miracle at ten weeks. Unsure if she was pulling my leg, I thumbed through several of the baby books and scoured the web. In black and white, each source verified her truth. Supposedly, most babies don't sleep through the night for several months.

Devlyn also appears to be sleeping better. Since the blowup with his mother, a new version of calm has washed over him. An incomparable tranquility he has needed for years. Before the verbal altercation with his mother, Devlyn had been pretty chill. Mostly. I'd only seen him upset or angry a few times—two of those three occasions involved his mother.

Now, Devlyn is the ultimate definition of relaxed. Zen master extraordinaire.

"Who's my little princess?" Devlyn says sweetly to Desirée as she drinks from the bottle in his hand. Swaddled in the crook of his arm, he rocks her side to side. His eyes on hers as she stares up at him and curls her little fingers in his shirt.

Each time he speaks to her, a small smile tips up the corners of her mouth and she makes a bubbly sound around the nipple. Ovary. Explosion.

When she finishes the last of the bottle, Devlyn sets it on the table before lifting her to his shoulder and gently patting her back. It isn't long before a ferocious belch echoes through the living room.

"Good push, princess." Devlyn sets Desirée in her bassinet before twisting to face me. "Want to finish shopping today?"

Last year, Christmas was a bust. Leading up to the holiday, things had been weird between me and Devlyn after our first kiss at the end of November. And until things started to mend, my mood had been sour. Christmas didn't feel merry or bright.

But this year… bring on all the holiday cheer.

For the first time in my adult life, I get to *really* decorate. Not just a measly little tree in the house with a few candles and decorative pieces. I get to pull out all the stops and decorate without limits. And Devlyn gets his first dose of Festive Shelly.

I close my eyes and picture all the merriment.

Outside lights strung along the roofline, around the windows, and on the trees. A blow-up tree for the front yard and an artificial tree for the back patio. Reindeer figurines for the lawn. I wanted the animated deer, but Devlyn mentioned the likelihood of them breaking easier. So I found a beautiful set of lifelike deer figures.

Today, since Devlyn offered, I'd like to get more holiday items for inside the house. Last time we browsed Target, I spied a whole section of holiday decor that called my name. Soft colors with a vintage feel. Classic.

"Are you trying to butter me up, Mr. Templar?" I tease.

His lips tip up on one side. "Maybe."

I'd meant it as a joke, but now I'm curious. What is up Devlyn's sleeve?

I narrow my eyes at him. "What're you up to?"

Leaning in, he presses his lips to mine and kisses me breathless. All too soon, he breaks the kiss. He rises from the couch, swipes the empty bottle from the table and takes a step away. Peering over his shoulder, he taps his temple then leaves the room.

I love this side of him. Happy and optimistic and flirty. Much as I want to pry the plans from his lips, I won't ask what he has in store. Something about the surprise has me jittery, in all the right ways.

While I lock Desirée's carrier in the car seat cradle, Devlyn loads our purchases in the back of the car. Warm air floats from the vents and replaces the cooler December air. Jolly holiday music echoes from the speakers at a low volume. The sky a little more gray than blue as the sun hides behind puffy clouds.

Once he has everything stowed, Devlyn hops in the driver's seat and holds his hands in front of the vents.

A minute passes. Then another. Devlyn has yet to put a hand on the steering wheel or gear shifter. *Is he really that cold?* I note the outside temperature on the dash display. Fifty-seven. Chilly, but not cold.

"Everything okay?" I ask as he rubs his hands together.

Green eyes flick in my direction. I study the lines of his face that are a hint deeper. The corners of his lips and eyes turned up a touch. And I swear I see his eyes twinkle a second before he blinks.

"Fine. Just trying to feel my hands again." He makes a fist with each hand, then flattens them out again.

"It's not *that* cold," I tease as I reach for his hands and sandwich them between my own. Immediately, I note how warm his hands feel. Not warm. Hot. I loosen my grip on him.

A soft chuckle spills from his lips. "They *were* cold. Now I'm just trying to feel them again." He jerks his chin toward the back of the car. "My fingers went numb after store number two."

Heat crawls up my neck and floods my cheeks. While I pushed the stroller through the mall and ogled all the festive decorations, Devlyn walked beside me and carried all the bags from our purchases. We visited ten stores over the last two hours, easily. Which means Devlyn grinned and trudged through the numbing pain for more than half that.

"Why didn't you say something?"

He waves a hand. "It's no big shake."

"I could've put bags in the stroller basket or carried one."

"Shelly…" He cups my cheeks, leans in and kisses me softly. "I didn't mind." His words are calm and barely above a whisper. "I'll carry twice that to see your smile again."

My eyes dart between his and look for things left unsaid. As he stares back, all I see is his truth, out in the open.

"Okay." I press my lips to his. "Now take me home," I demand, sitting back in my seat and buckling my seat belt. "Time to decorate."

He blinds me with a bright smile before he buckles up and drives us home.

I'm going to be sick.

The blinker ticks at a deafening volume as I wait to turn into the neighborhood. *Ticktock. Ticktock.* I blink a few times in an attempt to clear the fog coming in from all sides. Swallow past the building lump in my throat. Breathe slow and steady as I tell myself everything will be okay.

It will be, won't it?

With a break in the traffic, I steer the car into the neighborhood. If I drive slow enough, I can stretch the minute and a half to two minutes without Shelly asking questions.

*Everything will go according to plan.*

Shelly sings to the Christmas song on the radio, a slight bop in her shoulders on every other line. I mentally soak up her joy. This time last year, we were finding our way back to each other after my freak-out. The weeks leading up to Christmas were a little less cheery as we tiptoed around our relationship.

But everything worked out. Slowly, steadily, we fell in love.

Now, I am about to stir things up.

"Eeee!" Shelly squeals as I park in the driveway.

Twisting to face her, I can't help but match the bright smile on her lips. Her happiness is my happiness. Period.

"Will we see you at all today?" I tease. "Or should I take little miss up to the studio while you decorate?"

Shelly play slaps my arm. "It won't be that bad." Her eyes veer up then left and right as her lips shift side to side. "Maybe a little. But only because I've never had so much space to decorate. Plus, I get to decorate, *really decorate*, outside for the first time."

I lean across the console and press my lips to her cheek. "Decorate whatever you want." And I mean it.

When we exit the car, she retrieves Desirée's carrier from the back seat while I fetch all the goodies from the back. With each step closer to the front door, my stomach twists in a new knot. I stay a pace or two behind Shelly so she doesn't notice the shift in my expression.

*It. Will. Be. Fine.*

Inside the house, Shelly goes about unbuckling Desirée and getting her a bottle. I take all the bags to the reading nook near the sliding glass doors. It's the most centralized room in the house and should make it easier for Shelly to go room to room and add splashes of holiday cheer.

I stop at the entrance of the living room and watch my girls for a beat. Desirée stares up at Shelly as she drinks her bottle. One of her little hands grips Shelly's finger while the other hand plays with the ends of her hair. I snap a mental picture of the sight and make note to bring the image to life with pencil on stock paper.

"Be right back," I say just above a whisper. Shelly tilts her head enough to flash me a soft smile.

Taking the steps two at a time, I dart up the stairs to my

studio. My eyes roam the room from the landing. Nothing is out of place, not that I expected otherwise. Shelly only comes up here when we are together or I am working in the studio.

In three long strides, I reach the entrance to the closet. Tucked away behind new tubes of paint is one of the biggest gifts I will ever give Shelly. Well, besides our sweet baby girl. I pick up the smallest, heaviest gift on the planet and stow it in my pocket.

I park on the stool at the drafting table and zone out. Minutes tick by as I breathe deeply and mentally work to unravel the knots beneath my diaphragm. Calm as I can be, I rise from the stool and make my way back downstairs.

*Now. Do it now.*

At the base of the stairs, I peer into the living room. No sign of Shelly or Desirée. The house is quiet as I pad past the kitchen, sitting room and down the hallway toward the bedrooms. Just outside the nursery, I hear Shelly whisper to Desirée.

"Nap time, little angel. When you wake up, the house will sparkle. Lights and snow people and a beautiful tree. Blue and silver and white. It'll be the best first Christmas ever."

The door slowly opens and Shelly startles and slaps a hand to her chest when she spots me just past the frame.

"Sorry. Didn't want to disturb while you got her settled."

She drops her hand. "It's okay. Just didn't expect you there."

Without a word, I take her hand in mine and walk us down the hallway. She doesn't ask where we are going as I guide her through the house. She doesn't ask what I am doing when I park us on the couch in the living room. I wrap an arm around her shoulders and tuck her into my side. Just like every other time, she melts into my side. Becomes an extension of me, of us.

"Love you," I whisper against her hair.

"Love you too."

I kiss her crown and give her shoulder a squeeze before straightening in my seat. She tips her head back enough to peek up. To steal my every breath with her shimmering twilight eyes.

The weight in my pocket digs at my thigh.

*Everything will be fine. Do it. Now.*

"Shell, I…"

She sits up straighter. Her hands come to my cheeks as her eyes scan every inch of my expression. "What is it?" A crease forms between her brows as horizontal lines mar her forehead.

My eyes drift shut for one deep breath. When they open and all I see is my Andromeda, every nerve in my body calms. Every doubt in my mind gets washed away.

This is Shelly. My Shelly. My Andromeda. Goddess and ruler of my heart.

Leaning into her, I press my lips to hers. Let her warmth blanket me. Let her vibrance and zeal soothe every ounce of skepticism. Let her love consume every molecule in my body.

Reluctantly, I break the kiss. Brush the hair from her cheek and tuck it behind her ear. Hold her blues with my greens. Then, I lay my heart in her hands.

"Shelly, will you marry me?"

*I'm sorry, what?*

Every muscle in my body, head to toe, locks up. I stare back at Devlyn, unable to breathe or think or form words. I blink to moisten my dry eyes. Then do it more.

Marriage is not something I am opposed to, but it isn't something I foresaw in the near future. I love Devlyn, but this seems… sudden. Unlike him. Questionable. Our relationship time line has flown by, one momentous occasion after another.

Is this because of Desirée?

I don't want Devlyn to feel obligated to marry me because we have a child. That shouldn't be why he proposes. God, please don't let it be the reason he is proposing.

I love this man more than imaginable. His heart is limitless. He gives without second thought. And in the past fourteen months, I've felt and experienced so much with him. A love to rival all others. A love I never thought I'd have in my life. He has gifted me so much.

That said, I pray the reason for his proposal is love and not obligation.

"Uh..." I tap my toes on the floor. Pin my lips between my teeth as I study the seriousness in his gaze. Tightness forms between my brows as my eyes narrow.

Why does this feel so weird? Me wanting to ask him the reason why he asked me to marry him. Prepregnancy Shelly wouldn't think such preposterous things. Prepregnancy Shelly would have been in his lap already, hands on his cheeks as she kisses him senseless.

So why isn't that me now? Why am I sitting here like he asked me to solve a quantum physics equation?

With each passing second, I watch the shimmer in his green irises fade. I witness the upward turn of his lips fall into a frown of despair.

*Shit.*

His eyes drop at the same time as his hands. Then his head begins to shake slowly. "I shouldn't have..." He scoots an inch away. "What was I thinking?" he mutters, moving back farther. "Idiot," he whispers.

Before he retreats farther, I wrap my fingers around his wrist and stop him. "No." His eyes shoot to mine, glassy. Agony pours off him in waves. I shake my head. "Not no to the question. No, as in don't pull away."

Tears brim his eyes that have reddened in less than a minute. "It's too soon." He shakes his head. "Me asking you was impulsive. Sorry for putting you on the spot. I just thought—"

"Devlyn, stop." I inch closer to him and press my lips to his. "It's not that I don't want to marry you. And proposals always put someone on the spot," I say on a laugh. "But we've never discussed marriage and I..." I pause as I try to gather the right words.

"You can be honest with me, Shell. Always."

I lift a hand to his cheek and he leans into my touch. His eyes fall shut as he takes a deep breath. Then another. And it is in this singular moment that I have my answer without even asking the question. Not like I didn't know the answer to begin with.

How could I ever think Devlyn would propose out of obligation? Nothing about us has ever been like that. Hell, he fought our relationship so hard in the beginning. Fought the inevitable with every breath we took.

"What I was going to say was I don't want you to feel obligated to marry me because we have a child together." I half shrug and work my lips between my teeth. "Before the words formed on my tongue, the thought tasted sour. Foolish. And I'm sorry it crossed my mind." I shake my head and laugh. "I swear… little Desirée sucked all my sensibility away while in the womb."

Devlyn takes my hands in his. A glimpse of a smile appears on his lips and disappears just as fast. He stares down at our hands as his fingers caress each of mine before cradling them in his. Left then right, he rocks his head on his shoulders as he sorts through what to say next.

"Desirée is not the reason I asked," he says as his head lifts. His greens lock onto my blues and all I see is vulnerability and love and hope. "Honestly, I didn't know if I'd have the courage to ask." My brows pinch together as I wait for him to elaborate. "After the way my parents' marriage played out, I didn't want that to happen to us." His eyes widen. "Not that we are anything like them."

I nod and squeeze his hands. "Agreed."

"I've never loved anyone the way I love you, Shelly. It scares me while my heart begs for more. Before you, I avoided things that scared me. With you, though… I'll gladly walk through hell. Because I know you'll be on the other side, waiting with arms wide open."

Tears sting the backs of my eyes. Emotion clogs my throat as I try to swallow the excess saliva flooding my mouth. The urge to wrap Devlyn in my arms and hug the breath from his lungs surges in my veins.

*What did I do to deserve this man?*

*Why did I question his reasons?*

Things between us have never been simple. From the start, we toed the line. Devlyn fought the undeniable love he had for me. At that point, it may not have been *love*. Perhaps, extreme like. As for me, I only sheltered my feelings because he was reluctant. Without a doubt, I knew he felt something stronger than friendship between us.

*Friends.*

God… Devlyn made that word my least favorite. I hated it more than *moist*. Only because I knew, deep in my bones, he wanted more than friendship. His resistance to see us beyond more than friends didn't hurt. He had been broken. Thrown away. Used until no longer necessary. Had that happened to anyone else, their trust and willingness to love would be shattered too. Hence why I didn't blame him.

But all that changed.

The night he gave in to what he felt for me, the night he kissed me, everything changed.

At first, not for the better.

We suffered on our own for several days. And when I finally found a way to breathe again, I opted to let go. To move on. To say goodbye.

That single text led us to where we are today. Lovers. Parents. Connected in a way I never thought possible with another person.

So why did I hesitate? Why did I question the path that led us to this moment?

Devlyn proposed and I doubted his reasons for asking. It was foolish and absurd. I love him, plain and simple. I love Devlyn more than I have loved another person.

"Ask me again," I whisper.

He scoots the table away from the couch, then drops down to one knee. One hand digs in his pocket while the other takes my left hand. Tears burn the backs of my eyes once more. Clasped tightly between Devlyn's thumb and forefinger is a ring with more diamonds than my eyes can count with one glance. At the heart of the ring... an oval-shaped dark-blue stone with the occasional sparkle.

His eyes lock with mine and I stop breathing. His thumb draws small circles over my ring finger as he worries his lips between his teeth.

"Shelly Nicole Reed," he says just above a whisper. "I have loved you longer than I was willing to admit. Maybe from the first moment I saw you more than two years ago." A small smile tips up the corners of his mouth. "But there's no use in denying it another minute. Shelly, you make me whole. Make life worth living. Your light and warmth and kind heart are what I was missing. Your love and passion and gaiety. *You*." He takes a deep breath and swallows. "Before you, I merely existed. With you, I see every color. Every facet. Every angle. Light and beauty and brilliance. With you, because of you, I know love. Real love. True love." His thumb trails my ring finger from knuckle to tip. "Will you marry me, Shelly?"

Tears spill down my cheeks in parallel lines. Though Devlyn is a blur, I refuse to wipe the tears away. I swallow past the thick ball of emotion in my throat and slowly nod.

"Yes," I croak out. Swallowing again, I repeat myself with more gusto. "Yes, Devlyn." My lips roll between my teeth. "I will marry you."

The biggest smile brightens his face. I get lost in the sight as he slides the ring into place on my finger. As he lifts my hand to his lips and kisses my ring finger. As he wiggles his way between my legs on both knees, frames my face in his hands, and kisses me senseless.

In a matter of seconds, our clothes are peeled away and we are connected in every way possible. Mentally, emotionally and physically. We make love on the couch, in the middle of the day, without a worry in the world.

It is simply him and me and a love to rival all others.

*June 30th—the following year*

If someone told me two years ago I would fall in love, welcome the most precious little girl into the world, and marry my best friend, I'd have laughed in their face. Because two years ago, love felt like an impossibility.

Until Shelly.

The love of my life. My fiancée. The woman who I get to call wife in… I look down at my watch. In thirteen minutes, Shelly will be my wife.

God, just thinking the word seems surreal.

*Wife. Shelly will be my wife. Mine. Forever.*

A knock sounds at the door. "It's Micah."

Not seeing my bride since yesterday afternoon is the only "tradition" Shelly enacted today. Last night, she stayed with Cora, Autumn, Penny and Erin at Cora and Gavin's house. All the guys crashed with me at my house. And all us parents got a night free of children, courtesy of our parents.

To say it has been odd to not have my girls close by for the past twenty-four hours would be an understatement.

Though it was nice to get a night off from dad duties, sleep evaded me for hours. Wouldn't put it past one of the ladies to offer to hide the dark circles I noticed in the mirror as I buttoned my dress shirt.

I'd let them put makeup on my face or style my hair, so long as Shelly and I exchange vows this evening.

"Come in."

The door swings open and in steps my brother, Micah. It's an odd feeling to have a sibling after being alone the past twenty-four years. Odd in all the right ways.

The Saturday after I proposed, we invited her family and Dad to the house for dinner. Considering we were weeks from Christmas, they assumed it was us wanting a small gathering before the main event. They weren't wrong, but they didn't know the extent.

That night felt weeks long. My knee had never bounced so much beneath the dinner table. I'd scooted food around my plate more than a child avoiding Brussel sprouts on his plate. And when Shelly finally flashed her ring to the group and announced our engagement, I'd never sweated so profusely in my life.

Thank god for dark-colored shirts.

Nervous as I was, each member of the Reed family welcomed me with open arms. Micah pulled me in for an unexpected warm hug. Not the *slap-a-shoulder, one-armed* kind. A true, genuine, constricting hug.

*"Congratulations,"* he'd said. *"My sister is lucky to have such a wonderful man love her. Welcome to the family."*

Not only does Shelly make me whole with her love, but so does her family. *My family.* A family I never saw coming and will never take for granted. These people—Nicole and George, Micah and Peyton—fill in all the gaps and holes my mother created years ago. These people make me feel like I belong. They give me purpose and strength.

Loving Shelly had been but the beginning. Receiving more love than I knew possible in return has been the greatest gift.

"You ready?" Micah shuts the door behind him. "Only a few minutes until showtime."

I have never been more ready for anything. "Was ready the second she said yes."

A brilliant smile lights Micah's face. His eyes shimmering with excitement.

Though Micah and Shelly shared the same eyes as their mother, the three sets sparkled in a different way. At first, seeing the three of them together was strange. I'd never seen such unique irises. But with each visit together, I began to notice the differences.

Nicole's blues were a hint lighter than her children's. The luster more noticeable when she was happy or excited.

Micah's irises were the darkest. Borderline black. And the first time I heard his wife, Peyton, call him starlight, I knew the reason why. The sparkle in his dark irises was visible, but faint in comparison to Shelly's.

I may be biased, but it is my opinion that Shelly got the prettiest version of their constellation eyes. *My Andromeda.* The blue of her irises is darker than her mother's, but lighter than her brother's eyes. A rich blue. Like royalty. A queen. A goddess. My goddess. And the golden flecks that formed my favorite constellation, I knew all the ways to make them glow. With my hands and lips and words.

It took a while to see the difference between the three sets of matching eyes, but Shelly's sparkling blues are the ones that hold my heart captive and steal my breath.

And then there is my sweet little Desirée. Eyes as ravishing as her mother's, but with a thin ring of tea green around her pupil. The addition of my eye color gives hers an almost ethereal look.

"Whenever you're ready, let's get in position," he states, coming in for a hug. "Not every day my baby sister gets married and I get a kick-ass brother." He releases me from his grip. In two lengthy strides, he reaches the door and twists the knob.

Inhaling deeply, I take one last look in the full-length mirror and exit the dressing room. My fingers brush over large leaves and grassy bushes as Micah leads us through the gardens to the north lawn. White chairs sit in lush green grass on either side of a brick aisle. Thousands of red, pink and white rose petals line either side of the aisle and add a pop of color. A color that will always be my Shelly.

Pink.

At the end of the aisle, the bricks extend left and right to accommodate the wedding party. An arch of greenery and flowers and brilliant colors showcase where the ordained minister will perform the ceremony.

Micah leads me down the brick aisle. The rows of white chairs filled with family and friends. As I pass each, I hear words of congratulations, but don't stop to chat. Because any minute, music will float through the air. Bridesmaids will walk the aisle in soft-pink dresses. And behind them, my bride will make her way toward me.

When I reach the front, I give each of the guys a hug. Dressed in sharp gray suits to match my own is Micah, Jonas, Gavin and Chet. White button-downs beneath suit jackets, accented with a black-gray-and-pink bow tie. Each congratulates me on the big day.

I open my mouth to thank them, but get cut off by the change in music.

We shuffle into position and my eyes lock on the start of the brick path where Shelly will enter. To my left, Gavin mutters, "No better feeling than watching the woman you love walk to you in a breathtaking dress." I simply nod, not daring to look away from the entrance.

In a pale-pink dress that brushes the brick as she moves, Clementine steps out from the lush gardens and into the north lawn first. In one hand, she carries a small wooden pail adorned with white and blush roses, moss, and vines that trail up the handle on either side. On the front of the pail is a white heart that reads *Here comes the bride.*

With each step she takes toward us, she reaches into the pail, grabs a fistful of blush rose petals, and tosses them along the brick path.

*This is happening. Shelly and I are getting married.*

When Clementine reaches the back row of chairs, the first bridesmaid comes into view. Erin. Her blush dress sweeps the ground with each step. Her hair in some fancy loose braid and secured at the nape of her neck. A small bouquet of pink and white calla lilies and roses gripped in her hands.

Three breaths pass before the next bridesmaid appears. Autumn. Her appearance the same as Erin before her, with an additional splash of color from her tattoos.

Jonas sucks in a sharp breath. "Gorgeous," he whispers. "Absolutely gorgeous."

Today is my and Shelly's day, but hearing these men, my brothers, revel over their wives… it makes my heart hammer harder beneath my rib cage. Makes my breath come in short bursts. Because in less than a minute, it will be my turn. My only prayer is that my knees don't buckle.

Seconds later, Peyton comes into view. Her eyes flit to Micah as a glowing smile lights her expression before she winks at her husband.

"Goddamn, I am a lucky man," Micah says loud enough to garner a few laughs from the crowd.

Only one more bridesmaid left. The maid of honor. Cora. The second she steps into view, Gavin leans toward her without taking a step. He doesn't say a word, but I *feel* the love radiating off him as he watches his wife. Feel the connection they share. A connection that rivals what I share with Shelly.

When all the ladies are lined up on the opposite side, the music in the garden shifts.

Without warning, my palms sweat. An electric vibration hums through my veins. I lean to the right and try to peek through the thicket of greenery blocking Shelly from view, but it is no use.

My eyes laser-focused, I catch movement through the thinnest part of the plants. An hour-long second passes as I hold my breath and wait.

Then, she steps into view. Everyone rises from their seats, but I still see her. The queen of my heart. Goddess of my soul. *My Andromeda.*

My eyes trail down the length of her body as I memorize her in this moment. Breathtaking in desert-pink tulle. Wide straps across her shoulders that come to a point at the base of her sternum. A thin band of satin around her middle. The skirt layered and in waves. Small white flowers and pearls decorate the bust and trail down half the skirt. A lush bouquet of white, blush, and dark-pink roses, pink calla lilies, baby's breath and greenery clutched tightly in her hands.

Speechless, I remind myself to breathe. My vision blurs

and I blink a few times, not wanting to miss a second of this moment. George rubs a hand over her forearm as they step closer, but I don't dare shift my gaze from Shelly.

Although we have forever, no day will replace this one. The day Shelly says she will be mine in every way. Always.

### SHELLY

My pace slows as I catch sight of Devlyn.

*Damn, he's handsome.*

I grip Dad's arm tighter with my bent elbow. He brushes his hand over my forearm ever so gently in silent reassurance.

"Got you, Shelly Bear." His hold on me tightens. "Promise."

The backs of my eyes sting. A thick ball of emotion rests dead center in my throat. Every nerve in my body comes alive with excitement, becomes overwhelmed with joy. I blink a few times. Tip my head back slightly. Tell the tears rimming my eyes they need to wait a little longer. I swallow. Then swallow again.

"Thanks, Daddy," I whisper.

The aisle straightens as we reach the back row of chairs and I pause for a beat. Rake my eyes over Devlyn in a smart gray suit, white dress shirt, and charcoal-and-pink bow tie. On the breast of his jacket, a dark-pink calla lily and blush rose makes up his boutonniere. His floppy brown locks, a little lighter from time in the sun, parted off-center and styled to look messy on purpose. Hands clasped at his waist, I take in the slight bounce in his stance. As if he can't contain the energy flowing through him.

Faster than imaginable, we reach Devlyn and the minister. Dad kisses my cheek and I close my eyes for one rapid heartbeat. Then he places my hand in Devlyn's and takes a seat in the front row.

"You're stunning," Devlyn whispers, his hand squeezing mine.

"Pretty handsome yourself."

I pass my bouquet to Cora, then Devlyn and I turn slightly toward the minister. The next few minutes pass by in a haze of watery eyes and white noise. The minister reads the wedding script he has undoubtedly read hundreds of times prior. Every now and again, I catch a word or two, but otherwise drown out his voice.

Instead, I focus on Devlyn.

*My husband.*

Technically, we are already married. Hours ago, the minister went to each of our dressing rooms and had us sign the marriage license. During and after the ceremony, many things get lost in translation or forgotten. When we hired him, he told us of the few times couples forgot to sign, too swept up in the moment.

Devlyn's fingers weave and stroke and warm my own as he holds my gaze. His green irises bright and glassy under the setting sun. A burnt-orange glow highlighting his skin.

The minister quiets. Devlyn releases one of my hands, digs in the inside breast pocket of his jacket, and retrieves a slip of paper.

*His vows.*

He breathes deeply and swallows before my favorite smile dons his lips. And as his lips part to speak, I block out everyone but him.

"Shelly… my Andromeda." His smile brightens infinitesimally. "A warm October day, more than two years ago, was the first time I saw you. The dazzling blonde who peeked through the windows of a flower shop. For days, I denied myself the sight of you. But it wasn't long before I caved. You'd seen me and I you, but we'd never spoken a word." He takes another breath and licks his lips. "And then I saw you again. In a bar, yelling your love for Karaoke Grandpa."

At this, the majority of the wedding party, including myself, bursts out in laughter. Several seated guests appear bewildered, but most smile or shake their head.

"Bars have never been my scene, but a friend was in town and we went out to catch up." Devlyn briefly glances over his shoulder to Chet. "Had I not seen you that night, I may not have had the urge to call Elizabeth. To insist on touching up the mural I'd painted the previous year." Devlyn looks up from his paper, a small half smile softening his expression. "You see, you'd already been my muse. The woman in the window." Subtly, he shakes his head. "I didn't know your name, but I knew *you*." He presses the heel of his palm to the center of his chest. "Here. And as much as I tried to fight it, I needed to know you more. Even if I was just a friend."

I roll my eyes and Devlyn laughs.

"Shelly, you were never just a friend. Not one second. From the very start, you've always been more. It was me who needed time to learn this." Paper still in his hand, Devlyn takes hold of my free hand once more. "Thank you for loving me. Thank you for putting up with my stubbornness early on. For giving me another chance." His eyes dart to my parents and his dad in the front row, Desirée drooling in Mom's lap. "And thank you for giving me something I never thought I'd have… a family. I love you, Shelly Nicole Reed. And I will love you every day of forever."

Over my shoulder, Cora hands me a tissue. I tip my head back and blot my eyes.

Cora and Autumn warned me about this moment. Listening to the person you love as they confess the biggest reasons for loving you. Sounds simple when said aloud, but hearing it while loved ones watch and listen... cue the messy, happy tears.

Once my tears seem to be under control, I stow the tissue in my dress and retrieve my own piece of paper. I stare down at the scribbled words and question the vows I'd written days ago. Compared to Devlyn's confession, my vows seem small.

I close my eyes and fill my lungs fully, opening my eyes on the exhale. Devlyn's thumb paints small circles on my hand. His eyes locked with my own. It is him and me and no one else in this moment.

"Devlyn... the *artist*." Behind me, Cora snorts. "If you asked my closest friend, she'd tell you, without hesitation, how I rambled on about *the artist* after you painted the first mural. She'd tell you how I talked about you for weeks. The guy I couldn't stop sneaking a peek at. God, the front of the shop had never been so pristine." At this, Elizabeth chuckles in the crowd. "That display window got so much love that week." I pause and hold his green irises for three quiet breaths. "Because I just knew... I didn't know who you were, didn't ask for your name, didn't say one word to you, but I knew."

Plucking the tissue from my dress, I blot my eyes again.

"And then you reappeared a year later. Your warm smile and addictive eyes. The way you looked at me... I couldn't breathe. Couldn't form intelligible speech, which is miraculous for anyone who knows me well." Chuckles float around us. "But more than anything, I couldn't stay away."

At this, Devlyn squeezes my hand. His silent way of reciprocating the feeling.

"Devlyn, my life was monotonous before you. I had love, but nothing compared to the love you give. I had family, but not like the family we created together." I inch closer to him and tighten my hold on his hand. "Loving you is effortless. The most natural thing I have ever done. Life and love didn't make sense before you. I'd read about love, the type that steals every thought and breath and moment, but I'd never felt it firsthand. And I wholeheartedly believe it was because I'd been waiting for you." The backs of my eyes sting as my vision blurs. "I love you, Devlyn James Templar, more than I have loved anyone. And as long as there is air in my lungs and a heartbeat in my chest, I will love you. Always."

The paper in my hand falls to the ground as I step forward, ritual be damned, and press my lips to his. Devlyn frames my face with his hands and kisses me back with equal fervor. The minister says something and cheers erupt around us. But neither of us moves to break the kiss. Lost in each other, we kiss until we are breathless.

And when we break apart, the world finally levels out. Colors are brighter, bolder, more vibrant. Life is warmer, fuller, more passionate. And love… it isn't just something I read about anymore. Love is this living, breathing force. Powerful and daring. Strong and profound. Abstract and impassioned.

Mom walks to us and hands over a wiggly Desirée. She kisses my cheek and congratulates us.

And there, in front of the most important people in my life, I feel whole. Fortunate. Loved.

~

Although this is the end of the Artist Duet and the Bay Area Duet Series, I have four chapters of bonus content on my website. Get a glimpse into Shelly and Devlyn's future, as well as the rest of this circle of friends.

Still need more in the Bay Area Duet world? Penny and Reese get their own HEA in two side novellas.

# Thank You

Thank you so much for reading the **Artist Duet**. If you wouldn't mind taking a moment to leave a review on the retailer site where you made your purchase, Goodreads and/or BookBub, it would mean the world to me.

Reviews help other readers find and enjoy the book as well.

Much love,
   Persephone

## The Click Duet

High school sweethearts torn apart. When fate gives them a second chance, one doesn't trust they won't be hurt again. Through the Lens (Click Duet #1) and Time Exposure (Click Duet #2) is an angsty, second chance, friends to lovers romance with all the feels.

## The Inked Duet

A man with a broken heart and a woman scared to put herself out there. Love is never easy. Sometimes love rips you apart. Fine Line (Inked Duet #1) and Love Buzz (Inked Duet #2) is a second chance at love, single parent romance with a pinch of angst and dash of suspense.

## The Insomniac Duet

He was her high school bully. She was the outcast that secretly crushed on him. More than ten years later, he's her boss, completely oblivious to their shared past, and wants no one but her. More importantly, he doesn't understand her animosity toward him.

## Transcendental

A musician in search of his muse and a woman grieving the loss of her husband. Two weeks at an exclusive retreat and their connection rivals all others. Until she leaves early without notice. But he refuses to give up until he finds her again.

## Depths Awakened

A small town romance which captivates you from the start. Two broken souls have sworn off love. Vowed to never lose anyone else.

But their undeniable attraction brings them together and refuses to let go.

## One Night Forsaken

One night. No names. No romance. Just fun. Nothing more–at least, that's what she tells herself. Until he appears in her coffee shop months later with that addictive smile. She swore off commitment. He vows to never love again. But the more they fight it, the more life brings them together.

## Every Thought Taken

As young children, an unshakable friendship brought them together. As teens, they discovered an undeniable love. Then life pulled them in different directions–into darkness and light–and slowly ripped them apart. Years later, he returns home in the hopes of a second chance with his first love and to conquer the demons of his past.

## Distorted Devotion

Swept off her feet by love, life takes a dark, unexpected turn. Now the love of her life may be the cause of her death. Check out this gripping, romantic suspense.

## Undying Devotion

A long-term couple with a secret life. Their friends envy the bond they share, but remain oblivious to their lifestyle and how deep the bond lies. A turn of events has her wanting to spill every secret.

## Beloved Devotion

She asks the love of her life to marry her. When her girlfriend hesitates, then says yes, she is determined to learn why. As the pieces start to fall in place, she discovers she doesn't know her fiancée at all.

Here are some of the songs from the **Artist Duet** playlist. You can listen to the entire playlist on Spotify!

Loveless | PVRIS
Touch | Sleeping At Last
Heart | Sleeping At Last
I'll Be Good | Jaymes Young
Fear | Sleeping At Last
Anger | Sleeping At Last
Big Love, Small Moments | JJ Heller
Hearing | Sleeping At Last
Power | Isak Danielson
The First Glance | Anna Yarbrough
Life | Sleeping At Last

_Acknowledgments_

First and foremost, I need to acknowledge this series as a whole. I started daydreaming about this series and wrote the first duet before I published my first book. From the beginning, Gavin and Cora were the heart of this circle of friends. Writing the final duet was a challenge—ending the series with such a difficult story and bidding farewell to characters I've been with for years. It's bittersweet, but also a little sad. I hope you loved reading this series as much as I loved writing it.

To my family and friends… Thank you for always being my biggest fans and cheering me on. Your love keeps me going!

To Ellie McLove and Rosa Sharon… Thank you for performing miracles with my punctuation and fixing the typos and boo-boos I miss after reading the manuscript a dozen times. You ladies are superheroes! xoxo

To Kat Savage… Thank you for making my books pretty on the outside and putting up with my nagging. You're a rockstar! Love you!

To my author friends… All the constricting hugs! This author gig isn't all rainbows and sunshine, but having you in my circle and corner makes each day better. Love you all!

To the readers and bloggers who read my words… sending you all virtual hugs. Every time I read one of your amazing reviews or see your posts about my books, I cry. Spilling pieces of yourself on paper isn't easy, but your kindness makes it worth it each time I start a new book. A million thank yous to each of you!

And if this is your first Persephone Autumn story… thank you for taking a chance on my words. I hope you loved Shelly and Devlyn.

# About the Author

*USA Today* Bestselling Author Persephone Autumn lives in Florida with her wife and psycho cat. A proud mom with a cuckoo grandpup. An ethnic food enthusiast who has fun discovering ways to vegan-ize her favorite non-vegan foods. Most days, you'll find her with a tea latte or fruity concoction in her hand. If given the opportunity, she would intentionally get lost in nature.

For years, Persephone did some form of writing; mostly journaling or poetry. After pairing her poetry with images and posting them online, she began the journey of writing her first novel.

She mainly writes romance and poetry, but on occasion dips her toes in other works. Look for her non-romance publications under P. Autumn.